PERFECT
SILHOUETTE

Books by Judith Miller

The Carousel Painter
The Chapel Car Bride
The Lady of Tarpon Springs
A Perfect Silhouette

THE BROADMOOR LEGACY*
A Daughter's Inheritance
An Unexpected Love
A Surrendered Heart

FREEDOM'S PATH
First Dawn
Morning Sky
Daylight Comes

BRIDAL VEIL ISLAND*
To Have and To Hold
To Love and Cherish
To Honor and Trust

BELLS OF LOWELL*
Daughter of the Loom
A Fragile Design
These Tangled Threads

DAUGHTERS OF AMANA
Somewhere to Belong
More Than Words
A Bond Never Broken

LIGHTS OF LOWELL*
A Tapestry of Hope
A Love Woven True
The Pattern of Her Heart

HOME TO AMANA
A Hidden Truth
A Simple Change
A Shining Light

POSTCARDS FROM PULLMAN
In the Company of Secrets
Whispers Along the Rails
An Uncertain Dream

REFINED BY LOVE
The Brickmaker's Bride
The Potter's Lady
The Artisan's Wife

www.judithmccoymiller.com

*with Tracie Peterson

A PERFECT SILHOUETTE

JUDITH MILLER

BETHANYHOUSE
a division of Baker Publishing Group
Minneapolis, Minnesota

© 2019 by Judith Miller

Published by Bethany House Publishers
11400 Hampshire Avenue South
Bloomington, Minnesota 55438
www.bethanyhouse.com

Bethany House Publishers is a division of
Baker Publishing Group, Grand Rapids, Michigan

Printed in the United States of America

Library of Congress Cataloging-in-Publication Data
Names: Miller, Judith, author.
Title: A perfect silhouette / Judith Miller.
Description: Bloomington, Minnesota : Bethany House Publishers, [2019]
Identifiers: LCCN 2018053284 | ISBN 9780764232206 (trade paper) | ISBN
    9780764234101 (cloth) | ISBN 9781493418633 (ebook)
Subjects: | GSAFD: Love stories.
Classification: LCC PS3613.C3858 P47 2019 | DDC 813/.6—dc23
LC record available at https://lccn.loc.gov/2018053284

Scripture quotations are from the King James Version of the Bible.

Cover design by Koechel Peterson & Associates, Inc., Minneapolis, Minnesota
/ Jon Godfredson

Author is represented by Books & Such Literary Agency.

19 20 21 22 23 24 25   7 6 5 4 3 2 1

In memory of
Dorothy Gliniecki

I'm so thankful God brought you into my life.
I cherish the memories.

Chapter
ONE

Manchester, New Hampshire
August 1850

"MANCHESTER! NEXT STOP, MANCHESTER!" THE CONDUC-
tor raised his voice as the train hissed and chugged to a shud-
dering stop next to the Canal Street Depot.

Mellie Blanchard pressed her hand to her churning stomach,
stood, and made her way down the narrow aisle of the passenger
car. A trainman offered his hand as she descended the steps onto
the wooden platform. So this was Manchester.

Rows of redbrick buildings loomed over the adjacent canal
like ominous sentries assembled to keep invaders out. Or were
they positioned to keep prisoners within? The thought caused
a chill to race up her arms.

"Excuse me, miss, I believe you dropped this." A young man
strode across the platform, holding her copy of *La Petite Fadette*.
His lips curved in a broad smile as he glanced at the cover. "Let
me guess. You've come to Manchester to accept a position as
governess for one of the mill owners?"

"No, I've come seeking employment at the mills." She extended her gloved hand and accepted the book. "Thank you. I didn't realize I had dropped it."

"If you've come to work for the Amoskeag Company, I doubt there will be much time for reading French novels in your future." The man's clear blue eyes glistened like sunlight sweeping across ocean waters.

His cautionary words underscored what she'd known to be true when she boarded the train in Concord. Her life would never be the same.

"Thank you for returning my book. If you'll excuse me, I need to see to the delivery of my baggage." A gust of wind captured the edge of her gold silk bonnet and nearly sent it flying. She held it in place with her palm, then tucked the book into the pocket of her lightweight cloak before waving to a drayman seated atop a small wagon. When he didn't acknowledge her, she hurried to the side of the wagon. "I have baggage I'd like delivered to Mrs. Richards's boardinghouse, please."

He spit a stream of tobacco juice toward the opposite side of the wagon. "This ain't no free service. You gotta pay before I deliver. How many you got?"

"Two." Mellie dug into her reticule and handed him the requested coins before nodding toward the side of the depot. "Follow me. They're over here."

He stopped short and shook his head when he caught sight of the two oversize trunks. "First off, them's gonna cost you more. Most gals come here with one small trunk. Them things are huge."

She stiffened her spine and squared her shoulders. "When you stated your price, you didn't qualify a size requirement. I've paid your requested fee, and I expect you to deliver my belongings."

His features tightened into a scowl, but at least he began moving toward the trunks. He reached for the leather handle on one side and tested the trunk's weight. "This thing is heavier than a grown man."

"You exaggerate, sir. I doubt it weighs more than a small child, and the baggage handlers in Concord had no difficulty loading it onto the train."

The drayman braced his foot against the end of the trunk and gave a hefty push. When it slid only a few inches, he glanced about. "I gotta go find my helper. He's likely inside the depot chewin' the fat with the ticket master. Ain't never around when I need him. I've half a mind to send him packing."

Mellie offered a slight nod and turned toward the adjacent hillside. Rows of brick boardinghouses marched up the incline, with their slate-covered, gabled roofs and white dormers providing the only disruption in a sea of red brick and granite. Gone were the white birch and towering pines that had likely proliferated on the graceful rise before the coming of the Amoskeag Company. Had the farmers willingly sold their homesteads knowing the pastoral countryside would be forever changed, or had they been hoodwinked like the landowners down in Lowell? Of course, it no longer mattered. The farmland had already given way to industry. Even now, she could see workers constructing additional mills across the canal. How many did they need?

The drayman reappeared with a muscular young man at his side. "Finally found him." He didn't look at her as he spoke. Instead, he pointed the young fellow to her trunks. "These is the ones. Let's get 'em on the wagon." He glanced in Mellie's direction. "I'm gonna wait for the next train before I bring your trunks, so you might as well get on over to Mrs. Richards's boardinghouse. We'll meet ya there in about a half hour or so."

"If you could direct me?"

"You gals come to town with no idea what you're in for. No wonder so many of ya end up in trouble." He shook his head and pointed to the incline. "First boardinghouse on the third street over—Pleasant Street. You're lucky you ain't got too far to go. Them fancy shoes ain't made for walking—or for working in the mills, neither."

Mellie thanked him before heading off. She stopped and attempted to wiggle her toes before she reached Pleasant Street. Though she didn't want to admit the drayman was correct, her right shoe was pinching her toes and she'd likely have a blister by morning. When she arrived at the front door, she took a moment to catch her breath and straighten her bonnet before knocking.

Before long, a plump dark-haired woman opened the door. Her gaze traveled from Mellie's bonnet to the hem of her blue-gray shot silk day dress. "Can I help you, miss?"

"I've come about a room. I have a letter from Mr. Brownell. He was in Concord hiring for the Stark Mills. Are you Mrs. Richards?"

"I am." The woman's forehead creased. "You're going to work in the mills?"

Mellie swallowed hard. "Is there some reason why I shouldn't?"

"No." She shook her head. "It's just that you're a little . . . um, a little fancier than most of the girls who appear at my door." A nervous mumble escaped her lips as she waved Mellie forward. "Come sit down and we'll sort this out."

Mellie's heart picked up a beat as she followed the older woman into a parlor off the hallway. Mrs. Richards gestured to one of the well-worn, overstuffed chairs. With her thoughts racing, Mellie forced a smile and sat down. What if Mr. Brownell hadn't been working for the company? What if she'd been too trusting? What if she'd made this journey and spent the last of her sister's savings for naught? What would happen to her only remaining family? Her sister, her niece, her nephew. She didn't want them to suffer for the wrongs of their father. They needed as much security and normalcy as Margaret could provide. Mellie knew what it was like to grow up without either. After her parents died, she was shuttled off to boarding school, and her life had been forever changed.

"What else did Mr. Brownell tell you?" Mrs. Richards leaned back in the overstuffed chair.

Mellie retrieved a letter from her bag. "He gave me this and said I should present it at Stark Mill, Number One, and they would put me to work." She offered the note to Mrs. Richards. "Someone at the train depot asked me if I was going to work for the Amoskeag Company, but I merely told him I was going to work in the mills. Are there several different companies? Mr. Brownell didn't mention the Amoskeag Company when we talked."

Mrs. Richards sighed. "Well, I'll give you the easiest explanation I can, but it does get a little confusing. The Amoskeag Company owns all the land where the Stark Mills are situated, and if my memory serves me right, they have the water rights to Amoskeag Falls. Somewhere along the way I was told the directors of the Amoskeag Company connected with some of the men in Lowell known as the Boston Associates, but that all gets too complicated for me. Anyway, sometime later, the Amoskeag Company decided there was money to be made if they opened some of their own mills and mechanic shops. Mr. Stark owns three mills and a few of the mechanic shops, but I couldn't tell you much more than that. None of the company business is of any great importance to me—so long as I get my pay each week."

"Thank you. I think I understand a little better now." Mellie gestured to the paper she'd handed the keeper. "Does Mr. Brownell's note appear in order?"

Mrs. Richards nodded. "I didn't know Sam—Mr. Brownell—had been in Concord, but it appears this is in order. If you're willing to room in the attic, I can offer you space. When one of the other girls leaves, you can move into another room—if no one else claims it first. Once you've signed your papers over at the mill, come back here and you can get settled." She glanced at Mellie's shoes. "You might want to change into your working shoes before you go." Her eyebrows dipped low on her forehead. "Where are your belongings?"

"I'm having them delivered by a drayman who was over at the depot. He said he'd bring them after the next train arrives."

Mrs. Richards nodded. "In that case, I guess you have no choice but to wear the shoes on your feet. Walk outside with me and I'll point you in the direction you need to go." She pushed up from the chair and led Mellie to the front stoop. She pointed across the road and to the left. "There's three Stark Mills. Number One is four stories high—that's where you'll be going—the far left. Number Two is the tallest one at five stories high. Then there's the connecting mill. It's also four stories—the one with the cupola." She pointed toward the center. "Once they constructed that center mill, folks said the three mills formed a cross."

Mellie stared at the vast buildings. A cross, or perhaps a giant man with outstretched arms pulling young women inside to profit from their labors. But no matter. She needed work, and it might help to think of the three mills forming a cross rather than greedy men taking advantage of the unfortunate.

Mrs. Richards rested one hand on her fleshy hip. "Mr. Walters is the man in charge of all the Stark Mills. The girls tell me he's a mite picky about who he hires, but I don't know if that's true. They say it's best to have a reference from someone back home."

Mellie touched her reticule. "I have one with me."

"Give your note from Mr. Brownell to the man at the iron gates. He'll let you in and direct you to the agent. When you get back, you can read the boardinghouse regulations. Single girls working in the mills are required to live in a boardinghouse and abide by the house's rules." She lifted her hand from her hip and gave a slight flick of her wrist. "Well, you best be off. I'll have the drayman take your belongings to the attic. I'm sure Mr. Walters will offer a nice-appearing girl like you a position. If not, you can apply at any of the other mills down the row."

Mellie's stomach growled. Had she taken the time to eat before leaving Concord, the contents of her stomach would now be defiling Mrs. Richards's tidy front stoop. She hadn't anticipated the strangeness of being set adrift in a town where she didn't know a soul, where she'd be required to sleep in a room with girls she'd never met, where she didn't even know how to navigate her way around. Fear mounted as she retraced her steps down the hill and crossed the street on her way to the black iron gates and brick walls that loomed like a fortress out of the hills. She must regain her confidence if she was going to secure a position, for she desperately needed the income. She uttered a quick prayer and then began to hum a hymn while striding onward.

Chapter

TWO

MORGAN STARK FOLDED HIS ARMS ACROSS HIS CHEST and stared at the sprawling brick complex that comprised the Amoskeag Manufacturing Company. While his father owned three of the mills, much of the land belonged to the Amoskeag Company, and they'd now constructed additional mills—each producing dissimilar woven fabrics. When Amoskeag's board of directors had decided to expand from mere landowners, they'd invited Morgan's father to purchase a stake in the company and become a director. While the various mills weren't in competition with each other, they were at times in competition with the mills in Lowell, Massachusetts. At first, Morgan's father had thought it a conflict that some of the directors of the Lowell Mills were also directors at the Amoskeag Company, but the majority of the directors believed it was an acceptable arrangement. After making his one argument, Morgan's father never broached the subject again, although he still believed he was correct.

The few times Morgan had returned to Manchester, the family holdings in the company had increased. If not a new building, then an added wing, a connecting structure, or at the very least a fancy cupola and new bell. His father was a determined and forward-thinking man set upon building up his family's fortune. The success of the Amoskeag Manufacturing Company and the Stark Mills depended upon men like his father—men who had the wealth and foresight to harness the power of Amoskeag Falls.

He hailed a carriage and settled back for the ride home. Years ago, their house had been somewhat modest, yet as his father's mills expanded, so had the family home. Rather than live close to the mills, his mother had requested they move to a house located on several acres on the outskirts of Manchester. While she insisted the expansive mansion wasn't overly indulgent, Morgan suspected his mother's selection had been to impress her friends, as it was far too large a house for a family of three, especially when one of them was seldom at home.

As the carriage pulled away from the depot, he took in the length and breadth of the mills. In earlier years, his father had leased the land, but then he'd joined with several Manchester investors as well as a group known as the Boston Associates— the men who'd established the textile mills at Lowell, Massachusetts. Success had come quickly to all of them, and the products manufactured in the various mills had expanded, as well. Though his father's mills continued to create textiles, locomotives were now being produced within the complex. No doubt there would be an even greater variety in the coming years. That thought excited Morgan, as well as the residents of Manchester. The town continued to expand, and that growth had been beneficial to all who lived there, whether permanently or only long enough to bolster a family living elsewhere.

It wasn't until his final year in college that Morgan planned a return to New Hampshire. During his earlier years, he'd thought the warmth of the South much more appealing. But now that he'd completed his education and earned his certification as an engineer, a return home could serve him well. The opportunities to use his education in the mills would be boundless. He longed to work alongside men who understood the complexities of machinery, as well as the need to expand and develop new methods in the workplace. In that regard he had specific ideas, and yet he feared that convincing his father would prove the most challenging of tasks.

He'd written his parents and asked they keep his arrival to themselves. His mother wasn't one who easily maintained secrets, so he could only hope she hadn't already spread the news among her social circle. For all intents and purposes, he'd been absent from Manchester for years—ever since he'd gone off to boarding school. There had been a few days at Christmas, time spent at their summer home in Virginia, and he'd taken two trips abroad with his parents. Overall, however, he'd had sparse opportunity to develop friendships in Manchester.

The carriage rolled along the circular driveway and came to a halt in front of the pillared portico. He pushed open the door and stepped down while the driver unloaded his baggage. After tossing several coins to the driver, Morgan strode to the front door. He hesitated for a moment, took a deep breath, picked up a bag in each hand, then stepped inside.

Fortunately, the servants were nowhere to be seen when Morgan entered the house. If his good luck continued, he would meet privately with his father before his mother discovered his arrival. He concealed his luggage behind an arrangement of giant Chinese urns in the foyer before stealing down the hallway. He slowed his stride when he neared the sitting room. If his mother had come downstairs, she'd be at her desk writing letters or reading a favorite novel, but this morning the pocket doors were closed. He heaved a sigh and continued on to his father's office.

Morgan stopped outside the door. His father's face was obscured by the daily newspaper he held in front of him. When Morgan cleared his throat, his father lowered the paper, then dropped it onto the oversize walnut desk, smiled, and pushed to his feet.

"Morgan, my boy. What a wonderful surprise." With his arm extended across the desk, he clasped Morgan's hand in his own. "I didn't expect you until next week. Does your mother know you're here? Sit down, sit down. Let me ring for the maid to bring coffee. Are you hungry? I'm sure we can arrange for some breakfast."

Morgan chuckled and sat down. "In answer to your questions, no, Mother doesn't know I'm here. Yes, I'd enjoy coffee. And no, I don't want breakfast, thank you."

"I'll have Lucy fetch your mother and bring us coffee." The older man rang for the maid. "You look good, Morgan."

"Thank you, Father, but before you send for Mother, I'd prefer some time for the two of us to speak privately."

His father's brows lowered a notch. "You're not in some kind of trouble, are you?"

"No, nothing like that. It's about my position with the company. I know Mother doesn't enjoy discussions regarding the business, and I'd like to present a proposal to you."

A middle-aged woman entered the room, her eyes fixed on Morgan's father. "You rang, Mr. Stark?"

"Please bring coffee, Lucy, and if my wife should come downstairs and inquire as to my whereabouts, please tell her I'm in a business meeting at present."

"Yes, sir." She nodded and turned to leave.

"And please close the door on your way out, Lucy." That said, his father turned back to Morgan. "Well, you've piqued my interest. What kind of proposal? You're not going to ask for a raise before you even begin work, are you?" His lips twitched into a smile.

Morgan scooted forward in his chair. "Of course not. In fact, if you agree to my idea, you won't be paying me much at all."

"Now, Morgan, you know the company managers make a fine wage, and if you take a position overseeing the managers of the three Stark Mills, you'll be paid very well indeed."

"My position is what I want to discuss with you." Morgan straightened his shoulders. "I don't want a management position. I'd like to work in the mill and see if I can discover any new techniques or possible improvements that can be made. With my engineering education, I believe I may even develop ideas for new products we could produce in the mills." His father's eyes reflected doubt, but Morgan pushed on. "You know I don't enjoy sitting at a desk, Father. I'm not cut out to spend my days signing checks and going through profit-and-loss sheets. That type of thing would bore me to death, and I'd leave the company before year's end." He inhaled a deep breath. "Working around the machinery, helping develop new ideas, discovering how I can make a genuine contribution—that's what excites me."

His father waved him to silence. "Hold up for just a minute. First of all, your plan has flaws you've not considered. And second, you wouldn't last in that kind of position for more than a day or two. Mark my words, Son, our mechanics perform dangerous, dirty work all day, every day. Trust me, it's not the kind of thing you imagine. You've envisioned some sort of fairy tale, yet life in the mills isn't an enchanted one." He made a sweeping gesture with his arm. "*This* is the fairy tale. A beautiful home, servants, money—this is what those men in the mills dream of at night."

"I know, but—"

"Let me finish, Morgan." His father rested his arms atop the wide desk. "The men would never accept my son working alongside them. Your presence would create chaos and discomfort. No matter what the workers might be told, they'd believe you were there to observe their work habits and eavesdrop on their conversations—a spy who would report to management. Even if I thought you'd be happy in such a position, the idea simply isn't feasible."

Before Morgan could offer an argument, Lucy returned bearing a tray laden with warm biscuits, peach jam, a silver coffeepot, and two china cups. She placed the tray on one end of the desk. "Shall I pour for you, Mr. Stark?"

"No need, Lucy. Thank you." The maid disappeared from the room as silently as she'd entered. Once the door had closed, his father poured the dark steaming brew into the cups. "Cream? Sugar? Both?" He looked at Morgan and arched his brows.

"Black is fine." He waited until his father balanced one of the cups on a saucer and handed it to him. "Thank you." He took a sip of the coffee before he continued. "I've already thought of the spying possibility, Father. I didn't plan to go to work as Morgan Stark. I planned to assume the name William Morgan—simply switch my first and middle names. I wouldn't go into the mills using the family name. None of the men know me. Even your agents and overseers don't know me. They may know you have a son, but they've never set eyes on me. This can work, Father. I believe you'll soon realize how much more beneficial it will be to have me working with the engineers and mechanics rather than stuck away in a stuffy office."

"We have been discussing a new project at Stark Mills." His father stroked his jaw. "Perhaps you could be of assistance, but we would need to be very careful how this is handled. And there's still the problem of your identity. Just because my managers haven't met you doesn't mean there isn't someone who might recognize you."

"Other than a few social contacts I've met during my occasional visits home, I don't know who it would be. My time in Manchester has been extremely limited, and if we can convince Mother to remain silent about my return to the city, I doubt there will be a problem—especially if I'm wearing work clothes like these rather than a suit and necktie."

His father stared at him for a moment, then picked up a biscuit, broke it in half, and carefully slathered a spoonful of jam over the warm flakiness. After indulging in a bite, he wiped the corner of his mouth with a linen napkin and tipped his head to the side. "There may be some merit to your plan, but I still have misgivings. I have been discussing the development of a new piece of machinery with Cyrus Baldwin. Like you, he's an engineer."

Morgan's pulse quickened. "What kind of machine?"

"A circular weaving machine that will change the way cloth bags are made. I've seen the initial drawings. Rather than the flat pieces of cloth woven on looms, this loom would weave cylinders of cloth. Since the sides would no longer require stitching, they'd be much stronger. Far fewer bags of grain tearing open during handling. I believe demand would prove tremendous, that is, if we are the first ones to bring such a product to market."

Morgan wanted to shout with excitement, but the Starks were expected to maintain their decorum—perhaps not the women, but certainly the men. And he hadn't forgotten his father's earlier remark about further misgivings. After hearing about this new machine, he was determined to eliminate any such concerns.

Best to meet the problem head-on. "You mentioned you still had misgivings. What might they be?"

His father downed a final gulp of coffee and rattled the cup onto the saucer. "Instead of what might they be, you should have asked *who* might they be. And the answer is, your mother. We both know she's not going to agree to it. She's been looking forward to your return like a mother hen who's found a lost chick."

Morgan swallowed a laugh. While he loved his mother dearly and acknowledged her many fine attributes, she possessed few maternal instincts. There had been a nanny until he was old enough to attend school. And although his father had suggested they hire a governess or tutor, his mother had been eager to send Morgan to boarding school. She argued that he would receive a much better education and be happier where he'd have friends his own age. She might have been correct about the education, but he hadn't been happier. Being away from home at an early age had proved a difficult adjustment, though eventually he'd adapted. Now, as an adult, he had no great urge to come home to the nest and take refuge under his mother's wing.

"I won't be able to live at home. If you agree to what I've suggested, I'd need to apply for a position the same as every other employee. And I'd need to live in one of the men's boardinghouses— not here. Any attempt to live elsewhere would raise too many questions."

His father nodded. "You're right, but I don't think you'll gain your mother's agreement to any of this."

"But I have yours?"

"I'll agree to give it a try, but I'm going to insist that we revisit the arrangement on a regular basis. I'm not convinced it's for the best. Still, we'll see where it leads. You need to remember that you'll be a mechanic, not an engineer. You'll be repairing flywheels, looms, and other equipment. It will be up to you to find some way to become acquainted with Mr. Baldwin and possibly form a friendship that will lead to your helping with the new project. There's only a slim chance of that happening. He has a small office in the mechanics' shop, but I don't think you'll have much time to talk with him. And after working ten hours a day with the mechanics and laborers and living in a boardinghouse, I wager you'll change your mind and return home within a month or two."

Morgan shrugged. "I'll do just fine, and I'll get to know Mr. Baldwin—one way or another."

His father rang for Lucy, and moments later she entered the room again. Mr. Stark motioned to the tray. "You can take this, Lucy. The biscuits were excellent, as usual. And would you tell Mrs. Stark I'd like her to join us?"

The maid bobbed her head and retrieved the tray. "Right away, Mr. Stark."

His father swiveled in his chair. "You might as well take these few minutes to prepare yourself, Morgan. I believe you're going to be in for the battle of your life."

A short time later, his mother whooshed into the room like a debutante attending her first ball. Morgan rose to his feet and extended his open arms. "Hello, Mother."

Mouth open wide, she stepped into his embrace. "When did you arrive?" She took a backward step and surveyed him from head to foot. "And why wasn't I told you were here?" She directed a frown at her husband.

22

"You can place the blame on me, Mother. There was a matter I wanted to discuss with Father. I needed to gain his approval before including you in the discussion."

"Are the two of you plotting against me?" She feigned a look of suspicion.

Morgan shook his head. "Not at all." He gestured to one of the chairs. "Why don't you sit down, and I'll tell you everything. But first, I have a question for you."

She tipped her head to the side. "What's that?"

"Did you do as I asked in my letter?"

"Of course. I know you and your father think I can't keep a secret, but I'm very good at sealing my lips when it's important. Yet I'm not sure why you didn't want anyone to know you were coming home."

"Thank you for keeping my confidence, Mother. Now I'm going to tell you why I made the request."

Morgan went on to detail the arrangement he and his father had agreed upon. While his mother attempted to interrupt on several occasions, he'd silenced her and asked her to wait with her questions and comments until he'd finished. Once he'd completed his explanation, she pursed her lips and waited a moment.

She arched her brows. "May I speak now?"

Morgan nodded. "Yes."

"What I have to say won't take long." She looked from Morgan to her husband, then back at Morgan. "That is the most preposterous idea I have ever heard, and I will not agree to one word of it. You have finally come home to Manchester, and I have plans to introduce you to several young ladies. Any one of them would make you a wonderful wife. Until then, I have readied rooms upstairs for you, and you'll live with us until you decide to wed. You will take over management of the Stark Mills so that your father can rest and relax in his old age."

"Old age? I'm not ready for the grave, Ruth." The older man directed a wounded look at his wife. "You're in charge of this house, but I decide who works at the mills and what positions they hold."

His mother paled. "While that may be true, you've said all along that Morgan was going to fill a management position when he returned home. Now I'm hearing all this nonsense about him working as a laborer and living in a boardinghouse. How do you expect me to react? Did you truly believe I would smile and send you off with my blessing?"

"I didn't expect a smile, but I thought that once you realized this is what I want to do, you'd at least consider the idea." He reached for his mother's hand. "This isn't going to be a permanent thing. Father and I agreed we would reevaluate how it's going after a time."

She shook her head. "Nothing you've said convinces me your idea makes any sense."

"That's because you're not involved with the operation of the business, Mother. I gave this a lot of thought before deciding to return home. To be honest, if Father hadn't agreed, I was prepared to accept an engineering offer in Philadelphia."

"*Phil-a-del-phia!*" She clasped a hand to her chest. "Morgan, I would not be able to bear it if you didn't come home and prepare to take over the business. Your father needs you here."

"Then I'm hopeful you will withdraw your objections and give me your blessing."

He spoke with more boldness than he felt, but when his mother sank back in the chair, he knew he'd won her agreement.

Chapter
THREE

LETTER IN HAND, MELLIE APPROACHED THE WATCHMAN with fresh confidence. "I'm here to apply for a position. Mr. Brownell spoke with me in Concord. I have a letter from him. He said I'm to speak with a Mr. Walters."

The watchman unfolded the letter, gave it a quick read, and unlatched the gate. Once inside, he pointed her to a door on the first floor of one of the buildings. "See that door down there? The one on the left?" He arched his brows.

Mellie bobbed her head. "Yes. Is that where I go to meet with Mr. Walters?"

He shrugged. "Don't know if he'll meet with ya, but that's his office. Ain't seen him today. 'Course, that don't mean he didn't come in before I got here. His clerk's there. He should be able to help ya."

Mellie thanked him and made her way across the muddy ruts caused by the summer rains. Before knocking, she inhaled a deep breath and straightened her shoulders. She needed to appear poised. A frowning reflection stared back at her in the window, and she forced a smile. There. That was better. She knocked and waited only a moment before a male voice called for her to enter.

Pen in hand, a gray-headed man was leaning over a ledger, scratching numbers on the page. She stood silently until he finally looked up. "What can I do for you?"

She withdrew the note from Mr. Brownell, along with her letter of recommendation from the Concord Bank president. "I'm a new recruit sent by Mr. Brownell. I also have a letter of recommendation." She proffered the items, but he shook his head.

"You can give them to Mr. Walters. I'll see if he has time for you." He glanced over his shoulder as he strode toward a connecting office door. "You can sit over there and wait." The clerk nodded at a lone wooden chair sitting against the wall.

Mellie mumbled her thanks and followed his bidding. The chair was straight—and hard—likely on purpose. The clerk didn't appear to be the type who wanted anyone lingering in his space. She glanced about the sparsely appointed room. Three sash windows intersected the outer brick wall and permitted the clerk a clear view of the muddy incline she'd just traversed. No doubt he'd seen her coming even before she knocked. No pictures or printed notices broke the monotony of the white plaster walls dividing the offices. But even in this tightly enclosed space, the whirring din of machinery invaded the silence.

She startled when the door opened and the clerk reappeared. "You may go in. Mr. Walters has agreed to see you."

"Thank you." She didn't expect a reply, and none was given. Before she reached the door to Mr. Walters's office, the clerk had returned to his ledger.

Though he hadn't advised her to knock, she tapped on the

door before entering—just in case it was expected. Mr. Walters looked up when she entered and appraised her with dark, piercing eyes. His rotund belly forced him to sit at a distance from his massive walnut desk. While she surmised him to be in his early forties, his thinning brown hair and the wrinkles around his eyes made him appear several years older than that.

"My clerk tells me you've brought a note from Mr. Brownell, as well as a letter of recommendation." When she nodded, he leaned forward and extended his hand. "I'll take a look at them."

Mellie retrieved the missives from her reticule and passed them across the desk. She remained silent while he examined the letters. He hadn't introduced himself or asked for her name. He hadn't even offered for her to sit down. Was that a bad sign?

"So, Miss Blanchard, I see you come highly recommended as a tutor." He looked up from the letter. "What experience do you have working in a textile mill?"

"None." She cleared her throat. "I told Mr. Brownell I didn't have any experience. He said good moral character was of greater import."

Mr. Walters wiped the perspiration from his forehead. "While our girls must be of good moral character, it's always pleasing if they come to us with some measure of skill. However, you've been working as a teacher, so you're obviously well educated and most likely a quick learner. Am I right?"

"I like to think I'm capable, Mr. Walters."

He shifted in his chair and gestured for her to sit down. "Tell me, Miss—" he hesitated and glanced at the letter again— "Blanchard. Why is a young lady of your education seeking work in the mills? You appear to be a woman of means." He touched his lapel. "The quality of your clothing far surpasses what my employees would own."

Mellie folded her hands and placed them in her lap. "My family has fallen upon difficult times and I've had to step forward. I can be of greater help to them by working here than continuing in my tutoring position."

"Well, I suppose that's your decision, but you'll find working in the mills more demanding than tutoring children." He opened a thick ledger and traced his finger down the page. "You should report to Mr. Fuqua in the morning. He's the overseer of the weaving rooms in Mill Number Two."

"The five-story building?"

He nodded. "There are over five hundred looms in the number-two mill, where we produce sheeting and drilling. You'll be expected to operate more than one loom, of course. Mr. Fuqua will see that you receive the proper training." He penned a note and handed it to her. "Give that note to Mr. Fuqua when you report tomorrow. He'll have you sign the regulations and file it here in the office. I hope Mr. Brownell told you that we require a commitment of one year."

"He did." She folded the note and tucked it back into her reticule. "He also told me to report to Mrs. Richards's boardinghouse. I've already done so."

Mr. Walters nodded. "I hope she had a bed available for you. Mrs. Richards is one of our best boardinghouse keepers. Unlike many others, she keeps impeccable records."

"I believe I'll be sharing an attic room with some of the other girls."

"Good, good! I'm sure you'll be quite comfortable there. No doubt she has other boarders who work at Number Two. You can have one of them direct you to Mr. Fuqua in the morning." He withdrew a watch from the pocket of his bulging vest. "I wish you the best in your employment with Stark Mills, Miss

Blanchard. Put forth your best effort and you'll be rewarded. Good day to you."

"Good day to you as well, Mr. Walters." She glanced over her shoulder when she reached the office door. "And thank you for your time."

When Mr. Walters didn't acknowledge her final comment, Mellie hurried from the room and through the clerk's office without a backward look. By the time she passed through the iron gates, her fears had lessened considerably. She offered a silent prayer of thanks that the meeting with Mr. Walters had gone well, with one of her favorite hymns having bolstered her strength.

She'd accomplished what she came here to do. Secure a position that would help support her sister, Margaret, and her children. Along with the tutoring wages her sister would earn back in Concord, Mellie's contribution should add enough for them to get by. She stopped short. She hadn't inquired about wages—and Mr. Walters hadn't mentioned the rate of pay.

While Mr. Brownell had declared the pay for a mill girl would far exceed what she'd been earning in Concord, he hadn't been specific. Instead, he'd touted the fact that all of the mill girls had ample funds to purchase fine clothes and still help support their families at home. Eager to find a solution to Margaret's financial woes, she'd taken Mr. Brownell at his word. She now hoped her trust hadn't been misplaced.

Perhaps Mr. Fuqua was the one who set the wages for his employees. She'd be certain to inquire before she signed the paper work. Thus far, it seemed as if rules and regulations were more important than wages—at least to those who ran things in the town.

A stiff breeze whipped Mellie's skirts as she rounded the

corner and began her ascent to the boardinghouse. Using one hand to hold her skirts, she used the other to hold her bonnet tight to her head. Come winter, a breeze such as this one would chill to the bone. For now, she would enjoy the fresh air and warm August sunshine and put aside thoughts of traversing this distance several times a day in rain, sleet, or snow.

"I see you've made it back." Mrs. Richards stood on the front stoop, clutching the wooden handle of a straw broom. "Did all go well? You secured a position?" She swiped several leaves from the doorstep. "Try as I may, I can't keep this stoop clean. What I don't sweep away ends up getting tracked in by the girls."

"With this wind, it's a never-ending task, I'm sure." Mellie followed the older woman inside. "I'm not exactly sure what work I'll be doing, but I'm to report to the overseer at Stark Mill Number Two tomorrow morning."

"Good for you." She gestured to the stairway. "Come on in. Your trunks arrived, and I had them carried upstairs. The drayman was none too happy. He said if he'd known there were two sets of stairs, he would have charged you more."

"I'm sorry. I hope he didn't badger you."

The older woman chuckled. "I've been dealing with the likes of that drayman for years. I handed him a couple of biscuits and he was happy enough. However, the girls you'll be rooming with in the attic may be a mite unhappy with you."

"Why?" A pang of uneasiness assailed her.

The keeper stopped in the small foyer and looked back at Mellie. "I've never had anyone arrive with so much baggage. Usually the girls come here with a small trunk and maybe a bandbox. Your two big trunks and bandboxes filled most of the empty space in the room. It's going to be a tight fit for the five of you and all your belongings."

"I didn't realize." Mellie caught her bottom lip between her teeth. She didn't want to start off on a poor footing with the other girls, but she hadn't known she'd be sharing a small attic room with four other boarders. The very thought gave her pause. She was accustomed to a large airy room that overlooked a beautiful garden, where she would sit at her writing desk and journal the day's activities. A room with pale blue walls, yellow flowered draperies, two large chifforobes, and a chest of drawers in which to store her things.

"This room to the left as you come in is my bedroom, and the parlor is also considered a part of my living quarters. However, I do permit the girls to use it from time to time if they're entertaining special company. There's another small room off the kitchen that was once used for kitchen help or an extra boarder, but we're now required to keep a sickroom." She furrowed her brows. "You don't have lung problems, do you?"

Mellie shook her head. "No, I'm quite healthy."

The older woman nodded. "Lots of the girls have breathing problems once they start working in the mills. When we had the cholera epidemic hit last year, they added a new requirement to our regulations. Sick girls have to sleep in a room away from the others." She grasped the railing and started up the steps. "Come. I'll show you the rest of the place."

She followed Mrs. Richards up the remaining steps and down a narrow hallway bordered by closed doors. Near the end of the hall, Mrs. Richards made a sharp turn and opened a door leading to an even narrower set of stairs. Little wonder the drayman had been upset. Mellie couldn't imagine how he'd gotten her trunks up the narrow passage.

Mrs. Richards tapped the back side of the door. "Last one down in the morning makes sure to close the door, and the last one up at night does the same. Heat rises. It gets too warm up there in the summer with the door open. Come winter, the girls down here complain all the heat is going to the attic and they get too cold."

Mellie wondered how the attic was to be warmed during the winter if the door was closed, but she didn't ask. When colder weather arrived, she'd inquire. For now, the windows could be opened to provide a breeze.

"Here we are." Mrs. Richards took only a few steps into the attic before she bent forward and breathed heavily. "Those stairs are going to be the death of me."

Mellie's eyes slowly adjusted to the dim light. Stale air permeated the space. Two dormer windows, the only source of light and ventilation, were closed tight. "Perhaps if you opened the windows, the fresh air would help your breathing, Mrs. Richards."

"Windows remain closed during the days you girls are at work. They can be left open in the evenings and on Sundays beginning the end of May until the last day of August."

Thinking the woman must surely be joking about such a rule, Mellie chuckled. "And if it is hot on the first day of September?"

The keeper shrugged. "It doesn't matter. The windows must remain closed—one of the boardinghouse regulations."

"I see." But she really didn't see. She doubted the company owners who lived in fancy houses kept their doors and windows closed according to the same schedule. Still, she pushed the thought aside. Complaining would yield her nothing but difficulty.

"You're sharing the attic with Cora and Clara Winters. They're twins who hail from Massachusetts. Sweet girls. You'll like them. Then there's Phebe Collins and Olive French." She pointed to a narrow bed as if the two young ladies were present. "Olive will move downstairs as soon as Susan leaves for home. That will give you a little more space."

Two narrow beds centered the room with only a small space between. A bowl and pitcher sat balanced on one of the trunks that lined the walls. Bandboxes teetered atop the remaining trunks, while shoes and nightshifts lay scattered on what floor space remained in the room.

Mellie nodded from one bed to the other. "Where am I to sleep, Mrs. Richards?"

"You and the girls can decide who you'll sleep with. If I were you, I'd choose Cora and Clara. They're smaller, so you'll have more space."

Mellie struggled to comprehend what she'd heard. Sleeping in a bed with two strangers? Could she? Before she could formulate her thoughts, Mrs. Richards motioned her toward the stairs.

"Come along and I'll show you the rest of the house before I return to my duties in the kitchen. Before long, the girls will whoosh in here for their noonday meal, and heaven help me if it isn't on the table." Several graying strands escaped the keeper's tightly wound braid and bounced in rhythm as she descended the attic stairway. She stopped and opened one of the bedroom doors that bordered the hallway. "You can take a peek inside."

Mellie edged around the buxom woman. She'd expected far more space in the second-floor rooms, but upon inspection she was sorely disappointed. The room was of reasonable size and would provide adequate space for two or possibly three young ladies, but four or five occupied this room. The two beds had been shoved together below one of the six-over-six sash windows. Trunks, boxes, and personal items crammed every remaining nook and cranny. She stared in wonder. How did they ever perform a proper toilette?

She waved Mellie toward the stairs. "No need to look any further. The other three are about the same." At the bottom of the stairs, she pointed to the front room of the house but continued walking. In the dining room, twenty place settings had been positioned on a long table.

Mellie let her gaze linger on the table and tried to imagine being gathered with twenty strangers for each meal. Of course, they wouldn't be strangers for long, but still, the idea was somewhat daunting.

Mrs. Richards continued into the kitchen. "As you can see, this is where the cooking gets done, and I need to get to it before the bells ring. There's a copy of the regulations on the parlor table for you to read before the noonday meal."

Mellie's emotions warred within as she returned to the parlor. Could she adjust to so many changes overnight? Her mind told her she must, yet her heart wanted to board the next train out of Manchester. Bells rang in the distance as she retrieved the printed regulations from an ornately carved mahogany table before sitting down.

A short time later, bells once again sounded, and then the front door burst open. Chattering voices sprinkled with laughter couldn't dull the sound of feet pounding against the wood floor. Mellie sat unnoticed as the flurry of cotton skirts and scuffed shoes trampled the hallway.

Mrs. Richards waved her forward. "Come on and join the others or you'll be starving by supper, Mellie. I've set a place for you."

Mellie cautiously approached the dining room. She steeled herself for the barrage of questions that would likely follow her introduction. However, her presence was barely noticed. One or two of the girls grunted and nodded while the others continued bolting down the food they spooned onto their chipped plates. There was no pleasant conversation or laughter, no mention of the morning's activities or plans for the evening—only the sound of silverware scraping on china.

She settled on the empty chair at the end of the table and spooned a small helping of boiled beef and creamed potatoes onto her plate. Those around her continued to eat as though they'd never see another meal. Before she'd taken more than a few bites, the girls pushed away from the table, ran for the hallway, grabbed their lightweight capes and bonnets, and were out the door.

Once the girls departed, Mrs. Richards bustled into the dining room, stacked the dirty plates, and gathered the utensils.

"I don't know how the girls are able to eat so rapidly," Mellie said. "Surely they must realize it isn't good for the digestion."

Mrs. Richards chuckled. "It may not be good for the digestion, but it's better than going back to work hungry. They have only thirty minutes for their meals. During that short time, they must leave their workstation, rush to the boardinghouse, eat their meal, and return to their machines." She stacked several bowls at the end of the table. "My house isn't as far away as some, so my girls are fortunate. They have a little more time than those who live in the houses farther up the hill. You'll soon learn that manners don't count around the boardinghouse table—not if you want to maintain your strength at the mill."

Mellie wondered if she'd ever count herself fortunate to be living here, but she didn't voice the thought. Realizing she was in the way, she handed her plate and utensils to Mrs. Richards.

"We all have to hurry if we're going to finish everything

that needs to be done in a day." Mrs. Richards blew out a long breath. "Right now I need to wash the dishes and then get to my ledgers. Since you're done eating, you might as well go up to your room and unpack your belongings. You can use the empty pegs on the wall." Her gaze traveled the length of Mellie's day dress. "You'll want to wear something more serviceable tomorrow. If you go in dressed like that, the overseer will think you've come expecting tea instead of a job."

"Thank you, I'll see what I can find." She hesitated. "I have a plain navy broadcloth."

The older woman shrugged. "Up to you, but you'll look like you were caught in a snowstorm within a half hour."

Mellie frowned. "I don't understand."

"Lint. The air's full of lint in the mills. If you've nothing but more fancy dresses in your trunks, you best wear the broadcloth. I can loan you an apron, or maybe one of the girls will let you borrow one of her calicos."

"I'll see if I have something that will do." Mellie turned her head and hurried from the room before the older woman could see the tears pooling in her eyes.

Chapter

FOUR

THE AFTERNOON HAD PASSED SLOWLY. DESPITE THE HEAT and stale air, Mellie had remained in the attic room until the evening bells announced the end of the workday. Hoping she'd appear more like the other boarders, Mellie had changed into her broadcloth dress before arriving at the dinner table.

Mrs. Richards stood at the side of the table until all the girls were seated. "I know you didn't have time earlier, but I want our new boarder, Mellicent Blanchard, to tell you a bit about herself. I believe she prefers to be addressed as Mellie, and she hails from Concord. Isn't that right, Mellie?" The older woman looked at Mellie and smiled.

"Yes." Twenty sets of eyes—twenty-one if she counted Mrs. Richards—stared down the table at her. The last time she'd felt such discomfort had been as a six-year-old when she'd been introduced to her class at boarding school.

When she didn't say anything further, Mrs. Richards continued, "Mellie has been assigned to Mr. Fuqua in Stark Mill

Number Two." She turned to the two girls sitting to Mellie's left. "Cora and Clara both work at Number Two, so you can walk to the mill with them in the morning."

The blond-haired girls bobbed their heads in unison and offered Mellie a smile.

A girl at the other end of the table leaned forward and pinned Mellie with a scowl as Mrs. Richards retreated to the kitchen. "I hope you didn't put her in our room. It's too crowded already."

"Well, so are all the rest of the rooms. So don't put her in ours," another called out.

Mellie shrank back, her nerves taut. Did they treat every new boarder this way?

Mrs. Richards hurried from the kitchen with a tray bearing a platter and three bowls. The sight of food seemed to have a quieting effect upon the girls—at least for the moment.

"Stop bickering or I'll make certain those who complain have at least five girls in their bedrooms every night." Mrs. Richards gave the group a hard stare. "Mellie has been assigned to the attic."

A girl sitting across the table groaned. "There's not enough beds, Mrs. Richards."

"She can sleep with us." The girl looked at Mellie. "Me and Clara don't take much space. We're twins, you know."

Mellie smiled and nodded. "Thank you. I don't snore, and I promise to keep to my side of the bed."

Mrs. Richards's lips curved in a broad smile. "Thank you, Cora. I can always count on you and Clara to be kind. Go on and tell the girls a little about yourself, Mellie."

Mellie glanced around the table, pleased to see that the girls appeared far more interested in eating supper than anything else. "I came to Manchester seeking work. My sister and her children live in Concord and have fallen on difficult times. I thought working in the mills would offer me enough money to help them."

"What'd you do in Concord?" The girl pointed her fork at Mellie's hands. "Those hands of yours ain't seen a lot of hard work."

A low murmur hummed around the table as the rest of the girls leaned forward to gain a look. Mellie longed to hide her hands beneath the table, but that would never do. Instead, she agreed with the girl. "You're right that I haven't performed much manual labor. I was employed as a tutor for a family in Concord. Though the work is different, educating children can certainly be laborious."

The girl sniggered. "We'll see if you think that's true after you've been in the mills a day or two. I, for one, think you'll soon change your tune." Her supper finished, she pushed her plate to the center of the table. "Anyone else going into town?"

The girls gobbled the remainder of their supper, and soon the clatter of shoes racing up the steps filled the house. Both Clara and Cora remained in the dining room with Mellie. Cora finished her last bite of the yeasty bread before touching Mellie's arm. "We'll go up to the attic with you. Olive might not like it if you change things around, but she won't complain if we do it."

Mellie silently rejoiced that she'd spent the afternoon writing in her journal rather than unpacking. She followed the twins upstairs. Who would ever believe that procrastination could prove to be advantageous?

⁂

Two shabby calicos and worn boots were a poor exchange for Mellie's lace fichu and French-beaded reticule, but Olive had insisted she'd agree to nothing less. The twins had attempted to convince Olive it was her Christian duty to loan Mellie a dress and shoes until she received her pay, though Olive remained steadfast. She'd been quick to observe Mellie's need and eager to benefit from the new arrival's situation. The twins' clothing was too small for Mellie, and Phebe's far too large. Olive's proved a perfect fit.

When Olive insisted upon both the fichu and the reticule, Mellie had considered bartering with one of the girls in a downstairs bedroom. Unfortunately, they'd returned from town only minutes before the ten o'clock curfew. She dared not prowl the house after bedtime, so she'd relented. The price had been dear, but she would have little use for her beaded reticule and lace fichu in the future—at least that was what she'd told herself during fits of wakefulness throughout the night.

No morning light had yet crept through the attic windows when Mellie was jarred awake by the clanging of the first morning bells. She moaned and struggled to roll onto her side when a quick jab of Cora's elbow warned that her attempt would fail.

"Roll out, Mellie. We've only thirty minutes before final bells ring. You don't want to be late or you'll be terminated before you ever begin work."

As Mellie suspected, there was neither time nor space for a proper toilette before rushing off to the mill. In turn, the girls washed at the pitcher and bowl, donned their calicos and boots, used the privy behind the boardinghouse, returned for their bonnets, and accepted a thick slice of brown bread slathered with jam from Mrs. Richards as they raced out the door and down the hill.

Clara nudged Mellie's arm. "Eat while you're walking, Mellie. You can't take that bread into the mill. And make sure all the jam is wiped off your fingers."

"I'm not hungry."

Cora nodded. "Clara's right. You need to eat whether you're hungry or not. You'll be famished in no time. That slice of bread will help stave off your hunger until we go back to the boarding-house for breakfast."

Grape jam smeared Mellie's mouth by the time they'd neared the gates. Using a lace-edged handkerchief she'd tucked into the pocket of Olive's shabby calico, she carefully wiped her face and hands.

Phebe huffed as she struggled to keep pace. "It won't be as bad as you think, Mellie. I remember my first day. I was so scared I thought I'd lose my breakfast. As you can see, I made it through that first day and all the rest, too." She made a sweeping gesture down her ample figure. "As long as you keep to your looms, you'll do fine." She grinned in a way that accentuated her plump cheeks. "Most of the girls are kind and will offer help if you have a problem."

"Phebe's right. There's no reason to worry yourself." Cora looped arms with Mellie as the huge iron gates swung open. "I'll take you to Mr. Fuqua before I go to my looms. I hope he'll assign you to work near us, but if he doesn't, you'll discover there's always a kind girl or two who will help when needed. You'll do fine. All of us made it through those first days."

The bread and jam settled like a brick in Mellie's stomach. She shouldn't have eaten. Worse yet, what if she expelled the contents of her stomach in front of the overseer? Her thoughts whirred, and her head ached from lack of sleep and worry.

Cora nodded toward the nearby towering fortress. "Come on, this is Stark Number Two. Remember—once they start the machines, you'll not be able to hear much, so you need to hol-ler loud to gain the attention of the overseer or other workers."

Inside Cora gestured to the winding steps leading to the upper floors. "Weaving room is on the top floor."

Phebe sighed. "Climbing these steps is the hardest part of the day for me."

By the time they'd climbed the four flights of winding steps, Mellie longed for a drink of water and a few moments to catch her breath, but Cora grasped her hand and pulled her along. As they continued along the outer row of looms, Cora waved to a wiry man holding a ledger, then leaned her head close to Mellie. "That's Mr. Fuqua."

When they drew near, he smiled and bid Cora good morning and then looked at Mellie. "You must be the new girl. Mr. Walters told me you'd be reporting today. We had planned to keep you in the weaving room, but two girls from the spinning floor left earlier this week and there's a greater need down there. I'll take you to meet Mr. Comstock. He's the overseer in the spinning room."

Mellie's lips began to tremble, and her hands shook. Her entire body converted into a quivering bowl of jelly. *Don't cry. Don't cry.* Over and over she silently repeated the words, her mind begging her body to listen. She fixed her eyes on Cora and prayed the girl would sense her fear and do something—anything that would keep her nearby.

Cora squeezed her hand and smiled. "You'll do fine in the spinning room. I know a couple girls who work there. When the bell rings, meet us at the bottom of the stairs, and we'll walk home together for breakfast."

Mr. Fuqua pointed to the steps. "We need to hurry downstairs. I must return before they start the machines."

After one final glance at Cora and Clara, Mellie followed Mr. Fuqua down the winding steps and into the spinning room. Mr.

Comstock's smile faded when he learned she had no experience, yet he didn't let her return upstairs.

He glanced at the paper Mr. Fuqua left with him before signaling her to follow him to a pedestal table, where he could stand and oversee the room. "You need to sign your papers."

Mellie lifted the paper and scanned the page. "Does this set forth my wages? No one has mentioned my pay."

"You have no experience, so you'll begin at four dollars a week. One dollar and twenty-five cents will be withheld to cover your room and board."

Mellie gasped. "I was told the company paid for my room and board."

"The company pays twenty-five cents and you pay the remainder." Mr. Comstock shrugged. "The keepers receive one dollar and fifty cents for each boarder." He turned away and quickly scanned the room before tapping the paper. "Sign on the bottom line. You have to get started working if you expect to be paid for today."

Mellie dipped the overseer's pen into the inkwell and scratched her name on the designated line while calculating how much money she'd be able to send home each week. She would need to maintain a portion of her weekly wages for incidental expenses. Even if she'd been able to send Margaret three dollars a week, it wouldn't be enough. She'd planned to send her sister at least four dollars a week. Why had she listened to Mr. Brownell's puffery? Her thoughts raced. She would need to find a solution—perhaps tutoring a child in the evenings or working as a clerk in one of the local shops.

Mr. Comstock cleared his throat and frowned. "No daydreaming while at work, Miss Blanchard." Heat rose in her cheeks as he crooked a finger at an operative standing near one of the machines. The young woman scurried to his side.

"This is our new girl. She has no training, so you'll teach her." He turned to Mellie. "This is Sarah, one of my best operatives. Listen to her." That said, he returned to the far side of the room and bellowed, "Two minutes!"

Sarah waved her forward to one of the roving machines. "The machines will turn on in two minutes and then it will be hard to hear." She tugged on her ear as if to emphasize her point. She indicated the spindles of thick cotton roving at the top of the machine. "The roving is pulled into the drawing roller where it is stretched. Then the spinning flyer pulls down the roving where it's spun into yarn." She pointed to the bottom of the frame. "Those heart-shaped cams provide even distribution of the thread onto the lower bobbins by slowly moving the bobbins up and down. If the machine isn't working properly, signal Mr. Comstock." She gestured to a young girl stationed nearby. "The bobbin doffers watch the frames and replace the bobbins when they're full."

Sarah had barely completed the explanation when the wood-and-iron beasts around them thundered and belched to life. Trembling sensations coursed from the bottom of Mellie's feet to the top of her head. Sarah pulled the handle of her machine, and it joined in the pulsing chorus. With amazing speed, the machine stretched and thinned the roving before spinning it onto the empty wooden bobbins. The two of them watched as the machine did its work. Soon Sarah moved to another machine and pulled the handle, and then another.

She leaned close to Mellie's ear. "You'll be able to manage more than one machine before day's end." Pointing to one of the idle machines, she gestured for Mellie to pull the handle and set to work. Though she didn't know what she'd do if the machine should malfunction, Mellie pulled down on the handle and watched as the spools of roving twisted and turned through the machine. Like the other girls, she stood watching the frame, amazed when one of the children rushed forward, removed the full bobbin, and slid an empty bobbin into place.

Sarah drew near and pointed to the next frame. "Go ahead and start a second machine. You're doing fine."

Mellie pulled the handle, and her second machine churned into action.

After nearly two hours standing in front of the frames, her eyes glazed and her legs ached. Lint filled the air, and the room was now warm and dank, making each breath more difficult than the last. The deafening noise worsened her headache. She longed for the peace and quietude of home. Closing her eyes, she envisioned the pastoral countryside, where she'd take the banker's children for afternoon picnics during the spring and early autumn. Then a tap on her shoulder jerked her back to the present.

Mr. Comstock stood at her side and hollered near her ear, "Keep your eyes open and fixed on your frames, Miss Blanchard! The roving can snarl or break. You need to be attentive at all times. If you're tired, go to bed early tonight."

"Yes, sir." The heat rose in her cheeks as he proceeded down one row of machines and up the next, his watchful eyes seeming to dart in every direction.

When the breakfast bell rang, Sarah shouted for Mellie to shut down her frames. Before she reached the handle on the second frame, the other operatives had raced toward the doorway and were clattering down the winding steps. She squeezed among the girls descending from the fourth floor and was pushed along with the throng to the outer doors. Once outside, she flattened her back against one of the cold brick walls and watched for Clara and Cora.

The twins spotted her. Clara grabbed her hand, and they began running. "How'd it go in the spinning room?" Clara asked.

"I grew weary of standing and staring at the frames, but I suppose it went well. While the work is tedious and mindless, I'm thankful for it." How could the twins run at this pace after standing the past two hours?

Her legs ached as she hurried alongside the twosome. Would she be able to stand at her frames until seven o'clock this evening? She wanted to ask the twins if they ever suffered cramps in their legs or fainted from the oppressive heat and humidity inside the workrooms, but talking would take more breath than she could muster while hurrying across the mill yard toward the boardinghouse.

Mellie and the twins were among the last to rush into the house, hang their bonnets on the pegs by the door, and scurry to find a place at the table. As Cora and Mellie sat down side by side, Clara found an empty chair opposite them.

Cora nudged Mellie and leaned close. "Be sure you eat fast and as much as you can. Breakfast and noonday meals are hearty, while evening meals aren't as plentiful."

Mrs. Richards handed a platter of sausage to a girl at the end of the table, followed by heaping bowls of scrambled eggs, gravy, and warm biscuits. Several crocks of butter and jam were centered on the table, along with pitchers of cold water and milk. No manners were observed. A grunt and a pointed finger signified that a bowl or platter should be passed. Forks clattered on plates, and arms gyrated from hand to mouth like spinning whirligigs. Mellie did her best to keep up with the others, but the rapid pace barely allowed time for tasting, much less chewing. She'd finished only a portion of the food on her plate when the bells rang.

Chairs immediately scraped across the wood floor as the girls rose and dashed toward the door like a swarm of bees seeking nectar. They made their return down the hill, across the mill yard, and up the winding stairs at the same breakneck pace. With her stomach aching as much as her legs, Mellie came to a panting halt in front of her frames. She shouldn't have eaten so quickly or so much.

Before she'd caught her breath, Mr. Comstock lifted his arm and jerked it in a downward motion, his signal to begin work. One by one, the operatives pulled the wooden handles, the frames rumbling to life. The noise seemed to be even more deafening than it had only a short time ago.

Along with the other girls, Mellie repeated the same rushed ordeal when the noonday bells rang. By midafternoon she was certain she couldn't bear to stand at the frames until seven o'clock. Every muscle ached and begged for rest. She directed a look toward the wall of windows. If only they'd open one of them. Perspiration dampened her body, the calico dress clinging to her thin frame. Her eyes itched, and she longed for a breath of fresh air.

When the bells rang to signal the end of the workday, the girls hurried to the stairwell, but not with the intensity they'd exhibited earlier in the day. This departure was more casual. Their supper would be waiting, yet they could take time to laugh and visit during the walk home. The bells would ring again to tell them when to go to bed, but they wouldn't call them back to work until morning. And for that, Mellie was most grateful. Though her aching body begged her to quit, she knew she couldn't.

Her family needed her.

Chapter

FIVE

MELLIE HAD BEEN WORKING AT THE MILL FOR ONLY A week when several girls suggested a walk into town after supper. While they continued to discuss ribbon and lace to transform old dresses, Mellie could think of nothing but sleep. Her weary body needed a night of peaceful sleep—a desire that would likely go unfulfilled until she could return to Concord for a visit. And with every cent needed to help her sister and the children, a visit home was a far-flung dream.

"Come with us, Mellie!" Jane, one of the girls who boarded in a downstairs room, leaned forward to capture her attention. "You need to see the town and walk through the shops. Trust me, you'll enjoy doing something other than sleeping and standing at your frames."

Mellie attempted a smile as she shook her head. "I'm too tired. I don't know how you girls do it every day. My body aches, and I fear it needs sleep more than shopping or sightseeing."

"We won't stay long," one of the other girls added. "Go up-

stairs and change into another pair of shoes—that always helps."
She looked around the table. "Everyone who's going, be at the
front door in five minutes."

Cora circled around to Mellie's side. "You should come. When
new boarders refuse, the other girls think they're being uppity.
I know you're tired, but Clara and I will go along. We won't
stay long. I promise."

"Unless you want to remain longer once we get there." Clara
grinned. "I think it will cheer you a bit, Mellie. Please say you'll
come."

She felt that she should remain behind and go to bed or even
write a letter to her sister, but instead she nodded her assent.
The idea that the other boarders might believe her unfriendly
or aloof had been a motivating argument. She'd be living here
for at least the next year, and she needed friends, not enemies.

Not all of the girls were waiting by the front door when the
twins and Mellie returned downstairs. Mellie glanced over her
shoulder. "Are the others coming?"

Jane shook her head. "Olive and Charity decided to remain
behind, and Ada said she doesn't feel well. She has trouble
breathing. Mrs. Richards said Ada needs to go home and breathe
some fresh air for a few months so she doesn't ruin her lungs.
Ada's been working in the mills since she was fourteen. She
keeps getting worse, but she says her family can't get along
without her wages."

"That's true for all of us, isn't it?" Mellie arched her brows.

"Not true for me." Abigail shook her head with such vigor
that her bonnet shifted. "Not true for quite a few of us. I came
here to gain a bit of independence and have money I could
spend or save as I pleased. None of my wages go back home."
She gestured to some of the others. "Same for you, isn't it?"

Several of them murmured agreement, but Phebe shook her head. "It's not like that for me. Except for a tiny sum, I send all my wages home. My pa hasn't been able to find work, and my little brother, Timothy, is sickly. They need every bit of my pay just to cover their necessities and the doctor's bill or medicine when Timmy's sick. The doctor won't come any more unless Pa pays him first—says we already owe him too much money."

Cora offered Phebe a sympathetic smile and gave a nod. "Me and Clara send part of our money home so that our brother can go to college, but we keep the rest. We save some in the company bank and spend a little on ourselves, too."

"Cora spends more than me." Clara pinned her sister with a defiant look. "And don't you try to deny it, Cora."

"There's nothing wrong with buying a pretty ribbon or piece of fabric from time to time, Clara." Cora turned from her sister and nudged Mellie. "This is Elm Street. Most of the stores where we shop are along here. I like to go into the shops at the Merchants Exchange. At Bachelder's they have hosiery and fancy goods of every sort. Putney's Confectionery is there, too." She licked her lips. "They have the most wonderful tea cakes, and you can get tea or coffee in the attached public house."

"And they sell horehound and coltsfoot candy. Both taste good and help with breathing problems and a scratchy throat." Clara's brows knit together. "Maybe we should pick up a stick of coltsfoot for Ada."

"How kind of you, Clara," Mellie said. "I wish I could offer to pay, but I gave the last of my money to the drayman who delivered my trunks."

The street was lined with granite and brick buildings, each glass window displaying the latest wares. Jane signaled them to a halt in front of Charles Pittney's Millinery. A sign in the window boasted sale prices on all their ribbons, laces, silks, velvets, satins, and embroideries, as well as the largest selection of fashionable bonnets to be had in all of New Hampshire.

Jane nodded toward the doors of the millinery. "We have to go in here. I need some ribbon for the dress I'm going to wear to the Grand Complimentary Ball, and they always have the best selection."

Alice chuckled. "The ball isn't until the middle of October, Jane. I don't think you need over two months to sew a bit of lace on your dress."

"You can wait until a few days before the dance to alter your dress, Alice, but I prefer to have mine ready ahead of time." Jane pointed to a sign in the window. "Besides, the sign says everything's on sale."

Mellie turned her attention to a storefront across the street. Though the sign advertised ambrotypes, the window revealed several paintings. "I believe I'll go over there and look at the artwork displayed in the window. There's no need for me to go into Pittney's. I can't afford to purchase anything tonight."

Jane hiked a shoulder. "Suit yourself, but we'll be a while. Come over and join us when you're through."

Cora drew near to Mellie's side. "I'll go with you. Clara's going to Putney's to purchase some candy for Ada."

Cora and Mellie waited for a carriage to pass before crossing to the other side of the street. Once in front of the photography shop, the two of them stared at several pastoral scenes in expensive gilt frames. After a few moments, Cora turned to Mellie. "Do you paint pictures, Mellie?"

"No. I can draw a little, and I've learned paper cutting, but I've never painted anything. Still, I admire those who can put brush to canvas and create beauty, don't you?"

"They're very pretty." Cora bobbed her head. "I've never been in this shop. I'd like to see what it would cost to have a likeness made of Clara and me to send home to our family." She grasped Mellie's hand. "Come on, let's go inside."

A bell jingled as they pulled open the door. Paintings hung along one wall of the shop. In an alcove on the opposite side, two upholstered chairs flanked a circular table covered with a burgundy velvet cloth. A still-life picture was centered above the chairs. The niche was effectively fashioned to resemble a family parlor. A camera sat atop a high table opposite the setting.

Mellie chuckled when Cora settled into one of the chairs, lifted her head, and folded her hands in her lap. "How do I look? Would this make a good pose?"

They both startled when a balding gentleman rounded the corner. He pointed toward the unoccupied chair. "I would suggest we remove the extra chair before I take your picture."

As he strode forward, Cora jumped to her feet. "I was only pretending. I don't think I could ever afford a picture, sir."

His blue eyes twinkled. "If you work in the mills, I'm sure you make enough money to purchase a small ambrotype." He motioned them to a counter at the rear of the room. "Take a look at these smaller ones. A picture this size is only one dollar."

Cora studied the picture he handed to her, then returned it to the counter and picked up one of the larger offerings. "This is much nicer. I doubt my father would be able to make out Clara and me in one of the smaller pictures." She touched a finger near her right eye. "Pa's eyesight is poor." She tapped the larger photograph. "How much is this size?"

"That is one of our finest. It is ten dollars."

Cora gulped. "I wouldn't want to spend that much on a picture. If I'm going to spend ten dollars, I think my folks would rather have something useful, but thank you for your time." After tracing her finger along the edge of the framed picture, Cora turned away from the counter. Her eyes shone with longing when she looked at Mellie. "I'd like to send them a likeness of Clara and me—one my pa could see—but the price is too much for me." Cora thanked the owner, and the two of them stepped outside. "Would you spend that much on a picture, Mellie?"

Mellie shook her head. "My wages are needed for my family's necessities. They don't need a picture of me."

Cora tipped her head and peered at Mellie. "Do your folks expect you to send your wages home every payday?"

The twosome crossed the street and stopped in front of Pittney's. "My parents died when I was a young girl. My sister and I were placed under the guardianship of my uncle, who managed my parents' estate. He sent me to boarding school and later to finishing school. My sister, who is eleven years older than me, married at a young age. When my uncle died, her husband took charge of the estate. Upon his recent death, we discovered he'd disposed of our inheritance. He left my sister and her children in dire financial straits, and I want to help them as much as I can."

She hadn't anticipated relating the past would be difficult, but it had been. Like tearing the scab off an old wound, she felt an initial sting and then an oozing flow of anguish and grief. For the life she'd left behind, for her future in the mills, but mostly for her sister and the children. They were suffering the most.

Cora turned to her. "You couldn't find a position in Concord that would have been more to your liking and offered decent wages?" Her brows arched. "Surely with your education . . ."

The unfinished question hung between them while Mellie

decided how, or if, she should reply. Yet Cora wasn't like the folks back home, those who were eager to spread every tittle and jot of gossip, no matter how painful. Cora's questions came from a place of curiosity rather than cruelty.

"I was a tutor for a wealthy family in Concord—their family owned the bank. They paid me very well, and I was happy with the position. But when my brother-in-law died, he'd left behind enormous debt, and then it was discovered he'd embezzled money. We were considered outcasts."

Cora's smooth features tightened into a frown. "So the banker terminated your position?"

"No. At my request, he permitted my sister to take over the position. She's able to tutor her own children while instructing the banker's children. It works perfectly, and he was most kind. My sister wouldn't have been able to find employment elsewhere. While I could have looked for a position as a tutor here in Manchester, I was told I would make much more by working in the mills. And families hiring a tutor closely investigate applicants. I'm sure I wouldn't have wanted to answer some of their questions."

"I didn't mean to pry, but I'm sure you understand that your fine belongings caused us to wonder."

"Of course, but I'd be thankful if you didn't share everything I've told you with anyone other than Clara, and perhaps Phebe. She seems a kind girl. I'll share with the others when I feel the time is appropriate."

"We wouldn't breathe a word. You can trust Clara and me. We learned how to keep a secret long ago." She grinned. "And you can trust Phebe, too. She's dependable. A good sort—does her best to help support her family."

Mellie nodded and gestured toward the door. "Shall we go inside and see what the others have found?"

While they made their way down the aisles, Mellie's thoughts returned to the photography shop. Perhaps the owner would be interested in hiring her to help during the evenings. Maybe she could somehow use her paper-cutting abilities to increase his business. Then again, perhaps he'd consider her paper cutting as competition for his photography business. She'd need to give the matter more thought—and prayer.

While a couple of the girls were looking at bonnets, several others were talking with a group of fellows who appeared more interested in the girls than in ribbons or lace. Cora glanced around, then nodded to Clara, who was admiring a display of lace. "I'll fetch Clara and Phebe. We can go back to the house if you'd like. I know you're tired."

"Thank you, but if you and the others want to stay, I believe I can find my way."

Cora shook her head and hurried off. "Just wait for a few moments." A short time later, she returned with Clara and Phebe following on her heels. "Clara and Phebe want to go back, too." Cora pointed to the door. "Shall we?"

When Cora told the others they were leaving, no one appeared to care. Only one of them waved in their direction as they departed. On the walk home, Mellie wondered why the other girls had been so eager for her to come along. Once they'd found a few young men to visit with, nothing else mattered.

Mrs. Richards greeted them upon their return. Her chair was turned toward the foyer, perhaps so she could keep account of each girl on her arrival home. During her first evening at the house, the twins had enlightened Mellie regarding the keepers and their ledgers. While she'd initially thought the ledgers were only to record the costs of the boardinghouse, Mellie soon learned the ledgers contained much more. Mrs. Richards maintained careful records about the habits of each boarder. She noted if they returned after the ten o'clock curfew, if they'd been keeping company with unsavory men, if they'd paid their full rent and board each payday, and if they were regularly attending church on Sunday. While those details were listed in the corporate rules signed by each girl, Mellie was surprised to learn the keepers chronicled all their shortcomings and then reported them to the company.

Mrs. Richards placed her open book on the table beside her. "You're home earlier than I expected. Did you enjoy seeing some of the town, Mellie?"

"Yes, thank you. It's very nice. The stores in Concord close much earlier. I was surprised to find so many establishments still open for business."

"They make much of their income from the mill workers. If they want their money, they need to remain open when the workers can shop—few close before nine-thirty." Her gaze settled on the small package in Clara's hand. "It appears you're the only one who parted with any of her wages, Clara. Did you find some pretty bauble?"

Clara frowned and shook her head. "No. I bought a stick of coltsfoot and two horehound lozenges for Ada. I thought they might help her throat."

"That was generous of you, Clara." She extended her hand. "I'll take them to her. While you were gone, I decided it was best to move her to the sickroom. She's got a fever, and I don't want the rest of you coming down with the same thing."

"I'd rather give it to her myself, but I don't want to get sick." Clara stepped forward and dropped the package into Mrs. Richards's open hand. "Tell her it's from me and Cora and that we'll be praying for her."

After bidding the older woman good-night, the four of them climbed the stairs and walked to the end of the hall. Clara opened the door leading to the attic but then came to an abrupt halt and signaled them to be quiet.

Cora drew close to her sister. "What's wrong?"

"There's someone up there giggling and talking to Olive. I heard them say something about Mellie and then laugh." Clara motioned Mellie forward. "Go up there real quiet-like. I think some of the girls are talking about you. Might as well give them a little surprise."

Holding tight to the railing, Mellie tiptoed up the steep stairway. With each step the voices became more distinct. Her breath caught as she heard Olive mention gambling debts and embezzlement. *Was she? Could she?* Surely not! With a burst of energy she didn't know she had left in her, Mellie ran up the final steps. Her mouth dropped open at the sight. Olive sat on the edge of her bed with Charity sitting beside her, the two of them poring over her journal.

Crossing the distance in three long strides, Mellie yanked her journal from Charity's hands. "How dare you go through my belongings and read my personal writings!"

Olive's dark eyes glimmered in the candlelight. "I can understand why you wouldn't want anyone reading what you've written in there. Looks like you've had quite a downfall from the days when you wore all those fancy dresses. I'd wager those society folks don't want anything to do with you anymore."

"Wager! You're so funny, Olive. I don't think Mellie wants to think about her brother-in-law and all the money he lost at the gaming tables." Charity poked Olive with her elbow. "It's wagering and stealing that caused all Mellie's problems and brought her to Manchester. Isn't that right, Mellie?"

Phebe circled around the twins and glowered at Charity. "I believe your parents chose the wrong name for you, Charity. There's nothing charitable about your behavior. I wonder what Mrs. Richards would think if I told her what the two of you have been up to while we were gone."

Charity's quick temper was a match for her fluff of red hair. She jumped up from the bed and pointed her finger at all of them. "You just try it and we'll see what everyone in town thinks about your friend Mellie when we tell them about her fall from grace back in Concord." She sneered. "If you knew what was in here, you'd choose your friends more carefully, Phebe."

Phebe remained toe-to-toe with the redhead. "I know I wouldn't want as a friend anyone who would sneak around and go through my personal belongings."

Mellie touched Phebe's shoulder. "Thank you, Phebe, but you don't need to come to my defense."

Olive's lips curled in a scowl. "That's right, Phebe. Stay out of this. Mellie knows what she has to lose if I tell others she's not who they think she is."

The angry girl's words slipped over Mellie like a rope tightening around her neck. Mellie clasped the journal to her chest. "I did nothing wrong. The debts weren't mine, and I didn't steal anything."

Charity hiked a shoulder. "Maybe not, but from the sound of that journal, folks in Concord were mighty angry when he took his own life and left them without any hope of recovering what was owed them."

Olive leaned forward. "And it looks like he owed most of the town. But if you don't mind us telling others about your past, that's fine. You and Phebe and the twins can go right ahead and talk to Mrs. Richards." Vengeance glistened in her eyes. "I forgot to mention that I'm close friends with one of the fellows who works for the local newspaper. I'm sure he'd be pleased to write a column about you and your family."

The slipknot drew tighter. "Nothing will be said to Mrs. Richards, and I don't want anything in the newspaper. Are we agreed?" Despite her attempt to sound forceful, Mellie's voice quivered.

Olive barked a laugh. "Not quite. Here are my terms. You don't speak to Mrs. Richards, we won't tell the other girls or my friend at the newspaper, *and* you'll loan us any of those dresses whenever we want."

Mellie gripped the journal tighter. How could she have been so foolish? Hadn't she learned to keep her personal belongings under lock and key all those years ago in boarding school? Though she doubted either of the girls would keep their word, she had no choice. If her character was called into question, she'd lose her job.

Olive pushed up from the side of the bed, her mouth twisted in an ugly smirk. "If you tell me yes, then we're agreed."

"We're agreed."

Chapter

SIX

MORGAN HAD RELENTED TO HIS MOTHER'S REQUEST THAT he remain home for a few days before beginning his "masquerade" at the mills—the word she had used when referring to his decision. In exchange, she promised to keep his secret.

Both he and his father had nearly finished their breakfast when his mother appeared at the dining room table. "Are you sure you can't stay with us another day or two, Morgan?"

"*William*, Mother. I'm referring to myself as William Morgan from now on."

She sat down and rang for Lucy. "I simply cannot do that, Morgan. It's far too confusing. Your father is William and you are Morgan. If I had wanted two Williams under one roof, I would have named you William. But I didn't. Morgan is my family name, but now it seems it isn't good enough for you."

"I'm now using your family name as my surname. You should be pleased." He gave her a fleeting smile.

His father pushed his plate to the side. "We both know there's no reason to be offended by the change of name. It's a necessity and it certainly isn't permanent. I believe that William Morgan is a good choice."

"Of course you do. You always wanted him to be named William." His mother turned to Lucy when she entered the room. "I'll have my coffee now, Lucy. And it appears my husband and *Mr. Morgan* need their cups filled, as well." Once Lucy had hurried off to the kitchen, his mother turned to him. "How soon are you leaving?"

"As soon as I finish breakfast and change my clothes."

She let her gaze travel from his necktie to his suit jacket. "Why would you change your clothes? You look very nice this morning. I do believe navy is an excellent color on you. It brings out the blue in your eyes."

Morgan stifled a laugh. "I'm going to the mills to apply for a position as a mechanic, Mother. I don't think many mechanics wear suits to work, and I don't think the overseer will notice if what I'm wearing brings out the blue in my eyes."

His mother sniffed. "It's rude to make sport of others, Morgan— especially your mother."

"I apologize." He stood, approached her chair, leaned down, and brushed a kiss on her cheek. "If you'll excuse me, I'm going upstairs to change."

"Don't you leave without telling us good-bye." His mother's response took him back to all the times he'd heard those same words. Each time he'd departed for school, she'd made that same comment.

He lifted his hand to signal he'd heard her request before he left the room. Once upstairs, he changed into a pair of worn work pants and a faded shirt. Yesterday he'd sent his father's stable hand into town to purchase three sets of new work clothes and then had traded the fellow for three sets of his worn clothing. The shirtsleeves were a little short, but otherwise the fit had been passable. He shoved the clothes into an old carpetbag and latched the leather tab. With the bag in one hand and a flat-billed cap in the other, he slung the jacket that still smelled of horses and hay across his shoulder and descended the steps.

He strode toward the dining room but stopped when he heard his mother call out from her sitting room, "Workmen to the back, young man. Who let you in the front door?"

Taking a backward step, he peered into the room. "I'll remember that in the future, Mother."

"Morgan!" She clasped a hand to her bodice. "You look positively . . . awful." She withdrew a lace-edged handkerchief from her pocket and dabbed the corner of her eye. "I can't believe your father has agreed to this. You know there's likely vermin in those boardinghouses, don't you?" She shuddered.

"I doubt that, Mother, but I don't think my sensibilities are as delicate as yours." He grinned and tipped his head toward the door. "I'm going to say my good-byes to Father and then be on my way."

"Well, do come here and give me a hug." She opened her arms as he approached her and leaned down for a hug. "Dear me, what is that horrid smell?" She wrinkled her nose and sniffed.

"The clothes are clean, but it may be the jacket." He glanced at the coat draped over one arm. "I believe the odor is musty hay and sweaty horse."

"Morgan! You need not be so crass with your explanation."

"Sorry, Mother. I borrowed the jacket from one of the men who works in the stable."

She brought her fingers to her lips as if she might cry. "I simply cannot believe this is something my son would do. Please promise me you will end this foolishness quickly."

"I can't promise how soon it will end, but I do promise I'll not work as a mechanic for the rest of my life." He glanced toward the hallway. "I really must go. I'll be sending reports to Father, which I'm sure he will share with you."

That said, he hurried to his father's office before she could further detain him. After a light tap on the door, he opened it and stepped inside. His father looked up and gestured toward Morgan's clothing. "I see you've dressed for the occasion. Let's see if you can fool Mr. Walters. He's a shrewd man. I wouldn't be surprised if he sees through that getup and calls your bluff."

Morgan brushed his hand down the front of his shirt. "I think I look like a workingman."

His father nodded. "You may look the part, but there's more to it than the clothes. Do you think one of those men down at the mill could put on your suit and pass for a gentleman?"

The cautionary words gave Morgan pause. "Perhaps not, but I think I'm prepared to convincingly answer any of his questions. If not, I'll be back home before the noonday bells ring."

His father stood and walked him to the door. He patted Morgan's shoulder. "Good luck, my boy. I'll be eager to hear how things progress."

Before Morgan approached the black iron gates, he mussed his hair and settled the cap at the back of his head. His father's comment had hit the mark, and he now worried that he might not get past the front gates. He pulled on the cord, and a man soon appeared behind the metal bars.

He looked Morgan up and down. "What can I do for ya?"

Using his thumb to point over his shoulder, Morgan met the man's gaze. "I saw a broadside in town saying there were openings for mechanics."

"Got a reference letter?"

Morgan swallowed hard. He hadn't thought he'd be asked for references. "No, but I'm plenty skilled."

"Ain't me you gotta convince. I'll go see if Mr. Walters wants to talk to ya. Wait right there." The man pointed his thick finger through the bars. "I'll be back in two shakes."

Morgan leaned against the far end of the gate, his eyes traveling down the expanse of redbrick buildings. Was this a foolish idea? Maybe he should have given it more thought. There was still time. He could leave before the watchman returned. He glanced toward the hillside, then back at the mills. No. It was a sound idea and he was going to see it through—if he could get hired on.

He startled when the gates rattled. "Come on. Mr. Walters's clerk said to send you in." He pointed to a door. "Right through there. He'll take care of ya, and good luck."

Morgan tipped his hat. "Thank you."

The clerk wasn't as friendly as the watchman. He looked up and motioned to a chair. "Sit there. Name?"

"Mor . . . Morgan, William Morgan." The clerk didn't appear to notice that he'd stumbled over his name. In the future he'd need to be more careful.

"The watchman said you have no references. Is that correct?"

He nodded. "I saw a broadside—"

"Yes, the watchman told me." He stood. "Follow me."

There was nothing friendly about this fellow. He hoped Mr. Walters would be more cordial. The clerk handed the older man sitting behind the desk a piece of paper, told Morgan to be seated, and disappeared.

"Tell me about yourself, Mr. Morgan. Start with your experience as a mechanic." Mr. Walters leaned back in his chair, stared at Morgan, and waited.

Morgan inhaled a deep breath. "To tell you the truth, my experience is somewhat limited. But I have a good understanding of machinery, and I think I could be useful to your company."

A half smile played at the man's lips. "Our mechanics are expected to resolve difficult situations in a hurry. Everything from repairing broken teeth on a carding machine to replacing worn belts on the looms and much more. From the looks of your hands, it's been a very long time since you've so much as tightened a bolt." He placed his arms atop his desk and leaned forward. "Care to explain why that would be?"

Morgan inwardly cringed. Why hadn't he thought about his hands? If only he'd kept them hidden or worn work gloves. He stared down for a moment. "I was attending college—studying to be an engineer. I was good at it, too." He met the older man's eyes. "I haven't been able to find work as an engineer, so I figured the best thing would be to get myself to work as a mechanic. At least then I'd be around machines."

Mr. Walters continued to stare at him. "I'm going to guess you dropped out before you got your certificate and that's why you couldn't find a job as an engineer." Morgan opened his mouth to speak, but Mr. Walters waved him to silence. "I'll give you a position, but it will be up to you and your overseer whether you keep the job. If I receive any complaints from him, you'll be gone. Understood?"

"Yes, understood. And thank you, Mr. Walters. Thank you so much. You won't regret this. I promise."

The manager nodded. "We'll see, Mr. Morgan. We'll see." He scribbled something on a sheet of paper. "Give this to my clerk. He'll write a note to your overseer and give you directions to the mechanics' building. And good luck to you."

Morgan smiled and nodded. How many times had he been wished good luck today? But if he was going to succeed in this endeavor, he'd need a lot more than wishful good fortune. He'd need the Lord's help every step of the way.

August soon faded into September, and although Mellie had planned to secure a second job, she'd been too weary to pursue the idea. She had settled into the daily schedule, yet her body continued to protest the long days standing in front of her frames. At night, cramps curled her toes and twisted her muscles with such ferocity that she'd awaken in pain. Not until she'd either paced the small space between the two beds or massaged her legs and feet could she go back to sleep. Clara suggested she change shoes each day, but that hadn't helped. Instead, she'd ruined her good shoes slogging through the ankle-deep mud and mire created by the late summer rains.

Mellie bowed her head against a gale wind as they neared the mills. The yawning gates would remain open only a few minutes longer. "Hurry, Cora." She looked over her shoulder and waited until Cora was at her side. Cora wasn't one to lag behind, but she'd been visiting with Abigail, one of the girls who roomed on the second floor.

"Sorry, but Abigail was telling me about dance lessons at Granite Hall."

"Dance lessons?" Clara circled around Mellie and came alongside her twin. "Since when are you interested in dance lessons?

We can't afford that kind of silliness—and you know the lessons won't be free. Any lessons come at a price."

"These lessons are free if you buy a ticket to the Grand Complimentary Ball that's hosted by Mr. Vance and some of his students. Tickets to the ball are a dollar, but Abigail says the price for ladies' dance lessons is only two cents."

"Don't you think it sounds like fun, Mellie?" Cora arched her thin brows.

"Yes, it likely would be fun." Mellie attempted to lift her foot and cringed as the mud sucked at her boot and threatened to topple her forward. How she wished she had a pair of galoshes. "Right now I want to get inside before I'm swallowed by all this mud. I'll be thankful when the rain stops and the mill yard finally dries."

Clara shrugged. "Once the rain stops, the sleet and snow begin. It will be springtime before this place dries out."

Mrs. Richards insisted the girls remove their galoshes or shoes and brush the mud off the hems of their dresses on an oilcloth she'd placed on the floor of the entryway. They did their best. Still, it was impossible to clean off all the wet mud, and the keeper's complaints were almost as bothersome as their plodding through the mud.

Cora tugged on Mellie's coat as they ascended the winding brick stairs. "Would you think about attending, Mellie? If you go, I might be able to convince Clara."

"I hear you plotting, Cora. I'm not going to any silly dance. I'm saving my money to buy Christmas gifts for Mama and Papa, and you should do the same."

When they'd arrived at the spinning rooms, Clara grasped Mellie's hand. They backed up against the cold, hard bricks while the other workers pushed around them and continued up the stairs. "There's an opening in the weaving room. I told Mr. Fuqua you were a good worker and he should see about moving you upstairs with us. He said he'd talk to Mr. Comstock."

Clara hurried up the steps before Mellie could reply. When she was assigned to the spinning rooms, she hadn't considered the possibility of being moved to another floor. The idea both excited and frightened her. Working near Cora and Clara would be pleasing, but learning to weave on the looms might prove more difficult than keeping watch over the spinning frames. She was a woman who had always enjoyed a challenge, yet working in the mills had already provided more of a test than she desired.

Mellie had been at her frames for over an hour when Mr. Fuqua stepped into the spinning room. He stood near the door and spoke to Mr. Comstock for several minutes. The men glanced in her direction while they talked, and a few moments later, Mr. Fuqua gestured. She pointed a finger to her chest, uncertain if she should leave her frames. He nodded in return.

"Keep a watch on my frames, Gertrude," Mellie said as she hurried by the girl.

Both men remained by the door when she approached, but it was Mr. Fuqua who spoke. "You're being moved upstairs to the weaving room, Miss Blanchard. Bring your belongings with you."

She glanced at Mr. Comstock, who merely nodded and strode toward Gertrude. She'd likely be assigned to Mellie's frames until another girl was hired. While gathering her lightweight cloak and bonnet, Mellie stole a final glance at Gertrude. With the girl's look of wretched defeat etched in her mind, Mellie followed Mr. Fuqua up the steps.

Before he opened the door to the weaving room, Mr. Fuqua came to a halt. Even with the door closed, he had to shout. "We won't be able to talk in there. I'm going to have Miss Winters, Clara Winters, train you on the looms. You'll work beside her. Listen and learn, Miss Blanchard. I'm fair with my workers, but I expect the same in return. No excessive visits to the necessary, no opening of windows, a note from your boardinghouse keeper or a doctor if you are sick. The contract you signed is valid no matter where you work in the Stark Mills. Understood?"

"Yes, sir."

"Good. Then we shall get along just fine." He opened the door and waved her forward.

On her first day at the mills, Mellie had been in the weaving room for only a few minutes before Mr. Fuqua had whisked her down to the spinning rooms. Back then, the overseer hadn't yet signaled to set the machines in motion. But today the looms had been in operation for nearly two hours. It took only one breath to notice the difference. Suffocating heat and humidity draped the room. The girls used handkerchiefs tucked at their waists to dab their brows. The clamminess of the place belied the brisk chill that had seeped through Mellie's cloak earlier in the morning.

She took a position beside Clara and forced a smile. The humidity and flying lint strangled her attempts to gain a cleansing breath. She'd encountered flying lint in the spinning room, but it hadn't compared to this.

Clara cupped one hand around her mouth and leaned close to Mellie's ear. "You'll be tending these two looms." She dropped her hand and pointed back and forth between the iron devices. Once again she cupped her hand to her mouth. "First you knot your thread, then place the bobbin in the shuttle." She tapped her finger over a tiny hole at the tip of the shuttle. "The thread must come through the hole." Holding the tip to her mouth, she sucked in. When she lowered the shuttle, she tugged on the thread that she'd sucked through the hole.

Mellie frowned. How many other operatives had held that shuttle to their mouths? Somehow the method didn't seem proper. "Isn't there some other way to thread the shuttle?"

Clara shook her head and handed Mellie a shuttle. "Try it." Mellie sucked the thread through the metal tip and handed it to Clara. After placing the shuttle in the track, Clara pulled down on the handle. The loom roared to life like a lion released from its cage, the shuttle flying back and forth at breakneck speed while the beams pounded a thundering rhythm.

Clara grasped her arm and pointed to the take-up roller. "Make certain the cloth stays in proper position on the roller and keep a close watch on the shuttles. You don't want any snags in the cloth or you'll hear about it from Mr. Fuqua."

Mellie had continued her watch over the loom for only a short time when Mr. Fuqua slowly walked down their row, taking note of each machine and operative. When he arrived at one of Clara's looms, he leaned down close to her ear and spoke before passing behind Mellie.

As soon as he'd walked by, Clara moved to Mellie's side with an empty shuttle in her hand before stepping to an idle machine. She handed a full bobbin and the empty shuttle to Mellie and gestured for her to thread the shuttle. "Mr. Fuqua said for you to begin working your second loom."

Though she didn't feel qualified to operate even one loom, she dutifully followed Clara's instructions. When yet another monster came to life and added its roar to the banging, crashing, and pounding, she wasn't certain whether moving to the weaving room had been a sound decision. Could she bear this thundering noise for ten hours a day? She hadn't pondered the question for long when the jarring clamor lessened. Startled by the sudden change, she glanced to her side. Clara and the other operatives were rushing for the door while her machines continued to clatter. Clara rushed back to her side. "Shut off your looms and hurry."

Mellie shook her head. How had the other girls managed to hear the bell? Careful to lift her skirt in one hand, she clambered down the stairs behind the chattering throng. Stragglers from the lower floors wove into their number as they scrambled for the smell of fresh air and food to fill their grumbling stomachs.

Cora was waiting when Clara and Mellie stepped outside. "Do you like being with us in the weaving room, Mellie?"

"I like being near you and Clara, but the noise is deafening. My head already aches."

"Snip a couple of small pieces from an old handkerchief and stuff them in your ears. It helps a little. After a while, you'll get used to it." Cora looped arms with the two of them. "Did either of you give any more thought to the dance lessons or attending the ball? I truly want to go, but I want at least one of you to go with me."

Clara sighed. "I suppose if it's that important to you, I'll go to one dance lesson, but only if you use your money to pay for both of us."

Cora laughed aloud. "I'll be happy to pay for you. Abigail said there's a class tonight, so we can begin this evening."

While Clara didn't appear nearly as happy as her sister, Mellie was certain they'd both have fun. She'd always enjoyed dancing classes when away at school. Perhaps she'd walk into town with them and visit the photography shop. She'd enjoyed viewing the display of artwork, and perhaps she'd gather her courage and speak to the owner about a part-time position. At the very least, there would be peace and quiet.

Nowadays, anything that would still the incessant drumming in her head was a welcome relief.

Chapter
SEVEN

September

WHEN MELLIE AND THE OTHER GIRLS ARRIVED HOME FOR
supper that evening, Mrs. Richards poked her head around the
door and called to Mellie, "You have a letter on the side table
in the parlor. There's one for Abigail, too." That said, she disappeared back into the kitchen.

Mellie stepped into the parlor and spotted her name on one
of the letters. Seeing her sister's familiar script, the noise and
chaos of the day faded from her memory. She longed to run
upstairs and devour every word, but if she didn't sit down for
supper, she'd hear about it from Mrs. Richards. After only a
week in the mill, Mellie had ceased any attempts to use proper
manners at the dining table. There simply wasn't time—not if
she was going to fill her stomach and be back to work before
the gates closed. While none of them ate with the power-driven
speed used at breakfast and noonday meals, supper was still
devoured with more haste than at a typical family dinner table.

This evening she put her newly acquired eating skills to use and was the first to finish her bowl of stew plus a thick slice of bread and butter. She gulped down the final swallow of milk and pushed away from the table. "Please excuse me. I'm going upstairs to read my letter."

Taking the first flight of steps as fast as she could, she hurried down the hallway. After drawing in two cleansing breaths, she continued upward and finally dropped onto the bed and tore open the letter. Margaret's flawless handwriting was like a balm to her soul. Mellie pressed the creases from the page while quickly scanning the contents.

Her breath caught.

She must have misread. She began again, this time reading each well-formed word at a slower pace. But as she continued, her stomach knotted around the mutton stew she'd eaten only minutes ago. The first few sentences were pleasing. The children's health had been good; Margaret continued to tutor the banker's children along with her own. They were most thankful for the funds Mellie sent each week. Then from that point forward, Margaret's letter described one difficult situation after another: more creditors had appeared, either sending letters or arriving at the front door; the banker had lowered her wages, since her children were present and learning while she was tutoring his children; the house had been advertised for sale; she wasn't certain where they would live after it was sold, but there was an old farmhouse they might be able to secure—still, she wasn't certain if the banker would be willing to bring the children out there each morning; she was now doing alterations and some dressmaking at night to help bolster their income. The final paragraph asked for her prayers and advised Mellie she shouldn't worry. God would see them through these difficult circumstances. Mellie's thoughts swirled. Certainly she would pray and ask God to provide for her sister, yet pushing aside her concerns would be impossible.

Chattering voices and the sound of footsteps in the downstairs hallway pulled her from her thoughts. She folded the letter and tucked it into her pocket as Cora and Clara appeared. Cora plopped down beside her on the bed. "You look as though you've received sad news. Is there a problem at home?"

Mellie forced a smile. "The same news most of us receive from home—not enough money."

Sympathy shone in Cora's eyes, and she patted Mellie's hand. "Come with us to the dance lessons. It will take your mind off your problems. I'll pay your two cents." Her bow-shaped lips curved in a beseeching smile. "Please?"

Cora's pleading voice reminded Mellie of her young niece when she wanted Mellie to play a game with her. "No dance lessons for me, but I will walk into town with you. I believe I'll stop at the photography shop. I enjoyed viewing the artwork."

On the walk into town, laughter and excitement filled the evening air. During supper, Cora had enlisted several other girls to come along, but she'd still insisted that Clara attend. Her reasoning had been quite simple: They always did everything together and this should be no different.

When they neared the photography shop, Mellie bid them good-bye and squeezed Clara's hand. "Try to enjoy yourself. I think you'll discover the lessons are an entertaining distraction from our work at the mills."

Cora dropped back and looped arms with her sister. "Come on, Clara. I'm not going to let you disappear into the photography shop with Mellie."

The bell over the shop door jingled when Mellie stepped

inside. She recognized the owner of the shop when he turned and glanced over his shoulder. He was sitting at a canvas with a paintbrush in hand. She stepped closer and stood behind him, watching as he continued to paint.

"May I assist you with something special?" He brushed a fine line of blue paint on the canvas before looking up.

"Not at the moment. I was going to admire some of your paintings."

"Ah, these aren't my paintings. I exhibit them for others." He pointed the tip of his brush at the canvas. "As you can see, I'm merely an amateur. I'm much more skilled with a camera than with paints." He narrowed his eyes. "I remember you. You were in here with another young lady. You looked at the paintings, and she inquired about the cost of a photograph. Am I right?"

"Yes. You have a good memory."

He ran a palm over his bald head and then drew his fingers through the fringe of graying brown hair that rested on his collar. Muttonchop sideburns masked a fair portion of his thin face, but his blue eyes revealed kindness. "I'm afraid you'll not find any new paintings, but you're welcome to examine any of the current renderings for as long as you'd like."

Mellie thanked him and slowly circled the shop, examining each painting as she proceeded. She attempted to gather her courage to ask if he needed any help in the shop, except the words caught in her throat.

He leaned across the counter and arched his brows. "Do you paint?"

His question startled her. "No, I'm merely an admirer. One of my teachers thought I possessed some artistic talent. I soon proved her wrong, however."

"I believe art is like beauty—it's in the eye of the beholder.

Perhaps your teacher saw a raw, hidden ability in your work."
He smiled. "Is that possible?"

Mellie laughed. "No, I'm afraid not. I can produce a decent
sketch, and I believe I'm good at paper cutting, but that's the
extent of my ability."

He arched a brow. "Paper cutting?"

"Yes. *Scherenschnitte*. Are you familiar with it? It's the art of
German paper cutting. In truth, that's why I came here this
evening."

"To talk about paper cutting?" He chuckled. "You've come to
the wrong place, miss. I know nothing about the art of paper
cutting." He glanced about the shop as if to emphasize there
weren't any paper cuttings on display. "Why did you think I
could be of help?"

Mellie offered a silent prayer of thanks. He had just given her
the opening she prayed for only a few minutes ago. "I don't need
assistance with my cutting. I need to earn additional money to
help my family. I work in the mills."

He nodded. "I assumed as much. And how can I help you
earn this extra income, Miss . . . ?"

"Blanchard. Mellicent Blanchard—from Concord, although
now I live at Mrs. Richards's boardinghouse."

"And I am Mr. Asa Harrison. A pleasure to meet you, Miss
Blanchard."

She smiled and inhaled a deep breath. "I thought perhaps
you would permit me to cut portraits here in the shop—and
other cuttings of scenes or whatever customers might request.
Usually, though, folks want portraits more than anything else.
I'm really quite good at portraits, and I work quickly."

Mr. Harrison gave her a lopsided grin. "So you want me
to offer you space to work in my shop, and in turn you will

compete for my photography business by cutting portraits of customers?"

Before stepping inside the shop, she'd considered what she would say if he posed such a question, but her thoughts now twisted and turned like tangled fishing line. She drew another breath and slowly exhaled. "I know there are folks, like my friend, who can't afford a photograph. I can provide paper cuttings at a lesser cost than a photograph, and I would be willing to pay you two cents for each cutting I make."

"And what will you charge for your cuttings?" He appeared somewhat amused by her answer.

"A small cutting would cost five cents. They don't take long." She was suddenly struck by an idea. She gestured to the picture frames at the far end of the room. "I would encourage them to purchase a frame for their portrait. You would make a profit from those sales, as well. And you wouldn't be required to provide me with anything other than a small space where I can sit and do the cutting."

For a moment, he didn't respond. Instead, he stepped toward the front of the shop. "Perhaps we could have you sit in front of the window so that you could be seen while cutting the portraits. It would create curiosity and bring shoppers inside."

Her enthusiasm mounted, and she bobbed her head. "I agree." She hesitated for only a moment. "Shall I begin tomorrow evening?" She didn't want to appear presumptuous, yet she didn't want him to overthink the idea and turn her down, either.

"Let's not move too quickly." He stroked one of his broad sideburns.

Her heart thudded in her chest. At first, she had thought he was going to agree.

He cleared his throat. "While I'm certain you're a very honest and talented young woman, I've not seen any of your work. If you can't create what customers expect, then your work will shine a poor light on my business, and that wouldn't be good for me."

Mellie brightened. "You're right—it wouldn't. But I have cuttings I brought with me to Manchester. I'll bring them to the shop and you can see what you think of my work." She glanced toward the door. "I'd be pleased to go and get them right now, if you'd like."

"I would very much like to see them. I'd also like to see you cut a silhouette. In fact, you can use me as your subject. Seeing what you can create and how long it takes will serve as the best proof of your ability." He cocked a brow. "Don't you agree?"

She nodded. "I do. I have special scissors and a paper used only for my paper cutting. It won't take long for me to go back to the boardinghouse and get them." She'd completed the sentence with a question in her voice, then awaited his response.

He looked at the clock. "If two hours is enough time for you to fetch what you need, get back here, and complete my silhouette, you go right ahead. I'm eager to see what you can do."

Mellie prayed while hurrying to the boardinghouse, and she continued to pray as she rushed back to Asa Harrison's photography shop. If he didn't like her cuttings, perhaps he'd hire her to assist customers in the shop. For now, she needed to remain positive about her paper cuttings.

During her absence, Mr. Harrison had returned to his painting. When the bell rang, he swiveled around on his stool. His gaze settled on the small case in her hand. "I see you have your supplies. You should remove your cape and bonnet, so you are comfortable while you work." He moved a chair closer to the stool where he'd been sitting. "Will this arrangement work for you?"

She nodded. "That's fine." He obviously wanted her to complete his silhouette before he looked at any of her other work. Removing a piece of black paper and her scissors from her case, she sat down opposite him. "Please turn to the side so I have a good view of your profile."

He turned and remained still while she quickly snipped tiny cuts to reveal the fringe of hair at his collar, then continued in a circular fashion to form his bald head before a slight outward protrusion of the forehead and then turning inward before cutting his slightly crooked nose. Beneath his lips, she cut an indention before creating his chin and the edge of his collar.

Once finished, she extended the cutting to him. He held it at a distance and narrowed his eyes. "Hmm." His lips made a downward turn before he looked at her. "I was hoping to see myself portrayed as much more handsome, but I see you've captured my true likeness." He laughed and shook his head. "That is amazing, Miss Blanchard. I must say, I didn't expect such fine work and in such little time. I do believe it would be beneficial to have you here in the shop."

"Would you like to see my other cuttings? I don't have many portraits, just ones of my family members, but I do have a number of scenes and some snowflakes. The children always enjoy the snowflakes. Of course, I do those using white paper." She didn't wait for his response before removing a worn scrapbook from her case. "I keep them in here so they won't get wrinkled."

"I'd say that's sound thinking." He extended his hand to accept a cutting of two doves encircled by a decorative heart while she placed several other cuttings on the counter. He declared the work exquisite and marveled at the intricate cutting. "These are superb, beyond anything I imagined. They're works of art that must be exhibited, not hidden away in your scrapbook."

"Thank you." His kind words struck a chord, and she swallowed hard to keep her emotions in check. "Then you're willing to have me begin tomorrow evening?"

"I am. If you'll leave a few of your cuttings with me, I'll frame them and place them on display in the window. You'll need to put a price on each one, so I'll know what to charge if a buyer should come in when you're not here."

Together they looked through her cuttings and decided upon several to be framed and a price for each. He made a list of what she'd left with him and the prices they'd decided upon, including a frame. When a cutting sold, Mr. Harrison would be reimbursed for the cost of the frame, and when she offered a percentage of the displayed cuttings, he refused. "Your offer is very kind, but such a charge would be unfair, Miss Blanchard. I'm pleased with our arrangement. I believe that having you create your cuttings in the shop will prove beneficial to both of us."

They'd chosen frames for Mellie's paper cuttings and she was tying her bonnet when Cora burst into the shop like a gust of wind. "Mellie! I'm glad you're still here. We had such a wonderful time. You must come with us next time. The lessons weren't overly difficult, and there were enough fellows for each of us to have a partner. Mine was quite nice, although Clara's was better looking. And the music was good, too. Some of the men who play in Mr. Dignam's band played for us. Not the whole group, of course, but enough to offer fine dancing music." Her attention shifted to Mr. Harrison and the cuttings displayed on the counter once she'd stopped long enough to take a breath. "Those are lovely." She drew closer and traced her finger down one of the cuttings. "Were these on display when we were here before?"

Mr. Harrison shook his head. "No. These are the work of your friend Miss Blanchard. She's agreed to have me place them for sale in the shop."

Cora's mouth gaped. "Really, Mellie? You made these?"

Before she could respond, Mr. Harrison answered for her. "Indeed, she did. And look at this." He held up the silhouette Mellie had cut only a few minutes ago. "A fine representation, don't you think? And it took her only a short time. She's going to begin work in my shop tomorrow evening. What do you think of that?"

Cora appeared dumb struck. She stepped closer and examined Mr. Harrison's silhouette. "Are you going to cut silhouettes like these, Mellie? Could you cut one of Clara and me? What would it cost? Less than a photograph? We could send it to our folks for Christmas." She beamed at Mellie.

Mellie wished she'd have thought of cutting their silhouettes before she'd agreed to work for Mr. Harrison. The girls had been so kind to her, cutting their likenesses was the least she could do in return. Mellie gathered her belongings, then edged Cora toward the door. "We can talk on the way home. It's getting late and we want to be back before curfew. Where are the others?"

"They're over at Pittney's, all of them looking at ribbon and lace. Now that they're enjoying the dance lessons, they're hoping for invites to the ball."

Mr. Harrison followed behind them. "Be sure you mention your new position here at the store to your friends, Miss Blanchard. I'm hopeful many of them will want to purchase one of your cuttings as a gift."

Cora remained close by her side as they walked toward Pittney's. "How'd you learn to do that? Make those cuttings, I mean? I've never known anyone who could make something so pretty."

"When I was in boarding school, one of the housekeepers was an old German lady. The other girls didn't like her much, but she was kind to me—almost like a grandmother. We spent a great deal of time together. One day when I was around seven or eight years old, I saw her doing paper cutting and asked if she would teach me."

Cora stopped in her tracks. "You've been able to make those since you were eight years old?"

Mellie chuckled. "No, not like the ones you've seen. My first cuttings were horrible. I've kept a few of them all these years just to remind me how much I learned from her. Paper cutting is like most everything else—the more you practice, the better you become at it. And it helped that I enjoyed creating with scissors and paper. Now it's providing a way for me to increase my income and help my family a little more."

As they neared the store, Mellie frowned. "When did Olive and Charity join you? They weren't along when we parted at the photography shop."

"They told me they weren't going, but then they showed up just before lessons began. Charity said she already knew how to dance, but it sure didn't look like it once the music started. Her partner kept complaining that she was stepping on his feet."

Cora giggled, yet Mellie didn't join in. Ever since she'd caught the pair reading her journal, Mellie had avoided both Olive and Charity as much as possible. She'd been relieved when Olive had finally moved downstairs, where she now shared a room with Charity. As far as Mellie was concerned, they were cut from the same cloth and would likely enjoy each other's company.

Cora and Mellie joined the group, and they walked toward home, the girls laughing and chattering about their dance partners. When they stopped before crossing the street, Olive moved to Mellie's side. "I'm sure glad to see you, Mellie. There's something we need to talk about."

Mellie's earlier excitement over the new position at Mr. Harrison's shop fizzled like water poured on a fire. Mellie remained silent and continued moving. No need to ask what Olive wanted. Questioned or not, Olive would make her wishes known.

She nudged Mellie's arm. "I'm planning to wear that pretty blue shawl of yours tomorrow evening when my beau comes calling for me. You know the one I'm talking about? It's got that real fancy edging?"

"Yes, I know the one, but our agreement didn't include shawls or any of my other belongings. Only dresses."

She leaned close to Mellie's ear. "Well, I've changed my mind. I want to wear that shawl, and if I don't have it in my room by tomorrow evening, I'm going to have a fine story for my newspaper-reporter friend." Her warm breath smelled of onions and the peppermint she'd likely sucked on to sweeten her breath. It hadn't helped.

And it hadn't sweetened her behavior, either.

Chapter

EIGHT

"MORGAN! GO WITH JOHNSON. THERE'S A WORN BELT IN the weaving room in Stark Number Two that needs to be replaced." The overseer's hands remained cupped to his mouth until Morgan picked up his toolbox and strode toward Harold Johnson's workbench.

The older man waved his acknowledgment to the overseer, picked up his tools, and grinned at Morgan. "Let's go, young fella. Looks like you're gonna get another lesson today."

Back when Morgan had reported to Mr. Hale for the first time, the machine shop overseer had expressed doubts about Morgan's lack of experience. Still, he'd agreed to give Morgan a fair chance before making a final decision about his abilities or his future. In turn, Morgan had agreed to take instruction from an experienced mechanic. "You'll be an apprentice of sorts," Mr. Hale had told him. That said, he introduced Morgan to Harold Johnson, a man close to his own father's age.

When Morgan had addressed him as Mr. Johnson, the overseer

was quick to correct him. "Around here, the men are known and addressed only by their surnames." He then glanced down at Morgan's paper work. "I see your name is William Morgan, but around here you'll just be Morgan. Understand?"

Delighted with the arrangement, Morgan had nodded his agreement. Ever since he'd decided to change his name, he'd been worried that he wouldn't respond when someone addressed him as William. At least in the workplace, he wouldn't have that concern.

The two men shrugged into their coats before exiting the low-slung building that housed the mechanics, who constructed and serviced the machinery used in the mills. An unexpected blast of air hit them as they exited the building. Morgan tugged on his cap and lowered his head against the cool wind. "Seemed warmer when we got here this morning."

Johnson grunted. "From the look of those dark clouds, we probably got us another thunderstorm moving in. Can't tell about the weather this time of year. Or any other time for that matter. One thing's for certain in New Hampshire—there's gonna be lots of winter and not much fall, spring, or summer, so we've got to enjoy any weather that don't include snow or ice while we can. 'Course the ankle-deep mud caused by these recent rainstorms isn't any fun, either."

They walked across the canal bridge, their work boots clomping a steady rhythm on the wooden slats. Morgan bowed his head against the gusting wind. Johnson might think the weather fine, but Morgan wasn't convinced. "Think this will take long?" He clamped his jaw tight to stop his teeth from chattering.

"Better not. Them overseers in the weaving rooms get mighty angry if their machines are down for long. But I say they got only themselves to blame. They're supposed to check those belts at least once a week to make sure they ain't worn." His chest rumbled with a low laugh. "'Course, I ain't about to say that to any of them. They'd for sure report me to Hale, and I don't want that." He nudged Morgan's shoulder. "And neither do you."

Morgan would make a note of Johnson's remark this evening. Whenever one of the men mentioned something that could be changed to make things operate more efficiently, Morgan jotted an entry in a small notebook he carried in his pocket. Since he'd begun work at the shop, he hadn't returned home for a visit. Instead, he'd sent two letters to his father describing his work assignments and his living conditions at the boardinghouse. In both letters, he'd cautioned his father not to respond to his letters. Any mail coming to the boardinghouse was received by the keeper, and she seemed an inquisitive sort. Morgan didn't want to take any chance of being discovered. In his last letter he'd promised to make a brief visit when he could safely get away. In truth, he feared that if a visit wasn't soon forthcoming, his mother would take matters into her own hands—and he didn't want that to occur.

The entrance into the mill offered relief from the wind and threatening storm. They weren't in the weaving room for long before both he and Johnson shed their jackets and hats. The overpowering heat and humidity soon erased all thoughts of the cooler walk from the mechanics' building and replaced them with memories of a long-ago summer vacation in Charlotte, North Carolina. The humidity had been so overpowering that his mother had insisted upon a hasty departure.

He wondered if his mother or father had ever stepped foot in one of these weaving rooms. Most likely not, for the humidity alone would have dissuaded them. And the thunderous clamor of the machines would be sufficient to turn his parents in the opposite direction. Yet the conditions in the Stark Mills were no different from those in Lowell or any of the other textile-producing mills around the country. Pointing out the working conditions to his father would be of little consequence, as he already knew they would be ignored. He'd overheard his father discuss such matters with the other owners, and they always came to the same conclusion: Conditions in their mills far exceeded those in England, and they could all be proud of the care and provision their workers received. However, Morgan wasn't so sure of that.

The weavers charged with operating the looms dependent upon the shut-down line shaft appeared less than pleased to see them arrive. No doubt they were grateful to have a short respite. Johnson leaned close to Morgan's ear as he pointed to an upper portion of the leather belt that slipped over an iron gear near the ceiling and traveled through an opening in the floor down to the basement where it was slipped around a flywheel. When power from the turbine set the crown gear in motion, the leather belt circulated on the flywheel, traveling up to the weaving room and creating the needed energy to power the looms.

The overseer rushed across the room toward them, his face glistening with perspiration. "Get that belt replaced immediately! This whole section of looms is unproductive."

Johnson focused on the belt for a moment. The thick leather had a weakened spot that was nearly worn through. He stepped close to Morgan. "Go down to the basement. I'll pull on the belt and move the worn spot downward. When it gets to you, give it a tug so I'll know to stop. Then use that saw blade in your toolbox and cut it. Pull it through once it's cut. Shouldn't take much to saw through that worn leather." He pointed to the spot. "If one of those belts ever breaks, it could kill anyone in its path. The gears could swing it every which way until it was under control." Morgan didn't miss the look of condemnation that Johnson directed at the overseer. Either the overseer hadn't heard Johnson's remark, or he chose to ignore it. Morgan decided it was the latter. He also decided he'd record this item in his journal. While maintaining a high humidity might be the only way to keep threads from breaking during the weaving process, there was no good argument for using worn belts that placed the workers' lives in danger.

Removing and replacing the belt had taken longer than the overseer had hoped—and he hadn't failed to let Johnson know how he felt about it. Johnson didn't bother arguing with the overseer.

He continued replacing his tools in the wooden toolbox. "If you're not happy with our work, you can send word to John Hale, our supervisor in the machine shop. My name is Harold Johnson." He tipped his head toward Morgan. "And this is William Morgan. Just in case you want to mention us by name. After reviewing your complaint and talking with Morgan and me, I'm guessing Mr. Hale will be quick to file a report with management." He shrugged into his coat. "Anyway, that's what he usually does when he gets a complaint." Johnson gestured toward the door. "Let's be on our way, Morgan."

Morgan followed Johnson down the spiral staircase, worry dogging each step he took. The moment they were outside the mill, Morgan came alongside Johnson. "Do you think he's going to take you up on your suggestion? It almost sounded like you wanted him to report us." The last thing Morgan wanted was for some overseer in the weaving room to write a scathing report about his work. Mr. Hale would likely terminate him. After all, the supervisor hadn't been keen on hiring him in the first place.

Johnson barked a laugh. "I was calling his bluff. He won't do nothin' 'cause he knows he's in the wrong. If I report what we saw in there, he's the one who will be in trouble. I don't know if he's been reported before, but if he has, he'd lose his job this time. Those worn belts are dangerous, and the overseers have strict rules about making sure they're in good condition."

"But it would be his word against ours. Hard to tell who they'd believe."

Johnson shook his head. "No, it ain't. They'd believe us." He slapped a hand on his toolbox. "I cut out that piece of worn leather, and I made sure he was watching when I stuck it in my toolbox. There's a work order that shows exactly where we went to replace the belt plus the name of the overseer." He clapped Morgan on the shoulder. "No need to worry, lad."

Once they returned to the mechanics' building, Morgan put down his toolbox, shrugged out of his jacket, and hung it on a metal wall hook.

"Morgan! Over here!"

He startled and spun around. Mr. Hale was waving for him to hurry. The urgency of the supervisor's command and his frantic gestures were enough to erase Johnson's assurance that the weaving room supervisor wouldn't report them.

As Morgan wended his way through the workbenches and machinery, Mr. Hale continued to wave him onward. Drawing closer, Morgan caught sight of a man about Mr. Hale's age, wearing a suit and holding an overcoat across one arm.

Mr. Hale grasped Morgan's elbow as he approached. "This is the young man I was telling you about, William Morgan." He turned to Morgan. "This is Cyrus Baldwin. I mentioned his circular weaving machine to you when you first applied for your position here."

Mr. Baldwin extended his hand. "Pleased to meet you. Mr. Hale tells me you've acquired some education in engineering and expressed an interest in the design of my new machine." He glanced at Mr. Hale. "We've been discussing possible production. Mr. Hale assures me that since the tradesmen here in Manchester can produce all of the equipment for the mills as well as locomotives, there should be no problem producing my circular looms."

Morgan glanced back and forth between the two men. "But you disagree, Mr. Baldwin?"

He hiked a shoulder. "My primary concern is one of time and also willingness on the part of management. I have faith in the men who work in Mechanics' Row, but I'm hoping to arrive at a time for completion of a prototype. While I prefer to have the looms made in Manchester and see them put into production at the Stark Mills, there are others who have shown an interest in my project. I'd like to have a reliable opinion on how long it would take to produce a prototype and, using my detailed drawings, how much it would cost to do so. I've spoken briefly to Mr. Stark, and once I'm armed with the necessary information, I can present it to him and ascertain if it's possible to move forward with the project."

"I'm sure he'll be very eager to hear your proposal."

"We'll see. I've heard a few rumblings that financing the project may be problematic. So, if you're willing, I'd like you to work with us on development of the proposal. Mr. Hale believes there may be some new machinery required to produce certain parts of this loom, and I agree." He patted Morgan's shoulder. "We'll see what you think once we've inspected the equipment in the other mechanic shops."

Morgan tamped down his excitement, and for the rest of

the day he remained careful, both with his questions and with the knowledge he had regarding Mr. Baldwin's invention. By the time the three men had parted, Morgan was certain of one thing: He must speak with his father, and soon.

Several of the unmarried mechanics joined Morgan on their return to the boardinghouse that evening. "We're going into town after supper, Morgan. Care to join us?"

In truth, he didn't want to go into town, yet he'd already turned them down several times. The last time, a couple of the fellows made comments that maybe he thought he was too good for them. If he was going to discover ways to improve conditions in the mills, he needed to maintain a rapport with the men. "Sure, I'll go along."

It wasn't until they were on their way that one of the fellows mentioned the dance classes at Granite Hall. "We don't care about the classes, but it's a great way to meet girls," one of them said. "And it's worth the three cents he charges us. It's only two cents for the gals, which I don't agree with, but Mr. Vance says he wants to be certain we're there for the dance lessons."

Another fellow guffawed. "Even if he charged five cents, it wouldn't be the lessons that interested me. I met a real sweet gal the other night. I'm hoping she'll be there again this evening. She promised she would be."

"Well, if she's not, there's sure to be others who are just as nice," yet another called from the back of the group.

"You interested in dancing lessons, Morgan?"

Morgan inwardly groaned. The last thing he wanted to do was attend a dance class. "Can't say as I am." He slowed his pace. "But I am interested in photography. I think I'll stop in here and have a look at what kind of equipment the owner has in his shop."

The group stopped outside the glass window, and one of the men chortled. "You're not fooling me, Morgan. You're going in there to meet that pretty gal sitting in the window."

Morgan winked and grinned. "Maybe I am and maybe I'm not. You fellows go on and meet your gals at Granite Hall, and I'll take my chances here."

They all laughed. "Your odds are better if you come with us," one of them hollered as they continued on their way.

Morgan waited until they were out of sight before entering the shop. His comment about photography had been truthful. He did have an interest in photography, but it was the delicate paper cuttings displayed in the window that had captured his attention. A moment later, he'd caught sight of the lovely girl. There was something familiar about her; she reminded him of someone he'd seen before. And yet he couldn't place her. Without a doubt she was one of the most composed young women he'd ever observed. Even with passersby stopping to stare at her working in front of the window, she remained intent upon her task.

A bell jingled when Morgan opened the door. She looked up at him and smiled. "Good evening. Are you interested in an ambrotype? Or perhaps you'd like to view the paintings on display in the shop?" When he shook his head, the young woman continued, "We also have framed paper cuttings for sale. If you'd like, I can cut a silhouette of you while you pose for me."

He nodded. "I'd very much like a silhouette, thank you." He pointed to several framed silhouettes on a table behind her. They were of different sizes. He pointed to the largest one. "I'd like mine to be that size."

"The larger ones are eight cents. The smaller size is five cents." She hesitated. "Do you still want the larger size?"

"Yes." He glanced at the stool opposite her. "Do I sit there?"

She nodded, got up, and moved the stool a bit closer. "Sit facing the rear wall, please. I need a good view of your profile while I cut."

He positioned himself on the stool with his feet propped on one of the rungs. "I promise I won't move a muscle."

She smiled as she returned to her chair. "So long as you don't talk while I'm cutting, we'll do fine. I doubt you'd be pleased if I portray you with your mouth open in your finished silhouette. Why don't you wear your cap? If you don't mind, pull it forward just a bit."

He did as she requested and promised to remain silent until she was finished. It was while he sat staring at the wall that he recalled where he'd seen her before. She was the woman from the train station, the one who had dropped her book—a French novel—which he'd retrieved for her. During their brief encounter, she'd said she was going to work in the mills. He wanted to ask her if she'd been hired there and how she was faring, but he dared not. He'd been dressed as a member of the gentry during that meeting, and today he was a member of the working class. He couldn't reveal his identity and risk the consequences that might follow. If his fellow workers discovered he was the son of an owner, they'd never speak to him again. And the loss of trust among the workers, who would think he'd been placed with them in order to spy on them, might never be regained. No, he couldn't reveal his identity—not now.

He turned toward her and tilted his head. "You've been able to capture my good looks in such a short time? I can hardly believe it."

She laughed and held up the silhouette. "I'm not responsible for your outward appearance—you have God to thank in that regard. However, I've done my best to capture your profile."

Morgan stared at the cutting. How had she been able to cut such a perfect likeness in so short a time? He took the cutting and placed it atop a piece of paper on the counter.

She moved from her chair and stood beside him. "If you're not pleased with the silhouette, you're not required to purchase it. I don't want unhappy customers."

"Unhappy?" He shook his head. "No, quite the opposite. I think your work is excellent." He reached in his pocket and counted out the coins.

She thanked him, then gestured across the store. "What about a frame? If you plan to give your silhouette as a gift, I think it's special to have it mounted in a frame. Mr. Harrison has a very nice collection here. If you'd like to select one, he can frame it for you. You can pick it up tomorrow evening."

"Yes, I believe I would like to have it framed. Could you help me choose one?"

Together they surveyed the collection, but he wasn't certain which one would be best. "What would you suggest?"

She picked up a black oval frame, then placed the silhouette on top of the white background. Only an inch of white surrounded the cutting, but it looked perfect. Giving a nod, she handed him the frame. "I like simple frames so that those viewing the silhouette or picture aren't distracted by the frame. But if you prefer something fancier—"

"No, no, this is perfect. I agree with your choice."

"Good. Besides, this is much less expensive than those gilded frames." She placed the frame and silhouette on the counter. "It will be ready for you tomorrow."

"And will you be here tomorrow?"

"Yes, of course. I'm going to be working here every evening. You can tell your friends. Perhaps they'll want to have silhouettes made to send to their families or sweethearts back home."

"I'll do that. And I'll see you tomorrow."

He glanced over his shoulder as he strode toward the door. For some inexplicable reason, he already missed her.

NINE

LIKE THE OTHER WORKERS, MORGAN LOOKED FORWARD to Saturday afternoons, when the mills closed at five o'clock and the gates wouldn't reopen until Monday morning. The boardinghouse keeper served supper early on Saturdays to allow the men extra time for their evening activities. Most Saturdays, the men had finished their meals and were on their way to town by five-thirty.

"Going into town this evening, Morgan?" One of the men pointed his fork in Morgan's direction.

"Maybe later. I have some other things I need to do first. What about you? Going back for more dancing lessons?" He hoped his questions would divert the conversation away from his plans for the evening. "I didn't hear if that girl you liked so much was at Granite Hall last night."

The fellow bobbed his head with such enthusiasm it looked as if it were attached to a spring. "She sure was, and she was waiting just for me." He wiped the gravy from his lips and grinned. "She stayed in my arms for every lesson—kept talking about the ball in October. I think she wants me to be her escort. I'm giving the idea some thought, but tickets are a dollar each. That's pretty steep for two tickets."

The fellow sitting next to Morgan shook his head. "Whew! That's more than I'd pay. Maybe if you don't ask her, she'll buy her own ticket and be there anyway. If I was you, I'd take my chances."

"What would you do, Morgan?"

Morgan looked across the table. "I suppose it depends on how much you want to be with her. If you like her and have enough money, I say you should invite her and pay for her ticket. You can't tell about ladies. If she must buy her own ticket, she may refuse you as a dance partner throughout the evening. Would it bother you to see her dancing with other fellows?"

"'Course it would."

Morgan nodded. "Then you've answered your own question." He pushed away from the table and made his way to his room.

He wanted to escape before one of the men made any further inquiries about his intended whereabouts for the evening. The additional free hours would permit him time to go home, visit with his father about the meeting with Cyrus Baldwin, and then head to the photography shop for his silhouette—and hopefully a visit with the young lady who'd captured his interest there.

During their time together last evening, he'd forgotten to ask her name. Come to think of it, she hadn't asked his name, either. That could mean a couple of things. Either she'd been so smitten by his good looks that she'd failed to ask, or she'd been completely unimpressed and didn't care enough to inquire. Then again, perhaps like him, she'd simply forgotten to ask. He preferred to believe his final thought was correct.

Once he was certain most of the men had departed, Morgan ran downstairs, walked a short distance from the boarding-house to be sure no one would see him, then hailed a carriage. Before long, the driver guided the horse and carriage around the circular entrance and came to a halt in front of the portico.

Morgan stepped down, tossed the driver a coin, and tipped his hat. He waited until the carriage rolled off, then hurried to the front door and entered the house. He'd made it through the foyer and was passing his mother's sitting room when her high-pitched command stopped him.

"Workers and servants to the rear door. How dare you walk—" She stopped midsentence when Morgan turned to look at her. She shook her head as if trying to make sense of the young man standing in her home.

"It's me, Mother." He grinned. "You're just not accustomed to seeing me in my work clothes."

Her gaze slowly trailed from the top of his head to the floor, where his work boots had deposited remnants of dried mud. "Morgan Stark! I can't believe you'd enter through the front door looking like that. What if we'd had visitors?" She clasped a hand to her bodice and visibly paled. "How would I ever explain? Why, I'd be the laughingstock of Manchester."

"No need for concern, Mother. There are no visitors at present. If there were, you could say I'm one of the hired help who hasn't yet learned to use the rear door." He shrugged. "Simple as that."

"It isn't simple at all. The truth is that you shouldn't be working in the mill with all those, those . . ."

"Common people?" He tipped his head.

"Well, yes. You come from good stock and you're well educated. I still can't understand why you insist on this silly experiment of yours—or whatever it is."

There was no use debating with her. It would accomplish nothing. "Is Father in his study?"

"He is. And I'm sure he'll be every bit as disgusted with your appearance as I am." She flitted her hand toward the doorway. "Just go and see if I'm not correct."

He hesitated a moment and arched his brows. "You did insist that I come and visit you."

She narrowed her eyes. "I did, but not looking like that."

Hiding a smile, he sauntered down the hallway. He rapped on the door and entered the room, where his father was studying figures in a ledger. Mr. Stark glanced up, and a look of surprise shone in his eyes before he gestured to one of the chairs. "Good to see you, my boy. From your appearance I'd say you're still employed at the mills."

"I am, and I apologize for not contacting you more frequently."

His father waved the comment away. "No need to concern yourself. It's more important that your identity remain a secret. Still, it's good to see you."

Morgan scooted forward in his chair, excited to share news of his visit with Mr. Baldwin. He related their discussion and his examination of Mr. Baldwin's drawings before detailing their time spent in the various machine shops to compile information about production of the looms.

"There's a great opportunity here, Father. But unless you move quickly, I fear Mr. Baldwin will take his invention to another company, and you could lose out on a product that may reap a fortune in the coming years."

"What's this about losing a fortune?" Both men turned toward the door. Morgan's mother quickly closed the distance between the doorway and desk and sat down in the chair beside Morgan. She folded her hands in her lap and waited.

"We're discussing business, my dear. We'll join you in your sitting room when we've finished our talk."

Instead of leaving, she settled back in the chair. "I believe I'll stay. Any talk of losing a fortune is a discussion that interests me."

Morgan arched a brow. "Truly? I seem to recall your telling me you considered such talk dull and tasteless. Even guests weren't permitted to discuss business during your dinners and social gatherings."

Morgan's mother removed a handkerchief from her pocket and toyed with its lace edge. "Your recollection is correct. However, we're not dining, and this isn't a social gathering. When there's talk of losing a fortune, I have an intense interest." She pinned her husband with a hard stare. "If we're in financial straits, I should know such a thing."

Mr. Stark tapped the ledger book resting on his desk. "We're not teetering on the edge of financial ruin, but I don't have sufficient funds to invest in the new project I've been discussing with Morgan."

"One that could greatly increase our wealth?" She pursed her lips and waited.

His father gave a slight nod. "Possibly, but there's never a guarantee when you invest in a new product or the development of an invention, and this project involves both."

Morgan wasn't certain if he should continue or if his father wanted to call a halt to any further discussion while his mother remained in the room. Finally, his father sighed. "If you're going to remain during this discussion, I need your word you will not breathe a word to anyone—not even one of your lady friends. This can't become tittle-tattle at your teas or garden parties."

His mother straightened her shoulders and tilted her head.

"Really, William. I do understand how to keep my lips sealed. Have I said anything about Morgan and—this?" She waved toward his clothing and curled her lip. "Besides, you never know when a woman can bring a bit of insight to a problem."

Morgan could have mentioned several times when his mother hadn't been able to maintain her silence. He worried she might drop an enticing tidbit while attempting to impress one of her friends. Nevertheless, this was his father's decision and so he wouldn't argue the point.

His mother frowned and gestured for them to begin. After a quick glance at his father, Morgan explained the basic idea of the circular weaving machine and how, if developed, it would be used. He then repeated details of the meeting with Cyrus Baldwin.

"Oh, I do like Cyrus. He's so eccentric, don't you think, William? Anything he invents will be wonderful."

"We're hoping his invention will prove sound." He offered his wife an indulgent smile. "Continue, Morgan."

Morgan nodded. "From what I could gather, Mr. Baldwin prefers the prototype and subsequent machines be produced and utilized in Manchester. And he wants work on the prototype to begin as soon as possible. Unfortunately, to do so means a substantial investment of funds with no guarantee the machine will function as expected." Morgan paused and looked at his father. "So, there you have it. He did say he would like me to continue working with him if the owners are able to raise the necessary funding."

His mother squared her shoulders and arched her neck. "I am so proud to hear Cyrus Baldwin is impressed with *my* son."

"I'm proud of him as well, Ruth, but we must be careful to remember that we can't whisper a word of this to anyone. Such pride and excitement could cause us to misspeak."

"You mean *I* might misspeak."

"Now, Ruth, I included myself in that remark. I have to catch myself from time to time, too. I know you wouldn't intentionally say anything, but it worries me that you're involved in this conversation. Sometimes not knowing can be a good thing."

"That may be true in some cases, but I think you'll be pleased I'm here after I tell you that I have a possible solution to your dilemma."

That was enough to spark Morgan's interest. "What's your idea, Mother?"

"Well, I need the answers to several questions before I know for sure."

"What sort of questions?" Morgan asked.

"The questions are for your father." She pulled her chair forward, rested her arms on the desk, and met her husband's gaze. "Are there any surplus funds available in either the Stark Mill accounts or the funds you oversee for the Amoskeag Manufacturing Company?"

"There are operational funds in the Stark Mill accounts to meet our month-to-month obligations without difficulty. However, the capital funds were depleted earlier in the year when we constructed the new building. That sizable project required significant loans from the bank. Securing any additional loans wouldn't be possible until I've paid off the current ones—and that won't happen for ten more years."

She gave a little nod. "What about the Amoskeag accounts that you handle?"

His brow furrowed. "That money isn't mine. Granted, I'm a shareholder, but my position as treasurer of the group doesn't give me access to use those funds for an investment in Stark Mills."

"Hmm." She tapped her chin with her index finger. "But this

project *is* going to benefit the Amoskeag Manufacturing Company. If the prototype for the circular loom proves successful, the future looms will be manufactured by the Amoskeag Company. They'll be making money through the production of circular looms just as they do from all the other looms and equipment in the shops."

"That may be true, but beyond monthly expenses, use of any Amoskeag funds must be approved by the board."

"Well, there is enough money in the Amoskeag funds if you had the board's approval, correct?"

"That won't help, Mother." Morgan shook his head. "The idea is to keep this entire project secret so that other textile mills don't manufacture the looms and begin production of the bags before us. We could always move forward later, but it's the first operation that will secure the customer base. And that's a huge advantage. In order to win them, we'd need to sell for a lesser price, which would likely be impossible given the expense of beginning a new operation."

His father nodded. "And given the fact that the Amoskeag Manufacturing Company has board members who are also partners in other textile companies, we wouldn't want to tip our hand before we're certain the design will be successful."

His mother appeared undeterred. "Here's my idea. You withdraw funds from the Amoskeag funds, so that Cyrus doesn't go to someone else with his design. I'll write to my father and ask that he give us a loan for whatever amount you'll be taking from the Amoskeag Company. You then replace the funds before anyone knows they've been withdrawn."

"No, absolutely not, Ruth. I simply will not consider your idea. Even if I did, there's no guarantee your father would agree to such a large loan."

"Don't be silly. Of course he will. After all, I'm his only heir, and one day the money will all be ours anyway. Besides, I'll let him know that his money will be returned in full—with interest if he'd like—just as soon as we begin to realize a profit." She inhaled a breath and continued. "I'd tell you to wait until I receive the funds from him, but arrangements for such a large sum may take a bit of time. And since Morgan has said that time is of the essence, we need to tell Cyrus the funds are available." She dropped back in her chair as though she'd presented them with a fait accompli.

Morgan cleared his throat. "I, for one, am opposed to this." He looked at his father. "You could be charged with theft and be sent to prison, Father." He turned to his mother. "I know you're well-intentioned, Mother, but I don't think your idea is wise. Frankly, I wouldn't want the Stark Mills involved in the project unless there's some other way to secure the funds—something aboveboard."

"Morgan Stark!" His mother's complexion burned red with anger. "How dare you speak to your father and me in such a manner. Accusing us of illegal practices. Why, I never! What I've suggested is no different from borrowing through a bank."

Morgan pushed to his feet. "I don't agree, Mother." He lifted his jacket from the back of the chair. "And I believe Father won't agree, either." He shrugged into his coat. "I'm going to leave so the two of you can talk in private." He moved to the door, then turned toward his father. "If you secure funding, I suggest you contact Mr. Baldwin. There are a few other matters I had planned to discuss with you concerning the mills, but those can wait for another time."

A host of chaotic thoughts plagued Morgan as he returned to town. In her desire to be of help, his mother had seemingly lost her moral compass. Surely his father would manage to set her thinking along a different path than the one she'd proposed. The fact that his mother would even consider such an idea nagged at him and caused him to question her principles. But for now he'd set aside all thoughts of her proposal and instead concentrate on visiting with the young lady at the photography shop.

Why hadn't he asked her name?

A mother and her three children who had visited the photography shop last evening entered the shop shortly after Mellie arrived. The mother drew near and gestured to the threesome. "I've decided to have you make silhouettes of the children. My parents live in Ohio, and they've never seen any of them. The silhouettes will make a wonderful gift—one I can afford." She stared longingly at Mr. Harrison's photography equipment. Mellie could almost read her thoughts. More than anything, the mother wanted a daguerreotype of her children. Perhaps if Mellie spoke to Mr. Harrison, he would lower his price a little for this woman. After all, if the mother was going to pay for three silhouettes and frames, it would end up costing her almost the same amount. And if she had a daguerreotype made, she could sit with the children, as well.

"Excuse me for a moment. I need to speak to the shop owner. I'll be right back." Mellie waved toward the paintings. "You and the children can look at the beautiful paintings while I'm gone."

"That's fine, but I don't have a lot of time." The woman grasped her little girl's hand and followed the two boys as they headed to where the paintings were displayed.

A short time later, Mr. Harrison followed Mellie to the front of the store and approached the woman. "Miss Blanchard tells me she thinks a daguerreotype of you and your children would make a fine gift for your parents, but you don't think you can afford the expense."

"That's right." Her eyes were clouded with confusion as she glanced at Mellie.

Mr. Harrison offered a gentle smile. "I believe I could do a daguerreotype of you and the children for about the same cost as three silhouettes and frames."

"Truly?"

He nodded. "Grandparents should have the pleasure of seeing their daughter as well as their grandchildren. Come sit over here, and I'll get everything set up."

Mellie stood at a distance while he guided the family into the small alcove that had been arranged much like the corner of a parlor. With the mother seated in the chair and the little girl on her lap, Mr. Harrison had the boys stand on either side of their mother.

Mellie turned as the bell over the front door jingled. She smiled at the young man who had entered and gestured toward the counter. "I have your purchase ready for you, sir."

Morgan chuckled. "Sir? You're making me feel like an old man."

"That wasn't my intention, but I didn't realize until after you left last night that I hadn't asked your name."

"Morgan." He cleared his throat. "William Morgan, but most of us call each other by our last name. I've gotten to where I prefer Morgan."

"Thank you very much for your business, Mr. Morgan."

He shook his head. "Just Morgan—please."

She nodded and smiled. "Thank you for your business, Morgan. I hope we'll see you again in the future."

"You will. I enjoy watching you do your paper cutting."

"It's Scherenschnitte."

His brows dipped low. "What is?"

She laughed. "The art of paper cutting is known as Scherenschnitte."

"Oh!" He raked his fingers through his hair. "I doubt I'd ever learn to say that word properly, so I'll just say *paper cutting* instead."

"Of course." The bell rang, and a group of several girls stepped into the shop. "If you'll excuse me, I need to see to these ladies."

He nodded and turned toward the alcove, where Mr. Harrison was photographing the mother and children, while Mellie moved to the front of the store.

Mellie was aware of the young man throughout the remainder of the evening. He was either studying the paintings or watching as she cut silhouettes. At nine-thirty, when Mr. Harrison announced it was time to close the shop, Morgan drew near. "If you don't have someone coming to escort you to your boardinghouse, I hope you'll permit me to do so."

She shook her head. "No, thank you, Morgan. I'm not in need of an escort." He seemed a nice fellow, yet she barely knew him.

"I understand. Still, I don't think it's safe for you to walk back to the boardinghouse unescorted."

"I'll be perfectly safe." At least she wanted to believe she would, but this would be the first night she would be walking home without Cora and Clara at her side. Though they'd offered to come by and walk home with her, she'd refused. It wasn't fair to expect them to leave the warmth of the boardinghouse every night just to walk her home.

He shrugged. "I don't think it's wise, but I won't pressure you to accept my offer. Even so, if it's all right with you, I'm going to follow you at a short distance in case there should be a problem."

His presence would offer a modicum of safety but without giving the appearance they were together. She gave him a slight nod. She slipped into her coat, tied her bonnet, and stepped outside. When he followed, she turned and glanced over her shoulder. "You must not follow me to the door of my boardinghouse. I don't want the keeper to see me in the company of a man."

He gave a solemn nod, smiled, and crossed his heart with his finger. "I promise."

Chapter

TEN

MELLIE HADN'T MENTIONED HER POSITION AT MR. HAR-rison's shop to Mrs. Richards. She had told only Cora, Clara, and Phebe, then asked that they remain silent about it. They understood Mellie didn't want Olive or Charity coming inside the shop and causing any problems. Both Olive and Charity appeared to like embarrassing others. At times Mellie believed they were insecure girls who longed to be accepted. At other times, she thought they both possessed a mean streak and enjoyed inflicting pain on others.

Eager to help Mellie keep her secret, Cora planned a new route to their dance lessons—one that wouldn't lead them past the photography shop. After proving it would take less time, they'd eagerly followed her directions to Granite Hall each evening. Of course, there was no way she could guarantee one of the girls wouldn't come to town on another evening and spot Mellie, but so far Mellie had been fortunate.

Immediately after accepting the position, she'd considered

telling everyone. After all, if most of the girls in their boarding-house came to have a silhouette cut, she could make a profit in a short time. Once word spread among the boardinghouse, it would likely move among the other houses, and then more customers might visit the shop. Yet the idea of having Olive or Charity make an appearance had deterred her. Mellie continued to avoid them whenever possible, both at home and at work. But when Olive wanted something bad enough, she'd wait until bedtime and then slip upstairs to the attic. That way, Mellie couldn't escape seeing her.

Even though she disliked doing so, Mellie had relented and loaned her shawl to Olive. The girl's threat to tell her newspaper-reporter friend had hit the mark. Right now, all Mellie wanted was to make enough money to be certain Margaret and the children didn't suffer any further. She decided that one loan of her shawl was a small price to pay to keep any gossip at bay. Still, she wasn't a fool. There was little doubt whether or not Olive's extortion would continue. Mellie could only hope that Olive would not eventually demand money. If that hap-pened, Mellie would draw the line. Borrowing clothes was one thing, but she wouldn't be forced to give away her hard-earned wages.

Lifting her skirts, Mellie stepped around several mud puddles. As the days of pounding rain continued, she'd begun to wonder if they should follow Noah's example and build an ark. Today the skies had finally cleared, but the mud left in the wake of the storms made both walking and riding difficult. Carriage wheels groaned in protest while horses strained to lift their hooves from the congealing mire, and those on foot would need their galoshes for days to come.

She stopped as she neared the shop. A hinged, two-sided

wood sign sat in front of the door. The profile of a child had been drawn and painted on the board, advertising that silhouette cuttings would be created each evening from seven-thirty until nine-thirty. The prices and sizes were listed below the picture, along with her name as the *Artist-in-Residence*. While the title was flattering, she didn't deserve or want such an unwarranted accolade. In truth, she would have preferred that her name had not been placed on the sign, either.

Upon entering the shop, Mellie removed her galoshes and set them on an old piece of newspaper Mr. Harrison had placed in a corner behind the door. She spotted Mr. Harrison at the rear of the store and waved her umbrella to gain his attention.

He strode toward her with a wide smile. "Did you see the sign?" His eyes shone with delight.

"Yes. I was taken by surprise. You didn't mention you were going to have a sign made."

"I painted it myself. I don't count myself an artist, but it turned out better than I expected."

"I didn't know creating signage was among your many talents. It is quite nice, and I'm sure it will garner attention." She didn't tell him how she'd nearly tripped over it as she tried to enter the store. "We might want to move it a little farther away from the door."

His brows furrowed as he glanced at the door. "I see what you mean. I'll go move it so it's in front of the window instead. Passersby will spot the sign, then look up and see you sitting in the window. It will be perfect."

She didn't wish to dampen his enthusiasm, yet she wanted him to remove her name and the gratuitous reference to her as an artist. He was the artist—not her. "Could you possibly make a few small changes before moving the sign to the window?"

Her question brought him to a halt. "Did I spell something incorrectly?"

"No, but if you could paint over my name and the wording below, it would please me."

"But why? That is your name, and you are my artist-in-residence. Customers prefer knowing our names when they come into the store."

She didn't want to upset him. No doubt he had spent hours painting the sign, and he'd done a good job of it. "I suppose you could leave my name, but I don't think it's proper to advertise me as an artist."

He waved his hand in a dismissive gesture. "Bah! You are one of the finest artists I've ever seen. Art comes in many forms. Some in sketching, some in painting, some in pottery, and some in your Scherenschnitte." He chuckled. "Did I pronounce it correctly?"

"You did." She offered a weak smile and decided not to argue any further. She'd worked here for a little over two weeks now, not very long. She couldn't chance losing this opportunity.

"I hope you won't feel I am taking advantage, but I have accepted a dinner invitation for this evening. I'll return before closing time, of course." He offered a sheepish smile. "I know you are capable of handling things while I'm out. If anyone should come in for a photograph, please offer to make an appointment tomorrow or tell them I will be in throughout the day and evening tomorrow."

Mellie's heart warmed. He'd come to trust her, and helping him was a small way for her to repay his kindness. "You go and enjoy yourself. There should be no problem."

"Thank you." He inhaled a deep breath before once again gesturing to the front of the store. "Because of the sign, I had four customers come in and make appointments to have silhouettes made this evening. I hope that you approve. I wrote the names and times on a paper." He pulled the note from his pocket and glanced at it. "The first lady should be in anytime now." He'd barely finished his sentence when a woman with two children entered the store. He smiled and made a sweeping motion with his arm. "Ah, Mrs. Franklin, do come in. Miss Blanchard is eager to create your silhouette"—he looked toward the children—"and your children's?"

She nodded. "I thought I would have their silhouettes made, as well. I'm sure my husband will be pleased." She turned to Mellie. "You will have time to do all three of us, won't you?"

Mellie looked at the appointment sheet and nodded. "Yes. Why don't we begin right away? Who wants to be first?"

The younger boy raised his hand, and soon Mellie had completed their cuttings, all of which pleased Mrs. Franklin. She was choosing frames when the bell over the door jingled. Mellie's throat tightened when she turned and saw who was entering the store.

Olive and Charity stepped inside, their features twisted into sneers. Olive moved a little closer. "We're here to see the *artist-in-residence*. But you don't look like an artist, and you certainly don't reside here."

Mrs. Franklin's satin skirt swished as she carried three frames to the counter and placed them alongside her silhouettes. She lifted her chin and cast a cold stare in Olive's direction. "The artist is currently assisting me. I would appreciate it if you would put your manners to good use. It is rude to interrupt." She looked down her nose at the two girls. "I highly recommend Miss Gilbert's classes on etiquette and proper comportment.

They are conducted two nights a week, and I'm sure that being under her tutelage would be helpful to both of you."

Olive stiffened but didn't respond. Instead, she turned away and pretended to study one of Mr. Harrison's paintings until Mrs. Franklin and her children departed.

Once the older woman was out of sight, Olive walked over to Mellie with purpose in her step and a blazing anger in her eyes. "How dare that woman speak to me like that! You're lucky I didn't tell her you're nothing more than a mill girl, just like us." Her lip curled. "Since you're such an artist, I want to pose for a silhouette. You can prove just how good you are."

Mellie sighed. This wasn't going to end well. She could feel it in her bones. Yet any attempt to dissuade Olive would likely result in another embarrassing scene. "Why don't you remove your bonnet and have a seat on the stool?" She pointed to the back of the room. "Please turn so I have a good view of your profile."

Olive gave a sly grin as she looked toward Charity.

Mellie's stomach clamped hard around her supper. Since they appeared determined to stay, she'd cut Olive's silhouette, then encourage them to leave before any other customers arrived. Picking up a piece of black paper and her scissors, Mellie stared at Olive's profile while she snipped tiny indentations, then made longer cuts down the forehead and at the neck. She rotated the paper and snipped a few wisps of hair at her nape.

Once finished, Mellie placed her scissors on the table and forced a smile. "All done." She extended the cutting toward Olive. "Would you like to choose a frame, or do you have one at home you'd prefer to use?"

The bell over the front door rang, and Mellie turned to see Morgan entering the shop. He nodded and offered a smile, but before she could acknowledge him, Olive squealed like a stuck pig. Startled, Mellie twisted around. Olive had extended her arm to its full length and was holding the silhouette between her thumb and forefinger. "Charity! Look at this. She's given me a nose that's much too large and made my chin as pointed as the tip of a knife." She swung the cutting back and forth like a fan and glared at Mellie. "How dare you!"

Morgan hurried toward the threesome, turning a frown on Olive as he drew near. "Are you suffering an illness of some sort, miss?"

"No, of course not. My health isn't the problem."

"Then I can't imagine what would cause you to behave in such an unladylike manner." Morgan shot a look of concern toward Mellie.

Olive scooted around on the stool and tapped a finger on the cutting that still hung from her fingers. "Look at this! She's done her very best to make me appear dreadful." She waved in Mellie's direction.

Morgan removed it from her hand and held it near Olive's face. He looked from the silhouette to her profile and back again. "I'm bewildered that you aren't pleased." He fastened his gaze on her. "If you don't mind my saying, you are a very attractive young lady, and this cutting exemplifies all of your best features." He turned to Charity. "Don't you agree?"

Before Charity could answer, Olive leaned toward Morgan. "I believe you may be correct. I think the inadequate lighting caused me to arrive at a hasty decision." She slipped off the stool and pressed close to Morgan's side. "I don't believe we've met. I'm Olive French." She batted her lashes at him. "And you are?"

"William Morgan." He took a backward step and glanced

toward the counter. "I believe you can pay over there at the counter—if you've decided you like the silhouette." He tipped his head. "If I were you, I'd certainly purchase it. I'm sure your beau would be pleased to have it as a gift."

"Mr. Morgan! Well, I do have my choice of gentlemen callers, but none of them is a steady beau. Of course, they've all asked, but I'm still waiting for the perfect match to come along."

Mellie thought Olive's attempts to look and sound coy were ridiculous. She stepped behind the counter. "You didn't say, Olive, if you'd like a frame for your silhouette."

Olive wrinkled her nose and shook her head. "No, I don't believe I want a frame."

"Then that will be five cents, please."

Olive tilted her head and looked at Morgan. "I'll buy the cutting, but only if you agree to walk me back to my boardinghouse. That way I'll know you meant all those things you said to me." She purred and preened like a cat seeking shelter.

"I don't see any reason why I couldn't escort you home, miss." Morgan pulled his flat-billed cap from his back pocket and held it in his hand.

Mellie found it difficult to believe that Morgan agreed. He'd been so eager to walk her home over the past weeks. Perhaps he did find Olive attractive. She picked up the coins Olive had flung onto the counter, then watched as the girl slipped her hand into the crook of Morgan's arm.

Something poked at her insides. Jealousy? No, it couldn't be. Disappointment? Yes, that had to be it.

None of Olive's behavior had come as a surprise to Mellie, but she now wondered if Morgan was the man she'd first thought. After appearing at the store and walking her home for the past couple of weeks, he no longer seemed worried about her safekeeping. Was he truly interested in a girl like Olive—one who would fawn over him and boost his ego?

Before she could dwell on the thought of Morgan and Olive walking arm in arm, Mellie's next appointment arrived. This time it was a young man who appeared to be thirteen or fourteen. He doffed his cap and ducked his head, seemingly embarrassed.

Mellie glanced at the list of appointments, then smiled at him. "You must be Benjamin Rourke. Am I correct?"

He nodded and raked his fingers through a shock of auburn hair. "I . . . I made an appointment with Mr. Harrison yesterday." He glanced at the clock. "I'm a little early."

"That's quite all right. I've already completed my previous appointment. Why don't you have a seat on the stool there?"

After she'd finished cutting his silhouette, she helped him choose a frame. Over the next hour, the remainder of her appointments arrived on schedule, and there were several other customers who came in and were willing to wait their turns. They'd stand and watch, transfixed as Mellie snipped away the outer edges of black paper until the likeness of her subject appeared, with the remnants of paper fluttering to the floor.

It was near closing time when the bell over the door rang and a young mother with two children arrived. The red-cheeked toddler was cranky, and the smaller child slept on her shoulder. "I hope I'm not too late. I wanted to come earlier, but I couldn't manage it."

With one look at the harried young mother, a surge of sympathy swelled in Mellie's chest. "There's more than enough time. I can't leave until Mr. Harrison returns, so there's no hurry. Did you want a silhouette of both children or one of yourself?"

Her lips curved in a half smile. "I'd like a small one of each of us, but I don't know if the children will cooperate. If I wake the little one, she'll cry, and I'm not sure Isabelle will hold still for you."

"I think if you sit down in this chair, I can cut her profile while she's sleeping on your shoulder. Let's try. If you don't like my first attempt, we can wake her and try again."

Soon realizing her mother was occupied, the toddler scampered around the shop, reaching for anything within her grasp. Her mother's admonitions did nothing to deter Isabelle, and Mellie was hurrying across the room when Isabelle started to grab hold of Mr. Harrison's tripod.

Thinking that Mr. Harrison had returned when she heard footsteps behind her, Mellie scooped up the child. "Nothing harmed," she said. She took a backward step and turned. "Oh, I thought . . ."

"Would you like me to entertain her while you finish?" Morgan extended his arms to the toddler. "Want to come and play over here?"

Arms outstretched, Isabelle strained toward him. He lifted her up in a swoosh, and little Isabelle giggled.

Mellie's thoughts raced. When had he returned? Hadn't Olive invited him to sit in the visiting parlor so she could show him off to the other girls? Did he realize how irresistibly endearing he appeared while entertaining little Isabelle? She stared at him a moment longer and erased the thought from her mind. He'd been walking Olive home only a short time ago.

She frowned at the remembrance and strode back across the room, where Isabelle's mother was still holding the infant. "If you can hold the baby in the crook of your arm, I'll position my stool so you won't have to move. Then we can see if Isabelle will cooperate."

A short time later, it was Morgan who held Isabelle on his lap while Mellie cut her silhouette. In truth, she couldn't have completed the cuttings without his help. But she wouldn't let down her guard with a man who seemed to toy with the affections of young ladies.

Mellie's customer was paying for her silhouettes when Mr. Harrison rushed inside and came to her side. "I'm sorry to be so late. We were talking, and I wasn't careful about the time."

"Everything is fine, Mr. Harrison. It's not quite nine-thirty. I knew you would return on time. I wasn't worried." From the corner of her eye she could see Morgan moving toward the door. Was he leaving without a word to her? "Business was good this evening. I've listed everything that was sold and left an accounting of the payments. Your share from the silhouettes is in the drawer."

"Thank you, Mellie. I don't know how I managed my evening hours before you came to work for me." He moved behind the counter. "I'll see you tomorrow evening."

Morgan slipped out the door while she was donning her bonnet and cape. He'd obviously noticed she wasn't happy with his earlier behavior and taken his leave. After bidding Mr. Harrison good-night, she picked up the case with her scissors and paper. She'd promised to cut a likeness of Cora and Clara after she returned home this evening. Though she was tired, she didn't want to disappoint them.

She'd gone only a short distance when she heard the distinct sound of footfalls behind her and glanced over her shoulder.

"No need for concern, Mellie. It's just me."

Morgan! She recognized the deep timbre of his voice, even before seeing his face. "I don't need you to follow me. Unlike Olive, I didn't beg you to escort me home. I'm perfectly fine."

He moved to her side. "Why are you angry with me? I've done nothing but try to help you."

She gasped in surprise. "Help me? Other than entertaining Isabelle, how do you think your actions helped me this evening?"

"I got Olive to leave the store before she created another incident. And, I might add, I convinced her to purchase the silhouette, even if I did have to stretch the truth a little. She does have a rather large nose and pointed chin." He sighed. "That was the longest walk of my life."

Mellie couldn't restrain a laugh. Morgan joined her laughter and fell in step beside her.

After their laughter died away, neither of them spoke for a while, though a current seemed to glide between them as smoothly as a bird taking flight. Morgan cleared his throat. "Thanks to that sign in the window, I finally know your full name is Mellicent. I don't believe I've ever known anyone named Mellicent."

She should put an end to his attentions right now. She was here to earn money for her family, not find a beau. Yet his nearness made her stomach flutter in a most delightful manner. Besides, he seemed determined to keep her safe at night whether she enjoyed his company or not.

But in truth, she did enjoy his company. She paused and turned to him. "Please call me Mellie. Mellicent is much too formal."

Chapter

ELEVEN

MORGAN SWALLOWED HARD WHEN HE CAUGHT SIGHT of Mr. Hale and Mr. Baldwin hunched over a worktable. Had Mr. Baldwin come to announce he'd found another investor to fund his project? Morgan hadn't heard anything from his father. He could only assume the Stark Mills had lost their opportunity to produce the circular loom and Mr. Baldwin was here to pick up the drawings he'd left with Mr. Hale.

Gathering his courage, Morgan approached the two men. Mr. Baldwin glanced over his shoulder and locked eyes with Morgan. He jerked upright and clasped Morgan's shoulder.

"Good morning!" Mr. Hale smiled and echoed Mr. Baldwin's cheerful greeting.

"Good morning, gentlemen. You both seem in good spirits for such a gloomy day." Morgan nodded toward the windows, emphasizing the gray clouds that threatened to spill either rain or snow—the type of moisture dependent upon New Hampshire's changing fall temperatures.

"Ah, but it's a glorious day, in spite of the clouds." Mr. Baldwin tapped the drawings spread across the worktable. "Today we begin work on the circular loom prototype. Thanks to Mr. Hale, constructing the prototype isn't going to be as time-consuming as I'd once thought." He clapped Mr. Hale on the shoulder. "Because he was confident Mr. Stark would acquire funding, Mr. Hale has been making inquiries at some of the other shops in the mill yard."

"Without divulging why I was making such inquiries." Mr. Hale leaned forward to look at Morgan. "I didn't want anyone to know about Mr. Baldwin's invention."

Mr. Baldwin bobbed his head with such enthusiasm, a shock of his dark hair dropped across one eye. "Of course, of course, and I appreciate your caution." Fingers spread wide, he raked his hair back into place. "The use of forging dies in the locomotive shop will markedly speed the entire process." He nudged Morgan. "We won't need to worry over production of the circular frames. They can be manufactured with the dies used for the locomotive wheels. I think we can adapt without any problem, especially for the prototype. If there are problems, we'll be prepared for them when we begin production of additional looms."

Morgan did his best to keep pace with the conversation swirling around him, yet it was proving difficult. When had the funds become available to move forward with the project? Why hadn't his father gotten word to him? If nothing else, his father could have used an anonymous name and sent a letter to the boardinghouse.

"You haven't said a word, Morgan. I thought you'd be overjoyed by the news." Mr. Baldwin's brows dipped low, and he rubbed his chin. "Have you lost interest in the project?"

"No, not at all. I'm very excited. It's just, well, a surprise. I didn't know the finances had been received. So, is it Stark Mills that will invest in the project, or has Mr. Stark arranged for some other financial plan?"

Both men stared at him as though he'd spoken in a foreign tongue, but Mr. Hale was the first to answer. "We aren't privy to the financial records of Stark Mills, yet Mr. Stark has sent word that we are to move forward posthaste. Mr. Baldwin and I have been tasked with keeping a record of the costs as we proceed, and funding has been placed in a special account for our use during this first step."

Morgan silently chastised himself. Mentioning the financing wasn't an inquiry a mechanic would make. He'd better keep on his toes or his identity would be discovered before he accomplished anything.

"I'd like you to go over to the locomotive shop with me so we can talk to the foreman. He needs to meet you and know that he'll be dealing directly with you much of the time. He talked like he'd want you to meet several of the men in his shop, as well." Mr. Baldwin shifted from Morgan to Mr. Hale. "Are you coming with us, John?"

The overseer shook his head. "I'll let the two of you go ahead and meet with him. I have work here that needs my attention. But Morgan has been removed from his previous assignment and will be working only on the circular loom until further notice. You'll be reassigning his work until we move further along with production."

Mr. Baldwin smiled at Morgan. "I think we're going to get along quite well."

For the remainder of the day, Morgan shadowed Mr. Baldwin's every move, listening carefully as he spoke to various foremen and workers. He committed their names to memory, and he did sketch a few drawings of the forging dies they'd be using for the loom.

When they had departed for the shop where the power looms were produced, Morgan stepped alongside Mr. Baldwin. "Is there some reason you decided against the circular dies that are used for the power looms? I thought you were considering adapting those."

"At first we thought they might work, but it turns out they aren't large enough and the dies can't be enlarged. We have more latitude with the ones in the locomotive shop."

Mr. Hale and Mr. Baldwin had obviously continued their meetings with the belief that the necessary funding would become available. Yet Morgan hadn't been included in any of those meetings. And when Mr. Baldwin revealed they'd already ordered the leather strapping and redesigned the pulleys and other equipment made in the power-loom shop, Morgan was sure he'd been intentionally excluded. The idea niggled at him. Had his father consented to the project earlier but cautioned against sharing the news with anyone else until he sent further approval? If so, why? Had he decided to use funds that didn't belong to him? Had Morgan's mother convinced him there was no danger in doing so? Or perhaps she hadn't needed to convince him. Maybe his father had been unable to set aside the possibility of losing huge financial gains, especially to a competitor. The thoughts plagued him throughout the day.

Shortly before quitting time, they returned for a brief meeting with Mr. Hale. Morgan longed to know more about the financial arrangements, but the older man had made it clear he didn't know. Besides, further questions might cause them to speculate about his interest, and deep inside he feared what he might discover. Maybe this was one time it was good to be in the dark. Once their meeting ended, Morgan grabbed his coat from atop the worktable.

"Before you go, you should take this with you." Mr. Baldwin rolled up a copy of the diagrams and handed them to Morgan. "Study as you have time. The more you commit the plans to memory, the easier it will be once we begin work. If you must stop and study a diagram each time a screw or bolt needs to be placed, it will take much more time." He tapped his finger on the roll of documents. "And remember to keep these away from prying eyes. The last thing we want is for the design to fall into the wrong hands. If the corporate bigwigs in Lowell or Nashua caught wind of this invention, they'd try to develop the loom and beat us to production." He patted Morgan on the shoulder. "I've made notations so you will know the size and number of each item that must be on hand when we begin."

Morgan turned to Mr. Hale. "Did you have someone in mind to take charge of procurement for the project?"

"Why, you, of course. I thought you understood that I appointed you as Mr. Baldwin's second on this project."

A cradle of fear lodged deep in his belly. "I understood you relieved me of my other duties so that I could act as Mr. Baldwin's assistant, but I didn't realize that would include taking charge of procuring all the materials and tools necessary for producing the machine."

Mr. Hale shrugged. "To my thinking, that's what a second does—everything his superior either can't or doesn't want to do. I know you're one of our most recent hires, but you're also one of the brightest. Still, this is a large and important undertaking." He glanced around, looked at the list of men on the employee board hanging above his desk, and pointed. "I'll assign Jake Marlow to help you assemble the tools, materials, and equipment. Don't share the details with him. I'll tell him all he needs to know, and if he asks further questions, tell him he needs to speak with me." He perched on the corner of his desk, one leg dangling. "Most of the men don't mean to cause problems, but sometimes they talk too much. Makes them feel important if they think they know more than the other fellas. One thing leads to another and before you know it, you've got rumors flying around like a flock of geese headed south for the winter."

Mr. Baldwin nodded his agreement. "I'm all for giving Morgan as much help as he needs, but I concur. We don't want anyone spreading rumors. Once we've completed the prototype and are ready to move forward, it will be difficult to keep things quiet. For now, however, secrecy is critical."

Morgan nodded and tucked the design inside his coat. He wasn't certain where he'd find a place to study the renderings. Obviously, Mr. Baldwin didn't understand that living in a boardinghouse didn't permit privacy. With two other men sharing his room and a parlor where the boardinghouse keeper permitted poker games if there was no gambling, Morgan would be hard-pressed to find a safe place in which to study the drawings.

Even so, he'd have to figure out something. The project was far too important for him to fail.

On Sunday morning, Mellie entered the recently constructed brick-and-granite church on the corner of Franklin and Market Streets. On her first Sunday at the boardinghouse, the twins had invited her to attend church with them. Mellie had agreed, but she was taken aback when, the following Sunday, the girls had attended a different church. It was then that Mellie had learned the girls had a routine they referred to as "circulating church."

Each Sunday morning they attended a different church until they'd attended every church in the city—and then they started anew. Sunday by Sunday, church by church.

Mellie had continued the routine for only two rounds before she expressed her desire to attend the Franklin Street church every Sunday. While she'd enjoyed visiting the various churches, this church reminded her of home. Phebe had said the same about the Methodist church that she attended each week. Cora and Clara continued their weekly routine but attended with Mellie when the Franklin Street church rotated to the top of their list, and with Phebe when it was "Methodist Sunday." When Mellie had inquired about their odd habit, Cora told her that choosing a church had been one of the very few times they hadn't been able to agree. Between them, they'd decided to circulate among the Manchester churches until the two of them finally decided. Thus far, that hadn't happened.

While company rules stated that church attendance was required, the workers were permitted to attend any church of their choosing—a far cry from the early years in Lowell when the mill girls were required to attend St. Ann's and a portion of their pay was involuntarily deducted and given to the church. Yet some of the workers continued to rebel quietly against the rule by heading off to the river rather than attending Sunday services. From time to time, Mellie had heard gossip about the girls who had been discharged for lying about church attendance or breaking company or boardinghouse rules, especially the girls already considered to be of weak moral character.

With the passage of time, Mellie had become increasingly comfortable in her new surroundings. It wasn't the same as living at home in Concord, but she'd learned to navigate the city and could locate most any establishment on her own. Though she enjoyed the company of Phebe, Clara, and Cora, she no longer felt dependent upon them. But for some reason, while sitting alone in the church pew, she was struck by a sudden sense of loneliness. Perhaps it was caused by a group of girls who'd entered in a cluster and were whispering among themselves, or perhaps it was because she was seldom alone in her new life.

She hadn't completely overcome the feeling when, from the corner of her eye, she glimpsed someone at the end of the pew. Mellie looked up and inhaled a sharp breath.

Morgan leaned sideways toward her. "May I sit with you?" He didn't wait for a response before sitting down beside her. "I hope you don't mind, but when I saw you sitting alone, I thought you might like some company."

Some of the girls who'd settled in a pew only a few rows forward glanced in their direction. They quickly turned around, and several of their bonneted heads bent together as they tittered. Mellie didn't know any of them by name, but she recognized more than one who worked in the spinning room. Word would soon spread that she'd attended church with a beau.

She offered a faint smile. "I don't visit during church services."

"Then perhaps you'd join me afterward?"

Her stomach fluttered as though butterflies had taken up residence there and were now attempting an escape. She wanted to welcome Morgan, yet she remained silent. Olive hoped to call Morgan her beau, and Mellie didn't want any more difficulty with her.

Although Morgan continued to escort her home each evening, Mellie still insisted he leave her at the corner before her boardinghouse. His presence continued to pique her curiosity, and she wanted to learn more about the gallant young man who insisted upon protecting her.

Thus far, the exchanges about their pasts had been limited, and she'd always been careful not to divulge too much. Interestingly, she thought he was even more cautious about his earlier life. Yet who was she to question how much or how little he wanted to reveal? She was thankful he didn't press for more, and she offered him the same consideration. It was enough to know he worked on Mechanics' Row, lived in one of the boardinghouses, and had attended college to study engineering but hadn't immediately found work as an engineer and had accepted the lesser position. Knowing he could understand how quickly life could take an unexpected turn had given her comfort and created an unforeseen bond. Those facts aside, she hadn't agreed to have him call on her—or have him sit with her in church. She didn't want anyone to assume he was her beau.

After the final hymn had been sung and the pastor had recited the benediction, Morgan turned to her. "It's a fine afternoon for a walk. Care to join me?"

She didn't meet his eyes. "Thank you for your offer, but I have clothes that need mending and letters to write. I have little time to complete such tasks during the week."

"May I at least walk you home, then?"

Not wanting Morgan to think she didn't care for him, she gave him a lighthearted smile while she shook her head. "That wouldn't be wise. Besides, you already walk me home six days a week. Sunday should be your day of rest."

"Is there some reason why you don't want to be seen with me, Mellie? The company has no rules that would prohibit us from spending time together."

How could she explain to him that if Olive saw them together, she would do everything in her power to ruin Mellie's future in Manchester? Based upon the stories Olive had been telling the other girls, Morgan was one step away from offering a proposal of marriage.

Mellie dug her nails into her palm. "I have little free time, Morgan. If you want a young lady to escort, I suggest you contact Olive French. She continues to seek your attention."

He frowned. "Olive French doesn't interest me in the least. She's a mean-spirited young woman who has little kindness for others and a rather large nose." He grinned when he mentioned Olive's nose.

"Then I suggest you ask one of the other girls who are frequently at Granite Hall for dance lessons. You might find one of them to your liking."

He sighed. "It's you who I find to my liking, Mellie, but I'll remain content with walking you home after you finish work each evening—at least for now."

He tipped his hat and turned toward the falls. She longed to call after him and tell him she'd changed her mind, but she tightened her lips in a thin line. That would never do. She dared not let Olive see them together.

Only two days had passed when Mellie felt a tug on her cape while walking home for the noonday meal. "I hear you're out to steal my beau. I had two girls tell me they saw you sidling up to him. And in church, no less." She leaned close to Mellie's ear. "You're what's known as a slow learner, aren't you?"

Mellie wanted to escape Olive's grasp, but workers swarmed around them, blocking any possible path through the crowd. Olive's fingers pinched into the flesh of Mellie's lower arm. "We can talk at the boardinghouse. I'll meet you in my room after supper. Before I leave for work."

Olive tightened her hold, and a sharp pain raced up Mellie's arm. "There's nothing to talk about. You quit seeing him or I'm going to have a talk with my friend."

"We had an agreement. I've already loaned you my shawl and a dress."

"Well, now we have a new agreement. Stay away from Morgan or you'll see your name in print, and you won't like the story—and neither will the overseer at the mill."

Mellie's chest tightened. She could not lose this job over anything or anyone—including Morgan.

Chapter
TWELVE

DESPITE HIS REPEATED ATTEMPTS, MORGAN COULDN'T discover why Mellie had recently become distant and stand-offish. She'd consistently refused any invitation he extended. When he attempted to sit beside her at church, she'd either flanked herself with Cora and Clara or moved to another pew. She couldn't stop him from following her home from work at night, but he'd once again been relegated to following behind her rather than walking at her side.

Her actions baffled him. She professed he'd done nothing to offend her, yet she wouldn't say why things had changed between them. Tonight, he was going to persist until he got an answer—one that made sense. He'd become weary of studying diagrams in one of the back rooms in the photography shop until closing time. Granted, it had given him ample time to learn the details of the circular loom, but now that work on the prototype had begun, his need to study would soon be completed. He longed to visit with Mellie during her free time between customers, although each of his attempts had failed.

Determined to break through Mellie's tough-as-nails exterior, Morgan walked into the store with his memorized speech on the tip of his tongue. He didn't see her, so he stepped to the rear of the shop, where he spotted her talking and laughing with a gentleman, a customer perhaps.

The stranger glanced in Morgan's direction, and Mellie turned. She took a sideways step and motioned Morgan forward. "I'd like you to meet Samuel Knoll. He's a dear friend of Mr. Harrison and has come for a visit. He tells me he's an engineer, so the two of you have much in common. I told him you'd been using the back room to study some business drawings over the past two weeks."

Morgan winced at the remark. "Did you?" His voice cracked, but he did his best to appear calm. Instead of carrying the drawings home each evening and possibly having them discovered by one of his fellow boarders, Morgan had stored them in an old cabinet in the back room. Had Mellie shown this Mr. Knoll the drawings? Fear shrouded him. His breathing turned shallow, and his ears filled with the sound of rushing water. He grasped the back of a nearby chair. "I'm sorry. I'm suddenly not feeling well."

Mellie's bright smile—the loveliest smile she'd given him in a long time—faded and was replaced by concern. "Sit down, Morgan. Let me fetch you a glass of water."

"No, I'll be fine." Using his palm, he swiped the beads of perspiration from his forehead. "I don't know what came over me." He forced a smile. "I think that must be how ladies feel before they swoon."

The bell jangled, and Mellie glanced toward the front of the store. "I need to go help the customers, but please sit still until I return." Her eyes shone with compassion. "Mr. Knoll will stay with you." She looked at the visitor and smiled. "You will stay here, won't you? I don't think he should be alone."

"Of course. My pleasure." Mr. Knoll settled in a chair next to Morgan. "Would you prefer quiet or would you like to converse?"

Morgan's mind reeled. "You talk, and I'll listen. Tell me about yourself and your work, Mr. Knoll."

"Samuel. To my friends, I am Samuel, and I hope that you will soon consider me a friend." He hesitated a moment, his dark, narrow eyes capturing Morgan's attention. "As the lovely Miss Blanchard told you, I am an engineer by education, but it isn't what I enjoy." He gestured toward the paintings that adorned the studio walls. "Painting, that is what I love."

Relief washed over Morgan like a spring freshet. "So, you're an artist?" He looked toward the walls. "Are any of these yours?"

"No, no." Samuel shook his head. "I wish I could tell you even one of them was mine, but I am a connoisseur of art, not an artist. I have several wealthy clients, who have come to trust my judgment regarding artwork. When I find exceptional pieces, I purchase them. Fortunately, my clients all have differing taste, so I seldom have a problem selling a painting to one of them." He raised a shoulder. "I suppose you could call me a capitalist of sorts. I sell the pieces at a profit—sometimes large, sometimes small. However, I take great pleasure in searching for excellent artwork, so I don't concern myself with the profitability. If need be, I can always find other ways to increase my income." He gave a wry smile.

"I see." Morgan wanted to ask what he did to supplement his income, but such an inquiry would be rude. The fact that this man was an engineer continued to trouble him. "And what of your engineering abilities? Do you put them to use during your travels or only when you're at home?"

"I use my skills wherever and whenever there is a need or an opportunity. I hope I didn't offend you when I said that art is my real love. Engineering is an honorable profession, but I believe that no matter what a man chooses, he should find fulfillment in his work. For me, that is art. There have been times, however, when my engineering talents have profited me."

The response didn't eliminate Morgan's concerns. It sounded as though Mr. Knoll might avail himself of any opportunity. "Was it your engineering abilities or your love of art that brought you to Manchester? Or was it merely your desire to travel?"

Samuel pursed his lips and tipped his head. "I do enjoy travel, though I usually have good reason for leaving home—whether for work or visiting friends or both." He glanced toward the stairs leading to the upstairs apartment. "I haven't visited with Asa for several years, but he wrote and said he might have some items that would interest me."

"And does he?" Morgan asked.

"Yes. Asa never disappoints, only this time I believe one item he mentioned will provide a windfall for us both."

"Is it a painting or a sculpture?"

He shook his head. "I can't reveal much right now, but I suppose you could say it's a combination of art and sculpture."

"I see. Well, it sounds intriguing, yet I won't question you further. When it comes to business, I know it's important sometimes to keep secrets."

"True, but usually not a good idea when it comes to affairs of the heart." He grinned. "Are you and Miss Blanchard enjoying an affair of the heart?"

"I had thought we were headed in that direction, but right now I'm not so sure."

The older man clapped him on the shoulder. "Then I suggest you have a talk with her. Someone so lovely should not be permitted to slip through your fingers so easily."

Morgan looked up at him. "I've tried."

"Well, then you must try harder, my friend." Samuel nodded to the stairs leading from the back room to the upstairs apartment. "If you'll excuse me, I need to go upstairs and change. Asa and I are going out for a late supper."

Mr. Knoll had managed to avoid detailing what had brought him to Manchester, although his answer had alleviated some of Morgan's concern—but not all. He waited until the upstairs door closed before getting up from his chair. Moving as quietly as possible, he crossed to the cabinet and turned the skeleton key that remained positioned in the lock. When the store was open for business, it was easier to retrieve necessary supplies if the cabinet remained unlocked. Besides, Mr. Harrison had assured Morgan no one would bother his papers. Still, Morgan wanted to make certain the drawings remained intact.

When the cabinet door creaked, he shuddered and peeked around the corner, but Mellie was busy cutting a silhouette for a customer and no one else was in the shop. He heaved a sigh and studied the contents of the cabinet. Nothing on the second shelf appeared out of place. He knelt and retrieved the drawings. He'd arranged and tied them in a precise manner so he'd know if they'd been disturbed. He placed them on the desk and smiled. They were exactly as he'd left them. He briefly considered taking them home but decided they were safer in the cabinet than under his bed. One thing was certain: He wouldn't be studying the drawings until after Mr. Harrison and his friend departed for supper.

After replacing the drawings, Morgan stood at a distance and watched while Mellie finished her cutting. When the customer left, Morgan walked to the front of the store and sat on the stool opposite her—the one used for customers. "Could we talk, Mellie?"

"Not out here where passersby can see us."

He frowned. "What difference does it make? They'd likely think you're cutting my silhouette. I can turn and pretend if you think that makes my presence more suitable."

She shook her head. "No, that won't help. It doesn't matter if you're posing or not. I can't be seen with you."

His mouth dropped open. He couldn't make sense of her sudden aversion to him. "Why? I understand you don't want Mrs. Richards to see us together, but there's something more to all of this, and I want to know what it is." He folded his arms across his chest, stared at her, and waited. If a customer should come into the store, he'd simply move off the stool, let her work, and return later.

Her shoulders sagged, and she avoided his eyes. Finally, she whispered, "I can't tell you."

"You can tell me anything, Mellie. I won't betray your confidence."

"Even if I told you, there's nothing you can do about it, so it's better if you just honor my wishes and stay away from me."

How could she make such an assumption? Did she believe him so powerless? "You don't know whether I can do anything to help or not. Besides, I don't believe that you truly want me to stay away from you. At least I don't want to believe it."

Distress reflected in her eyes as she turned away from the front window and met his gaze. She drew a deep breath. "You already know that Olive French is sweet on you. She's told the girls at the boardinghouse and others she works with at the mill that you're her beau."

"But I'm not her beau. You—"

Mellie held up her hand. "Please. Now that I've started, let me finish before I lose my courage." He nodded for her to continue. "Shortly after I moved into the boardinghouse, Olive found my journal and read it. There were private matters written in it about my family. If she sees me with you, she's threatened to go to a friend who works at the newspaper and reveal what she read—information that would be embarrassing and hurtful to my sister and her children and could also raise questions about my character. If that occurred, I could lose my job." She heaved a sigh, then looked him in the eyes. "Now you know why I can't be seen with you, so please move away from the window. Olive and her friends walk past the shop every evening."

"Thank you for telling me. I don't want you to suffer on my account, but please understand that I have no interest in Olive French."

"I believe you. And I hope you understand that if it weren't for Olive, I'd be pleased to have you call on me."

He grinned. "That's good to know. One day I may hold you to that, Mellie, but for now I'll continue to work in the back room and escort you home at a distance."

She pressed a shaking hand to her heart, and he regretted he'd been so persistent with her. The fear she'd expressed was painfully real. If he had offered to take care of her dilemma with Olive, it would only have deepened Mellie's fear. And that was the last thing he wanted to do. He hoped instead to convince Olive she should change her ways.

Chapter

THIRTEEN

ON THE FOLLOWING SUNDAY AFTERNOON, MORGAN made a visit home. He'd rented a horse at the livery and been careful when he rode out of town. Rather than riding directly to his parents' home, he'd taken a circuitous route. While he doubted anyone had followed him, he didn't want to take any chances. Instead of approaching the front of the house, he circled around to the stables, left the horse with the groom in charge, and walked to the house.

He greeted Lucy with a broad smile. "Good afternoon, Lucy. Do my parents have guests this afternoon?"

"It's good to see you, young man." She continued preparing a tea tray and gave a shake of her head. "No visitors today. Your mother will be pleased to see you. She's been fussing over the fact that you've not been 'round for a visit lately. Are ya hungry? I can put some more sandwiches on the tray."

Morgan gave her shoulder a gentle squeeze. "I had my fill at the boardinghouse before I left town, but I wouldn't refuse a few of your delicious tea cakes."

The color in her cheeks heightened at his praise. "I'll put some extras on the plate and wrap a few in a napkin that you can take with you when you leave."

"That's kind of you, Lucy." He nodded toward the doorway. "Is my father in his study?"

"I believe they're both in the parlor. Your mother asked your father to join her for tea. She didn't go to church this mornin', and I think she's curious to know if she was missed." Lucy chuckled and returned to her preparations.

Morgan strode down the hall and stopped in the parlor doorway. "I heard tea was about to be served, so I thought I'd stop by and join you."

His mother jerked around at the sound of his voice. "Morgan! I was just telling your father that he should send word that I wanted you to come for a visit."

"Well, I'm glad I could save him the trouble." He took a seat in one of the side chairs near his father. "How have you been, Mother? Lucy tells me you didn't attend church this morning." He arched his brows. "Not feeling well?"

"I've been suffering with headaches and some stomach ailments. Nothing that won't go away once your father stops quarreling with me."

Morgan chuckled. "Surely Father isn't arguing—he usually gives in to you so readily."

His father grunted. "Which, in this case, has proved to be a reprehensible error."

"Now, William, it isn't quite that bad. If you'll agree to my plan, we'll still be able to resolve our problem."

"*Our* problem? I'm the one who will be held accountable—and likely go to jail."

Morgan sucked in a lungful of air. "Hold up a minute. I'm at a loss. What are you talking about? Does this have anything to do with the money to finance production of the prototype?"

His mother's clear blue eyes widened in surprise. "I thought your father had told you."

Mr. Stark shook his head. "No, Ruth. There was no need to worry Morgan. Besides, if he had wanted to know how the money was acquired, he would have come and asked me." The older man's gaze traveled from his wife to Morgan. "The fact that he hasn't come for a visit until now is a sign, at least to me, that he didn't want to know about the financial arrangements." He arched his brows. "Am I right, Son?"

Morgan sighed and nodded. "When Mr. Baldwin announced we were moving forward with the prototype, I hoped you hadn't done anything improper, but I couldn't bring myself to ask."

His father's eyelids closed to half-mast. "You mean illegal, don't you?"

"I suppose I do." Morgan's voice was no more than a hoarse whisper.

"Now, now. We don't need to become maudlin. We'll resolve this." At the sound of footsteps in the hallway, his mother lifted a finger to her pursed lips.

They remained uncomfortably silent while the maid was arranging the tray. When Lucy dawdled longer than necessary, his mother waved her from the room.

As soon as the maid was out of earshot, Morgan turned to his father. "Does this mean you took money from the Amoskeag Company without the consent of the directors?"

"It does." His father's eyes flashed defeat.

"And you haven't received the funds from Grandfather to repay what was taken?" Morgan stared at his mother, his stomach churning like a summer storm.

Mrs. Stark bowed her head and picked at the edging on her handkerchief. "I'm sure I will. He'll send the money any day now. I know it."

Morgan didn't want to ask, but her answer begged yet another question. "And have the two of you decided what you'll do if the money doesn't come soon?" He shifted back to his father. "How long before someone discovers the money is missing?"

Clearing his throat, Mr. Stark turned toward the bank of windows overlooking his wife's flower garden. "We haven't made any further decisions about how to replace the money." His hand shook when he raked it through his thick white hair. "There's an audit due the first day of November."

"First of November!"

His mother started and clasped a hand to her chest. "No need to shout, Morgan. We both realize that doesn't give us a great deal of time, but my father will help."

"How do you know that, Mother? Is this supposition on your part?" His question was somewhat overbearing, but the seriousness of their situation frightened him. "I don't want Father going to jail because he agreed to your idea."

Lifting the handkerchief from her lap, she dabbed a tear from her cheek, then pointed to her husband. "He could have told me no." Her voice cracked.

All three of them knew the truth. Telling Ruth Stark no wasn't an option. Her mother had died in childbirth, and her father had granted Ruth's every wish from that moment forward. Little wonder she was certain he wouldn't fail her now.

"I'm sorry, William. I shouldn't have insisted, but I didn't want the circular loom to go to another mill. I don't usually interfere in your business matters, except I thought this was one time when I could help." She swiped another tear away and gave her husband a soulful look.

"Have you heard anything at all from Grandfather?"

She shook her head.

"Is there a possibility he's traveling? That he's gone to Europe or that he's ill? Perhaps you should send a telegram."

"I have. There's been no response."

Morgan frowned. "What about sending a telegram to the housekeeper? Ask her to send word of his whereabouts."

His mother gave a slight nod. "I can do that, but if your grandfather is traveling, the staff will be away, too. He closes the house when he travels."

Morgan shook his head. "There must be someone who would know his whereabouts. We must do something."

"I am doing something." She pursed her lips and lowered her brows. "I've been trying to think of a plan to recover the borrowed money."

Morgan wanted to correct her and say *stolen* or *taken*, but such a comment would likely cause further tears. "A plan? Does it have your approval, Father?"

His mother sighed. "I didn't say I'd developed a plan yet— but I will. You wait and see. I'll take care of this. The two of you need not worry yourselves any further. I'll take care of everything."

His mother's words did little to relieve Morgan's concern, but he decided against saying as much. To belabor the matter wouldn't resolve anything.

He offered her a feeble smile. "In the meantime I'll be praying that your attempts to contact Grandfather are successful, and that he agrees to send the money."

꧁꧂

A short time later, Morgan rode back to the boardinghouse. He attempted to read but was unable to think of anything other than possible methods to contact his Grandfather. Returning the book to his bedside table, he left the house and walked into town. Perhaps the fresh air would help calm his mounting fear.

Lost in his thoughts, he didn't hear the approaching footsteps as he continued down Elm Street. He startled when a hand grasped his arm. Pulling loose, he spun and looked into the eyes of Olive French. He sighed. Could this day become any more difficult?

Her lips curved into a bright smile that didn't quite reach her eyes. "Now, isn't this a wonderful happenstance?"

He frowned at the sound of her syrupy-sweet voice. "Were you following me?"

His tone was harsher than he intended. Her eyes widened, but she remained by his side. The sharp retort hadn't been enough to send her scurrying back to wherever she'd come from.

"No, I wasn't following you. We're just going in the same direction, I guess."

"And where were you going, Olive? It's Sunday evening and the stores are closed."

"I just was out for a walk and saw you, that's all."

He couldn't deny her response might be true. After all, he too was out for a walk tonight with no destination in mind.

She continued alongside him. "It's a nice evening for a walk, don't you think?" A grunt was his only response, which did nothing to deter her. "I was wondering if you've asked anyone to the Grand Complimentary Ball. There's not much time to alter or purchase a dress." She glanced up at him. "I mean if a girl was going and if she wanted a new dress."

"But if you were going, you wouldn't need to alter or purchase a dress, would you, Olive?"

Her brows danced up and down on her forehead. "I might."

"Come now, Olive. I think I know better. One of the fellows at work courts a girl who lives in your boardinghouse. He tells me that instead of worrying over dresses, you've been threatening one of the other girls and wearing *her* dresses to parties and dances."

When Joshua Stanley had mentioned Olive's scheme as the men walked home from work several days ago, Morgan had been startled. Upon further questioning, he'd discovered several of the girls in Mellie's boardinghouse had related the tale to their beaus. At first he'd been disheartened to learn the girls had spread the story, but now he was pleased to be armed with the knowledge.

In the waning light, he saw wariness crowd Olive's features. "You know what else he told me?"

"No. What?" Her voice warbled.

Morgan tipped his head so he could watch her expression. "He told me you've been telling the girls at Mrs. Richards's boardinghouse that I'm your beau and that I asked you to the Grand Complimentary Ball."

Even with the lack of bright light, Morgan could see that she had visibly paled. "Well, I . . . I may have said I was hoping you'd be my beau and ask me to the ball."

He came to a halt and folded his arms across his chest. "No, Olive. That's not what you said. You see, I did a little checking around. I was surprised by how much girls tell their beaus about what happens in their boardinghouses. Your story has come to me through several of the fellows at work."

Morgan was doing his best to be careful how he framed his conversation. He didn't want to say anything that would implicate Mellie. But if he was going to get Olive to confess her wrongdoing, he'd need to be shrewd.

"I have to admit that you're a clever girl, Olive." He lightened his tone and chuckled. "Not many girls would have gone to such extremes."

As her shoulders relaxed, she let out a long breath. "I'm good at getting what I want, and I hope that will include you."

"We'll see. First you need to tell me a little more about your clever ways." He winked at her.

The wink did its work, and soon she'd related the whole ugly story of how she'd read Mellie's journal and then threatened to have a scandalous story printed in the newspaper. She giggled. "I told her I have a friend who works there, but I don't. She was foolish enough to believe me, which means I'll be wearing her fine clothes for as long as I like."

"I see." He offered a forced smile. "That answers my question about the dresses, but what about me? How did I become a part of this? How do you gain me as a beau by reading that girl's journal? Was she writing things about me and you threatened to tell others?"

She shook her head. "No, there was nothing about you in there. I just heard her mention your name one time, and I thought maybe she was sweet on you. I told her you were already spoken for and she needed to stay away from you or I'd tell all the secrets in her journal." They'd been standing in front of the bookseller's shop, and she nodded. "Shall we continue walking?"

Anger swelled in Morgan's chest and threatened to cut off his breath. How could this young woman be so mean-spirited?

"No, Olive, I don't want to walk with you. In truth, I think you should apologize to the young lady you've threatened and ask her forgiveness." He inhaled a sharp breath. "And after that, perhaps you should consider seeking God's forgiveness."

Chapter
FOURTEEN

MELLIE SMILED AND WAVED TO MORGAN WHEN HE walked into the shop. She was eager to tell him about her answered prayer, but until she finished cutting the silhouette of an uncooperative little boy, her news would have to wait.

Morgan strode to her side and nodded toward the boy. "Looks like you've got an unhappy little fellow on your hands."

Mellie sighed. "Yes, even with his mother holding him, he won't settle. If he doesn't quit crying, she'll likely leave without purchasing a cutting."

"Let me see what I can do." He walked a short distance from the child, then snapped his fingers over his head. The little boy looked in his direction, and once Morgan had the child's attention, he pulled a bandalore from his pocket, wound the string between the two wooden disks, slipped his finger into the loop at the end of the string, and flicked his wrist. The bandalore flew in an outward direction and then whirled up the string and back into his hand. The child watched with rapt attention while Morgan continued to dance the bandalore up and down the string, first in one direction and then in another. While he was entertaining the little boy, Mellie deftly snipped the profile.

Once Mellie had helped the young mother select a frame for her son's silhouette and the two had departed, she hurried to Morgan's side. "You're not going to believe what has happened."

He tipped his head to the side. "Seeing that smile of yours makes me think it must be something good."

"More than just good—it's wonderful. God has answered my prayers."

"How so?" He sat down on the stool and faced her.

"Olive came to my room last evening. At first, I thought she was going to force me to loan her another one of my dresses or make some other demand. Instead, she apologized for her actions and promised she'd never reveal the contents of my journal. She then told me how she'd lied about having a friend who worked at the newspaper office and asked for my forgiveness." She leaned toward him. "I shouldn't be amazed that God answered my prayer, yet I could barely believe my ears when Olive revealed her change of heart." When he didn't appear surprised, she arched her brows. "Don't you believe me?"

"Yes, of course. But rather than a nudge from God, I think it was a giant push from me that may have caused Olive to change her ways."

Mellie listened as he revealed a portion of the recent discussion he'd had with Olive. "It may have been a push from you, but it was God who nudged you to speak with Olive. Don't you see? He used you to answer my prayers."

He chuckled. "So I'm a go-between, am I?"

"I suppose you could say that, but you're in good company. Do you recall how God used Ananias to restore Saul's sight?

God uses His people to carry out His will and to answer prayer all the time. To be used by God in such a way is truly an honor, don't you think?"

"Yes, but it's a little overwhelming to think that what I did was carrying out God's plan." He gave her a sidelong glance. "Did she go into detail about what happened to cause her change of heart?"

"No. She said she didn't want to discuss how or why she'd decided to ask my forgiveness, and I didn't press her. I was overjoyed by her newfound attitude and didn't want to make the situation more difficult for either of us. Knowing I didn't need to worry about retribution if she saw us together or that she'd be skulking in my room when I returned home provided ample relief. The apology was significant, and I care little about the details."

"I'm pleased you were willing to accept Olive's apology. You know, there are times when accepting an apology can be almost as difficult as offering one."

"I suppose that is true." Her thoughts drifted back to Concord and the unkindness that had been heaped upon her sister. "If healing doesn't take place, bitterness usually follows."

Mellie stared at a silhouette she'd cut earlier in the day of two children and thought of her niece and nephew. She hoped Margaret had discovered some way to overcome the pain caused by her husband. If not, anger and resentment would take root in her sister's heart and affect the children. Mellie longed to do more than pray and send money, but living in another city didn't permit the closeness they'd once taken for granted. Margaret's letters remained silent regarding the pain and humiliation she'd been forced to bear. Yet Mellie could read between the lines. The foreclosure on the house had been completed, and Margaret and the children were now living in a ramshackle farmhouse—the one she'd mentioned in an earlier letter. The banker still brought his children but constantly complained about the distance. And now he was seeking a capable tutor who lived closer to his home.

The click of snapping fingers pulled Mellie back to the present, and she smiled at Morgan. "I'm sorry. My thoughts wandered."

When the bell over the front door jingled, she turned to see Mr. Knoll and Mr. Harrison enter the store. Mr. Knoll carried a sign in one arm while Mr. Harrison carried a metal canister. After placing it on the counter, he turned toward Mellie and Morgan. "Come see what we've got. I think there are going to be a lot more customers in the store."

Mr. Knoll held the sign in front of him. Mellie took a step closer and then gasped. "A lottery? Is this some sort of misguided prank?" She shook her head. "This can't be true." Her stomach tightened as she looked from one man to the other. "Who would want to promote such a thing?"

Mr. Harrison frowned. "I don't know. Perhaps several of the shop owners decided it would be a good way to develop more business. No matter who decided, I think there will be folks coming into the shops who haven't in the past. And we can all use more business."

Mr. Knoll nodded his agreement.

Mellie looked back and forth between the two men. Did they truly think this was a sound idea?

Mr. Harrison removed several smaller signs and placed one of them on a metal stand atop the counter. "There are tickets inside the envelope, Mellie. When you sell a ticket, you must write down the name of the purchaser and the ticket number so we can provide a record prior to the drawing." He walked behind the counter and gathered a pen, ink, and piece of paper, then placed them beside the envelope.

"I'm sorry, but I won't sell lottery tickets, Mr. Harrison."

He continued speaking as though she hadn't said anything. "Samuel and I were talking on the way. I'm certain every shop in town will participate. People will come in to purchase a ticket, and once inside, they're more apt to look around and have you cut a silhouette or sit for a portrait, maybe even purchase a painting." Mr. Harrison smiled at Mr. Knoll.

"I don't believe you heard me, Mr. Harrison. I said that I will not sell lottery tickets—not in your store or in any other store. I do not believe in gambling. I've witnessed the ruination that can be caused by wagering, and I'll not be a part of it."

Mr. Harrison's mouth fell open. "A lottery isn't the same as betting on horses or wagering at cards, Mellie. This isn't going to be something that occurs all the time. I don't believe you can place this lottery in the same category as gambling."

"I am speaking only for myself and my beliefs, Mr. Harrison, and I do not wish to participate in either purchasing or selling tickets for a lottery. If you insist that I must sell the tickets, I will regretfully give you my notice to quit."

"Quit? You would quit working here because I'm selling lottery tickets?"

If she quit, how could she make up for the money she'd been earning in his shop? There were a few other shops that might hire her, but if all the stores were participating in the lottery, she'd be faced with the same problem. And yet if she agreed to sell the tickets, it would appear as if she approved of the lottery. She simply couldn't agree—not after the trouble gambling had heaped upon her family.

"No." Her voice cracked. "I will quit if *I* am required to sell the tickets. This is your store and you have every right to sell whatever you'd like. However, you will need to have someone other than me take care of those sales when you're away from the shop."

Mr. Harrison traced his index finger along the edge of the sign. "I certainly don't want you to quit, Mellie. I suppose if someone came into the store and I wasn't here, you could direct them to another shop. I'm not making any profit from the sale of the tickets, so it wouldn't matter if the purchase was made elsewhere. Would that be acceptable to you?"

She didn't realize she'd been holding her breath until she blew out a lungful of air. "Yes, that's acceptable. Thank you for your understanding."

"Of course. I don't want you to do anything that goes against your principles."

Mr. Knoll chuckled and patted his friend's shoulder. "That's true, Asa. We both know that there are far too few principled people in the world today, don't we?"

Mr. Harrison frowned at his friend and gave a slight shake of his head. "If you'll excuse us, Samuel and I need to finish a few things upstairs." He glanced over his shoulder. "No need to worry about the lottery tickets. I'm not scheduled to begin selling them until tomorrow."

During her conversation with Mr. Harrison, Morgan had stood at a distance, listening but not entering into the discussion. He remained leaning against a case where Mr. Harrison stored canvases. Once the two men had disappeared, he said to Mellie, "You're quite courageous. I know how much the extra income means to you." He tipped his head. "And you would have quit if he hadn't given in to your request?"

"Yes. Difficult as it would have been, I couldn't stay here and have any part of selling those tickets. I feel it would be a betrayal to my sister and to what I believe." She shrugged. "I don't expect everyone to agree with me, but I had to do what is right for me. I can tell you that I was frightened he'd tell me not to come back."

Morgan shook his head. "You're better for his business than those lottery tickets will ever be. And for what it's worth, I don't agree with the lottery, either."

"I'm glad to know I'm not alone. I fear this lottery is going to create heartache for many of the mill girls who purchase tickets rather than sending the money home to their needy families."

Morgan nodded. "And for the families living in Manchester, as well. I don't see how anything good can come of this."

She reached for a stack of black paper beneath the counter. "Only one person can win, but each person who buys a ticket believes they'll be the lucky one. I wonder if those in charge of this lottery weighed the consequences against the benefits of their plan."

Morgan sighed. "I doubt much thought was given to the disadvantages." He gestured toward the back room. "I need to return the drawings to the mill. I thought I had them completely memorized, but it turns out it's more difficult than I thought to recall every small detail."

Mellie glanced up after the bell over the door rang. She stepped from behind the counter and sent Morgan a quick smile. "I must go and serve the customers who just came in. Why don't you gather your drawings while I help them? Afterward we can walk to the boardinghouse—together."

As Morgan walked toward the rear of the store, he considered their conversation. Mellie's willingness to stand her ground no matter the consequences impressed him. Had the situation been reversed, would he have had that same resolve? He hoped so. His father had given in to his mother rather than stand his ground. Morgan didn't want to think of what that choice might cost his father. He shook off the thought and continued into the back room.

There was at least another hour before closing time. If the customers wanted silhouettes, it might take even longer. He strode to the cabinet, but instead of retrieving the loom drawings, he removed a copy of *The Three Musketeers* from the shelf. He'd borrowed the book from the Manchester Athenaeum, the private circulating library that many of the mill workers frequented. Morgan had read *The Count of Monte Cristo* while attending school, but he'd never gotten around to *The Three Musketeers*. Truth be told, he felt a bit guilty reading the novel. The Mechanics' Lodge was well supplied with trade publications. He could be reading a copy of the *Mechanics' and Engineers' Trade Journal*, but he sometimes needed a book that would take his mind off his day-to-day life.

After reading the first few pages, he realized he hadn't absorbed a word of what he'd read. His thoughts hadn't been on the antics of the three swordsmen, but on the future of his parents and the Stark Mills. He hoped they had received word from his grandfather. He closed the book with a snap, returned it to the shelf, and reached to the back of the cabinet. As he removed the drawings, his eyes fixed upon the two corners he'd fastened with thin cords and tied in a unique knot.

One look at the knotted ties and fear bristled down his back. Mr. Baldwin had been clear with his instructions: The drawings must be protected. Granted, the prototype was close to completion, but few had seen the loom in its near-completed state. Though parts of the machine had been produced by men working in various mechanic shops, sharing why or where the parts would be used hadn't been necessary. In truth, the men producing the parts cared little. So long as they had a work order signed by a superior, they performed their jobs, not bothering to ask any questions.

Morgan studied the knots. There was no doubt that the documents had been disturbed. He'd arranged the drawings so that anyone wishing to view the entire page would need to untie at least one of the knots. When he'd arranged the pages and tied the knots, he'd thought the idea excessive. Now he realized he'd not done enough to protect Mr. Baldwin's design.

His chest heaved as he attempted to draw in a deep breath. Who'd been in the back room since the last time he'd looked at the drawings? His gaze shifted to the front of the shop. Mellie and Mr. Harrison were in and out of the room every day and knew the location of the drawings. Mr. Harrison was the one who had given Morgan permission to use the room. He'd also assured him the papers would be safe here. He glanced toward the stairs. Mr. Knoll sometimes came through the back room on his way upstairs to Mr. Harrison's apartment. Morgan raked his fingers through his hair. Had there been anyone else? Anyone who could have been in the cabinet and looked at the plans?

He rolled the drawings in a tight cylinder and walked to the front of the store. Mellie smiled at him. She was helping a customer select a frame. He waited, his eyes riveted upon her as she moved about helping the customer. Could she have betrayed him? He didn't want to think so, yet how could he be certain of anyone?

Mellie bid her customer good-bye and came to his side. "What's wrong, Morgan? You're white as a sheet. Are you ill?"

"I'm not feeling well, but it isn't due to illness."

Her brows crinkled. "I don't understand. What's the matter?"

He tapped the cylinder of drawings. "Have you ever looked at these papers, Mellie?"

She shook her head. "Are those the papers you were studying in the back room? The ones you stored in Mr. Harrison's cabinet?"

He nodded.

"No, I've never seen them." She pointed to the stool. "You look like you should sit down."

Panic rose in his chest as he dropped onto the stool. "Besides you, me, Mr. Harrison, and Mr. Knoll, can you think of anyone else who has been in the back room in the past week?"

Her forehead lined with creases as her attention drifted to the back room. "There have been a few children who wandered back there while I was cutting silhouettes, but they weren't in there long enough to bother anything." She hesitated a moment. "There was a man who came in to sit for an ambrotype, and you had to leave the back room while he changed into his suit."

Morgan nodded. "I left the drawings on the table, but I turned them over. I doubt he would have looked at anything on the table, and nothing appeared out of order when I returned to the room."

"You're probably right. He came back to the shop three days later to decide on which photograph he would purchase. He was having difficulty deciding and asked if he could sit at the table in the back room and think over his decision. He was here before you arrived to walk me home." She shook her head. "Other than that, I can't think of anyone who was back there."

Morgan massaged his temples. Mr. Knoll was the most likely suspect. He was an engineer and, by his own admission, a man always on the lookout to turn a profit. And when questioned about his business dealings, he was less than forthcoming. In addition, Morgan doubted a man having his photograph taken would have gone rummaging through the cabinet. He needed to consider every possibility, however. While Mr. Knoll was the more likely suspect, Morgan now wondered if the drawings had been moved when he returned that first day. "Do you know who that man is—the one who sat at the table in the back room?"

"No, but I can check the receipt book. His name and address would be listed there." She crossed to the counter and began flipping through the pages. "Here it is." She tapped the page.

He walked to her side and looked at the listing: *Ezekiel Snow, 23 Merrimack Street, Lowell, MA.*

"Lowell." His voice cracked, and his thoughts scattered like a round of buckshot. Had someone in Lowell learned of the new machine? If the owners of the Lowell Mills secured copies of the drawings, could they begin production of the new loom before the Stark Mills? If the owners at Lowell did manage to build a prototype and assemble a workable loom, it was possible they would be first to manufacture and sell the seamless bags.

His mind reeled at the thought. He needed to gain a hold on his imagination. A man from Lowell was in the back room on two occasions. He was having a photograph taken and choosing a picture for his loved ones.

Nothing more.

That was what Morgan told himself. That was what he wanted to believe.

Chapter

FIFTEEN

AFTER LEAVING THE SHOP THAT NIGHT, MELLIE WALKED alongside Morgan. She gave him a sideways glance. He was with her, but his thoughts were elsewhere. Twice now she'd asked him something, yet he hadn't responded to either question.

Her hand rested in the crook of his arm, and she gave a slight tug. "And then a cat flew into the room and landed on my loom."

"Oh."

"Morgan, are you listening to me?"

He turned with a jerk. "Yes, of course."

"Excellent." She grinned. "What did I say a moment ago?"

"I'm sorry. I guess I wasn't listening." He shot her a doleful look. "I'm still trying to recall who was in the back room of the photography shop. Maybe someone was back there during the daytime and got into the cabinet. Do you think that might have happened?"

"Anything is possible, but there have been very few occasions when a customer was in the back room, at least while I was there. I assume it's the same during the daytime hours." She gave his arm another tug. "I don't understand all this concern. Even if someone saw those papers, why does it matter?"

"Depending on who sees them, it could matter a great deal." In the shimmering moonlight, his eyes reflected distress. He stopped and grasped her hand. "I didn't tell anyone, including you, but those papers are extremely important. If anyone has seen them, it could mean huge financial losses for Stark Mills."

"Truly?" She giggled. "You've been entrusted with papers that could cause a downward spiral for the Stark Mills?" When a pained look spread across his face, she sobered. "I'm sorry, Morgan. I didn't mean to make light of a matter that is causing you such concern. But you must admit it is difficult to believe that you hold the future of Stark Mills in your hands. Wouldn't you agree?"

He nodded. "I promised I wouldn't divulge the details, so . . ."

"And I don't want you to break your promise. That's not what I was implying. I want to be understanding and help you, but I didn't expect *you* to hold such important company papers. You must realize that it comes as a surprise."

"Those papers—drawings, actually—pertain to my work with the machines, and I was entrusted with them so that I could memorize the details. I was told to keep them in strict confidence."

A weight of responsibility settled on Mellie's shoulders. Why had she suggested he study them in the back room, and why had she gained Mr. Harrison's approval for this? If she'd remained silent, Morgan would have found some other place to study and store the papers. Why hadn't he mentioned the papers were of a secretive nature? At least then they would have been more careful about customers going into the back room. "I'm so sorry, Morgan. If I'd have known—"

"It's not your fault, Mellie." Morgan squeezed her hand. "It's mine. I should have found another way that didn't involve you or the photography shop. I could have studied them at the Mechanics' Lodge or at the Athenaeum, but I couldn't have stored them there. I thought about keeping them at the boardinghouse but then decided they wouldn't be safe there. So, at the time, the photography shop was the best solution. Still, I should have asked Mr. Harrison to keep the cabinet locked at all times."

Mellie sighed. "I know it's easier said than done, but worrying won't change anything."

"You're right, although I still need to discover who has seen those drawings." His shoulders sagged. "If I'm going to succeed, it seems prayer is my only hope."

She squeezed his arm. "Prayer is our best hope—in all circumstances—don't you think?"

"True. Once again you're right, and I'll try to remember that in the future." He smiled down at her. "Now, what was it you were saying to me a short time ago—back when I wasn't listening?"

"You mean besides the cat? Well, Horace Mann is speaking on the common school movement at the Lyceum tomorrow evening. I've asked Mr. Harrison if I can be away from the store, and he agreed. I thought we could go together—I mean if you have an interest in hearing Mr. Mann. I'm told he's a very engaging speaker, and the Manchester Brass Band is going to play before and after the program."

He pushed his cap to the back of his head. "With you at my side, I'd be pleased to go almost anywhere. You tell me the time and I'll be at the front door of your boardinghouse waiting for you."

For a moment she considered telling him they should meet at the photography shop, but then decided that was silly. Now that Olive had revealed a change of heart, there was no reason Morgan shouldn't call on her at the boardinghouse. "The program begins at eight o'clock, so we should leave by seven-thirty, don't you think?"

She shouldn't be taking time away from work, yet she longed for something more than the same old routine she followed most days. Sundays allowed for a slight departure from her daily routine, but once church services were over, the rest of the day was filled with mending, letter writing, and other necessities she couldn't complete during the week. Up until now, she'd turned Morgan down each time he'd asked to escort her somewhere after church, not because she didn't want to go with him but because duty called. This one time she would push duty aside and enjoy an evening of entertainment together.

He nodded and smiled. "Seven-thirty it is. I'm glad you've decided it's important to do something other than work. I was beginning to think I would never have any time with you except at the store and walking you home."

"And you should spend more time with your friends."

Together they climbed the front steps of her boardinghouse. "Why would I want to be around those fellas I work and live with every day when I can be with the kindest, most beautiful girl I've ever met?"

His words caused a blush to color her cheeks. "Thank you for the compliment, Morgan, but—"

"Don't tell me you aren't beautiful and kind, Mellie. Anyone with eyes can see you are lovely, and I've never heard anyone say anything but words of praise regarding your kindness toward others."

She smiled. "Except for Olive French. You may recall that she didn't have too many good things to say to me or about me."

"I think Olive's jealousy overcame her good sense, but thankfully she saw the error of her ways." His brows dipped low. "She hasn't reverted to her threatening behavior, has she?"

"No. We're not close friends—not like with Phebe or Cora and Clara—but we're cordial to each other. She seems to regret her earlier actions."

"You see? You're not only kind and beautiful, but you can even get along with your enemies."

She chuckled. "It's because of you, Morgan, that Olive came to me and apologized, and I'm certainly thankful."

Without warning he leaned forward and kissed her cheek. "It was my pleasure." Before she could say another word, he dashed down the steps. "I'll see you tomorrow evening."

She watched him disappear into the darkness, her heart pounding a new beat.

⪻⪻⪻⪼

The following evening at supper, the girls chattered about the Lyceum program, their escorts, and the dresses they planned to wear. For once, Mellie felt a part of the excitement around the table. Yet, for some reason, Olive remained unusually quiet.

When Olive glanced in her direction, Mellie tipped her head. "What about you, Olive? Will you be attending Mr. Mann's lecture?"

"I haven't yet decided." She clamped her jaw and stared straight ahead.

Mellie couldn't imagine waiting any longer to decide, but it was obvious Olive didn't want to discuss the evening's event. After finishing the last of her lamb stew and biscuit, Mellie pushed away from the table. Phebe, Cora, and Clara followed, and soon the three of them were completing their toilette and slipping into their dresses.

There was a light tap on the door, and Mellie leaned forward and turned the knob. Olive stood in the doorway with a forlorn expression and a dress draped over her arm. "I have a problem with my dress. That's why I wasn't sure I could go tonight."

Mellie stepped aside so that Olive could enter. "What kind of problem? Did a seam rip?"

Olive shook her head. "No." Her voice quivered. "I spilled punch on it at the last dance, and I thought I could remove the stain. I tried to wash it out with soap and water, then wrung out as much water as I could and left it to dry. Now there's an even bigger stain than I started with. Do you think there's any way I can hide the stain?"

Mellie spread the gown across her bed. She looked up at Olive. "No, I don't think there's anything to be done in time for you to wear this tonight."

Cora ran a hand down the wrinkled dress. "Twisting satin isn't a good idea. That's why you've got all these creases."

Moving to one of her trunks, Mellie lifted the lid and removed a dress of gold alpaca with forest green accents. "I think this will fit." She held it in front of Olive. "The color is perfect for you. You're welcome to wear it tonight, if you'd like."

Mellie didn't know who looked the most surprised—Olive, Phebe, Cora, or Clara—but it was Olive who dropped onto the edge of the bed. "You would loan me one of your dresses after what I did to you?" She stared up at Mellie.

"Yes, of course."

"I asked all the girls downstairs to help me and not one of them would. Not even Charity."

"They may not have offered their help because there was

nothing they could do to remove the stain." Mellie wanted to give the other girls the benefit of the doubt, for truly there was no way anyone could have done anything to make the dress wearable.

"Yes, but none of them offered to loan me a dress—so why would you?"

"One of the first Bible verses I learned when I was a little girl was John 15:12. Do you know it?"

Olive shook her head. "I don't think so."

"It says we're to love one another as Jesus loves us." Mellie pointed to an embroidered scarf lying atop her other trunk. "After I learned that verse, my teacher had me embroider it. I was young, and the scarf was my first attempt at embroidery. It took me a long time—especially since any flaws had to be ripped out. I don't recall how many stitches I replaced, but since then that verse has held special meaning for me. I've tried to live by what it teaches."

Olive hung her head. "I'm sorry for being so awful to you, Mellie."

"You've already apologized. No need to do so again." Mellie smiled and reached for Olive's hand, pulling her to her feet. "Now go and get into this dress. I'll help you with your hair. If we hurry, we'll all be dressed on time."

When the girls descended the stairs a short time later, Morgan and several other young men were being held captive by Mrs. Richards. Sitting in her wing-back chair, she was quizzing the men like a queen holding court. And the men were perched on the edge of their chairs like birds eager to take flight.

The instant Morgan spotted Mellie in the doorway of the parlor, he jumped to his feet and hurried to her side. He leaned close to her ear. "Mrs. Richards does enjoy the attention, doesn't she?"

Mellie chuckled. "It does appear that way, but this is the first time I've been here when a group of young men came calling, so I'm as surprised as you."

"Well, I'm glad you arrived and saved me. I would have been next in line to answer a barrage of questions. She is one inquisitive lady."

Mellie slipped her hand into the crook of Morgan's arm. His eyes remained riveted on her, and she tingled with excitement. There was something about his look that made her feel as if she'd known him forever—or at least that she'd gazed into those ocean blue eyes of his before. Other couples walked in front and behind them, but he made her feel as though they were the only ones strolling along the crowded street.

They entered the Lyceum amid the crush of ticket holders, with Morgan leading her down the carpeted aisle to their as-signed seats. His eyes widened when he stopped at their row. He glanced at Mellie, then back at the seats adjacent to their own. Olive French and her escort looked in their direction.

He leaned close to Mellie's ear. "Let's go back to the entry hall. I'll see if there are any other seats available."

"No need. These are wonderful seats." She smiled at Olive, sat down beside her, glanced up at Morgan, and patted the empty seat. "Sit down, Morgan."

Olive turned her gaze on Morgan. "Are you and James ac-quainted?" She nodded toward her escort. When Morgan shook his head, she made the introductions, then settled back in her seat.

"What's going on? Why is Olive being so nice?"

Mellie was thankful he'd kept his voice at a mere whisper. "I'll explain later." She gestured toward the stage. "Oh, look! The band is going to begin."

The band's performance lasted only fifteen minutes, but the conductor promised they would return after Mr. Mann's lecture. The preacher from the Methodist church stepped to the podium, cleared his throat, and arranged his notes. He looked out over the crowd for a moment before beginning his introduction.

After a quick glance over his shoulder and a nod to Mr. Mann, who was seated on the stage, the preacher raised his voice for everyone to hear. "Horace Mann is a gentleman who has done much for mankind, and history will not forget him. While serving in the Massachusetts House of Representatives, he led a movement that established the first hospital for the insane in the United States. He served in the Massachusetts Senate, but later he gave up his political career to serve as the first Secretary of the Massachusetts Board of Education. Since his appointment to that position, he has worked tirelessly for the cause of universal, nonsectarian education throughout the country. He is an advocate for the education of all and believes in free public education for children of all social classes. In addition, he is a fierce critic of slavery. Ladies and gentlemen, I give you Horace Mann."

Applause filled the auditorium as the distinguished white-haired man with well-carved features strode to the lectern. For the next forty-five minutes he held them captive with his skillful storytelling interspersed with facts and figures that revealed the need for an educated society, and his efforts to make that education free for all. Nearing the end of his lecture, Mr. Mann rested his arms on the podium and leaned toward the audience. "I tell you this: Young children should not be working in textile mills, where their very lives are in danger. They should be sitting in a classroom, where they can be educated to meet their future with the ability to make wise choices."

He pointed to the rows of empty seats at the front of the auditorium. "I am told these are the seats reserved for the wealthy patrons of the Lyceum. Please notice only a few are in attendance this evening. Why?" He arched his thick white brows. "Because they do not agree with me. They prefer costly private schools where their children are educated among their own class while poor children work in the mills and coal mines. I tell you, this is wrong. And they dislike my views on slavery, as well. These men of wealth don't want anything to interfere with the cotton crops raised by slave owners. Cotton that's needed to keep their mills operating while making them wealthy. However, men of wealth need to step forward and think of others. Offer funding to educate the masses and free the slaves from their lives of hardship."

Murmurs spread throughout the room, and Mr. Mann pointed a finger at the crowd. "It is easy to agree with what I say until you realize it may impact your own way of life. But believe me, we will all be judged by how we treat our fellow man. Think on that as you take up your banner for or against the cause of education and freedom for all." He gave a nod, and a shock of his white hair dropped across his forehead. "Thank you and good night."

The ovation was not as fervent as it likely would have been earlier in his speech—before Mr. Mann made many of them uncomfortable with the idea that it might cost something to agree with his views. When the brass band once again took the stage, the applause increased. Mellie didn't miss the disappointed look that crossed Mr. Mann's face as he exited the stage.

While the band was playing, Mellie thought of her own education at an elite private school, which had cost a dear price—the school she'd been attending when her parents traveled abroad and died, the school where she'd remained a lonely child. She agreed that education should be free for all. Education was one thing that could never be taken away. Yet she wondered if Mr. Mann espoused equality for women in the workplace or only in education. Her schooling hadn't provided her with the ability to remain close to home and make a wage that was comparable to a man's. She wished she could ask Mr. Mann if he would favor such legislation.

As they left the auditorium later, her thoughts seesawed back and forth in an attempt to sort out all she'd heard. Morgan reached to the crook of his arm and patted her hand. "The café at Putney's is open. Would you like to stop and have tea and something to eat?"

"A cup of tea sounds wonderful."

Though a few other couples had stopped at the café, most had continued onward. After purchasing tickets for the Lyceum, few would have enough money for tea and cake afterward. Mellie and Morgan sat at a table in a far corner, away from the other guests.

After placing their order, she leaned toward him. "Tell me, what did you think about Mr. Mann's speech?"

"I agree with much of what he said. The issues he addressed are all challenging, and I doubt any of them will be easily resolved."

She nodded. "Unfortunately, that's true. Arriving at equitable solutions will be difficult, but I think it's important to do what we can to help."

The waiter placed tea and a slice of pound cake for each of them on the table. Once he'd retreated, Mellie poured tea into their cups.

"Yes, and I'm glad you suggested we attend the lecture," Morgan said. "Mr. Mann is an eloquent orator who gave us all food for thought." He forked a bite of cake. "And speaking of food, this cake is excellent. You should try yours."

She took a bite of cake and nodded. "You're right. It's delicious." She lifted her cup and sipped some tea. "Cora said the Lyceum has offered a number of enlightening speakers. I hope they'll continue to do so."

He pushed aside his cake plate. "And now I'd like you to enlighten me about this new friendship between you and Olive."

While they were finishing their tea, she recounted the earlier events of the evening with Olive.

"You are far too kind, Mellie. I hope Olive is thankful you not only memorized that Scripture but you live what it teaches."

She could feel the warmth rise in her cheeks. "I did what I would hope someone else would do for me in a similar circumstance. Your flattery is embarrassing me, so let's not turn my actions into martyrdom."

"If you insist, but Olive is privileged to know you. And I'm the most fortunate man in the whole of Manchester—perhaps in all of New Hampshire." He glanced around the darkened room before he leaned forward and placed a soft kiss on her lips.

Chapter

SIXTEEN

MORGAN ROLLED OVER, GROANED, SAT UP, AND PLACED his feet on the cold wooden floor. Morning had come, and yet he'd slept little. A nagging fear that the drawings had been copied continued to gnaw at him. He'd revealed nothing of his suspicions to anyone other than Mellie. Each time he saw Mr. Harrison and Mr. Knoll, he longed to ask what either of them might know—if either man had removed the drawings himself or seen anyone else do so. Yet such questions would likely prove unfruitful. If one or both of them were responsible, they'd deny any wrongdoing.

There was also the fear of insulting the men, especially Mr. Harrison. Morgan didn't want his actions to cause problems for Mellie. Besides, if they'd seen anyone looking at the drawings, wouldn't they have told him about it? If the circumstances were reversed, he wouldn't withhold such information. Of late he'd begun to wonder if he'd only imagined the drawings had been seen by someone else. Again, that was what he wanted to believe. But he knew better and just didn't want to accept the truth.

Now he must hope that someone else seeing the drawings was mere happenstance, that the person had no interest in looms or machinery and wouldn't try to profit from what had been seen.

He'd been doing what Mellie had advised, praying and trying his best to trust that the Lord would protect him—and those drawings. Each time he saw Mr. Baldwin, he considered mentioning his fears, but he still hadn't been brave enough to do so. He wanted to trust that all would go according to plan and God would protect him.

Thus far, it seemed to be working. The prototype had proved a success, and work had begun on the first of three machines. Although they could have begun a limited production of the new bags, Mr. Baldwin insisted they wait until they could manufacture in greater quantity and so secure the lion's share of the market before any competitors came along. While Morgan could understand the man's point, he worried Mr. Baldwin's rationale might be somewhat skewed. But then who could say what the future held? Mr. Baldwin could change his mind at any time. He hadn't been in the mill yard for the past two weeks, so who knew what he was thinking?

Morgan had inquired about the inventor's whereabouts, but Mr. Hale was evasive. He'd shrugged and said Mr. Baldwin had business elsewhere and hadn't given a date for his return. While the response had seemed odd to Morgan, he was relieved that he didn't have to face Mr. Baldwin right now.

This morning, as he strode into the machine shop, his thoughts were occupied with seeing Mellie later in the day. He was eager to ask if she'd consider a Sunday afternoon outing together. Though he was pleased to spend time with her at the shop, they were seldom alone. Mr. Harrison had recently advertised her silhouettes in the Manchester newspaper and in several other nearby towns, as well. Except for their walks home, he hadn't much occasion to visit with her.

He walked into the last building on Mechanics' Row and placed his belongings in one of the wooden cubbyholes along the far wall. Behind him, he heard Mr. Baldwin's deep voice echo across the room. He turned and lifted a hand in a feeble wave. Mr. Hale gestured for Morgan to join them. With great effort, he took one step and then the other. Each attempt felt as if his shoes were being sucked into a merciless, thick muck.

"Hurry, my boy! We need to have a talk." Mr. Baldwin waved in a wild circular motion, like a windmill blade gone awry.

Morgan forced a smile as he approached the man. "We've missed seeing you around here, Mr. Baldwin. Mr. Hale tells me you've been traveling elsewhere on some sort of business."

"That's true." He gestured toward Mr. Hale's small office. "Let's go inside." He looked over his shoulder as they entered. "Close the door behind you, Morgan." The older man pointed to a chair. "Sit down."

Morgan tried to calm his breathing as he lowered himself into the chair. A sharp pain cut through his chest, each breath sharper than the last. What was happening to him? The room revolved at a dizzying whirl.

"Something wrong, Morgan?" Mr. Hale's brows dipped in concern. "Sit still and put your head between your knees. You don't look well at all."

Morgan did as he was told. Slowly the pain and light-headedness disappeared. Embarrassed, he lifted his head again. "I apologize. Go ahead with what you wanted to say, Mr. Baldwin. I believe I'm all right now."

Mr. Baldwin hesitated and glanced at Mr. Hale before turning back to Morgan. "If you're certain you don't need a doctor . . ."

Morgan shook his head. "I'm fine. Truly. Please, go ahead."

Both men sat, Mr. Baldwin placing his palms on his knees. "As you mentioned, I've been doing a little traveling. I wanted to see if I could determine where we might develop our best markets once production of the bags commenced. I had thought it would be wise to go south and discover where the milling and bagging was most prevalent, so we could export bags to the larger markets first."

Mr. Hale nodded. "That's certainly sound thinking."

Morgan settled back in his chair. It appeared his fears were unfounded. This was a meeting about how best to market the bags. He inhaled a cleansing breath and smiled. "I agree. Your plan seems to be well thought out."

"Mmm, yes." Mr. Baldwin gave a slight nod. "However, before I embarked south, I decided to make a stop in Lowell to visit an old acquaintance. I thought he might want to join me on my journey."

At the mention of Lowell, Morgan immediately thought of the man who had recently come from Lowell to Manchester to have his photograph taken. The one who'd been in the back room of the shop on two separate occasions. Morgan quickly searched his mind for the name . . . *Ezekiel Snow*. Yes, that was it. Morgan's heart thrummed a rapid beat.

"Was your friend able to accompany you?" Mr. Hale asked.

Mr. Baldwin shook his head. "No, but I was his guest for several days. Being a lawyer, he's well known in the town. I wanted to visit with him about the patent for my loom."

Morgan breathed a sigh of relief. He thought Mr. Hale had told him Mr. Baldwin hadn't obtained a patent on the machine. This was the best news he'd heard in a long time. If the machine was patented, there was no need for concern. "So, you've obtained a patent. That's wise. I'm happy to hear the design is protected."

"I wish that were true," Mr. Baldwin said. "Unfortunately, my application has been delayed."

Those few words erased Morgan's short-lived calm. Renewed fear gripped him in a tight hold. "Why?" Both men stared at him. He hadn't meant to raise his voice. "I'm sorry. I was taken aback by your news."

"Yes, well, there are a multitude of patents for a variety of looms. In order to secure a patent, any differences in the design must be shown in detail. From what my friend explained, it's a rather lengthy process and I'll need to remain patient."

"If it does prove to take a long time, no one else could come along and patent a circular loom before you, could they?" Morgan held his breath while he waited for a response.

"I'd like to believe that would be impossible, but I can't be certain there wasn't a similar design submitted before mine. Much depends upon the differences and, of course, the date of submission." He let out a sigh. "Getting the patent approved was another reason why I wanted to hold off before beginning production." He folded his large hands together. "Besides the lack of a patent, my friend has heard some other disturbing news."

Morgan didn't realize he'd clenched his hands until his fingernails now bit into the flesh of his palms. He waited, his anxiety mounting with each passing second. He wanted to ask, but the question stuck in his throat.

"What was that, Cyrus?" Mr. Hale leaned his arms atop his scarred wooden desk, his gaze fastened on the inventor.

"While he was attending a social function, he overheard some of the wealthier members of the Boston Associates having a discussion." He looked at Morgan. "The Boston Associates are the investors who own and operate the Lowell Mills, and I believe a few of them are investors in some of the mills here in Manchester, too."

Morgan nodded. "I see." He dared not mention that he was well aware of the Boston Associates and who they were.

"So, as I was saying, these men were discussing a new piece of machinery they are in the process of developing. My friend didn't hear a great deal, but later he spoke to one of the men who was deep in his cups."

Morgan scooted forward in his chair. Part of him wanted to shout that he was responsible, that he'd left the drawings unprotected. But another part warned him to remain silent. The latter part won the battle. He stared straight ahead, held his breath, once again waiting.

"And?" Mr. Hale arched his brows.

"My friend told me the man spoke of a machine that would create a new kind of fabric. But his words were slurred, and we don't think he knew what he was talking about. Nevertheless, I remained in town hoping to discover more information, but it proved fruitless. My fear is that this man may have been talking about the seamless bags. He said the idea was something new, yet it was also old. Well, the production of fabric for bags is old, while the seamless bag will be entirely new." Mr. Baldwin shook his head. "I don't know what to make of it. Apparently, the man became suspicious when my friend continued to question him, so he stopped. He didn't want the man to alert anyone else that some stranger had been making inquiries about the machine. And it was difficult to know just how inebriated he was by the time the two parted company."

Mr. Hale leaned back in his chair and stroked his jaw. "I don't know, Cyrus. Maybe I don't want to believe there's a problem, but what that man shared with your friend doesn't make much sense. I don't think you can jump to the conclusion that he was referring to our circular loom." He frowned. "It's just not possible that anyone's gotten wind of what we're doing here. Up until the prototype was assembled, none of the workers even knew what was being created. They still don't know what it makes—they simply think it's a strange-looking new loom."

Mr. Baldwin pushed to his feet. "I hope you're right. I would hate to think we've gone to all this work and great expense only to fail."

Minutes later, the three men parted, Mr. Hale to oversee the workers, Mr. Baldwin to his home, and Morgan to work alongside the men producing the new machines. The hours passed in a slow procession of mixed emotion and worry. By day's end, Morgan left the mill yard feeling like a failure. He feared the worst about the new machine being produced in Lowell. He feared he hadn't properly protected the drawings. He hadn't yet been helpful in improving working conditions at the mills. And given the financial condition of Stark Mills, he doubted there would be sufficient funds available to make any changes that would benefit the workers.

With his parents' decision to move forward with the circular loom by "borrowing" money from the Amoskeag Company, they had placed the Stark Mills—and themselves—in jeopardy. To make matters worse, a competitor might secure a patent for the circular loom before Mr. Baldwin—and it could be Morgan's fault. His world seemed like something out of a dark comedy. Right now, the only good thing in his life was Mellie.

Morgan groaned when he spotted his father's groom waiting near the canal bridge. This could mean only one thing: He was being summoned by either one or both of his parents. The groom leaned against one of the bridge supports. As Morgan passed by, the man discreetly slipped a note into Morgan's hand.

He slowed his pace as the throng of workers walked around him. Once alone, he opened the missive and stared at his mother's impeccable handwriting. His assumption had been correct. He was being summoned home to meet with his parents. The note said it was imperative he come to see them this evening.

This evening? Did his parents not recall how difficult it was for him to make an appearance on such short notice? If he departed for home before eating supper at the boardinghouse, there would be numerous questions along with a stern reprimand from the boardinghouse keeper. A day's notice was required from residents wanting to be absent during mealtime. He would hear about the keeper's need to be frugal and the cost of wasted food. Of course, the food wouldn't go to waste—there were several men who would be happy to eat Morgan's share. That fact wouldn't appease the keeper, however.

He climbed the steps of the boardinghouse, his decision made. He'd quickly eat supper, rush to see his parents, excuse himself in time to get to the photography shop before closing time, and escort Mellie home.

After shoveling down his supper, he hurried toward the front door. His hasty departure resulted in a volley of hoots and hollers that followed him out the door. The men were certain he was off to meet Mellie. He wished they were right, for he expected the meeting with his parents to be far less enjoyable.

⚜

His parents were waiting in his father's office when Morgan arrived home. His mother *tsk*ed as she greeted him. "I do wish you'd take the time to change into proper attire before you come home, Morgan. Seeing you in those shabby work clothes distresses me." Disgust laced her words. "I hope you at least brushed off some of the dirt before you came inside." Her attention settled on the empty upholstered chair.

"I can stand if you'd prefer, Mother."

"Don't be silly. Sit down. We have some good news to share."

After giving the back of his pants a swipe, Morgan dropped into the chair beside his mother. He could use a bit of good news. "I'm eager to hear." He glanced back and forth between his parents.

His father cleared his throat. "First of all, we've repaid the money to the Amoskeag Company. I know that was of great concern to you, as it was to me."

His mother frowned. "I was worried too, William."

His father offered a weak smile. "Yes, of course, my dear." He returned his gaze toward Morgan. "In any event, your grandfather has been most generous, and the company books are once again in balance. There should be no problems arising from the brief loan that was made to fund the new looms."

Morgan couldn't meet his father's eyes. That his parents continued to refer to the stolen money as a *loan* weighed heavily on him. He was thankful they'd returned the money, but that didn't change the fact that it wasn't a loan. He shuddered to think what would have occurred if they'd been unable to return the money before the missing funds were discovered.

"Thank you for letting me know the money has been returned. It's still difficult for me to believe the two of you . . ." He shook his head and let his voice trail off. "Never mind. I'm thankful it's over." He looked at his father. "I will sleep better at night knowing you won't be going to jail."

His mother squared her shoulders. "All's well that ends well— as I knew it would."

"I'm glad to see that one of us was so confident." Morgan glanced at the clock on the mantel. "I need to return to town now."

His mother reached over and placed her hand atop his. "Not yet. There's one more thing. Your grandfather is coming for a brief visit at Christmas. He'll be here for my annual Christmas party, and we expect you to be present."

"But—"

"I don't want any excuses. If someone recognizes you, so be it. I don't know if anyone you're in contact with at the mills will be in attendance, but it matters little. Time with your grandfather is of greater importance than pretending to be a common workman in the mills."

His father nodded. "You need to be here, Morgan. Even if you should be recognized, your work in the mills is nearly complete. By Christmas we should be in production with the seamless bags, so—"

"But that isn't why I originally wanted to work in the mills, Father. We haven't even discussed the working conditions and some of the improvements I think would help the employees and also increase production."

His father shook his head. "If you go unrecognized, there's no reason you can't stay and continue your investigation. However, that isn't going to be your life's work. And if it happens to end in the next few weeks, then that's that."

His father's words cut the air like the slash of a sword. He'd thought his father supported what he was doing, but now it appeared as though he cared little about making changes at the mills. Instead, he was willing to maintain the status quo. But after the things Morgan had witnessed in the mills, and the things he'd heard from Mr. Mann, he didn't feel he could be content with the status quo ever again.

Chapter

SEVENTEEN

MORGAN RETURNED TO TOWN WITH HIS MIND HOP-scotching from one troubling thought to the next. Perhaps his father was right and Morgan shouldn't have posed as a mechanic and gone to work in the mill. Maybe he should have taken his father's advice and accepted a manager's position.

No matter which way he turned, it seemed he couldn't be completely honest with anyone. On several occasions he'd considered telling Mellie the truth, but each time he'd backed down. How did one tell a person he'd come to care deeply about that their relationship had been built upon a lie? Would she still want to be with him once she learned he was Morgan Stark and not William Morgan? What would Mr. Hale and Mr. Baldwin think when they discovered who he was? He'd stepped into this new identity thinking he could do good, yet each lie had required another. He was beginning to have trouble sifting the lies from the truth.

He bowed his head against a blast of cold wind that pricked his cheeks. Though he was shivering in his wool coat, he continued to plod through the icy weather at a listless pace. It was near closing time and he should hurry, but his eagerness to see Mellie was mixed with dread. He'd have to explain his late arrival, another lie needing to be told. He was building their relationship on a heap of lies that he feared was going to crumple and destroy any hope of a future with her.

Mellie was tidying up the shop when he arrived. Broom in hand, she looked up as the bell over the door pealed its familiar jangle. From the look on her face, he couldn't determine if she was angry, hurt, or simply surprised that he'd finally appeared. With her eyes downcast, she continued sweeping the plank floor. "I was worried something had happened to you. An accident at the mill or that you'd taken ill."

He wiped his shoes on the rug inside the door. "I'm sorry. I should have let you know I was going to be late."

When he didn't offer anything further, she stilled the broom, held it against her shoulder, and waited. There was little doubt she expected something more. Instead of lamenting his earlier lies, he should have been thinking of another one—one that would explain *why* he'd been late.

"I had to attend a meeting about a project at the mill, which I didn't know about until closing time. There wasn't time to get word to you. I had to be at the meeting immediately after supper."

After another swipe of the broom, she looked up. "Sounds like a unique meeting if it was after working hours and they required a mechanic to be present. Were all the mechanics present for this meeting?"

He swallowed hard. She didn't believe him. He couldn't fault her—he wouldn't have believed it, either. "No, just me." He attempted to gather his thoughts. "It had to do with the draw-ings I was studying in the back room. Mr. Stark needed some additional information."

"Mr. Stark? Then that truly was an important meeting. I've never seen Mr. Stark. One of the girls told me he seldom comes down to his office at the mill yard anymore. Tell me, what does he look like? Is he kind or fearsome?"

Morgan wasn't certain if she now believed him and was simply curious, or if this was a test because she hadn't trusted a word he'd said. "During our meeting, I'd say Mr. Stark was rather neutral, neither overly kind nor overly fearsome. He was pleasant, probably because he was relieved to hear there had been good progress on the project. What else was it you asked?" He hesitated, but before she could answer, he con-tinued. "Oh yes, about his appearance. He has white hair and rather sharp features. I'd say he's about my height with a medium build."

She placed the broom and dustpan in a tall cabinet, then turned to him. "And is his office quite fine? Where is it located? I was told it was in Stark Number One. Is that correct?"

"I believe that's right."

"How did you get into the mill yard? I thought the gates were secured throughout the night. Did Mr. Stark use his keys to let you in?"

She definitely didn't believe him, of that he was certain. She was asking too many pointed questions. Either she wanted to trip him up or hoped he'd come around and tell her the truth.

"The meeting was at Mr. Stark's home. That's why I was so late. He lives a fair distance from town."

"Oh? And you walked, or did he send a carriage?"

He withheld a sigh. He was digging a hole so deep, he'd likely never claw his way out. "I rode a horse. I was told there would be a horse at the stables near the edge of town."

"I see." She took off her apron, tucked it beneath the counter, and removed her coat from the closet. He hurried to her side and helped her. "I'd enjoy hearing about the Starks' home. I'm sure it must be magnificent. Perhaps you can tell me on our way home."

He nodded. "If you'd like."

After fastening the thick braid clasps on her coat, Mellie walked to the rear of the store. Morgan remained by the counter while she advised Mr. Harrison she was leaving for the night. When she returned, he pulled open the door and followed her outside. She placed a gloved hand in the crook of his arm and held tight to her bonnet with the other. The cold, stinging wind had worsened in the short time he'd been in the shop. Although he disliked the unfavorable conditions, the freezing air had curtailed any further conversation. Most evenings he would have been disappointed, but tonight he was thankful for the silence.

Arriving at her boardinghouse, she opened the front door and then turned to him. "I look forward to hearing about the Starks' home tomorrow—unless you have another meeting."

Before he could kiss her cheek or bid her good-night, she hurried inside and closed the door against the churning wind that threatened snow at any moment.

⋘⃮

Mellie had rushed up the main flight of stairs before she stopped to catch her breath. After walking home in the freezing wind, her teeth were still chattering. When she reached the end of the hallway, she let out a long sigh. Someone had closed the attic door. She didn't want to accuse the girls who slept in the second-floor bedrooms, but she didn't think Phebe, Clara, or Cora would have closed the door. They wanted as much heat as possible during these cold nights.

Her thoughts skittered back to Morgan and his account of the evening's events. His tale had taken her by surprise. She would never have guessed he had been attending a meeting at the Starks' home. That a mechanic would be summoned to the home of the mill owner to discuss a project made her mind reel. Still, she'd been told by more than one person that Mr. Stark seldom came to his offices. Perhaps he preferred to remain at home and have his employees meet with him there. Who could say? Certainly not a lowly loom operator like herself.

As she ascended the steps, Mellie heard whispers and moaning—or was it crying? When she arrived at the top of the stairs, she stopped short and struggled to take in the sight. Cora sat on one side of Phebe, Clara on the other side. Phebe rocked back and forth on the bed with both hands covering her face. Low, soulful moans escaped from deep in Phebe's chest.

At the sound of Mellie's footsteps, Phebe dropped her hands and looked up. Her dark lashes were wet with tears, her eyes swollen and red. Tendrils of damp black hair clung to her face and heightened her pasty complexion.

Fear shot through Mellie as she struggled to speak. "What's happened?" She took a step closer to the bed, but Cora stood and motioned Mellie to the other side of the room.

Phebe grasped Cora's hand. "You don't have to go to the corner and wh-wh-whisper." She hiccupped.

Cora motioned toward the stairway. "Did you close the door?"

Mellie nodded as she moved to the bed and sat beside Cora. She wasn't certain if she should direct her questions to the twins or Phebe. She extended her arm and touched Phebe's hand. "Are you ill, Phebe? Would you like me to go fetch the doctor?"

Phebe shook her head. "No." Her chest heaved as she inhaled a breath and lifted a crumpled paper from her lap. "This says it all. I wi-wish I could die. It sh-should have been m-me." Her body collapsed against Cora as she wept.

Mellie leaned closer to the candlelight and smoothed the wrinkles from the letter as she attempted to read the scribbled note. She squinted, gasped, and turned to Phebe. "Oh, Phebe, I am so very sorry. I know how much you loved your little brother." Rather than providing comfort, Mellie's words seemed to offer little consolation.

Phebe continued to rock back and forth. "It's all my fault. Forgive me, Lord. It's all my fault. Forgive me, Lord." Over and over she repeated the incantation.

Mellie knelt in front of Phebe. "His death is not your fault, Phebe. You told us that he was a sickly child. From your mother's letter, it appears he contracted the croup and that led to pneumonia. His frail body was unable to fight off the infection. I don't understand why you're holding yourself responsible."

Phebe swiped at her eyes with the back of her hand. "I'll tell you why." She hiccupped and gulped a lungful of air. "Instead of sending home money so that my folks could buy enough firewood to keep their rooms warm, I spent my money on lottery tickets." She withdrew a handkerchief from her skirt pocket and wiped her nose. "I was so sure I would win, and when I did, they'd be all set for a long time to come. They'd be able to afford a doctor for Timmy whenever he was sick, they'd be able to buy medicine and food, and they wouldn't have to worry about having enough wood to heat their rooms or whether they'd be able to pay the rent. Don't you see, Mellie? If I would have sent my money home, Timmy would still be alive." She hunched forward and once again began to rock back and forth.

Mellie grasped Phebe's hands in her own. "I know there's nothing I can do or say to ease your pain, but the three of us love you, Phebe, and we know your intentions were to help your family. If you'd like to go home for a visit, I'm sure the overseer would grant you permission. You're a good worker, and they'd let you come back after you've had some time at home."

Phebe shook her head. "You read the letter. Ma said there was no reason to come home—they've already buried Timmy."

Mellie nodded. "But it might give you some peace to go home and spend a little time with your mother and father."

"No. I think it would make it harder. Ma didn't say so, but I know they blame me."

Mellie rocked back on her heels. There was nothing she could do to change the situation, but she could ask God to grant her friend peace and comfort in the days to come. In the meantime, she'd do her best to offer Phebe solace and reassurance. She knew Cora and Clara would do the same.

⸮⸜⸜⸜

The three girls had comforted Phebe until she fell asleep several hours later. Though exhausted, they sat on the bed across the room, each of them saddened and weary.

Mellie turned to the twins. "Did the two of you know Phebe had been purchasing lottery tickets?"

They shook their heads in unison. Cora sighed and glanced toward the other bed. "Before you came home this evening, she said she hadn't been sending much money home since the shops in town began selling those lottery tickets. She showed them to me. I couldn't believe she'd purchased so many. I do wish she would have said something to one of us. We could have tried to convince her it was foolish. She thought if she bought enough tickets, she'd be sure to win, but when she received that letter, she blamed herself and said she'd never be able to go home and face her family."

A cloak of darkness wrapped around Mellie's heart. The life of a small child had been lost, and who could say what other tragedies would occur before the merchants stopped selling those tickets? The cost of this lottery was far too great.

Chapter

EIGHTEEN

THE NIGHT HAD BEEN LONG, AND NONE OF THEM SLEPT well. Phebe was restless and cried through most of the night. Even when Phebe was quiet, Mellie's sleep had been interrupted by thoughts of what had happened. As the night wore on, remembrances of her niece and nephew marched through her mind, and tears had pricked her eyes. She couldn't imagine the depth of Phebe's anguish.

After hearing the sad news, fearing that Phebe would be overcome with grief, Mrs. Richards agreed that one of them should remain home from church to be with her. Clara insisted she be the one to stay behind, and Mellie didn't argue with her. She doubted she would win. Clara seemed to feel a deep responsibility to care for Phebe, perhaps because she'd been the first one to speak with Phebe after she received the news. Or perhaps because Clara wanted to reveal God's love to her friend.

Before leaving for church, Mellie carried a tray of food upstairs for Clara and Phebe. When she entered the room, Phebe was sitting on the edge of the bed while Clara brushed the girl's hair.

"Thank you, Mellie," Phebe said. "Even though Mrs. Richards said she told the others they shouldn't ask me any questions, I don't think I could go downstairs and sit with them. It would be too uncomfortable."

Mellie placed the tray atop one of the trunks. "I'll be happy to bring your meals upstairs for as long as you like, Phebe." She smiled at the two girls. "I hope you're both hungry. I piled your plates so full, Mrs. Richards wondered if I was going to have a second breakfast with the two of you."

Clara continued brushing as she met Mellie's gaze. "I'm so hungry my stomach's been growling loud enough to wake the dead." Phebe flinched at the words. Realizing what she'd said, Clara froze for what seemed an eternity. She returned to slowly stroking Phebe's hair with the fine-bristled brush. "I'm sorry, Phebe. I spoke without thinking. I didn't mean to . . ."

"It's fine, Clara. You can't watch every word you say around me." Phebe shifted on the bed and attempted a smile. "I appreciate everything you three have done for me."

Mellie removed her good bonnet from a wall hook near her bed. "We know you'd do the same for us, Phebe. I must hurry now or Mrs. Richards will be coming upstairs to scold all of us. Just know that if there's anything you need, we'll do our best to help."

"Thank you, Mellie." Tears pooled in Phebe's eyes, and she looked away.

"Mellie! We need to leave for church right now!" Mrs. Richards's voice echoed from the lower hallway.

Mellie waved to the two girls and hurried down to the second floor, where Mrs. Richards was waiting with her hands on her hips and a scowl creasing her face. "You're going to cause me to be late for church, Mellicent."

Mellie continued along the hall and down the next flight of stairs with Mrs. Richards following in her wake. When they arrived at the front door, Mellie glanced over her shoulder. "Since we are caring for one of God's grieving children, I believe He will forgive you if you're late, Mrs. Richards. I think the Lord reserves His wrath for greater offenses, don't you?"

Mrs. Richards sniffed. "Since you've become an authority on what God thinks, perhaps the members of the clergy would like to visit with you. Most of them don't claim such deep insight."

Mellie sighed, shoved her arms into her coat, and tied her bonnet in place. She walked with Cora, Mrs. Richards, and several other girls who had required Mrs. Richards's urging to be present for services. When they arrived at the corner of Franklin and Market Streets, Mellie waved to the others. "I need to turn here. I attend the Franklin Street church."

Mrs. Richards nodded. "I know where you attend, Mellie." Ada tried to follow along with Mellie, but Mrs. Richards grasped her arm. "I'm no fool, Ada. You don't attend the Franklin Street church—you're hoping to sneak off and return to the boardinghouse. Well, that isn't going to happen."

Ada frowned and attempted to argue with Mrs. Richards, but even without looking back, Mellie knew Ada wouldn't win. Above all else, Mrs. Richards wanted high praise that she was operating her boardinghouse within her allocated budget and that her girls were following the rules. When she presented her ledgers to the boardinghouse supervisor, Mrs. Richards wanted a balanced financial sheet and, if she had her way, a notation by all the girls' names that they regularly attended church, hadn't been absent from work, and had been home by ten o'clock every night. If one of her girls did anything to cause an imperfect report, the rest would suffer. No doubt, Phebe's illness, along with Mellie's tardy appearance this morning, had set the keeper's nerves on edge.

The bells chimed in the distance, and Mellie quickened her step. There was a bite in the frosty air, but at least the wind wasn't howling anymore. For that she was grateful. Warmth greeted her as she stepped into the sanctuary and made her way down the aisle. She slid into a pew, leaned back, closed her eyes, and let the sounds of the pipe organ wash over her. The familiar hymns soothed her worried thoughts of Phebe. The pastor stepped to the pulpit, lifted his hand for the congregation to stand, then recited a blessing. The organist played the opening chords of "Hallelujah, Praise Jehovah," and the congregation lifted their voices in worship.

Before the song had finished, a man's form moved into Mellie's peripheral vision, and she edged to the center of the pew. Morgan's tardiness was unusual, and she had begun to think she wouldn't see him this morning. During the sermon, she rested her hand at her side. He placed his hand atop hers and gave a gentle squeeze. A quiver raced up her arm. She considered withdrawing her hand, but she needed to feel the warmth of his presence. After what had happened to Phebe, Mellie could use all the strength Morgan could offer.

She did her best to give the pastor her full attention, though her thoughts wandered back to Phebe on several occasions. She hoped her friend would find the ability to forgive herself for what had happened and understand that her intentions of helping her family, though misguided, had been good. She had hoped the lottery would pull her family out of poverty. Yet, even before the drawing had taken place, her dream had been shattered by death.

After the final stanza of "Just as I Am," the congregants made their way out of the pews, stopped to shake hands with the pastor, and dispersed toward their homes, girded by God's Word and hopefully prepared to accept life's challenges in the coming week.

Mellie rested her hand in the crook of Morgan's arm as they walked down Franklin Street.

"I was hoping you'd accept an invitation to go ice skating with me this afternoon. The pond is frozen, and I think there's going to be a large group there. It should be fun. I've even managed to borrow some skates I think will fit onto your shoes. Since you don't have to work, I was hoping you'd join me."

His smile was charming, and she didn't want to disappoint him, but she couldn't spend her afternoon ice skating. Not after what had happened last night. Even if she agreed to go, she wouldn't be good company. She'd be thinking of Phebe and her little brother.

"Thank you for the invitation, but I can't."

"But why? You need to take some time for yourself, Mellie. You know that old saying: 'All work and no play makes Jack a dull boy.' We all need to play a little, don't you think?"

"I do, but not today. I made a commitment, and I need to be back to the boardinghouse by three o'clock."

He stopped short and grasped her hand. "Then let's go to the livery. I'll rent horses and a sleigh. We can go for a ride, and I promise I'll have you back before three o'clock."

She wanted to agree, yet the rules stated she must advise the keeper if she wasn't going to return home for a meal—and she hadn't done so. "I can't. I didn't tell Mrs. Richards I wouldn't be there for the noonday meal."

He shaded his eyes and looked down the street. "Isn't that

Mrs. Richards and a couple of the girls from your boardinghouse coming this way?"

Mellie turned around. "I think so, but—"

"Wait here! I'll be back in no time."

He took off at a run, and when he'd neared Mrs. Richards, he slowed and walked alongside her. Before long, he was racing back. He panted for breath and gestured toward the boarding-house keeper. "I asked her permission, and she said it would be fine this once since she wasn't serving a large meal until supper. She said if we stopped by the house, she'd give us some bread and cheese to take with us."

Mellie gasped, surprised by Mrs. Richards's generosity. The woman wasn't known for such kindness. "You must have charmed her."

"The only one I want to charm is you, Mellie." He grinned. "So? Are you going to say yes and join me?"

Mellie nodded. How could she refuse? Besides, she needed to talk to someone she trusted. He would listen and empathize with what had happened.

A short time later, he helped her into the sleigh and, after a brief stop at the boardinghouse, they were on their way out of town and into the countryside. She was surprised at his ability to maneuver the horse-drawn sleigh along the rutted, narrow road encrusted with muck, snow, and ice. "You act like a man who has handled horses all his life."

"I've been around my share. I promise I'll do my best to make certain the sleigh doesn't tip over. You're safe with me." Humor glinted in his blue eyes.

Along the way, they passed several large estates that sat back from the road, each one with its own private drive and entrances that boasted magnificent porticos. Seeing them, she recalled that Morgan had never described for her the interior of the Stark home.

"Is this the area where the Starks live?" Mellie asked. "Our conversation was cut short, and I never did get to hear what their home is like."

"Yes, they do live near here. We passed their house a short time ago."

"Oh, I do wish you would have told me. Would you please point it out on our return?"

He nodded. "I'll try to remember."

She longed to talk with Morgan about what had happened last night, but she wanted to wait until they stopped to eat. Right now, he was concentrating on his driving, and she wanted his full attention when she told him about Phebe. While she was somewhat interested in the Stark home, she'd been inside many fine estates in Concord. In truth, she was more curious what Morgan thought of such a fine dwelling. From what she'd learned about him, he'd not had the same opportunities she'd experienced in her earlier years. "Why don't you tell me about the Starks' home? Were the furnishings lavish? Did they have lots of servants? Did Mr. Stark serve refreshments?"

He gave her a sideways glance and grinned. "Let me see if I can recall each of your questions. "Yes, the furnishings were lavish. I saw only one servant, but there may have been others. No, Mr. Stark didn't serve refreshments. Was that everything?"

She gave him a look of mock indignation. "Tell me what rooms you were in and what they looked like. I want more details."

"Details? Let's see. I went in the rear door—it's in the back of the house."

"Morgan!"

He tipped his head back and laughed. "All right. The kitchen was large, although I didn't get to see much more than the huge wooden worktables because the maid hurried me through a hallway, where there were pictures of relatives—at least I would guess they were relatives—hanging on the walls. There was a carpet runner in the main hall, and Mr. Stark's office was at the end of it. The doors into the other rooms were closed. Mr. Stark sat behind a large desk that looked as though it was made of walnut. There were chairs upholstered in dark colors, with Mr. Stark's chair covered in leather. Over the fireplace was a painting, a simple bucolic scene with some sheep." He hesitated. "Oh, and there was an impressive winding staircase leading to the upper floors of the house."

"It sounds quite lovely. Did you think it quite remarkable?"

He shrugged. "I don't think such a large house is necessary, but yes, it was very nice." He pulled back on the reins. The horses slowed, then came to a halt not far from a pond. There was a spot where logs surrounded a charred site used for fires to keep skaters warm. After tucking the blanket around her, he jumped out of the sleigh. "Stay here and I'll get a fire started. I don't want you to get too cold."

Mellie pulled the blanket tight beneath her chin. While this outing had sounded like a wonderful idea a short time ago, she wasn't sure eating bread and cheese in the snowy countryside was the best idea. She peered over the edge of the blanket and watched sparks skitter around the stacked wood, take hold, and send flames shooting heavenward, then settle to a welcoming fire.

Morgan hurried back to the sleigh, helped her down, wrapped the wool blanket around her shoulders, and grabbed their basket of food. "You'll be warm in no time. I promise."

She hoped he was right. If not, her chattering teeth would prevent her from eating a single bite. He led her to a log he'd brushed free of snow, and once she was seated, he skewered a chunk of bread onto a stick to toast for her.

He returned a few minutes later with the warm, crispy offering. "Hurry and put your cheese on the bread so it'll melt some."

Mellie did as she was told and then took a bite. The gooey cheese and toasted bread exploded with flavor on her tongue.

Once Morgan had toasted his piece, he took a seat beside her. By then her thoughts had turned away from food and were focused on Phebe and what had happened last night. "Morgan, I need to talk to you about something."

※

Morgan's chest tightened. Mellie needed to talk to him about something. Had his lies finally caught up to him? He swallowed hard. "What is it?"

Sadness washed over him as he quietly listened to Mellie recount the contents of Phebe's letter. When she'd finished, Mellie shook her head. "She loved Timmy dearly, almost as though he were her own child—likely because he was so much younger than her. Through her tears she told us how she'd cared for him from his birth until she left home and came to Manchester." She looked up and met his eyes. "Phebe cried so hard while telling us about him that she could barely get the words out."

He couldn't fathom the extent of Phebe's grief. To have her brother die at such a young age, especially while she was living far from home, had to be overwhelming.

"I admire the three of you and what you're doing for Phebe," Morgan said. "I'm sure she's going to need continued support as the days and weeks go by. I'm told grief can be as crushing as a debilitating illness. Do you think it would help if she took time away from work and went home for a visit?"

Mellie shook her head. "That's the worst of it. She says she doesn't know if she can ever go home again. I think she'll change her mind after some time passes, but she's refused to go right now."

"But wouldn't it comfort her to be near her parents?"

Mellie's shoulders slumped forward as she detailed the facts surrounding Phebe's misguided decision to purchase lottery tickets rather than send the money home. She sighed and shook her head. "I wonder how many victims this lottery will claim before it's finally over. And there's nothing we can do."

Morgan let his gaze momentarily settle on the fire's burning embers. "There's nothing we can do about the lottery, but perhaps Timmy's death won't be in vain if we gather a large group and appear at the next town meeting to protest against the operation of any further lotteries in Manchester. What do you think?"

"Oh, Morgan, that's a grand idea. Perhaps there will be a few adversely affected folks willing to speak out against any future lotteries. The wealthy men who run the city need to hear that such gambling entices folks to spend their hard-earned wages on purchasing tickets rather than providing for the needs of their families. If we furnish them with facts, they'll surely agree that any lottery is a sham and a lie."

Morgan flinched at her final word. *Lie.* What would she think when she discovered he had been dishonest with her? When she learned he wasn't a mechanic but an engineer and the son of William and Ruth Stark? When she discovered he'd been living a lie? After she learned the truth, how could she ever believe that his feelings for her had been genuine?

NINETEEN

MELLIE COULD FEEL THE COLD, WET SNOW SEEPING through her boots as she walked toward the mill. The girls paraded down the hill and across the bridge in soldierlike formation, their faces covered with woolen scarves and their heads bowed against the frigid wind. At first, the arrival of the snows was greeted with enthusiasm, but already the beauty and novelty had been replaced by a longing for spring. Yet the seasons wouldn't change again for many months. This was New England, where winters were harsh and long, even for the heartiest of souls.

The only place where they were too warm was inside the weaving room. Heat and humidity were maintained year-round to keep the threads from breaking. It mattered little if the girls were damp with perspiration when they walked home in freezing temperatures or if they fainted in the summer heat. Little wonder many of them suffered with chest coughs, colds, and pneumonia. So far, Mellie and the twins had remained healthy.

Phebe, who had returned to her looms after only two days off, hadn't succumbed, either. Mr. Fuqua had granted the girl permission to remain at home for a full week, but after the end of the second day, she'd decided it was easier to keep her mind off Timmy when at work. Besides, with the onset of the frigid weather, she'd been unable to keep warm throughout the day.

Even with the attic door open and the quilts piled high, there was little warmth to be found in their room. The first one out of bed each morning had to chip an icy layer from the pitcher of water before washing and dressing in the chilly room. Each of them took her turn, wrapping in a heavy quilt to keep warm while preparing for another day at the mills. Although the downstairs rooms were a bit warmer, the only room without frost layering the inside of the windows was the kitchen. While biscuits baked, the frost on those windows melted and trickled down the glass like tears on the cheeks of the heartbroken. Truth be told, Mellie doubted whether the boardinghouse keeper cared much about the other rooms, since most of her waking hours were occupied in the kitchen.

One thing was certain: It would be much more difficult to leave the boardinghouse each morning if Mrs. Richards ensured all the rooms were warm and cozy. While the keeper avowed she was simply doing her best to maintain her allotted budget, the girls thought she pocketed any extra money when the household expenses decreased. Mellie had no idea if that was correct, yet she'd heard girls from the other boardinghouses claim the same thing about their keepers. Though she hoped the keepers wouldn't do anything so unconscionable, she knew that money could influence even the most respectable. After all, her own brother-in-law's desire for more money had caused his death and the devastation of his family.

Mellie climbed the winding stairs and stepped inside the weaving room. She leaned forward and coughed, her lungs immediately rebelling against the thick, humid air. In a few moments, her body would adjust to the sudden change in temperature, but until then, each breath was difficult. She did her best to ignore the unpleasant sensation as she hurried to hang up her coat and get to her looms before the bell rang.

She glanced around, looking for the twins. She'd thought Clara and Cora had followed her up the stairs, but neither was at their looms. The clock was ticking off the seconds. If they were late, they'd be in trouble. Her breath caught when the door opened and her two friends raced into the room, tossed off their coats, and skidded to a stop in front of their machines just as the bell rang.

"Where were you?" Mellie mouthed the words, not expecting a response. With the noise from the looms, she wouldn't be able to hear Cora's reply.

When the bell finally rang and they were free to return home for breakfast, Mellie hurried to join Cora and Clara. "Where did you go? You scared me. One minute you were behind me, and the next minute both of you were gone."

Cora grabbed her coat from a hook and shoved her arms into the sleeves. "Clara and I were talking to Billy and Jimmy Bobeck. Do you know them? They're brothers who work in the carding rooms."

Mellie shook her head. "No, I don't think I've met them. Why did you stop to visit with them?"

"They invited Clara and me to the ball. Can you believe it? I didn't think either of us would get an invitation." A wide grin spread across Cora's face.

Clara had already donned her cloak, and the twins waited until

Mellie had fastened the clasps on her coat. The three of them descended the stairs, careful to stay close to the brick wall, where the wedge-shaped steps were wider. Even stepping on the widest portion could be dangerous. Melted snow and ice left the stairways wet and slick. Just yesterday one of the girls had slipped down several steps before she was able to grab the rail and break her fall.

Mellie looked over her shoulder. "The ball isn't far off. The two of you will need to decide what you want to wear. If you'd like to wear any of my dresses, you can have your choice."

Clara frowned. "Aren't you going to attend with Morgan?"

"I don't think so." Mellie's stomach tightened at the thought of her recent conversation with Morgan and how she'd disappointed him. "I told him that since they were having the lottery drawing during the dance, I didn't want to attend. He says I shouldn't let that influence my decision, but I've been so opposed to the lottery, and after what happened to Phebe, it seems wrong to be at an event where they're going to celebrate the cause of such tragedy."

"I suppose that's true. Still, you shouldn't base your decision upon what happened to Phebe."

"And why is that?"

Clara leaned around her sister. "Because Phebe told me she's going to attend. She was invited yesterday and said she accepted. When I appeared surprised, she said staying at home wouldn't change what had happened in the past. Since Phebe has decided to go, I think you should reconsider."

"I do, as well. Have you considered that your decision may cause Phebe to feel guilty because she's decided to attend?" Cora pinned Mellie with a warning look. "Phebe's been doing much better these last few days. I know none of us want her to relapse and once again blame herself."

Mellie sucked in her breath. "That's the very last thing I want."

Throughout a breakfast of sausage, gravy, scrambled eggs, biscuits, and cinnamon-spiced apples, Mellie remained oblivious to the chatter swirling around her. Instead, her thoughts centered upon her quick decision to avoid the lottery drawing. The ball was an annual event that had begun several years ago. None of the girls seemed to know the exact year or why, but Mrs. Richards said it mimicked the seasonal "lighting up" and "blow out" balls that had begun in Lowell each September and March. However, the girls argued against the keeper's assessment. The balls in Lowell were a mingling of employers and company officers with the factory workers. Most of the girls thought the ball had begun in order to promote Mr. Vance's dance lessons. Mellie tended to agree with the girls. The businessmen in Manchester were always eager to find new ways to increase their profits. The lottery was evidence of that fact.

After breakfast, Cora looped arms with Mellie as they traversed the snow-shoveled path through the mill yard. "Are you going to give further thought to attending the dance?" She tightened her hold on Mellie's arm. "I truly want you to be there. We'll have such fun. Please tell Morgan you'll attend."

They stepped into the entrance of Stark Number Two and crossed to the stairway. She'd love to be at the ball beside Morgan, but perhaps it was too late. "I'll see what he says," Mellie said. "Maybe he's already asked someone else."

Cora untied her bonnet as they ran up the steps. "You know that's not possible. He's in love with you. Every time he looks at you, I can see it in his eyes."

Mellie stared after her friend as she hurried up the steps, stunned by her revelation. She thought Morgan was fond of her, but love? He'd never used that word, and neither had she. In truth, she wasn't sure they knew each other well enough to profess love, though her feelings for him ran deep. During her time in Manchester, she'd come to depend on him. He was a God-fearing, reliable, strong, truthful, hardworking man, and she doubted she could find anyone more thoughtful and caring than Morgan. Even so, she was glad he hadn't yet declared his love—they needed more time.

She pressed her hand to her fluttering heart. Who was she fooling? With or without declarations, Morgan had already woven his way into her heart.

✦

Morgan crossed the canal bridge, eager to begin the day. He was to meet with Mr. Baldwin and Mr. Hale this morning to select a group of mechanics who would assemble the circular looms. In order to maintain secrecy, production of the loom's numerous components had been forged in a variety of shops throughout Mechanics' Row.

On his way across the mill yard, he hadn't noticed the numbing cold, although he welcomed the warmth the moment he stepped inside the brick building. However, one look at Mr. Hale's pale complexion and Mr. Baldwin's dour appearance and Morgan's chest tightened until he could barely breathe. Something was amiss.

He forced a tentative smile. "Good morning, gentlemen." He reached inside his pocket and withdrew a paper. "I've made a list of the possible employees I thought the two of you might consider. They are excellent mechanics, and more important, I believe they can be trusted to conceal all information regarding the new looms until we begin production."

Neither of the men extended a hand to take the list. Instead, Mr. Baldwin gestured to a nearby chair. "We need to have a talk, Morgan."

"Yes, of course." He gripped the arms of the chair with clammy palms. "Is there a problem of some sort?" The room was alive with an electrifying tension, and while he feared learning the cause, he needed to know.

Mr. Baldwin sat down beside him. "You may recall that some time ago I went to visit with my attorney in Lowell regarding my patent on the circular loom."

Morgan nodded. "Yes, he said it could take a good while."

"Exactly. Well, I received word from him today that my design was being examined for a patent, and something quite strange happened during the process."

"What's that?" Morgan asked nervously.

"It seems that while the patent authorities were in the process of examining my design, another submission was received for a circular loom. One of the clerks brought it to their attention, and they asked to see the submission. And do you know what they discovered?"

"I have no idea." Morgan's voice cracked.

"The design was submitted under the name of Franklin Montee. Do you know a Franklin Montee?"

Morgan's mind reeled. He'd expected to hear Mr. Baldwin say the documents had been submitted by Mr. Knoll or perhaps Mr. Snow, but he had no idea who Franklin Montee might be. "No, I don't. I've never met anyone by the name of Montee."

"Here's the thing, Morgan. The attorneys working in the patent office wrote to my personal attorney and said it appeared the submission made by Mr. Montee was an exact duplicate of my plans. It doesn't seem possible someone could submit the exact same plans unless they had copied the original. Yet how could that occur? We've gone to great lengths to protect the design. There isn't a man working in the various shops who knows of the design." He pointed his finger at Mr. Hale, then moved it to point to Morgan, and ended by pointing at himself. "Other than my attorney, the three of us were the only ones who had access to the design." He leaned forward, his face only inches from Morgan's. "Am I right?"

"I believe so, Mr. Baldwin."

"Then tell me this, Morgan. How did someone get an exact copy of my design? I gave you the drawings to study, and you took them home. Am I right?"

"Mostly."

"What does that mean?" Mr. Baldwin's eyes flashed with anger.

"I didn't take them to the boardinghouse. I don't have my own room, and I was afraid someone would see the drawings. Besides, there would be no time alone in my room when I could study them." He went on to detail how he'd studied and stored the documents in Mr. Harrison's shop.

Mr. Baldwin pushed to his feet and paced the room. "Who could have seen the drawings?"

Morgan sighed. "Mr. Harrison or his houseguest, Mr. Knoll, may have had access to them. The cabinet wasn't locked at all times. I do know that someone saw the renderings. I could see they'd been disturbed, but I remained hopeful it wasn't by anyone who wanted to steal the design—simply someone who'd happened upon them and then returned them to the cabinet."

Mr. Hale folded his arms across his chest and frowned. "When you first suspected the documents had been compromised, you should have told one of us, don't you think?"

Morgan shifted in his chair. "I had hoped to discover who had seen them and whether there was any real concern. Although it could have been Mr. Knoll or Mr. Harrison, there was also a gentleman from Lowell, Ezekiel Snow. He came into the shop for a photograph. He was also in the back room and could have seen the documents in the cabinet."

"I met Ezekiel Snow at a gathering hosted by Abbott Lawrence some time ago." Mr. Baldwin nodded. "I understand the two are longtime friends. I believe Mr. Snow invested in the cotton and wool mills that Abbott has established in Lawrence, Massachusetts." His lips curved in a wry smile. "He named the town after himself, just as Francis Cabot Lowell did before him. Not that those details are of any importance at the moment."

"I'm sorry, Mr. Baldwin. I didn't want to cause undue concern, and when this occurred, you weren't in town." Morgan glanced at Mr. Hale. "I considered telling you, Mr. Hale, but I didn't know that there was anything to be done. I'm still not sure there is. Did your attorney offer any insight regarding whether we should continue?"

Mr. Baldwin snorted. "He's a lawyer. I'm a businessman. My future is what's at stake here, not his, so the decision on what to do will be mine. He believes it will be easy enough to prove the second submission is a forgery. He has hired a detective to see if we can locate this Franklin Montee and if criminal action should be pursued against him."

Morgan frowned. "I don't see how they could beat us to production, Mr. Baldwin. We've been developing our loom for more than six months."

Mr. Baldwin sighed. "We've been going about this in a methodical and precise manner because we want the ability to produce more looms. They are likely moving in a haphazard manner with only one thought in mind—being the first ones to market. If they can show they were first to produce, they likely believe they will win any patent argument."

"And will they?" Morgan arched his brows.

Mr. Baldwin shook his head. "Not if I have my way. We're not only going to be first in submitting our drawings, we're going to move at full speed to get one of our looms producing before the end of the month. Now, let me see that list of names you brought with you."

Morgan handed him the paper. "I'll understand if you no longer want me to work on the project, Mr. Baldwin."

The older man glanced at the list before looking at Morgan. "Of course I want you to remain. Your intentions have always been honorable. In considering the matter, I must say the fault is my own. I shouldn't have asked you to take the drawings home to study them. That was foolish of me." He pointed to the list. "Now, let's decide who we want on our team and have them begin work as soon as possible."

Once they'd made their decision, the men were called together, sworn to secrecy, and promised a bonus if they had the loom in production before the end of the month. Morgan had no doubt they'd be successful. Still, guilt had settled hard in his gut.

As he walked back to the boardinghouse later that evening, Morgan's thoughts skittered about in his head. He needed to do something to make this right. He had no idea who Franklin Montee was, but somehow he was going to find out.

Chapter

TWENTY

Mid-October

A DRY, POWDERY SNOW FELL AS MELLIE WALKED BESIDE Morgan, her hand tucked in the crook of his arm. The fresh snow glittered in the moonlight.

Morgan covered her hand with his own. "Mellie, is something wrong? You're so quiet this evening."

"No." She drew in a deep breath. "Remember when you asked me to attend the ball?"

"Yes. You didn't want to attend because of the lottery. I understand, and I don't want you to feel any remorse about your decision."

She paused. "What if I've changed my mind?"

He stopped and turned to her with a smile. "Truly?"

"Not about the lottery. I still abhor that, but I've learned Phebe is going to attend. If I don't go, she may think her decision is improper. I don't want to do anything that would cause her further difficulty."

"And?"

"And what?"

"And you'd love to be by my side."

She rolled her eyes and grinned. "I would indeed."

He kissed her forehead. "You have no idea how much I needed some good news today."

Mellie's heart soared at the look in his eyes. Her news had delighted him, and now she couldn't wait for the ball.

Thankfully, Mr. Harrison hadn't objected when Mellie requested the evening off work. He'd agreed there wouldn't be much business in town on the evening of the Grand Complimentary Ball, especially on the night when the winning lottery ticket would be drawn. Mellie had ignored his remark about the lottery, knowing that Mr. Harrison and Mr. Knoll would be in attendance for that portion of the ball. The two men had both purchased tickets, and Mr. Knoll said he wanted to be there to pick up his winnings. Mellie doubted either of the men would win, yet it seemed everyone who came into the store or worked in the mills had the same opinion—the winnings would be theirs by the end of the ball. All but one would be sorely disappointed.

Over the next few days, Mellie did her best to help Phebe, Cora, and Clara with their dresses. They had to work by candlelight in the attic room long after they were supposed to be in bed, and she hoped the end result would be worth their lack of sleep. Before leaving for work at the photography shop, Mellie detailed what they could work on while she was gone. If each of the girls was going to have properly fashioned attire, the dresses would require alterations. Seams would need to be tightened or loosened, necklines lowered, and lace, bows, and trim added to transform Mellie's day dresses into fashionable gowns for her friends.

On the day of the ball, the girls rushed home more quickly than usual. Most days they walked a little more slowly in the evening, but not today. They would need to eat and be dressed before their escorts arrived at eight-thirty. The ball was scheduled to begin promptly at nine o'clock, and no one wanted to miss even a minute. The evening meal consisted of leftover dishes from the noonday meal—cold mutton, bread, pickles, cheese, beets, and fried potatoes, the only warm dish on the table.

Mrs. Richards scurried into the room with a deep blue shot-silk gown draped across one arm. "Eat what you want. I don't have time to worry over your meal tonight. I've been busy pressing my gown. I'm going to my room to dress." She started out of the room, then stopped in the doorway. "Is there anyone who isn't going to the ball this evening?" Two of the young-est girls raised their hands as though they were students in a classroom. Mrs. Richards smiled and gave a nod. "Good. You two clear the table and do the dishes. I'll decrease your room and board for next week."

The two girls bobbed their heads in unison, and Mrs. Richards continued toward her bedroom. Mellie had been surprised to learn several of the boardinghouse keepers would be in atten-dance this evening. Mrs. Richards had been clear regarding her own intent: She hoped to find a suitor who would eventually propose marriage so that she could resign her position as a keeper. Maybe that was the intent of all the keepers who planned to attend. On the other hand, perhaps some of the others simply wanted to enjoy an evening of fun or see if they'd won the lottery.

The minute they'd eaten enough to ward off their hunger, the girls rushed upstairs to their rooms. Cora and Clara performed their toilettes and then returned downstairs to the kitchen, where they could heat their curling tongs. As soon as Phebe and

Mellie completed their toilettes, they slipped into their wrappers and ran downstairs. Phebe and Mellie had considered forgoing the curling tongs entirely, but they finally decided upon braided chignons with curls only at the sides of their faces. It would take less time yet permit them to be more fashionable than usual.

Phebe followed Mellie into the kitchen and pointed to a chair. "I'll do yours first." She lifted a long strand of Mellie's hair and coiled it around one of the hot tongs. "One of the things I disliked the most when I came to work in the mills was how I had to be careful to keep every strand of my hair tucked and pinned tight to my head." She lifted another strand of Mellie's hair. "Did they warn you about that on your first day?"

"Yes. Cora told me there had been girls who would let their hair loose after beginning work and it would get caught in the looms and tear their hair from their heads. She told me it tore the scalp from one girl and she died." Mellie shuddered. "I can't imagine anything so horrible. Hearing that was enough for me to be certain my hair is always pulled back in a tightly braided knot."

Phebe placed the tongs back on the stove. "There's a looking glass in the hallway. See if you want more curls. I like it with three on each side, but I'll do more if you want."

After standing on tiptoe to see over several other girls, Mellie returned to the kitchen. "This is lovely. Thank you, Phebe. Now let me get started on your hair."

Afterward, they returned upstairs, where the girls each donned their gowns. Mellie wore a deep violet one, Phebe a rich emerald, Cora a pale yellow with mauve flounces, and Clara a bright poppy. They attempted to twirl for each other, but the effort proved impossible in their tight quarters.

Cora giggled. "We look like flowers in a colorful garden, don't you think?"

Mellie agreed. "I think Billy and Jimmy Bobeck will consider themselves very fortunate when they lay eyes on the two of you." She glanced at Phebe. "And the same can be said for you, Phebe. I know your beau is going to be delighted to show you off to his friends."

Phebe's cheeks pinked, and she lowered her eyes. "I know I said this before, but I want to thank all of you for everything you've done for me. If it weren't for the three of you . . ."

Phebe's voice trailed off as tears pooled in her eyes. Mellie stepped to her side and embraced her. "Just having you with us is thanks enough, Phebe. Now, let's put on our brightest smiles and go downstairs to await our beaus."

~~~~~

When Mrs. Richards announced Morgan had arrived, Mellie carried her cloak to the foyer. She smiled at him. "I was beginning to wonder if you'd forgotten me."

"I'm sorry. I was late leaving work, but I could never forget you." He leaned close and placed her cloak around her shoulders. "You look beautiful, Mellie." A shiver raced down her arms as he spoke. "Trust me, we'll be there on time. I rented a carriage for the evening."

"You shouldn't have gone to such expense."

He offered his arm, then opened the door. "Nothing is too good for you, Mellie. One day I hope to offer you much more."

~~~~~

The Grand Complimentary Ball was nothing like the formal balls Mellie had attended in Concord. A few of the men were attired in suits, although most wore mismatched jackets and trousers. The only man wearing a formal black waistcoat, studded white shirt, vest, and well-fitting pants was Mr. Vance, the director of the dance school. Likewise, those ladies unable to afford ball gowns were clothed in their Sunday day dresses with added lace at the bodice or fancy trim along the hem. A few owned fichus and had draped them around their shoulders for a more festive appearance. Mrs. Vance appeared at her husband's side in a modest lavender gown. Either she didn't own a ball gown or she didn't want to outshine the other ladies.

Noticeably absent were the wealthy residents of Manchester. None of the owners or managers of the mills was in attendance, at least as far as Mellie could see. Perhaps they would make an appearance later in the evening. Surely those in charge of the lottery would appear to conduct the drawing. For now, it appeared as if Mr. Vance and a small committee of his dance students were in charge of the festivities, and they'd gone to great effort to replicate the setting of a fancy ball.

Even though they'd paid for their tickets to attend the dance, the attendees were announced as if they'd received an engraved invitation to a private affair. Mellie smiled at Morgan as one of the young men cupped his hands to his mouth and called out their names.

Morgan chuckled. "I believe he's auditioning for a position in the queen's court."

"I think Mr. Vance must have instructed him to be certain everyone could hear the names of the attendees, though I'm not sure why. Perhaps it has something to do with the lottery drawing."

Morgan's brows dipped. "I don't think the lottery drawing will bring out the society folks. I doubt it would prove enough incentive for them to mingle with the working class."

"You're probably right." She gestured toward the large white urns that had been filled with sparkling greenery and situated throughout the room. Candles glowed from gold sconces and illuminated the space in a glowing halo of light. "They've done a fine job with the decorations, don't you agree?"

"Yes, it appears Mr. Vance and his committee have dedicated many hours to the decorations. Let's hope they have hired some excellent instrumentalists, as well."

"We'll soon see." She nodded toward the platform, where the musicians were taking their places.

They plunked and tooted until they were certain each instrument was in tune before nodding to Mr. Vance. Acting as floor manager, Mr. Vance stepped forward and directed the orchestra to begin. There were no programs or dance cards and no promenade. The gathering was a distant cousin to the balls held in the grand homes of high society. Yet this dance had a unique charm of its own, a spirit of camaraderie and equality.

Mr. Vance and his wife took a turn around the dance floor before he beckoned the others to join in. As the couples danced in time to the music of a waltz, the hanging garlands of white feathers swayed overhead and created an almost ethereal atmosphere. After another waltz, the musicians announced a galop followed by two polkas.

To Mellie's surprise, Morgan proved to be an admirable dancer, never missing a single step. When she praised his skill, he brushed it off, saying he danced well only when his partner was as talented as she.

Completing the second polka, Mellie tugged on Morgan's sleeve. "I think I'd like something to drink and a few minutes to catch my breath."

He chuckled. "You're willing to leave the dance floor and miss the mazurka?"

"I am. If they had announced another waltz, I might have waited for refreshments, but I don't think I could complete a mazurka after a galop and two polkas. Maybe Mr. Vance should tell his musicians we aren't all accustomed to so much spirited activity."

"Perhaps this is Mr. Vance's way of letting us know we all need to be participating in his dancing lessons, so we can strengthen our endurance." Morgan grinned.

"Or he's trying to help the doctor with added business. Maybe he thinks this strenuous dancing will cause heart palpitations." Mellie clasped a hand over her heart and chuckled. "If so, I do believe he's succeeded—at least with me."

"In that case, let's hurry and locate the refreshments."

They made their way to a room across the hall, where tables had been arranged and covered with crisp, white cloths. Several young men stood in readiness, handing Mellie and Morgan china plates when they neared the serving table. An array of biscuits, crackers, cheeses, and sandwiches filled the silver serving trays. And assorted cakes, fruits, and meringues were nestled onto tiered serving stands, each one more inviting than the last. At a separate table, urns of coffee and tea, along with ices and lemonade, were offered. Mellie accepted a tall glass of lemonade before they were escorted to a small private table to enjoy their repast.

"Mr. Vance and his students are to be commended on a lovely event. I doubt the cost of tickets covered all the expenses." Mellie glanced toward the serving table. "I hope the party will garner him additional students so that his expenditure proves worthwhile."

"So do I, because these cakes are delicious. I'd attend his dances just for the opportunity to enjoy the cakes." He leaned toward her and winked. "And to enjoy your company, of course." He popped another piece of lemon cake into his mouth.

"With the number of those little cakes you've eaten, I think my company is quite secondary to the treats being served." She pursed her lips in a mock pout.

Their laughter was interrupted by several short blasts of the trumpet, followed by Mr. Vance calling for everyone to join him in the ballroom. Mellie and Morgan moved back to the ballroom and weaved through the crowd until they were near Cora, Clara, and the Bobeck brothers.

Mellie tipped her head close to Cora's ear. "What's happening, do you know?"

"I think Mr. Vance is going to conduct the lottery drawing." She nodded toward the stage, where a large brass urn had been placed center stage.

"Truly? I wonder if Mr. Vance is one of those who decided the lottery would be good for business. If so, I suppose it makes sense that he would conduct the drawing."

Morgan hiked a shoulder. "I don't believe anyone has ever said who originated the lottery. Perhaps it was Mr. Vance, although it seems unlikely he would have organized it on his own." He scanned the room, then leaned close to Mellie's ear. "I do see a number of other business owners in the room, including Mr. Harrison and Mr. Knoll."

She followed his gaze across the room. "Mr. Harrison said they'd be here for the drawing. They both think they're going to win." She gave a wry grin. "I'm not sure how they believe that's possible."

Morgan chuckled. "Wishful thinking from both of them, I suppose."

Mr. Vance cleared his throat. "I'm going to reach into this urn and draw the winner's name in just a moment. I had hoped that the sponsor of the lottery would be here to draw the winner's name, but she is ill and requested I do the honors. However, I'd like all of you to know that Mrs. William Stark is the fine lady who originated and executed this lottery. I have a note from her that I'll read to you."

Morgan gasped, but before Mellie could question his reaction, Mr. Vance called for quiet in the room.

A fellow in the back slipped through the crowd and cupped his hands to his mouth. "Draw the winner first! Then you can read that note." A roar of agreement rose from the gathering.

Mr. Vance looked at the crowd with wide-eyed shock. The man's unruly behavior, followed by the hooting and hollering of the crowd, had obviously unnerved the dance instructor. Without hesitating, he stepped up to the urn, sifted through it with his hand, and removed a ticket. He held it close to his nose. Each ticket bore a name on one side and a number on the other. "The winning number is—"

"Just read the name," a man shouted.

Mr. Vance turned the ticket over. "The winner is Henry Walters."

A mill manager had won. "He don't need the money!" a young man called out.

A host of others shouted their disapproval, until Mr. Vance called for quiet. When the crowd finally settled, he unfolded the letter. "I'm now going to read the note, and I would appreciate your attention." Coughs, the shuffling of feet, and loud sighs emanated from the crowd while he read a lengthy message regarding the benefits that would be derived from the lottery. While nothing specific was mentioned, the note assured that the funds would be used for the betterment of the community. "I think a large round of applause is due Mrs. Stark for her efforts."

As the applause quieted, Mellie leaned toward Morgan. "Do you think Mrs. Stark wrote that speech?" Before he could answer, she continued, "I wonder why we weren't told exactly what the money would be used for."

Clara edged close to Mellie. "It makes me wonder, as well. If I was raising money for a charity, I'd want folks to know who was going to benefit." She arched her brows. "Wouldn't you, Morgan?"

His lips tightened into a thin line. "Yes, I would. I plan to make some inquiries and see if I can find out how the funds will be used. I'm sure there are others who will be seeking answers, too."

Mellie grasped his arm. "Perhaps this is something else that should be mentioned when we attend the town meeting to protest further lotteries. If they won't agree to halt these lotteries, we should insist upon oversight of the funds." She exhaled a long breath. "Surely Mrs. Stark plans to give a full accounting of how the money will be spent. No doubt she'll want residents of the town to know. After all, the Stark family doesn't need lottery proceeds to maintain their way of life."

Soon the ballroom filled with couples again, who swirled around them as Morgan danced with her. What was wrong with him? He'd been acting odd ever since the lottery drawing. Was there something he hadn't told her? Did he believe the drawing had been rigged? Was he ill? He'd visibly paled during the drawing. Even if the drawing had been manipulated, he'd have no way of knowing. Something was wrong. And why was he suddenly asking her to trust him?

Trust. It had never come easily to her, especially when something didn't feel right. Perhaps she was being ridiculous. Since learning of her brother-in-law's deception, it seemed she'd seen deceit in everyone. She looked into Morgan's clear blue eyes. Did she, like Cora, see the love in them?

Pushing such thoughts aside, Mellie determined to simply soak up the evening. Before long she forgot about lotteries, charity funds, the mills, the Starks, everything but Morgan and this moment. She caught sight of their dancing shadows on the wall—a perfect silhouette—and smiled.

She trusted Morgan. Perhaps she even loved him. She was not going to let her ridiculous suspicions ruin this magical night.

Chapter

TWENTY-ONE

SIX WEEKS HAD PASSED SINCE THE BALL, AND MORGAN still hadn't spoken to his parents. Not that he hadn't tried. After attending church the following day, he'd set aside his fear of being discovered, rented a horse, and traveled home. Lucy had greeted him at the rear door with a look of surprise, as well as the unexpected and distressing news that his parents were in Boston and wouldn't return until two weeks before Christmas. When he'd asked about their exact whereabouts, she'd shrugged and said they hadn't provided the particulars, only that they were going to Boston and when they would return.

Their sudden departure had given him pause. Was that why they'd had Mr. Vance announce the winner? So they could make a hasty departure and avoid questions about the lottery? Did they believe interest in the distribution of lottery funds would wane? But what if they had mishandled the funds and curiosity continued to mount during their absence? What if there was a public outcry for an investigation? If the funds were mishandled by his parents, what would that mean for their future? Had his mother calculated the risks when she decided to organize a lottery? Morgan was certain there was more to this lottery than collecting money for charity, and while he didn't want to believe his mother had planned to reimburse the Amoskeag Company with lottery funds, he couldn't rule out the idea. She had told him she'd come up with a plan to repay the money to the company. He wanted to believe she wouldn't stoop so low, but he couldn't erase the thought from his mind. Had his father agreed to this scheme? He didn't want to believe his father had given his approval, yet he doubted his mother could have managed without his knowledge.

Morgan now dreaded going to bed at night. The darkness produced more worries than rest. If his parents had misused the money, would they step forward and admit their wrongdoing? And if they didn't, would he have the courage to speak out against his own parents? The thought was chilling. Night after night, he prayed he wouldn't be forced to make that difficult decision. Morgan attempted to tamp down his rising alarm. He prayed his mother could offer him answers. Answers that would ease his fears and foreboding.

As the cold wind howled and blew a frigid December snowstorm into Manchester, Morgan longed to set matters aright with Mellie—not in bits and pieces but in one cleansing confession. But until he knew more details regarding the lottery, he could offer no more than bits and pieces. When Mr. Vance announced his mother had organized the lottery, Morgan had been stunned. Since then, thoughts of Mellie's potential rejection mingled with worries about his parents paraded through his mind like soldiers marching into battle. While he'd anticipated revealing his identity to Mellie would prove difficult, he'd never considered the truth would be compounded by his mother's involvement in the lottery. Once she learned everything, he doubted Mellie would want to become a member of the Stark family.

Walking toward town, his thoughts bounded between the lottery and the situation with the copied drawings and patent. But his worries momentarily melted when he entered the shop and Mellie graced him with a dazzling smile. He stomped the snow from his boots and lifted his hand in greeting.

A customer sat posing for his silhouette, and Mellie returned her attention to snipping his profile. Morgan wished he could cut a silhouette of Mellie perched on her stool with scissors and paper. What a perfect keepsake that would make, sitting on his bedside table.

After shaking the snow from his coat and draping it across his arm, he strode toward a display of frames. There were several new photographs arranged in Mr. Harrison's studio, as well as a new painting hanging on the wall—a sweeping landscape that portrayed the beauty of an autumn afternoon in New Hampshire. At the sound of footsteps, Morgan turned.

"Admiring the new painting, I see." Mr. Harrison moved to Morgan's side. "It's quite something, don't you think?"

Morgan nodded. "Did you purchase this for one of your customers?"

Asa shook his head. "No. It was a gift from Samuel—for acting as his host while he was in Manchester. Quite a lovely gift of appreciation. I attempted to refuse, but he wouldn't hear of it."

"He's left?" Morgan arched his brows. There were so many questions he'd wanted to ask Mr. Knoll. Questions about what objects he'd purchased—or stolen. The thought raced through his mind, and he silently chastised himself. It wasn't fair to condemn the man without proof.

"He left several weeks ago."

"So, he was returning home?" Morgan shoved his hands in his pockets.

"No, he had unfinished business elsewhere that required his attention." He drew his hand along his angular jaw.

"I didn't realize he'd completed his business here in Manchester." Morgan had hoped to question Mr. Knoll, but maybe Mr. Harrison could provide a few answers. He couldn't let the moment pass without at least trying to discover more. "Did Mr. Knoll locate that artwork he was intent upon finding? I believe he said you had news of some new piece—a combination of art and sculpture."

"You have a good memory. Mr. Knoll said he had mentioned the piece to you. No, we haven't completed that transaction as yet, but I'm hopeful he'll have good news to share and soon."

Morgan's stomach tightened. "Where did Mr. Knoll go? Somewhere interesting, I'm sure."

"A visit to Washington. He wanted to spend a brief time with friends and hoped to accomplish some business while there."

Fear crawled up Morgan's spine. Was Mr. Knoll going to make inquiries at the patent offices in Washington? He grasped Mr. Harrison's forearm. "Who is Franklin Montee?"

Mr. Harrison's gaze dropped to his arm. "What's come over you, Morgan? I have never heard of Franklin Montee, but from the way you clenched my arm, I assume he is of great importance to you."

Morgan's face and ears tingled with heat. "Surely Mr. Knoll mentioned Mr. Montee's name when the two of you were discussing your latest project."

Mr. Harrison frowned. "As I said, I've never heard of the man.

Do you think he might have been a customer?" He looked over his shoulder toward the counter. "I could look in my ledgers and see if I've photographed a customer by that name."

"No. He wasn't a customer. But perhaps he has some affiliation with a patent or the patent office in Washington?"

The older man shook his head. "I don't know anyone who works in the patent office. Samuel was going to meet an attorney friend who handles patent work, Lawrence Bledsoe. They planned to visit the patent office. Other than that, I don't know anything about patents. I'm sorry I can't help you."

Morgan knew he shouldn't continue pressing Mr. Harrison, but he couldn't help himself. "What did Mr. Knoll think of the drawings I had stored in your back room?" He arched his brows. "As an engineer, I'm sure he offered his opinion to you?"

Mr. Harrison's eyes clouded with concern. "Are you feeling unwell, Morgan? I don't know why you're asking me these strange questions, but I can't help you. I don't know this Franklin Montee, and Mr. Knoll never spoke to me about your drawings."

An unbearable roar vibrated in Morgan's ears as he watched Mr. Harrison walk toward the stairs.

"Are you ready to go?" Mellie placed her hand on his arm.

He turned and noticed she had already donned her cloak and hat. Why did everything seem easier to endure when she was near? Still, the last thing he wanted was to cause her more concern, so he forced a smile and offered her his arm. "I'm ready for anything with you by my side."

As they walked, Morgan's thoughts returned to his earlier discussion with Mr. Harrison. Mellie prodded him to confide in her, but he revealed very little. They were a short distance from the boardinghouse when she pulled him to a stop.

Taking his hands in hers, she faced him. "I can see that something has upset you. In fact, something has been bothering you for quite some time. You're not yourself. What's so terrible that you can't tell me? What is wrong, Morgan?"

"Mellie, it's nothing for you to worry about."

"If it concerns you, it concerns me. So long as you're honest with me, there's nothing you can say or do that will change how I've come to feel about you."

His stomach lurched, and he drew her into his arms. He wanted to tell her the truth about everything—who he really was and what he was doing at the Stark Mills, but he didn't want to do it now. How could he tell her when he didn't have all the answers himself? Right now, with the rest of his life in chaos, she was the only stable thing he could hold on to.

Mellie finished her supper and pushed away from the table. If she didn't hurry, she'd be late getting to the shop. Her shoulders slumped with weariness from the long hours at the mill. She longed to go upstairs with the other girls and lie across her bed. Granted, cutting silhouettes wasn't difficult, but between her job at the mill and her cutting portraits at the photography shop, she never seemed to get enough sleep. She went to bed weary and woke up the same way. And now, with Morgan out of sorts since the night of the ball, she was having difficulty going to sleep at night.

He wouldn't discuss what was bothering him, but ever since he talked to Mr. Harrison last week, his odd behavior had compounded. She'd expected to see a quick return to his usual cheery nature, but that hadn't happened. Instead, he remained troubled and lost in his own thoughts.

The most he'd shared with her was that he needed to resolve several difficult problems, which he couldn't discuss with anyone at the moment. She'd suggested he use his free time in the evenings to work toward a solution—partly because she hoped the added time would help him overcome his problems and partly because his moody countenance caused her customers discomfort. While he'd agreed with her decision, he insisted he would still come by at closing time to walk her home. And for that she was most grateful. Their walks were her favorite time of the day.

She shrugged into her coat, preparing body and mind for her trek in the freezing nighttime air. On nights such as this, most of the girls remained at home, and Mellie doubted there would be many customers. Still, she had to go. Tying a woolen scarf over her lower face, she started down the front steps. Keeping her head bowed against the cold wind, she felt her fingers beginning to turn numb after walking only a quarter of a mile.

Finally arriving at the store, Mellie rushed to the stove and stood facing the fire, hoping to warm herself before any customers came in. When she'd thawed a bit, she removed her coat, scarf, and bonnet, grabbed her chair, and positioned it near the stove. She might as well enjoy a bit of heat while she could, for there would be no comforting fire when she returned home to the frigid attic later this evening.

Her eyes were at half-mast when the bell over the door jingled and startled her to attention. She jumped to her feet and forced a smile at the well-dressed matron, who surely would be interested in a photograph rather than a silhouette. Mellie approached the woman, all the while thinking that once she fetched Mr. Harrison, she could return to her cozy spot in front of the fire.

The woman, wearing a carriage dress of green satin and a black satin pelisse trimmed in ermine, let her gaze wander around the shop before picking up one of Mellie's Scheren-schnitte cuttings of a bucolic scene with deer, rabbits, and children leading a cow and goat. She returned it to the shelf and exchanged it for an intricate cutting of butterflies and flowers.

She glanced at Mellie. "These are quite lovely. I'd heard Mr. Harrison had someone creating lovely paper cuttings in his shop, but I didn't imagine anything so beautiful."

"Thank you," Mellie said with a nod. "Is there something I can help you with? Mr. Harrison does the photography. If you'd like to speak with him, I—"

She lifted her hand and stayed Mellie. "No. You're the one I want to speak with."

"Would you like a silhouette?"

The woman shook her head. "No, thank you. What I would like is to have you attend a party I'm hosting Saturday evening." Mellie's mouth dropped open, and the woman quickly continued, "Not as a guest, of course, but to perform."

Mellie arched her brows. "Perform? I'm not sure I understand."

She cleared her throat. "I didn't phrase that properly. I would like to have you cut silhouettes of my guests—at least those who would enjoy having a profile made of them—as a form of entertainment, as well as a gift. I believe ten dollars would be a fair payment. I realize it's not much notice, but I've been out of town and now find myself rushing to make all of the party arrangements. You wouldn't need to begin until nine o'clock, and I would provide you with a separate room in which to work." She smiled. "I wouldn't expect you to sit in the midst of the party to cut the profiles."

Mellie didn't miss the woman's intended slight. She didn't want the hired help mingling as though she were a guest. And

Mellie did wonder at the belatedness of the offer. Had the woman truly been out of town? Had she hoped to engage some-one else to entertain her guests and been refused? Was Mellie an afterthought when the woman's preferred entertainment wasn't available? A part of her wanted to say she wasn't inter-ested, but to make ten dollars in a single evening was more than she could decline. Earning a week's wages in one evening was unheard of—at least for her. Part of the money would provide her sister with an unexpected and welcome surprise. The rest Mellie would use for Christmas gifts for her niece and nephew.

She set aside her earlier thoughts and nodded. "I would be pleased to provide paper cuttings for your guests on Saturday evening."

The woman turned toward the front of the shop. "Dear me! Look at it snowing out there. I need to be on my way. I don't want my carriage getting stuck in the snow." She strode toward the door. "Do wear the most appropriate dress you own, and I'll send my carriage here to the shop at eight-thirty to provide you transportation."

She was out the door before Mellie could ask her name. And now that the woman was gone, Mellie realized she'd need Mr. Harrison's permission to be away from the shop an hour before closing. And what if Mrs. Richards wouldn't grant her special permission to return home late that evening? There would be no way to send word to the woman. If she couldn't keep her appointment, there would be nothing to do but send word with the carriage driver the night of the party. No doubt the hostess of the party would arrive at the shop the following Monday and make a scene.

First things first. There was no need to dwell on the negative. She walked to the rear of the store and called to Mr. Harrison.

No doubt he was developing pictures. She disliked disturbing him, but a moment later he appeared at the top of the steps. "Is there a customer desiring a photograph?"

She shook her head. "No, but I need to speak with you when you can spare me a few minutes."

He jogged down the steps. "No time like the present. My photographs need more time to develop in the solution. What can I do for you?"

Mellie detailed her conversation with the woman. "I feel foolish for not asking her name, but judging from her attire and the coach that awaited her outside, I feel certain she's a member of Manchester society."

Mr. Harrison sat down in the makeshift parlor he used for photographing customers. "I see. Well, this sounds like an excellent opportunity for you to show off your talents and to make a handsome sum. You've improved my business in the shop, so how could I refuse you?"

"Thank you, Mr. Harrison. Now, I must hope my boarding-house keeper will give me permission to return home after ten o'clock on Saturday night. If she isn't agreeable, I'll be here instead of entertaining guests at a society party."

"If she doesn't readily agree, I'm sure the promise of a few pastries from the party and an extra twenty-five cents will do the trick." He chuckled. "Or perhaps a free silhouette?"

Mellie nodded. "I'll keep your idea in mind, but let's hope I don't have to resort to such devices."

When Morgan arrived, she didn't mention the Saturday night engagement. In his current mood, she doubted whether he'd hear a word she said. Besides, part of her ten-dollar payment would go toward a Christmas gift for him, and she wanted it to be a surprise.

Chapter

TWENTY-TWO

A FRIGID WIND CUT THROUGH MORGAN'S WOOL JACKET as he rode toward home. He'd received a brief message from his mother stating she and his father had arrived home, she would be hosting her annual Christmas party on Saturday, and he was expected to be present. Nothing more. No mention as to why they had gone to Boston without a word, no mention of the lottery, and no mention of the funds owed to the Amoskeag Company. Morgan needed answers, and now that his parents were home, he hoped to learn the truth.

He circled around to the rear of the house and dismounted. Though Lucy was nowhere in sight, the aroma of biscuits and baked chicken greeted him the moment he stepped inside. His mouth watered as he continued down the hallway to his father's study. The older man sat at his desk shuffling through a stack of papers. Morgan tapped on the doorjamb and cleared his throat.

His father smiled and pushed to his feet. "Morgan! Good

to see you, my boy. I wasn't expecting a visit from you. I was certain you'd be here for the party on Saturday, but—"

"Is Mother here? I'd like to speak to both of you. It's important."

His father's smile faded. "Something wrong?"

"Yes. And it will be easier if I can speak to both of you at the same time."

His father gestured to one of the chairs. "Sit down and I'll fetch her. I believe she and Lucy are going over the place settings for dinner on Saturday."

Morgan dropped into one of the chairs opposite his father's desk and gathered his thoughts. He'd need to remain calm. If he was accusatory, his mother wouldn't be forthcoming. He'd tried that approach with her in the past. She'd fold her hands in her lap, tighten her lips into a thin line, and stare into the distance.

At the sound of murmuring voices in the hallway, he clenched his jaw. The veins in his neck constricted into tight cords. He forced himself to inhale a deep cleansing breath when his parents appeared at the doorway.

"Morgan!" His mother beamed at him. "I am delighted to see you, but I must say your visit is unexpected. I hope you haven't arrived to tell me you can't attend Saturday night's party." She wagged her finger. "I won't hear any excuses. Your grandfather is arriving on Friday, and I want the entire family, small though it be, in attendance on Saturday."

Morgan sighed. She was prepared to wage war before the first skirmish. "You may set aside your concerns about the party, Mother. I've come to speak with you and Father about more serious matters." He gestured to the chairs. "Please sit down."

His mother momentarily looked at the chairs before turning her gaze toward the hallway. "I do hope this will be brief. What with our travels to Boston and the party only days away, I have pressing details that require my attention."

"My questions will be brief, but your answers may require more time."

Her eyes clouded with reluctance as she slowly lowered herself into one of the chairs. She glanced at her husband before turning to face Morgan. "Well? We're here. Do begin."

"I have a number of questions about the lottery you initiated, the funds that were taken from the Amoskeag Company, and your sudden departure for Boston."

He inhaled a deep breath, but before he could say anything more, his mother interrupted. "I still haven't heard a question, Morgan. Please get to the point."

"If that's what you prefer, then here are my questions. Did the two of you agree to initiate the lottery? Was it your plan to use the lottery proceeds to repay the Amoskeag Company the money you'd taken?" He glanced at his father. "How have the lottery proceeds been used? Why did you depart for Boston without a word—and before the lottery drawing?"

His father leaned back in his chair. "That's a lot of questions, Morgan, and I suppose you deserve answers."

Morgan rested his arms on his thighs and met his father's gaze. "The town deserves answers, Father. There are concerns about the use of the money raised through the lottery." He turned to his mother. "That lottery may have raised a great deal of money, but it also inflicted pain and suffering on families in Manchester and beyond."

"Pain and suffering? You always did have a flair for the dramatic, Morgan. How could a lottery—?"

"I'll tell you how, Mother. A little boy died because one of the mill girls purchased lottery tickets rather than send her earnings home for her parents to purchase medicine or heat their home. Other families suffered in much the same way. Workers bought those tickets, certain they'd be the one to take home the winnings—and their families suffered as a result."

Anger flashed in his mother's eyes. "That isn't my fault. If their families suffered, it's because they made a poor choice."

"I agree they made poor choices, but it was you who presented them with that choice. Don't you see?"

Her eyes softened, and she leaned back in the chair. "I was trying to help so the Stark Mills would be the first company with circular looms. I didn't consider the possibility that purchasing lottery tickets would inflict harm on anyone. Truly, I didn't." She directed a beseeching look across the desk toward his father. "Did you consider such a thing, William?"

"No, although I should have. I know there are men who gamble at cards or bet on horses without regard for the well-being of their families. But I never thought a lottery could create such misery." He looked at Morgan. "If I'd given the matter the thought it deserved, I would have more fervently objected. It doesn't change anything that happened to those families, but the funds weren't used to pay back the Amoskeag Company."

His mother nodded. "That's true, Morgan. Your grandfather wired money to the bank, but I had already initiated the lottery. The advertising had commenced, the tickets were distributed to the various shop owners, so I moved forward and decided we'd donate the money to charity." She twisted a lacy handkerchief between her fingers. "What were your other questions?" Her voice faltered.

"The lottery funds?"

"Oh yes. Well, I've invited a number of children from the orphanage to Saturday's party, as well as those from poor families in town." She continued to thread the handkerchief through her fingers. "What if we donated a portion of the funds to the family of the child who died? Would that help? I've only used a small portion toward the children's party. The money is in your father's personal bank account."

Morgan forced a weak smile. "I'm not certain that's wise. Perhaps a separate account should be set up at the bank and a committee appointed to decide how the funds will be used."

"That's a wonderful idea, Morgan. I'll take charge of the—"

Morgan shook his head. "No, Mother. I don't think any member of the Stark family should be on the committee. Perhaps the president of the bank and representatives of the working class would be more appropriate than a group of wealthy residents."

"I suppose you're right." She turned to her husband. "I'm sure you can arrange matters at the bank, can't you, William?"

"Yes, and I'll ask Mr. Frederick to serve as chairman of the committee. Very well, my boy. I will give you or Mr. Frederick an accounting of the funds received and then replace any of the money your mother has used for Saturday's party. The lottery was a tragic mistake. I should have insisted we find another way to secure the funds or let a competing mill be first with the circular looms. My decision to agree with your mother was influenced by my desire for wealth and respect."

His mother lifted the corner of her handkerchief to her eye. "I was only trying to help."

"I do believe you were trying to help, Mother. I've made mistakes in my efforts to help others, too." Thoughts of his double life came to mind. What would Mellie do when she learned the truth? "Unfortunately, those mistakes can lead to heartbreak." He hoped that wouldn't be true for him, but he couldn't blame Mellie if she never spoke to him again.

"Thank you for expressing some understanding, Morgan." She began to push up from her chair.

"Wait. Neither of you has mentioned why you traveled to Boston. Was it to avoid any questions about the lottery funds?"

His father shook his head. "The journey to Boston was totally unrelated to the lottery. I received word that my dear friend Amos March was in poor health, and he wanted me to visit as soon as possible."

His mother chuckled. "From the wording of his telegram, we thought he was going to die within the month."

Morgan arched his brows. "And?"

His father shrugged. "Amos said it was the only way he could get me to Boston for a visit. Once there, we decided to stay for a while. Your mother enjoys his wife, Harriet, and when the two of them weren't shopping, Harriet was hosting teas or insisting we attend the theater. We should have sent word, but you aren't able to come to the house much and the thought didn't enter my mind. I'm sorry if we worried you."

"As am I." His mother patted his arm. "I do have a great deal to complete before the party on Saturday, so if we've cleared the air, I trust I can return to sorting decorations and place settings."

Morgan nodded. He wasn't certain his mother understood the depth of the myriad problems created by the lottery, yet her willingness to step back and let others decide how the proceeds would be distributed pleased him. For that much he was thankful.

⁓

Morgan moved to the washbasin and stared at his image in the small oval mirror hanging from a nail. He wanted to believe he was a man who simply longed to prove himself and help others. Had his desire to succeed become more important than helping others? He had to admit he'd made mistakes. Concealing his true identity had begun with good intent, but what if someone at the party recognized him? His plans to discover problems and create better conditions in the mills would likely come to a halt. He needed to face that reality, for tonight one of his mother's guests might identify him. Though she'd said none of her guests would be managers from the mills who might know him, he couldn't depend upon that. After all, she didn't know all those he'd met.

Morgan glanced at his pocket watch. In order to arrive before the other guests and have time to change into his formal attire, he needed to be on his way. If he could have come up with any excuse to avoid attending, he would have.

After shrugging into his heavy wool coat, he pulled open the front door and hurried toward the livery. He'd arranged for a horse the previous day and hoped the animal would be saddled and ready. Walking into a roomful of guests wearing work clothes wouldn't bode well for him.

When he arrived at the mansion a short time later, he took the horse to the stables and entered through the rear door. Bounding up the steps two at a time, he hurried to his bedroom and slipped inside. His mother hadn't doubted his arrival, for a tub filled with warm water awaited him, his evening suit already set out. He shed his work clothes and settled into the cast-iron enameled tub. He hadn't bathed in a tub since he'd moved into the boardinghouse, and the heated water soothed his worries. Leaning his head against the back of the tub, he closed his eyes.

A knock on the bedroom door jarred him to attention. "Morgan! You need to hurry. I trust you're not asleep in the bathtub. The guests will be arriving soon." When he didn't immediately respond, his mother knocked again, this time with more vigor. "Did you hear me?"

He sighed. "Yes, Mother. Every word."

Once he'd completed his bath and dressed, Morgan returned downstairs, again using the rear stairs. He stopped at his father's study. After a light tap on the door, he opened it and peered inside. Both his father and grandfather looked up and greeted him.

Morgan stepped to his grandfather's side and embraced him. "It's good to see you, Grandfather. You look well. I trust you're feeling healthy?"

His grandfather motioned to the nearby chairs, and the two of them sat down opposite his father's desk. "My health isn't important. We all know your mother will be pleased to see me die so she can have all my money." He snorted and shook his head. "After listening to your father, I'm thinking you've lost your mental faculties. What you're doing at the mills makes no sense to me, Morgan. I'm sure there's more to it than what we've had time to discuss, but this plan of yours seems foolhardy."

Before they could talk further, his mother entered the room. "Come along, all of you. The guests will be arriving at any moment." When Morgan neared her side, her lips curved in a smile. "I know you won't be pleased, but I've partnered you with Isabelle Armstrong, your childhood sweetheart. She's looking forward to reviving your friendship." His father and grandfather continued down the hallway toward the large foyer while Morgan remained behind with his mother. "She has remained enamored with you for all these years."

Morgan took a backward step. "That's impossible. I haven't seen her since I left for boarding school."

"That isn't true, Morgan. Isabelle said you saw her during the summers when you came home."

He frowned. "I was in Manchester for only a week or two during my summer vacations. The remainder of the time was spent at our summer home or traveling abroad." He tilted his head. "Surely you haven't forgotten all those summers spent on the coast."

With a dismissive wave of her hand, she said, "Well, regardless, she remembers you, and she's eager to fan the embers of lost love."

Morgan burst into laughter. "Fan the embers of lost love? Really, Mother? Have you been reading romance novels? I hear they've become quite popular, even though most women deny reading them."

She clasped a hand to her heart. "Morgan Stark! How dare you speak to your mother in such a manner?" She scowled and tapped his chest with her index finger. "I expect you to be on your best behavior tonight and to show Isabelle Armstrong every attention. The two of you would make a perfect match. She's from a good family. One with a great deal of wealth to their name, which is always a good thing."

Morgan shook his head, disgusted his mother was attempting to match him with one of her guests. Even worse, she wanted him to marry someone who would bring wealth into the marriage. She obviously cared little about compatibility. If she had, she wouldn't have married his father.

"Come along." She marched off, leaving him in her wake. This night was proving to be even more difficult than he'd imagined.

Slowly, he followed his mother down the long hall that was decorated with greens and holly berries. He stopped and looked into the grand parlor that adjoined the oversize dining room. His mother had spared no expense with her decorations. An assortment of candles and bows of every size, shape, and fabric, more greenery, and myriad crystal had been arranged on the mantels and side tables. A glowing candelabra centered the dining room table. He couldn't deny the decorations were more beautiful than any she'd ever displayed. He wondered if his grandfather had paid for these, as well.

His parents began introducing their guests to Morgan and his grandfather. Although Morgan had likely seen or met most of them at some time in the distant past, he hadn't yet recognized anyone.

Then his mother nudged him with her elbow. "Isabelle has just arrived with her parents. Don't embarrass me."

"I only intentionally embarrassed you when I was a child. As an adult, such incidents have been pure happenstance." He tipped his head to the side and grinned.

Isabelle entered, holding her father's arm. She was a beautiful young woman. Any available man would be proud to court her, so why did his mother believe she cared for him? Truth be told, he never believed Isabelle thought of him as anything other than a playmate and friend. Besides, their times together had been short-lived, and they'd been too young to develop serious feelings for each other. Still, if any portion of what his mother said was true, he didn't want to humiliate Isabelle in any way. If she indicated she was interested in him as a suitor, he'd gently let her know he wasn't available. Mellie had already won his heart.

For a brief time before dinner, the guests mingled in the grand parlor, allowing them time to admire the decorations and compliment the host and hostess. At least that was how Morgan viewed the interval before dinner. Since he'd been paired with Isabelle, he decided to use the time to his advantage.

Isabelle's jeweled hairpins shimmered in the candlelight as she glanced around the room. "The house is truly festive. Your mother always decorates with such fine taste." She looked at him with a sweet smile. "I hope you won't mind my saying, but you've changed a great deal, Morgan. I wouldn't have recognized you. Of course, it's been a number of years since we've seen each other. You've gone through quite a transformation. I've always remembered you as a rather gangly young fellow with few interests other than riding and skipping rocks." She chuckled. "I suppose we all change once we leave those younger years behind us."

"Very true." He returned her smile. If she remembered him as a gangly youth with few interests, why would she now be interested in him as a suitor? Had her mother encouraged her to consider him as a possible husband? "I've discovered there's much more to life than riding and skipping rocks, just as I'm sure you've come to enjoy more than your dolls and play tea sets."

"Oh, you remember how I forced you to pretend to have tea with my dollies. I'm charmed." She removed an ivory fan from her waist and snapped it open. "Yes, like you, my interests have evolved through the years, and the list of those I consider dear friends has progressed, as well." She hesitated. "I find it difficult to believe a lovely young lady hasn't captured your attention by now."

She had opened the door to exploring other romantic possibilities, and he decided to enter in. There might not be another opportunity this evening. "And I find it difficult to believe you haven't been besieged by an onslaught of marriage proposals. Have none of those men met your expectations? Or perhaps your parents haven't approved of them?"

Isabelle lowered her eyes. "In truth, you've hit upon my dilemma." She lifted her gaze again and sighed. "My parents don't know I am in love and have promised him my hand. He wants to meet them and pledge his love and ask permission to marry me, but I know my parents need to adjust to the idea that I would wed someone who is, in their estimation, beneath me." A tear formed in the corner of her eye, and she dabbed it with a lace-edged handkerchief. "He is a good and honorable man who loves me—and I love him. Sometimes I wish I had been born into a normal family, one that didn't place all their value on wealth." She took a step closer and lowered her voice. "I don't want to offend or hurt you in any way, Morgan, but before coming here this evening, I determined that I would be truthful with you."

One part of Morgan wanted to weep with her, for he understood her pain; the other part wanted to jump in the air and click his heels, for he now knew she didn't desire him as a suitor. "Thank you for your honesty, Isabelle. You need not harbor any concerns about hurting me. You see, I find myself in the same predicament as you. I'm in love with a young woman, and she, too, is of a different social class. I haven't told my parents—they won't approve. At least my mother won't approve. I haven't yet asked the young lady for her hand, since there are some other obstacles to be overcome before that can occur. But I know she is the one I want to have by my side for the rest of my life." He grinned. "So, it seems we can now enjoy the party without the worry of meeting our parents' expectations. Am I right?"

She returned his smile. "I'm beyond belief that both of us find ourselves in the same situation. Yet I am so relieved. I arrived here overwhelmed with both worry and heartache. I knew my parents had spoken with your parents about a possible match, and my mother indicated you would be delighted at the prospect."

He stepped closer to her. "My mother suggested you would be delighted if I asked to court you. I doubt they had any idea this conversation would ever take place." He nodded toward the fireplace. "Right now, our mothers are deep in conversation and looking this way. I'm sure they're watching us with our heads together and think they can begin planning a wedding for next year."

She laughed and nodded her agreement. "It appears we're lining up to go in for dinner. I'm so thankful we had our talk. Now we can enjoy a delightful evening of conversation and dancing."

"And let our parents think whatever they like throughout the evening. I'm sure my mother will be dismayed when she discovers you found me a bore and rejected my suit."

Isabelle slipped her hand into the crook of his arm. "I do hope that when both of us are wed to the people we love, we can remain friends. I know you would find my fellow good company."

They proceeded into the dining room, and he smiled down at her. "I would like that very much."

Strange how things could change so quickly. What he'd decided would be a dreadful night had now made a complete about-face. He took a deep breath and looked forward to an evening of relaxation and fun.

Chapter

TWENTY-THREE

Mid-December

AFTER WORK ON SATURDAY, MELLIE WALKED HOME WITH Cora, Clara, and Phebe, her thoughts a jumble. Tonight she'd be cutting silhouettes at the party being hosted by the woman who'd come to the photography shop earlier in the week. Ever since the woman had departed the shop in such a rush, Mellie had been chastising herself for not asking her name. To make matters more difficult, Mellie hadn't been given any particulars. How many guests would be attending? Would there be children there as well as adults? Would someone be available to assist her? If too many guests came into the room and expected to have their silhouettes cut at once, that could easily lead to mayhem. Perhaps when Mellie arrived, she should suggest that the hostess give each guest a piece of paper indicating the approximate time the person's cutting would be done.

During the day, her thoughts had swirled and she'd been unable to focus on her looms. After having to shut down one of the looms to repair broken threads on five occasions, the overseer had issued her a warning: Any further broken threads and there would be less pay in her envelope this week. For the remainder of the day, she'd forced herself to keep her eyes fixed on the flying shuttle and the cotton threads. Working extra hours at the photography shop would do her little good if her pay at the mill was reduced.

"What's wrong with you, Mellie?" Cora nudged her arm as they neared the boardinghouse. "Did you hear Clara ask if you could slip out of work and go with us tonight?"

Mellie jerked to attention and looked at the twins. "What? No, I guess I didn't hear you. Where are you going?"

"You must be thinking about Morgan. You've had a faraway look in your eyes all day." Clara giggled. "Are you thinking about marriage?" She clasped a hand to her chest. "He's asked you to marry him, hasn't he?"

"No, he has not mentioned marriage, Clara. But if he does, you and Cora will be the first to know." Mellie pulled her cloak tight against the bitter wind. "Where are you going tonight?"

Clara grinned. "To the Lyceum. L. N. Fowler, the famous phrenologist, is going to be there. He's going to give a lecture, and afterward he'll choose several members of the audience and conduct head readings and analyses of their skulls. I do hope he chooses me." She looked at her sister. "Wouldn't it be grand if he chose both Cora and me? I think he might be interested in us since we're twins. Please say you'll go with us."

"Thank you for inviting me, but I can't go, Clara." Mellie opened the front door of the boardinghouse, then turned to Clara while she removed her cloak.

"You're going to miss out on a wonderful lecture. I do hope he'll choose Cora and me. Do you think he might?"

Mellie shrugged. "Perhaps, but if he should select you or Cora, I hope you won't place any value in what he says. I've read there are many scientists who say phrenology isn't scientific."

Clara draped her cloak across one of the hooks in the hallway and frowned. "I've read articles that say it is most scientific, but I'll see what I think after the lecture." She started toward the dining room. "Do you think Mr. Harrison would let you leave for a couple hours this evening?"

Mellie shook her head. "No. I'll tell you why when we go upstairs after supper." Thus far, she hadn't mentioned the party to anyone other than Mr. Harrison and Mrs. Richards. Morgan had been so detached she hadn't mentioned it to him. And she hadn't told the twins or Phebe because she'd half expected the woman to send a cancelation.

After supper, they all went upstairs. Phebe, Cora, and Clara rummaged through their dresses, each one trying to decide what to wear. While they were dressing, Mellie removed a pale blue shot-silk dress from her trunk and carried it to her bed.

Once Cora had fastened her dress, she did a quick turnabout. "What do you think about this one?"

"It's perfect," Mellie said.

The words had barely escaped Mellie's lips when Cora's gaze fastened on the dress lying across the bed. She pointed a finger at the gown and looked at Mellie. "You're not going to wear that beautiful gown to work at the photography shop, are you?" She shot Mellie a look of disbelief.

Mellie loosened her hair from the tight knot at the back of her head and picked up her hairbrush. "Yes, but I'll be at the shop only until eight-thirty."

Clara moved to her sister's side, and together the two of them stood staring down at the dress. Clara shook her head, a slow smile curving her lips. "And then where are you going? Do you and Morgan have some secret plans?"

"This has nothing to do with Morgan." Mellie explained to the twins about the request she'd received. "I agreed to attend, but other than what I've told you, I have no other details."

Cora's brow furrowed. "Truly? I know you wouldn't tell us an untruth, but I'm surprised you wouldn't at least ask the woman's name."

Mellie nodded. "I know. I've been upset with myself ever since I accepted the request. But when the lady saw it was snowing, she rushed from the shop before I could ask her. Please don't mention this to the other girls. If the carriage doesn't arrive for me, I wouldn't want to explain to everyone."

Clara nodded. "You know we can keep a secret."

"I do." Mellie nodded toward the bedroom door. "All three of you better hurry or you're going to be late for the Lyceum. You'll need to locate seats at the front of the auditorium if you want Mr. Fowler to choose you."

Mellie's comment was enough to send the girls into a flurry of activity. Soon they were out the door and on their way into town together.

When they neared the photography shop, Mellie bid them good-bye, but Cora stopped beside her outside the shop door. "We'll come by after the lecture and make sure you're not here. If the carriage doesn't arrive, we can walk home with you."

Clara bobbed her head. "But if you do go to that fancy party, we'll want to hear all about it. I would love to see all the beautiful gowns—and the food! I wonder what they'll serve. You'll tell us everything, won't you, Mellie?"

Mellie smiled. "Of course. I'll do my best to remember every detail."

Clara grasped her sister's coat sleeve. "Come on or we're going to be the last ones to arrive. We'll be eager to hear all the details."

Mellie waved as they disappeared from sight.

⚘

The carriage arrived promptly at eight-thirty. The driver stepped inside Mr. Harrison's shop and announced his arrival. Mellie stepped to the rear of the shop, retrieved her cloak, and bid Mr. Harrison good-night before she returned to the front of the store.

"I'm ready," she said to the driver after gathering her scissors and materials.

He held open the front door for her, then hurried ahead to open the carriage door. With a light touch to her elbow, he assisted her inside. Mellie leaned back against the carriage's thick leather seat as they started down the snow-covered street. She was gazing out the window when the coach departed town and rolled into the adjoining countryside. Moonlight glistened on fresh-fallen snow, and the distant glow of light could be seen in the windows of an occasional house as they passed by. After a short time, she leaned forward to gain a better view. Though it was dark outside, she was certain this was the same route she'd taken with Morgan on their sleigh ride.

A lump rose in her throat when the carriage turned into a driveway that fronted a stately white mansion. She was sure this was the house Morgan had pointed out as the Stark home. Another look out the window and there was no doubt. This was the house. She was going to be attending a party at the home of the woman who had arranged the lottery. She wanted to escape the carriage and flee back to town. Yet that was a ridiculous idea. She had to go inside. She had to appear pleased to be there. And she had to cut flawless silhouettes.

The carriage door opened, and the gloved driver extended his hand to help her down. "Mrs. Stark gave instructions for you to enter through the front door. Hired help usually enters at the rear, but I was told you're an exception." His features pinched into a tight expression as he looked her up and down.

"Thank you for your assistance." She could feel him staring after her as she walked toward the front door. He was likely feeling slighted—and she couldn't say that she blamed him.

The brass door knocker had barely had time to sound when a maid dressed in gray with a white apron and cap opened the door. Mellie offered a smile. "Good evening. I'm Mellie Blanchard." She nodded toward her bag. "I'm here to—"

"I know why you're here. Follow me, miss." She glanced over her shoulder. "The guests are having supper in the dining room, and all those children will be served in the upstairs playroom. That's going to be a fine mess to clean up come morning." She continued to mumble under her breath while she escorted Mellie into a well-appointed sitting room on the top floor of the house.

Mellie glanced around. "Will Mrs. Stark be directing the guests upstairs for their silhouettes?"

"She didn't give me all the particulars. Just said this room would be close to the ballroom, so it would be the best place for you." She nodded toward the hallway. "The ballroom is across the hall—behind those big ivory-and-gold doors. I can bring you tea or coffee, if you'd like."

"Thank you, but I'm fine. I'll just get my scissors and paper set out. Do you think it will be a while before supper is over?"

"The way they sit and take their time between courses, who can say?"

Mellie withdrew her paper, scissors, and three framed silhouettes she'd brought along to display. One was a child's profile, another was the figure of a man standing at a table, and the third a winter scene.

The maid leaned forward and peered at each one. "Them are sure pretty, miss. Maybe I'll come to your shop one day and have you make one of me." A splash of dark pink spread across her cheeks. "I think my man would like it if I had one made for him."

Mellie smiled at her. "In that case, why don't you sit down on that footstool and I'll cut your profile?"

"Oh, no, miss. I don't have . . ."

"There's no charge. My hands are cold and stiff. Cutting your silhouette will be of great help to me."

"Really? Then I'd be pleased to sit for you."

Mellie nodded. "Turn sideways and hold your head up. Do you want me to cut your cap into the profile? If not, why don't you take it off? You can arrange your hair however you'd like."

The maid quickly removed the cap and sat down. "I can't do much with my hair. The missus makes us keep it up and tucked under our caps as much as possible."

Mellie stood and pulled a few curly tendrils around the girl's face, then returned to her chair and snipped a perfect outline of the maid's face. After she had finished the cutting, Mellie extended the silhouette to her. "What do you think? Is it a fair likeness?"

The maid beamed as she traced her finger over the thick paper. "It's lovely, miss. And you even cut my eyelashes and my side curls. You're very kind. I'm beholden to you."

"It was my pleasure." Mellie returned her scissors to the side table alongside the paper. "When I came in, you mentioned some children. Do the Starks have several young children?"

She giggled and shook her head. "Oh, no, ma'am. They just got the one son, and he's grown now. The children are charity cases—youngsters of the poor folks who work in the mills and such. And a group from the orphanage too, I think. It's a Christmas party with a visit from Saint Nicholas, and I suppose she'll have you do their silhouettes. I heard she's using the lottery money to have the party and give the children gifts."

"I see. Well, Mrs. Stark was in a rush when she stopped by the shop, and I didn't understand there would be children in attendance. Not that I mind doing cuttings of children—they're always fascinated when I produce their likenesses."

"Don't you worry none. She'll keep them as far away from the other guests as possible. They'll come up here if she wants you to cut their silhouettes, but she won't let them interfere with the dancing and such. This party is as much about entertaining her rich friends as it is about doing something for the poor." The maid held her silhouette close to her chest. "Thank you again. I better get downstairs now before Mrs. Stark sends someone to look for me."

After the maid had closed the door, Mellie settled into the overstuffed chair. If Mrs. Stark had met with her, Mellie would have suggested she begin cutting silhouettes of the children as soon as she arrived. Instead, she was sitting here twiddling her thumbs and later she'd likely be unable to keep up. She closed her eyes but jerked to attention a short time later when the laughter and chatter of guests drew near.

The door opened, and the woman she now knew to be Mrs. Stark stepped inside and closed the door behind her. "Good evening, Miss Blanchard. I trust you're comfortable. I wanted to stop in to give you a few instructions. You are going to be the big surprise for my guests." Her voice took on a conspiratorial tone. "My Christmas party surprises have become well known throughout Manchester, and friends vie for an invitation to my annual gathering." She preened like a peacock as she glanced about the room. "Is there anything you need?"

Mellie shook her head. "No, but if we could begin soon, it would prove helpful. I understand there are children in attendance. Perhaps I could begin with them? If you don't want them close to the dancing, I could go to their playroom."

"That's an excellent idea. I'll take you down there. The playroom is on the second floor. You can finish with them, and then during the dancing interlude, Saint Nicholas will be here to present their gifts that were purchased with lottery funds. I thought my other guests might enjoy seeing the reaction of poverty-stricken children as they receive their gifts." She shook her head and grimaced. "Poor little waifs."

Mellie inwardly cringed. Mrs. Stark was going to put the children on display so she could feel good about herself—pleased that a portion of the lottery winnings were being spent on the poor children in town. But there would be no presents for Phebe's little brother—not this Christmas, or any Christmas hereafter.

"When you return from downstairs, I'll announce you to my guests, and they can join you in here if they want their silhouettes cut. Is that agreeable?"

"Yes, of course." Mellie gathered her belongings and followed the older woman downstairs to the playroom.

This was going to be a very long evening, yet Mellie's fingers tingled with the excitement of it all.

Chapter
TWENTY-FOUR

WHEN THE MAID ARRIVED IN THE PLAYROOM AND AN-nounced it was time for dinner to be served, Mellie gathered her cutting supplies and promised to begin anew once they'd finished their meal. Several of the children appeared worried she wouldn't return, so she asked if she could remain with them.

The maid leaned close. "Of course you can. I'm thinking they're mighty hungry, what with it being so late. I told the missus it isn't good for children to eat so late at night, but my words fell on deaf ears. At least she agreed to serve them fried chicken, mashed potatoes and gravy, and some warm biscuits, rather than the terrapin soup and saddle of mutton stuffed with oysters that is being presented to her downstairs guests." She shook her head. "It's obvious she isn't one who spends time with children."

The children's eyes grew wide when the servants entered bearing huge platters of food. While most of the youngsters were old enough to serve themselves, Mellie helped serve the younger children. As she watched the children's excitement over the large meal, her thoughts returned to Concord and her niece and nephew. Was her sister able to provide enough food for them? Were they able to keep warm, or was Margaret still struggling to make ends meet? Her sister's letters had become less and less dependable, and she no longer answered Mellie's questions about their welfare. Instead, she wrote about the lessons she was teaching, the weather, or some incidental story about a former neighbor or acquaintance. Margaret's recent letters were so void of personal content, they could have been intended for a stranger rather than her sister.

The girl sitting beside Mellie tugged on her sleeve. "Could I take that biscuit home to my little sister?"

Mellie's heart fractured at the beseeching look in the child's dark eyes. "Of course you can. I'll wrap a few extras, as well." She nodded toward the door, where the servants were returning. "Look! I believe your Christmas dessert has arrived." She grinned at the child. "Maybe we can save a piece of that for your little sister, too."

The children oohed and aahed when a servant lifted the dome off the large silver tray and revealed dozens of cookies of every shape and size. Another servant moved from table to table, delivering cups of hot chocolate topped with whipped cream. Observing the children revel in their dinner and seeing their joyful faces as they chose their Christmas cookies afforded Mellie an hour of pure pleasure.

When the servant offered the tray to Mellie, she looked at her little friend. "What kind do you think your sister would enjoy?" The child pointed to two round sugar cookies frosted with thick white icing and smiled when Mellie removed them from the tray. "I'll ask for a cloth to wrap your biscuit and the cookies."

"Thank you, miss. You're very kind."

"I'm going to speak to one of the maids, and then I must return to cutting silhouettes. It was very nice to visit with you."

She squeezed the girl's hand, then crossed the room to where four servants stood ready to clear the plates. Mellie approached the maid she'd spoken with earlier. "I wonder if you could bring me a cloth to wrap some cookies for one of the children?" She hesitated a moment. "And if there is food left over from their dinner, it would be a lovely gesture if Mrs. Stark would permit the children to take it home to their families."

"Yes, it would, miss. I'll ask her before the dancing begins." The maid walked to a nearby cabinet. "I believe there are clean linens in this cupboard that will work for wrapping cookies." She slid open a drawer, withdrew a white square of cloth, and handed it to Mellie.

"Thank you. I'm going to announce that any children who have finished their dinner and haven't yet had their silhouette cut should come and join me at the other side of the room."

The maid nodded. "The rest can play games until Saint Nicholas arrives with their gifts. I'm sure some of them are more than ready for bed. I told the missus she should have this party in the afternoon, but I didn't win that argument, either."

After helping the little girl wrap her cookies and biscuit, Mellie returned to her earlier position in the room. Several children had formed a line. She inquired if any of them were related, and when two boys said they were brothers, she asked if they'd like to have a cutting made together. They readily agreed, and she posed them sitting face-to-face while she deftly cut their silhouettes.

She handed the cutting to the boy who appeared to be the older of the two. "I hope your mother will be pleased with it."

The boy shook his head. "Our ma died last year, but we'll

paste it on the wall over the bed me and Caleb share at the orphanage." He looked at his younger brother. "Won't we, Caleb?"

The younger boy nodded and smiled as his brother grasped his hand. "Thank you, miss. It's a fine likeness of us."

Mellie swallowed the lump that had formed in her throat as she watched the twosome walk hand in hand to the other side of the room where they joined the others in a game, their youthful exuberance a contradiction to the life they'd been dealt. She marveled at their ability to show joy in spite of their circumstances. But then wasn't that what the Bible instructed? She sighed. It appeared so much easier for children to marvel and find joy in the tiniest thing. What was it about losing one's youth that squelched that joy? She wasn't sure, but she hoped her niece and nephew were still able to experience joy in the small wonders God presented.

She'd finished cutting the silhouette of the last child when she heard the distant sound of music and one of the servants approached her. "You need to go back up to the sitting room across from the ballroom, miss. The missus says the dancing will soon begin, and she'd like you settled in the room before they head upstairs." The maid arched her brows. "You're her big surprise, and she wants to keep you hidden until she's ready to make the announcement."

Mellie attempted to withhold a chuckle. Never before had she been a *big surprise* for anyone or at any event. She hoped Mrs. Stark's guests wouldn't be sorely disappointed.

⚜

At their places at the beautifully appointed dining table, Morgan leaned toward Isabelle. "Tell me a little about this fellow who's captured your heart."

Isabelle swallowed a spoonful of terrapin soup before regaling him with all the fine qualities of the young man she hoped to marry. If he possessed only a few of the qualities Isabelle expressed, Morgan was certain the man would prove an excellent husband for her. His lack of money and social standing would likely be the biggest stumbling blocks in the couple's path to the altar—a fact, he noted, that remained at the forefront of Isabelle's concerns.

"He sounds like a good man, and if given a chance, I'm certain your parents will overlook his lack of financial means." He glanced toward his father. "My father was in much the same position when he asked for my mother's hand. Somehow he convinced my grandfather that he could provide for my mother, and he's proven to be quite a capable husband. However, there have been times when my mother has used her position and family money to manipulate my father and force her decisions upon him." He leaned back when the maid approached to remove his soup bowl. Once the servant stepped away, he offered a broad smile. "However, I'm confident you would avoid that practice if you married someone of lesser financial means."

"Absolutely. I don't think money and social standing should be used to influence and manipulate. Unfortunately, you and I may be the only two at this table who feel that way." Isabelle picked up her fork and knife and cut a piece of mutton. "Now it's your turn. Tell me about your young lady. I'm sure she's quite pretty. Am I right?"

"She is a beautiful woman, but it's her inner beauty and strength I admire the most. She's educated and, at one time in her life, enjoyed a somewhat privileged life. But then tragedy struck her family, and she was forced to leave her home. She's now working in the mills."

Isabelle's gasp caused his mother to look their way. Mrs. Stark frowned at Morgan before turning her attention to Isabelle. "Is there a problem with your dinner, or has my son forgotten his manners and offended you?"

Isabelle shook her head. "No, the dinner is delicious, and Morgan is excellent company. I was merely surprised to hear news of a mutual friend."

His mother's frown slowly disappeared. She turned to another guest, but Morgan stared at her for a moment, disappointed that his mother would think he'd somehow offended a woman in his company. Or perhaps he shouldn't be surprised. After observing his mother's recent behavior, it was clear he didn't know her as well as he thought he did, and she didn't know him that well, either.

After a dessert of French cream cakes, assorted fruit, and coffee, Morgan's mother directed the guests to the winding staircase. "If you'll follow me, we'll adjourn to the ballroom for dancing, and I'll announce my special surprise."

Once the doors to the ballroom opened, guests entered a winter wonderland. Morgan was taken aback by the extravagance of the décor. Candlelight glistened on strings of clear beads suspended from the ceiling. Round tables and chairs that surrounded the dance floor had been covered in white, and a sleigh filled with packages sat on a large white cloth in a far corner. There was a white stage for the musicians, but at least his mother hadn't ruined the wood floors in the ballroom with white paint.

When everyone had entered the room, his mother stepped onto the stage with the musicians. There was no doubt she enjoyed being the center of attention. "My surprise this year will be a special portrait for each of you." She beamed at them. "I will escort you to a room across the hall where you'll sit for your picture. You may pose as a couple or as individuals, but once you return to the ballroom, please don't reveal anything about your experience. At the end of the evening, your portrait will be ready for you to take home." There was a round of applause after the announcement, and then the room began humming with murmurs.

Like Morgan, the guests seemed somewhat perplexed as to the need for secrecy after their photographs were taken. Was his mother having the guests dress in some special attire? He frowned. Was Mr. Harrison the photographer? If so, Mellie hadn't mentioned he'd be at the party. Then again they hadn't discussed much of anything of importance over the past week. He'd been far too consumed with his attempts to discover who had copied the loom drawings. However, unless some itinerant photographer had come into town, Mr. Harrison must be across the hall.

His mother clapped her hands to regain the attention of her guests. "I have prepared a list, and I'll tap you on the shoulder when it's time for you to step across the hall with me. I know all of you will be good sports and participate." She gestured to Morgan's father and grandfather, then added, "Even you two."

Most of the guests, including Morgan and Isabelle, turned to look at the two men. Isabelle leaned toward Morgan. "Your grandfather doesn't look particularly happy about having his picture made."

Morgan hiked a shoulder. "I don't think it's the idea of his picture as much as the fact that he doesn't like to be the center of attention. Mother always manages to somehow embarrass him on his rare visits." He grinned. "Come to think of it, maybe that's why he doesn't visit very often."

His mother signaled the musicians to begin, and soon the guests took to the dance floor. Thankfully, his mother hadn't insisted upon the formality of dance cards, probably because she'd paired off all the singles beforehand, just as she had with Isabelle and him.

Talking with Isabelle had made one thing clear: He needed to share his life with Mellie and introduce her to his parents. Wouldn't his mother be disappointed to learn she could not orchestrate his life as though it were one of her galas to plan?

Mellie looked up as Mrs. Stark escorted her first guests into the room, a middle-aged couple dressed in their lavish finery. They reminded Mellie of her sister, Margaret, and Richard. She'd often seen them in their grand attire, going out for an evening of dining and dancing with members of Concord society. Those times now seemed so long ago, almost otherworldly. And while Mellie didn't miss the fancy clothes or fine food, she did miss teaching and being surrounded by students who were eager to learn. Her time with the children earlier had reinforced how much she had enjoyed her time as a tutor.

Mrs. Stark took pleasure in telling the couple that Mellie was accomplished in the art of Scherenschnitte, and they would receive a personal paper cutting of their profiles.

The woman clapped her gloved hands together. "Oh, how enchanting, Ruth! You always find an original way to entertain and delight your guests."

Mrs. Stark reveled in the praise as she led the couple to the seating area facing Mellie. "You'll find Miss Blanchard a true professional."

Mellie wondered if Mrs. Stark would have introduced her

as a "true professional" if she had known that Mellie operated three looms at the mill each day.

She sighed, picked up her scissors, and smiled at the couple. "I'm going to do a paper cutting of your profiles." She offered several different poses they could choose for their silhouette. Once they were in position, she picked up a piece of paper, looked at the couple, and began to cut a profile of the pair. When she had finished, she offered the likeness to the woman.

"If it meets with your approval, Mrs. Stark has asked that you place it on the table before you leave the room."

The woman studied the silhouette, then looked at her husband and beamed. "It's wonderful, isn't it?"

He nodded and returned her smile. "Perfect. Just like you, my dear."

The woman placed the cutting on the table before turning toward Mellie. "I do wish I could take it with me right now. You promise I'll receive it before we depart?"

"Yes." Mellie bobbed her head. "Besides, you wouldn't want it in the other room, where it could become ripped or creased while you are dancing."

"And it keeps Ruth's guests in suspense about the impending surprise throughout the evening," her husband replied. "Ruth does know how to host an exciting gala."

One by one, the couples and singles stepped into the room, listened to Mrs. Stark give her short speech, and had their profiles cut. All of them expressed delight with the finished product, as well as with Mrs. Stark's ability to surprise them.

Mellie's fingers began to ache. After cutting silhouettes of the children and now cutting the numerous adult profiles, she desperately longed to rest her hand. Mrs. Stark had given no thought to the fact that she might need a short break in which to rest her fingers throughout the evening. The only breaks she'd had were the brief periods when Mrs. Stark walked across the hall and then returned with another guest or two.

Each time Mrs. Stark appeared with more attendees, Mellie thought it might be the last of the evening. She'd cut the portraits of Mr. and Mrs. Stark as well as Mrs. Stark's father while the guests enjoyed refreshments and the musicians a short respite. Unfortunately, Mrs. Stark hadn't shared, and Mellie hadn't asked, how many guests were in attendance, but she truly hoped she was nearing the end of the list.

As though reading Mellie's thoughts, the older woman approached and tapped a finger on her list. "You'll be pleased to know there is only one more couple on my list. However, I would like their silhouettes to be particularly elegant. Rather than merely their faces, I'd like the silhouette to be full length, facing each other and perhaps clasping hands." She hesitated a moment. "Could you possibly frame them in a lovely archway of some sort?" She offered a slight smile. "Or is that too much to ask? I would, of course, pay you extra for this cutting."

"Yes, I can do that." Mellie didn't need a pattern to cut a lovely arch around a couple, though it wouldn't be as pretty as many she'd done in the past. The cramping in her fingers wouldn't permit the addition of dainty, thin vines or an edge of flowers around the arch, yet she'd make it as intricate as her aching hand would permit.

"I wouldn't ask, but it's my son and the young lady I'm hopeful he'll marry. I'll just go and get them."

Once Mrs. Stark left the room, Mellie flexed her fingers and arched her back. It would be good to stretch her legs too, but she didn't want to be parading across the room when Mrs. Stark returned with the remaining couple.

Moments later, the door opened. Mrs. Stark entered and immediately stepped to one side. The young woman and her escort were speaking in French when they entered the room. Mrs. Stark looked at Mellie and gestured to the man. "Miss Blanchard, this is my son, Morgan Stark, and his dear friend, Miss Isabelle Armstrong."

The scissors dropped from Mellie's hand and spiked into the Aubusson carpet as the room swirled in front of her like a child's spinning top. She stared into the clear blue eyes of the man dressed in formal apparel. Those perfectly blue eyes, the perfectly fitted attire, the perfectly spoken French—it all came back to Mellie in a startling flash. Morgan Stark was the man who had approached her on the train platform when she'd first arrived in Manchester. He was the kind young man who had returned her copy of *La Petite Fadette*. How many times had she unsuccessfully attempted to recall where she'd seen those eyes? Had he remembered her and been careful to avoid speaking of their meeting?

The stays in her corset pressed against her ribs, and the room suddenly became far too warm. She could barely breathe. Time stopped. Disbelief overwhelmed her. How could Morgan Stark and her William Morgan be one and the same? And yet they were. How had he so easily managed two separate lives for so long? How had he so easily deceived her while he loved another? How could he be so willing to shatter their trust—to shatter her love?

Chapter

TWENTY-FIVE

PERSPIRATION TRICKLED DOWN MORGAN'S NECK AS HE struggled to take in the scene before him. His eyes settled on the tiny scissors that remained stuck in the carpet. Without thinking, he leaned down, picked them up, and attempted to hand them to Mellie. When she didn't extend her hand, he looked away and placed the scissors on the table at her side. Slowly, he turned to his mother and forced as much of a smile as the grim situation would allow. "Why don't you return to your guests now? The three of us will be fine without your supervision."

The older woman looked at Mellie. "Do remember my instructions, Miss Blanchard." That said, she waved her lace handkerchief in the air and strode from the room.

The instant the door closed behind her, Morgan knelt in front of Mellie. "Please. Let me explain."

She leaned back in the chair as if she hoped to disappear into its plush cushion. "I think everything is quite clear, Morgan. It *is* Morgan, isn't it?" She didn't look at him. Instead, she retrieved the scissors from the small table. "Please stand over there, facing your young lady so that I'm able to cut your profiles."

Instead of standing, he gestured to Isabelle. "Isabelle, this is Mellie, the woman I told you about during dinner."

Isabelle drew near, her eyes shadowed with concern. "I'm very pleased to meet you, Mellie. Please don't listen to anything Morgan's mother may have told you about the two of us. I am in love with another young man whom I hope to marry, and Morgan tells me he feels the same about you. However, our parents have put their heads together and think they're going to make a match between us. It isn't true, of course. Neither of us will agree to it. I hope you can set aside any anger or mistrust that's been caused by this ill-fated meeting."

Morgan nodded. "Every word she has said is true, Mellie. The two of us were friends when we were children. We haven't seen each other in years, and while I admire Isabelle, I've never had any intention of marrying her or anyone else other than you."

The entire time he spoke, Mellie had kept her gaze fixed upon Isabelle. "I do believe you, Miss Armstrong, and I thank you for your willingness to share the truth with me."

Isabelle beamed. "Then all is right between you and Morgan?"

Mellie slowly shook her head. "No, I'm afraid it isn't. You see, I thought the man kneeling before me was William Morgan, a mechanic working for the Stark Mills who lived in a boardinghouse and had grown up without all of this." She gestured around the room, then toward the gilded ceiling that danced above a candlelit crystal chandelier. She finally looked at Morgan. "And the lottery." She inhaled a long breath. "You renounced it as strongly as I did, yet it was your own mother who introduced and took charge of the idea. How could you? Were you laughing behind my back while I refused to sell tickets?" She shook her head. "Don't bother to answer. Thus far you've been able to fool me quite brilliantly, and I can't stomach another lie."

The rich foods he'd eaten earlier in the evening roiled in his stomach. How had this gone so terribly wrong? If only he'd known Mellie was going to be here. There was so much he needed to explain, but not in front of Isabelle. "Please, Mellie, I can explain everything if . . ."

She leaned to the side, gathered her supplies, and quickly tucked them into her bag. "I'm leaving now. Tell your mother that I was taken ill, or that I was rude and walked out, or whatever sorry excuse comes to mind. I'm sure you'll be able to think of something she'll believe. You seem quite practiced in that area." She pinned him with a hard stare. "Please move so that I may leave."

Morgan wanted to hold fast to the arms of the chair and keep her there until she gave him enough time to explain. Instead, he rose to his feet. "I'm begging you, Mellie. Everything I've done has been for a good reason. There are others who can tell you that my intentions have always been honorable. Just as Isabelle dispelled the idea of a romance between us, there are others who can explain why I've been living a double life. None of it was meant for anything but good."

She stood. "How can good come from lies? Trust is founded on truth, and it seems there's been very little truth between us."

"Will you at least give me an opportunity to explain?"

"I'm not sure you can erase all that has happened, but perhaps I'll be willing to listen one day. But not now. Everything between us has been based upon lies."

Mellie marched over and pulled open the door. Morgan followed behind her and watched as she disappeared down the hallway, uncertain as to how he was going to convince her of his love and that she could trust him. Isabelle approached and stood in the doorway beside him.

They both turned toward the ballroom when Morgan's mother opened the door. Surprise shone in her eyes when she caught sight of them. "There you two are. I was just coming to see what was taking so long. I know I asked Miss Blanchard to cut a decorative arch around your profiles, but I never expected it to take so long." She motioned for them to follow her. "Do come along. It's almost time for the grand march." She glanced at the envelope in her hand. "Do wait a moment. I need to give Miss Blanchard her pay."

Morgan shook his head. "She isn't in there, Mother."

"Did she escape to the refreshment room? I can take it there."

"She had to leave, Mrs. Stark," Isabelle said, stepping forward. "She received some distressing news and simply couldn't remain here any longer."

"When? What kind of news? Did one of the guests say something to her? I don't think anyone attending the party knows her. She certainly should have sent word to me if she needed to leave. Of course, you can't expect proper manners from the lower class, can you?" She arched her brows at Isabelle. "Still, there's no denying she is talented."

Morgan withdrew the envelope from his mother's hand. "I'll see that Miss Blanchard receives her pay. I can deliver it tomorrow."

He expected her to argue, but the musicians sounded the chords for the grand march, and his mother didn't object or await answers to her earlier questions. "Come along. Your father and I need to lead the march."

When Morgan didn't move, Isabelle said, "I don't believe

we're going to participate in the grand march, Mrs. Stark. Morgan and I need to talk—in private."

Mrs. Stark's lips curved in a coy smile. "Well, of course. It's much more important that the two of you have some private time to talk." She patted Isabelle's shoulder. "I'll explain your absence to your mother." She dipped her head close to Isabelle's ear, though she spoke loud enough for Morgan to hear. "I'm sure she'll be as delighted as I am to hear that you and my son desire time alone."

After giving Morgan an approving look, she quickly returned to the ballroom. Morgan nodded toward the side parlor, where Mellie had been cutting profiles only a short time ago, and the two of them stepped back inside. Closing the door behind him, Morgan turned to Isabelle. "I don't know how I'm going to get her to listen to me. I can't explain the truth of what's happened unless she's willing to listen."

Isabelle sat down and gestured for him to sit in the empty chair beside her. "If Mellie cares for you as much as I think she does, she's going to want to learn what caused you to mislead her." Isabelle hesitated. "You have misled her, haven't you?"

"Unfortunately, I have, but it was never intentional. Keeping my identity secret was necessary during my employment and—"

She held up her hand to stay him. "You don't need to explain to me, Morgan. I'm not judging what you've done, but I do understand the need for trust, so I hope you can convince Mellie that whatever you've done was for good reason. After you've explained, you might point out that in addition to trust, there's a need for forgiveness between those who love each other. We all make mistakes, but we can't move forward unless we're willing to truly forgive." Concern reflected in her eyes. "If you believe it would help if I spoke with Mellie, I would be willing to do so. I would suggest you wait until tomorrow, however, or the next day before you go to her. Let her have a little time to digest what's happened this evening."

"I fear that if I give her too much time, she's never going to let me near enough to tell her the truth. There are so many layers to all of this, some are connected and some aren't, yet all of them have affected Mellie." He leaned forward and covered his face with his palms. "What a mess I've made of things."

For the rest of the evening, the two of them remained in the upstairs parlor, Morgan lamenting his failures with Mellie, and Isabelle worrying if her parents would accept the man she loved.

When a tap sounded at the door, Morgan glanced at Isabelle. "That will be my mother, hoping to find me on my knee proposing to you."

She chuckled. "Thank you for making me laugh, Morgan. We needed something to lift our spirits for a moment."

The door opened. Only his mother's head appeared in the doorway. "May I come in?"

He had been teasing when he mentioned his mother might expect to see him proposing to Isabelle, but now he thought perhaps it hadn't been a joke. She'd entered the room as if she expected to discover them locked in a passionate embrace.

"Yes, Mother, do come in. Has the party finally come to an end?"

She frowned at his question. "Yes, and you need to come and bid farewell to the guests."

"Most of them don't know me, and I don't think they'll notice if I'm not at the front door when they leave." He massaged his forehead between his thumb and fingers. "I don't feel up to it,

Mother. I'll remain in here until they've all departed. I need time to think."

~~~~~

The clock in the parlor of the boardinghouse struck twelve as Mellie climbed the stairs to the attic bedroom. Being as quiet as possible, she changed into her nightdress. Most nights the icy conditions in the attic were more than she could bear, but the coach ride home had been so terrifying and cold, the attic seemed a balmy haven. There had been little doubt the coachman wasn't prepared for her departure when she made her hasty exit out the rear door of the Stark mansion. He'd been huddled among the other drivers near one of the fancy coaches, all of them imbibing to keep themselves warm. At least that was the reason he'd given when she'd expressed concern about his condition. Too late, she realized her remark had angered him. There were no warming bricks for her feet, and he made no effort to close the window flaps before slamming the door. The carriage careened along the snow-and-ice-covered roadway, pitching like a ship in a storm.

All thoughts of Morgan and the evening's revelations temporarily fled from her mind as the rough ride lobbed her from one side of the carriage to the other. Her shoulders, hips, and arms received a brutal pounding. When the carriage finally came to an abrupt halt in front of the boardinghouse, Mellie's head snapped back and hit the seat. She waited a moment, but when the driver didn't appear at the carriage door, she was left to her own devices. They both understood he wouldn't be reported for his horrid conduct. No one would care, for she wasn't of any greater importance than the driver who'd mistreated her. And there was no reason to dwell upon the mistreatment. She needed to sleep. Morning would arrive far too soon.

She was certain she hadn't yet slept when Cora jostled her arm and leaned close. "Time to get up, Mellie. If you don't hurry, you're going to miss breakfast and be late for church."

Mellie forced open her eyes. All three of the other girls were dressed for church. She sat up, turned sideways in the bed, and slipped her feet into a pair of thick flannel slippers. "I don't know how I managed to sleep while all three of you scurried around."

Cora plopped down beside her. "What time did you get home? Was it great fun? Were the dresses beautiful? We want to hear all about it, but we knew you'd need your sleep."

"The clock was striking midnight when I came upstairs to bed, although the party hadn't yet ended when I left. Everything was lovely, and I was able to spend time with a group of children during the early portion of the evening. They were delightful. I believe my time with them was the best part of the entire night."

"I want to hear about the gowns. I do hope you were able to see the ladies dressed in their finery." Phebe lifted her bonnet from a peg and held it by its burgundy ribbons.

"Since I was cutting silhouettes of the guests, I was able to examine all of their dresses in detail. However, I don't think we have time for such a lengthy conversation right now. I promise I'll regale you with all the particulars after church."

The three of them agreed and promised to snag a biscuit or two for Mellie if she didn't make it down in time for breakfast. After they'd descended the stairs, Mellie poured water into the washbasin, splashed her face, and let out a gasp. The icy water doused any lingering thoughts she'd had of sleep. After a quick toilette, she slipped into her dress, thankful for the added warmth. Her appearance wasn't as neat as what she usually attained on a Sunday morning, but she didn't want to be late. Mrs. Richards had granted her the privilege of remaining out late last night, but her kindness had come with a warning: *"Be late for church and I'll withhold any such favor in the future."* Though Mellie doubted she'd again have a need to return after curfew, she didn't want Mrs. Richards to regret her decision.

She descended the stairs and forced thoughts of the previous night from her mind. Her being late to breakfast might not please Mrs. Richards, yet it would allow less time for questions from the girls. And right now, the pain cut far too deep to be shared with anyone. After church she'd be able to discuss the gowns and the children, but it would take far longer before she could speak of the heartache and sorrow she'd endured at the Stark mansion.

Her feet had barely touched the final step when Mrs. Richards rounded the corner. "I see you finally made it out of bed. I was beginning to wonder." She glanced toward the dining room. "I'm afraid you'll have to go without breakfast this morning, and growling stomachs aren't appreciated during the Sunday sermon."

Mellie nodded. "I'll keep that in mind." She didn't know how anyone could control a stomach growl, but she didn't argue with the keeper.

Moments later, the other girls hurried to retrieve their cloaks, hats, gloves, and muffs. Cora edged her way close to Mellie and slipped her two warm biscuits wrapped in a checkered napkin. She leaned close to Mellie's ear. "Be sure you bring the napkin back. She counts them."

"I will. Thank you." She slipped them inside her muff, then hesitated before departing. "Where are you attending church this morning?"

"Methodist?" Cora glanced at Clara for confirmation.

"No, Presbyterian." She shook her head and giggled. "I don't think you'll ever learn the schedule."

Cora hooked arms with her sister. "Not as long as I have you around to keep me headed in the right direction."

The three of them proceeded down the brick sidewalk behind the other girls. There was little chatter this morning. They all kept their heads bowed against the stinging cold wind and walked as rapidly as the snowy conditions would permit.

Mellie parted ways with Cora and Clara and headed off toward Franklin Street. Now alone, her thoughts returned to Morgan, and she was once again struck by the deep pain he'd inflicted. His lies and deceit were monumental. She couldn't help but wonder when and how he had planned to confess to her. Or had he even given it any thought? Had he planned simply to disappear from her life as William Morgan and take his chances that she'd never discover his true identity? She silently scoffed at the idea, but after a few moments' consideration decided it truly might have been his plan all along. As Morgan Stark, the affluent mill owner's son, their paths were unlikely to cross. Perhaps he'd merely been toying with her affections until he resumed his life as Morgan Stark. The thought gnawed at her as she stepped inside the church.

Her gaze fastened upon the pew where Morgan usually sat at her side. She hadn't expected to see him there. She told herself she hadn't wanted to see him there. And yet his absence inexplicably compounded the loss that had hollowed within her like an empty space that couldn't be filled.

Mellie joined the other congregants as they blended their voices in song to the resounding chords of the pipe organ. She knew the words by heart and sang without giving thought to the lyrics or to the prayers the parishioners recited once the singing had come to an end.

The preacher walked to the lectern and opened his Bible.

"Today I would like to speak to you about two things. The first part of my sermon regards trust."

Mellie snapped to attention. Why wasn't Morgan here to listen to this? He needed to hear what the preacher had to say this morning.

"And the other is about forgiveness."

She frowned, not certain she wanted to hear that part of the message.

"We grow up placing our trust in our parents, our siblings, and close friends. Hopefully, we place our primary trust in God, because He is the only one who can meet our expectations as the perfect caretaker of our trust." He paused and let his gaze linger on the crowd for a moment. "Yet to go through life without trusting those we love would make us reclusive, withdrawn, and unlovable. Unless we extend ourselves to others, they can't connect with us, and connection requires a level of trust. Just as we all need to love and be loved, we need to trust and be trusted."

Mellie shifted in her seat. What he'd said thus far wasn't exactly what she had expected to hear.

"The problem arises when someone breaks our trust. Perhaps a parent doesn't keep a promise, a best friend repeats a confidence, or difficulty occurs in a marriage." He cleared his throat. "As Christians, we need to be open to restoring trust in those who have wronged us. Now, don't misunderstand me. After an offer of restoration, there must be more than an apology from the offender. There must be a change in the person's life that will rebuild trust. Those stepping-stones must be agreed upon by the parties involved. And I can assure you that, just as Jesus forgave us as He hung on the cross, He wants us to extend forgiveness to those who have wronged us and work toward the reestablishment of relationship." The pastor offered a fleeting smile. "Does it always work? Unfortunately, no. But you owe it to yourselves and to God to make the effort and reap the blessings of restoration."

Mellie walked out of church uncertain if she could meet such an expectation. Perhaps she did owe it to God and to herself to see if her trust could be restored. But first she'd need to discover the whole truth. And only Morgan could give her the answers.

Chapter
TWENTY-SIX

MORGAN HAD TAKEN ISABELLE'S ADVICE. INSTEAD OF appearing at the Franklin Street church and sitting next to Mellie, he'd attended with his grandfather and parents. Concealing his identity had resulted in a great deal of heartache, and he'd accomplished very little. Still, he doubted he would have ever met Mellie if he hadn't taken the job as a mechanic. In fact, if he hadn't returned home with the idea of working in the mills in this way, he'd likely be living elsewhere. Granted, such a decision might have caused a bit of difficulty with his parents, but it was nothing they wouldn't have eventually accepted. After all, he'd been living away from them for most of his life.

While he'd hoped to return to the boardinghouse after church, his mother insisted he return home for Sunday dinner. Her eyes flashed a warning that she'd not take no for an answer. "Your grandfather is expecting you to join us. He says he has something important to tell us all."

"Perhaps he's planning another trip abroad," Morgan said.

His mother sighed. "I hope not. He's getting too old for such trips. He needs to remain closer to home."

Morgan chuckled. "His health is excellent, Mother. If he wants to travel, he should do so."

"If he becomes ill while abroad, there would be no one to care for him. But then you young folks never think of these things."

Morgan gave a little shrug. "I'm sure if he needed care, a physician would recommend someone who could care for him. And it's not as though he couldn't afford such an expense."

"Perhaps, but it isn't the same as having a loved one care for you."

Morgan couldn't envision his mother acting as a personal nurse to his grandfather—or anyone else for that matter. In truth, she'd likely hire someone to care for him, so it mattered little if he were in New Hampshire or England. However, he withheld his opinion. No need to argue the point further.

When they'd all gathered around the table, Morgan's grandfather said grace. He'd barely whispered amen before his mother leaned forward. "We're excited to hear this news you mentioned, Father."

Morgan smiled across the table at his father. Both of them could have waited until after the meal, while his mother never could bear to wait on anything—especially a bit of secretive news.

His grandfather forked a bite of creamed potatoes into his mouth, swallowed, and looked at his daughter. "I thought we could wait until after dinner, but I know how you are, Ruth. I won't keep you waiting any longer." He inhaled a breath and let it out slowly. "You may recall my speaking of traveling to China?"

She shook her head. "I do, but—"

"I've booked passage for two."

His mother's brows shot up. "Two? Well, you'll need to find someone else to go with you. I'm not going to China."

The older man laughed. "I'm not inviting you, Ruth. My new wife is going to accompany me. It will be our wedding trip."

"New *wife*? Wedding trip?" Her fork slipped from her fingers and clanked against the china dinner plate. "Gracious, Father! You sound like an old man who's completely lost his faculties. First of all, you're not . . ." Her words trailed off as she stared at her father. "Wait. Did you . . . did you get married without telling me?"

"Remember who you're speaking to, Ruth. I'm your father, not your child. Yes, I did get married without telling you. I didn't bring her along because I thought it best to tell you we were married before making introductions."

Morgan's mother visibly paled. "A gold digger, no doubt. I cannot believe—"

"She is not interested in my money, Ruth. I do wish I could say the same for you." His mother gasped at the remark, but his grandfather shushed her. "She is wealthy in her own right, so you need not worry about any attempt to gain your inheritance. I'll bring her here to meet you after we return from China."

His mother stammered her apologies, then added how pleased she would be to meet her new "mother."

"No need to go that far with your acceptance of her," his grandfather replied. "I believe she'll be pleased to be addressed by her given name."

"Which is?" his mother asked.

"Aletha Williamson."

Her mouth gaped. "Not *the* Aletha Williamson of the Williamson Carriage Companies?"

"The very one. She's lovely, and I believe you'll find her quite gracious." His grandfather turned to Morgan and smiled. "I know you're eager to get back to that boardinghouse where you've been living." He glanced at Morgan's father. "Your father has told me all about what's been happening at the mill and the new invention. It sounds as though he wants you to step in and begin to take the reins of the company, so I decided that if you're soon to become a manager of some sort, you shouldn't be living with your parents—or in a boardinghouse."

His mother picked up her water goblet and took a sip. "There is more than enough room for Morgan to live here with us. I don't know why you think he shouldn't live at home."

"I'd like you to let me finish speaking, Ruth." He directed a sharp look down the table. "Morgan, your father and I did a bit of looking around and discovered a nice place that's closer to town than all these mansions around here. It will make a fine place for you to live—not too big, but enough space that if you ever marry it will be adequate, at least for a while." He looked at his daughter. "I don't want any argument about this, Ruth. You sent him off to all those fancy schools when he was a child and needed you. Now that he's grown, he doesn't need a mother to coddle him."

The gift was as much of a surprise as his grandfather's marriage announcement. "Thank you, Grandfather. I think I'll enjoy having a home of my own. And congratulations on your marriage. I'm glad to hear your new wife has your same adventurous spirit. I'm sure you're going to have a grand time in China."

His grandfather chuckled. "You're right on that account."

When Morgan departed later that day, his emotions remained a jumble. His grandfather had insisted upon taking him on a tour of his new home, and though Morgan had been pleased with the house and had enjoyed time alone with the family patriarch, he couldn't push aside his worries about Mellie. The house his grandfather gave him would mean little if he couldn't one day share it with the woman he loved.

⚜

Morgan walked alongside Mr. Hale to Stark Mill Number One, where they would meet Cyrus Baldwin for the initial runs on two additional bagging looms. The first of the looms was now in full production, and if all went well, they'd have the other two operating at full capacity by the end of the week. Orders already had begun arriving, and excitement was high at Number One, where the looms had been set up on the second floor. If needed, there would be room for at least two more looms on that floor.

Mr. Baldwin strode toward them and waved his hat in the air as they approached. "Good morning, gentlemen! It's a fine day, isn't it?"

Mr. Hale pointed toward the sky. "If you like freezing temperatures and snow, then you're right. It's a fine day, Cyrus."

"I don't care about the weather so long as we're ready to pull the levers on those other two looms." Mr. Baldwin drew near and clapped Mr. Hale on the shoulder.

The three of them stepped inside the building and brushed the snow from their coats. As they neared the winding brick stairway, Mr. Baldwin came alongside Morgan. "I know you've been as concerned as I have been about the patent and copies of my design."

Morgan's stomach clenched. Surely this couldn't be bad news. They'd already begun production. Another company having filed a competing patent would mean financial disaster.

He didn't want to believe his inability to protect the drawings might result in financial loss—for both Mr. Baldwin and the Stark Mills.

"Yes, I've been very concerned. Mr. Hale has likely told you that I'd been doing a bit of investigating until he called a halt to my inquiries."

"Indeed, he did." Mr. Baldwin offered a generous smile. "However, I pursued the final piece in the puzzle and called on Ezekiel Snow in Lowell."

"And did he tell you he didn't know a Franklin Montee?"

Mr. Baldwin laughed. "That's exactly what he said. Denied any connection to anyone with the name Montee."

Morgan's heart slammed against his chest wall. Why was Mr. Baldwin laughing? If Ezekiel Snow had denied knowing Franklin Montee, it closed all doors to locating the man. "What do we do next?"

"Not a thing." Mr. Baldwin shook his head. "You see, after I visited Mr. Snow at his office, I located his home and proceeded to pay his wife a visit. I said I was an acquaintance of Montee, had lost touch with him, and learned she or her husband might be related. Then I asked her if she could help me."

"And did she?"

"She did." Mr. Baldwin grinned. "Turns out Mr. Montee is her nephew. A sweet young man who isn't in complete control of his faculties and requires constant nursing care. Seems he was thrown from a horse a few years ago and suffered head injuries of some sort. Mr. Snow is his guardian and conservator, and he's taken to using Mr. Montee's name to hide some of his own business matters. There's little doubt Mr. Snow is the one who copied the documents and then attempted to gain the patent. Since he controls any assets that flow to Mr. Montee, it was safe for him to use his nephew's name." He shook his head. "Sad thing how a man who's revered as an upstanding businessman in the community would stoop to such lows."

While Morgan followed the other two men up the staircase, he thought of his own mother. Her misguided plans to finance the circular looms could have resulted in disastrous consequences for his father. If the money hadn't been returned to the Amoskeag Company prior to the annual audit, it was his father who would have been held accountable. And the fact that she'd organized a lottery for personal gain further grieved him. Granted, she was now contrite, but he shuddered to think that she had considered using those proceeds for her own benefit. Morgan wondered if she'd erased the entire matter from her mind, or if she had privately apologized to his father. He hoped the latter. He'd been convicted of the error of his ways, and though he hadn't yet spoken to Mellie, he'd asked God's forgiveness. Would she be willing to forgive him, too? At the moment, he wasn't certain she'd even speak to him.

Throughout the remainder of the day, the workers tested the looms. By the time they departed that evening, there was little doubt the looms were going to manufacture a product that would prove an economic boon for the Stark Mills.

While Morgan shared in the excitement with the other workers, nothing in his life could be thoroughly enjoyed until he'd set things right with Mellie.

Morgan didn't go to the photography shop until a half hour before closing time. He wasn't sure whether Mellie would expect him to appear and walk her home, but even if she didn't care to talk to him, he wanted to make sure she arrived home safely.

Mellie looked up when the bell over the front door jangled, but she didn't smile or greet him. Instead, she turned back to her customer and continued her cutting. Not wanting to disturb her, Morgan circled around to the parlor area used by Mr. Harrison. He was surprised to discover Mr. Harrison and Mr. Knoll sitting in the two wing-back chairs, conversing together.

Mr. Harrison caught sight of Morgan as he rounded the corner. "Morgan! Come and join us." He pointed to an empty chair nearby. "I think Mellie will be a while longer. Her customer hasn't been here long."

Morgan hadn't spoken with Mr. Harrison since his aggressive inquiry regarding Franklin Montee and Mr. Knoll. Even though Mr. Harrison had denied any knowledge of Mr. Montee, Morgan hadn't been entirely convinced at the time. Now, knowing the truth, he felt a sense of embarrassment that he'd secretly questioned Mr. Knoll's involvement. While there had been reason to suspect him, Morgan was pleased the real culprit hadn't been Mr. Harrison's dear friend.

Morgan nodded and sat down beside Mr. Knoll. "Good to see you back in Manchester, Mr. Knoll. I thought you had plans to remain in Washington for Christmas."

Mr. Knoll adjusted the spectacles that rested on his narrow, sharp nose. "I considered remaining, but many of my friends who live in the city had departed to enjoy the holiday in warmer climes, and I had concluded my business." He glanced at Mr. Harrison. "I considered returning home, but there was no reason to do so. I'd stopped there on my way to Washington and delivered the artwork to my customers."

Mr. Harrison leaned forward and rested his forearms on his thighs. "So Samuel did what I asked and then returned to Manchester so we can continue to work on our little project."

Morgan tipped his head to the side. "What project is that?"

"Now that Samuel has spoken with his attorney and we're hopeful we'll secure our patent, I suppose we can tell you." Mr. Harrison smiled. "That is, we'll tell you so long as you give your word that you'll keep your lips sealed."

Morgan nodded. "You have my word. If anyone knows the importance of safeguarding an invention, it's me."

Mr. Harrison stood and walked to a cabinet in the back room. When he returned, he sat down beside Morgan and presented a daguerreotype that was unlike any other Morgan had ever seen. Instead of a single image, there were two identical images side by side. "When you look at these two images through a stereoscope, the images layer themselves and become dimensional." He stopped and looked at Morgan. "Have you ever seen a stereoscope?"

Morgan shook his head. "I don't believe so. And if I have seen one, I didn't know what it was called."

Mr. Knoll chuckled. "I have mine upstairs. I'll be back down in a moment."

When Mr. Knoll was out of earshot, Mr. Harrison leaned forward in his chair. "By the way, Mellie didn't seem herself when she arrived today. I expected to hear about the fancy party she attended Saturday night, but when I inquired, she merely said it was a disappointment and so I didn't pursue the matter." He shot a glance toward the front of the shop. "Has she spoken to you? I wonder if perhaps one of the men at the party made untoward remarks to her—or perhaps she didn't receive as much pay as expected."

"I know it was a difficult evening, and I hope to talk with her about it on the way home this evening."

"Good, good. She's usually such a cheerful young lady. It's unusual to see her without a smile."

Before Morgan could comment further, Mr. Knoll appeared. "This, my young friend, is a stereoscope." He handed Morgan a wooden box with gold hinges and gold-rimmed eyecups. "This is what has been used with the stereoscope since it was invented." He gave Morgan a thick piece of cardboard with hand-drawn images of a country scene. After placing the cardboard in a slot, he tapped the eyecups. "Now look through those and see how the drawing becomes dimensional rather than a flat picture." He waited as Morgan brought the stereoscope to his eyes. "Well? Do you see what I mean?"

Morgan gaped at the image. It was as if he were right there in the scene. The bridge, the trees, and the flowers all came to life in a new and unique way. He withdrew the stereoscope from his eyes. "This is wonderful. I'm amazed at the lifelike imagery."

Mr. Harrison grinned. "Now place this dual-imaged daguerreotype in the slot and look at it through the stereoscope."

Morgan did as Mr. Harrison instructed. "It's truly extraordinary." He returned the stereoscope to Mr. Knoll. "You've invented a method to create these dual images of daguerreotypes for use with the stereoscope?"

"That's right. We're calling them stereograph cards." Mr. Harrison beamed. "Think how exciting it will be for people to see images of different countries, artwork, animals, and spectacular events, and all with a clarity and detail never before imagined."

"Remarkable," Morgan said. He looked toward Mellie when the bell jingled over the shop's door. "I hope you will experience great success with your invention. And I promise I won't breathe a word to anyone." He rose from the chair. It was near closing time, and Mellie was gathering her belongings. He didn't want her to depart without him.

"Yes, I trust you'll keep your word, Morgan." Mr. Harrison

stood and patted his shoulder. "I believe it's time to close the shop. I'll follow behind you and Mellie and lock the door."

Mellie hadn't given any indication she was pleased to see him or that she'd expected him to come and escort her home. Truth be told, he didn't know how she would react to him when he approached. By the time he neared her side, she had already donned her cloak. He shrugged into his heavy wool overcoat and reached down for her case.

"I can carry that, thank you." She grasped the handles of the case and strode toward the front door.

He didn't argue but matched her pace, arriving at the front door in time to open it for her. She gave him a little nod, then glanced over her shoulder and bid Mr. Harrison good-night.

When they'd gone but a short distance, Morgan touched her arm. "Mellie, I'd like an opportunity to sit down together so that I might explain everything to you. Would you please join me for a cup of hot chocolate or tea at Putney's?"

She stopped and met his eyes. "I don't believe you can talk your way out of all that's happened between us, Morgan, but as long as you promise to speak the truth, I'll listen to what you have to say." He smiled, and she shook her head. "Please understand that my agreement to hear you out does not mean all will be well. I will listen, yet it will take more than words to heal the broken trust that now exists between us."

He could ask for nothing more than the opportunity to plead his case. A thin layer of icy snow crunched beneath their shoes as he silently prayed for God to give him the words to melt her heart.

Chapter

TWENTY-SEVEN

MELLIE'S THOUGHTS SKIPPED FROM ONE QUESTION TO the next. Her stomach twisted in a knot as they walked toward Putney's. There were so many things she wanted to ask Morgan, yet she worried his responses might not be truthful. She'd been so trusting, believed everything he'd told her, and he'd taken advantage of her trust. She was trying to recall the preacher's sermon. She needed to forgive and seek to restore trust between them, to listen with an open mind. Though she longed to mend their relationship, fear had gained a foothold, and she doubted if Morgan would be able to convince her to trust him fully again.

A blanket of warmth and wondrous smells enveloped her as they stepped inside the confectionery. The aroma of Mrs. Putney's baking permeated the shop. The couple lived in a small apartment at the rear of the shop, and each morning and evening Mrs. Putney baked the confections offered from behind the glass-covered cases.

Morgan helped with her coat, then pulled out a chair for

her. He lifted his nose and inhaled a deep breath. "I believe I smell Mrs. Putney's famous apple dumplings." He hesitated. "Or maybe it's apple pie. Either way, it makes me want to order a sweet dessert with my tea. What would you like?"

She hadn't planned to eat, but food could provide a small diversion, if needed. "A piece of gingerbread if there's any in the case. If not, one of Mrs. Putney's molasses brownies would be nice."

"I'll do my best," he said and strode toward the counter.

She stared at his strong shoulders and the fine cut of his wool jacket, and her heart swelled. He certainly looked handsome in both his work clothes and the suit, and he seemed equally comfortable in either getup. How could that be? Instead of his usual work clothes, he'd arrived at the shop wearing a suit that was as fine as those worn by any shop owner or businessman. Had Mr. Harrison questioned Morgan's change of attire? The three men had been deep in conversation during Morgan's visit, and she wondered what they'd talked about for so long. Did Morgan discuss with them the fiasco that occurred at the party? Did he hope to win the allegiance of the two men? She hoped not. The last thing she needed was pressure from Mr. Harrison about her relationship with Morgan.

Soon Morgan returned with their desserts. He placed the gingerbread in front of her and a piece of cake at his place across the table. She looked at his plate. "Is that nutmeg cake?"

He nodded. "Mr. Putney said the apple dumplings are still in the oven, so I decided on the cake. I'll be back with the tea."

On his return, he carried a tray with two cups and saucers and a dainty flowered teapot. After removing the items and placing them on the table, he nodded to the teapot. "I'll let you pour. I usually end up spilling some when I pour that first cup."

Despite her shaking hand, she didn't spill a drop. When they'd both added cream and sugar to their tea, he took a sip and settled the cup back in its saucer. "I've been trying to think how best to explain my situation in order to make everything clear, and I think the first explanation I need to give is the reason I didn't reveal to you my true identity."

She gave a slight nod. "I believe that's a good beginning, too. However, please don't try to be too proper with your details. I want the truth, not politeness."

"Of course. Some of what I told you about myself is true. I did study engineering in school. If I recall, I told you I hadn't immediately been able to find work and so I'd taken the job as a mechanic. That wasn't true. When I returned home after completing my education, I presented my father with a plan to start work in the mills, but as a laborer—not a manager. You see, I wanted to explore possible ways to improve conditions for the workers. If they knew my identity, they wouldn't have spoken freely about their experience. Nobody in the mills knows who I am. I let the agent at Stark Mills as well as my overseer and manager believe that I hadn't completed my education. I didn't tell them the truth because they wouldn't have hired me as a mere assistant if they knew I had completed my education."

"Yes, of course. When telling lies, you must include everyone."

Morgan's head snapped back as though she'd slapped him. "I hoped to somehow improve conditions for the workers. One day I'll be in charge of Stark Mills, so I wanted firsthand knowledge of the daily responsibilities and obstacles that confront the men and women who work there. The only way I could do that was to conceal my identity—from everyone. Surely you agree that the workers would have avoided me if they'd known I was Mr.

Stark's son. While my methods may have been dishonest, my intentions were honorable."

She carefully considered what he'd said, silently beseeching God for wisdom. There was little doubt the workers would have shunned him if they'd known who he was, and his desire to help would have been thwarted. She stirred her tea, then took a sip. "And you didn't believe you could trust me to keep your confidence?"

He sighed. "So many things had happened, each connected to the other, that I feared if I shared even one thing, I'd be forced to share it all. And I couldn't. Not back then. It would have been like pulling a loose thread and unraveling an entire piece of cloth."

She nodded, though she wasn't entirely satisfied with his explanation. "Go on. What came next?"

He detailed the secrecy surrounding the drawings for the new looms that he'd hidden and studied at Mr. Harrison's shop, and the fact that they'd somehow been copied. "If someone else had patented our design before Mr. Baldwin was able to, I would have been responsible. I became obsessed with discovering who had copied the design."

"It's good to know what had so captured your attention. You didn't seem to hear anything I told you. That's why I didn't mention I was going to the party. You'd been so preoccupied, I doubted you'd care."

"Yes, the party." He shook his head. "My mother insisted I attend, and you know the rest. Isabelle and I thought it great fun that our parents were plotting our futures when we'd already made our own decisions." He hesitated a moment. "She is a lovely young woman, and I think the two of you could become great friends in the future."

Mellie didn't comment. Her future remained unclear at the moment. If she continued working at the mill, she doubted Isabelle Armstrong would be interested in a friendship. Besides, there was much more that Morgan needed to clarify. She could see where he might have been justified in being hired to work in the mills, but the things they'd shared had gone beyond exchanging work experiences. She'd told him about her sister's marriage and how it had come to ruin. He knew her feelings about gambling, and now she knew his own mother had headed up the lottery that he'd claimed to dislike. Had he been lying about that, as well?

She cut a piece of the gingerbread with her fork and focused on the questions to which she needed answers. "I'd like to hear about the lottery. You declared great opposition to the idea, yet you had to know your mother was the one who initiated it."

"I didn't know about the lottery until Mr. Vance made the announcement at the ball. I was as surprised as you. My mother never mentioned one word of it to me. If she had, I would have done everything in my power to dissuade her from the idea."

Mellie wanted to believe him, she truly did. Yet she couldn't imagine there hadn't been some mention of the lottery in his presence.

"You don't trust what I'm saying, do you?"

She tipped her head and met his eyes. "I want to, but it's difficult to believe you didn't have some suspicion." When he shook his head, she continued, "I'm curious as to why she decided to start a lottery in the first place. Is this something she's mentioned in the past? Does she have plans to continue the practice?"

"Why don't we go and visit my parents and let them answer your questions? I want to regain your trust, Mellie, and if that's going to happen, I think you need to hear from them—not just me. Would you go with me?"

Her heart thundered at the thought of seeing his mother again. "I'll need to think about that. I'm not sure they would be open to meeting with a mill girl."

"Perhaps not, but they would likely be willing to discuss the entire matter with my intended wife."

She sucked in a breath. *Intended wife . . .*

Though the idea warmed her, warning bells sounded in her mind. He was taking a great deal for granted. Not only did he think she was going to forgive and forget, but he was also assuming she'd become his wife when he hadn't even proposed.

"I think you're assuming too much, Morgan. Do you understand how deeply I've been wounded by your actions? When I saw you at the party, my trust was completely broken. I felt as if I were staring at a stranger, not the man I'd come to love and care for over the past months. My trust can't be restored by an apology and a list of circumstances you believe justify your actions."

He nodded. "I don't expect you to immediately forgive me. However, I want you to know the whole truth. I realize I wasn't forthright, and I apologize for that. I give you my word that if you agree to build a future with me, I will never withhold the truth from you ever again. I understand that it may take time before you trust me again, but I'm willing to give you all the time you need."

"You're right. It will take time for me to trust that you'll be completely open with me."

She moved her plate to the side. Her heart wanted to forgive him on the spot and declare her undying love, but her head told her she needed more time. She'd already seen what lies could do to a marriage, and she would not join her life to his unless she could believe he valued the truth as much as she.

He pushed cake crumbs around the plate with his fork. "I know our situations aren't the same, but you weren't completely forthcoming about your past when we first met. How long do you think it would have taken you to tell me about your past if Olive and Charity hadn't found your journal?"

His question surprised her. She hadn't considered that she'd withheld a portion of her past from him. At least until she'd had to reveal the embarrassment that had been cast upon her by her brother-in-law's penchant for gambling and his subsequent suicide. When Morgan had learned of Olive's threats to have her supposed journalist friend publicize the humiliating realities, he'd come to Mellie's defense. He hadn't belabored the fact that she hadn't confided in him. He'd merely done what he could to help her. But this was entirely different. Withholding the truth about her family wasn't the same as what he'd done to her. *Was it?*

She tucked a strand of hair behind her ear. "If Olive hadn't threatened me, I don't know exactly when I would have told you about my past and why I'd come to Manchester, but I want to believe it wouldn't have taken me until now." She offered a fleeting smile. "I know that's easy to say, yet I do believe I would have told you months ago—at least I hope I would have."

"I believe you would have, Mellie. I merely wanted to point out that it isn't always easy to reveal the truth, no matter how much you love someone. I feared I would lose you, and I didn't want to take that chance." He reached across the table and enfolded her hand in his own.

She could sense his sorrow over what had happened, and her heart ached. She didn't want to add to his pain, but the closeness they'd shared couldn't be restored with a cup of tea and one conversation.

"I know you've said you aren't certain you want to speak with my parents, but I would be grateful if you'd give the idea some consideration. I want you to understand all of the circumstances that surrounded everything and have influenced my actions since I've met you. Otherwise I don't think you can ever truly trust me again."

While in her heart she had already forgiven him, if they were to share anything deeper, she needed more. She needed to know everything. Only then could she make her decision.

She swallowed hard. "Very well. I'll meet with your parents."

Morgan sat in one of the wing-back chairs opposite his father's sturdy walnut desk. There was much groundwork to be laid before his parents would agree to meet with Mellie. The decision to speak first to his father had been an easy one. Unlike his mother, his father was accustomed to listening and evaluating facts rather than interrupting and taking the offensive.

Admitting his love for Mellie hadn't taken long, but detailing the intricate events that had created the breach between them had consumed most of the morning. It was nearing noon when his father leaned back in his chair and tented his fingers beneath his chin. "I'm willing to speak to your young lady and explain the role I've played in all of this, if you believe that is what will restore her trust in you. However, you need to understand that if she betrays our confidence, you stand to lose a great deal. We all do. I would be asked to resign my financial position with the Amoskeag Company, and even though we'd still own the Stark Mills, our reputations would suffer. Even though the money was repaid to the Amoskeag, our customers would view us as untrustworthy. Business would suffer and much would be lost. If you're willing to take that chance, my boy, then I'll speak to her."

"Thank you, Father."

His father nodded. "In the end, I'm the one who's responsible, not your mother. She didn't have the authority to withdraw the funds from the Amoskeag accounts. It was I who signed the check. It was my lack of strength and my inability to reject your mother's idea that placed us in jeopardy."

"But she'd already set the plan in motion before you—"

His father held up a hand. "No. I'm the one who bears responsibility. Your mother has a strong personality, and I've never been able to tell her no. Once she sets her mind to something, I tend to let her have her way—even when I disagree. It's a weakness I need to overcome. I've given this matter more thought than you can imagine. I haven't told your mother yet, but I plan to meet with the board of directors of the Amoskeag, confess my wrongdoing in this matter, and resign my position. I'm prepared to suffer the consequences of my actions. Taking the easy way out of a situation isn't what builds character, now, is it?"

Morgan shook his head. "No, but building character can be painful."

His father chuckled. "On that we can agree." He sighed. "Your mother has plans to visit Eugenia Higgins late this afternoon. Could you bring your young lady around then?"

Morgan frowned. "She'll be at work."

His father reached into his desk drawer and withdrew a piece of paper. "I'll send a note to the mill with my groom, asking that she be released from work at two-thirty. You can meet her at the front gate and explain." He dipped the nib of his pen into a pot of ink and scratched out a quick message. After blotting the ink, he folded the paper and rang a bell on his desk.

Once the maid had taken the note and disappeared, Morgan leaned forward. "I need to speak with Mother and make it clear that I intend to marry Mellie—with or without Mother's approval."

His father arched his brows. "Perhaps you should join her for lunch. I'll take my meal here in my office and finish this paper work that's been piling up for several days. I think the two of you should speak privately. No need to tell her Miss Blanchard is coming to see me this afternoon. If your mother knows, she'll insist on being present so she can take charge."

As if on cue, a knock sounded at the door and his mother appeared in the office doorway. "Morgan! I didn't know you were here." She frowned at the two men. "Why didn't one of you tell me?"

"I'm going to join you for lunch, Mother. Just the two of us. Father needs to attend to his paper work, so you'll have me all to yourself." He pushed to his feet. "We need to have a talk."

Her lips curved in a generous smile. "Yes, we do. I'm eager to know if you've called on Isabelle Armstrong since the party. I told her mother you'd likely be knocking on their front door the following day."

Morgan's father shot him a pitying look before turning to his paper work. "You two have a good lunch. Don't forget you agreed to visit Eugenia this afternoon, my dear."

She directed a puzzled look at her husband. "I haven't lost the ability to read my schedule, William. I know I'm to see Eugenia at three o'clock." That said, she waved Morgan forward. "Come along, Morgan. I'll tell Lucy you're joining me for lunch."

After directing Lucy to deliver her husband's meal to his office and to set a place for Morgan, she rested her hand in the crook of his arm. "Let's sit in the parlor until the table is arranged for us." She smiled up at him. "Tell me what you thought of Isabelle."

They sat in matching chairs separated by a small round table bearing an ornate gold statue. He pushed it to one side in order to gain a better look at his mother while he spoke. "Isabelle is a lovely person. I enjoyed her company when we were children, and she remains a delightful young woman."

His mother clasped a hand to her bodice. "I am so relieved to hear that you appreciate my choice."

"Your choice?" He cocked a brow. "I said she is a delightful young woman. Nothing more."

Before he could further explain his position, Lucy appeared in the doorway and announced that their lunch was served. Morgan escorted his mother into the dining room and seated her at one end of the table and then sat in the chair beside her.

His mother waited until Lucy served them and left the room before she continued their conversation. "I adore the Armstrong family." She lowered her voice as though she were telling him a deep secret. "They are extremely well-to-do. Isabelle is an only child and would inherit everything. Together with the Stark family wealth, the two of you would hold a powerful position in Manchester—dare I say, in all of New Hampshire." She beamed at him. "You and Isabelle make a perfect couple. I doubt either of you could find a better match." She picked up her fork. "And Isabelle's mother agrees with me."

He reached for his crystal goblet and took a drink of water. "I'm not sure where you got the idea that I wanted your help with choosing a wife. However—"

"You don't need to thank me, Morgan." She patted his arm. "I've always known you would need help finding just the right woman, so I've been quite observant over the past few years. Believe me when I say that Isabelle is the perfect match for you."

He shook his head. "You're wrong, Mother. Isabelle is lovely, and I'm sure one day she will inherit a great deal of money, but she isn't the woman I want to marry. You see, I've already found the woman I plan to marry."

His mother gasped. "How is that possible? You haven't mentioned anyone." Her brow furrowed. "I watched you and Isabelle at the party. You were both having a grand time. I can't believe you don't care for her."

"I care for her as a friend—nothing more. We enjoyed renewing our friendship, but neither of us is interested in the other as a marriage partner."

"She said that? That she doesn't want you to court her?" His mother sniffed. "I find that difficult to believe."

Morgan chuckled. "I'm not so perfect that women are swooning at my feet, Mother."

"This isn't humorous, Morgan, and I didn't say she would be swooning at your feet. Still, I can't believe she would dismiss your suit without due consideration, unless she has . . ." Her sentence drifted off like a kite sailing on a breeze. She cleared her throat. "Did she tell you she has a suitor? If she did, her parents aren't aware. Her mother assured me Isabelle would welcome your suit."

"And I'm certain you assured Mrs. Armstrong that I would be eager to court Isabelle, but I'm not." He picked up his knife to cut a piece of chicken. "I'm sure she has already told her parents that we have no interest in anything more than friendship."

His mother dabbed the corner of her mouth with her linen napkin. "Who is this woman that holds your interest? Every eligible young lady in Manchester was at the party, and you didn't dance with any of them." She placed her napkin back on her lap. "I didn't even see you speak with another woman for more than a few moments."

"She was at the party, Mother, but not as a guest." His mother's forehead creased in tiny lines. He could almost hear her thoughts whirring. "Her name is Mellicent Blanchard, and she—"

"The girl who was cutting the silhouettes?" His mother visibly paled. "You're planning to court the girl who works in the photography shop? I won't have it!"

He patted her hand. "No need to shout, Mother. I want to talk to you about my plans, but only if the conversation can remain civil. If not, I can leave."

"I didn't mean to shout, but you must realize what a shock this is. I'd like to know what she said or did in the short time she was cutting your silhouette that has so mesmerized you."

Not wanting to further distress her, he forced back a laugh. "I didn't meet her at the party. I've known her for months, but our courtship hasn't been a formal one because she has little free time. I walk her home from the photography shop each evening, and we've enjoyed several outings. She's a fine young woman with high ideals. If she agrees to marry me, I'll consider myself the most fortunate man in all of New England."

His mother leaned back and inhaled a long breath. "I'm sorry, but for a Stark to marry a girl who works in a photography shop is simply unacceptable."

"I forgot to mention that during the daytime she works at Stark Mill Number Two as a loom operator." He tightened his lips into a thin line. "I'm sure that won't please you, either. Regardless, she's the woman I love, Mother, and the woman I plan to marry. She is more than acceptable to me."

His mother shook her head until a pin fell from her hair. "I will not hear of it! What will people think?"

He shrugged. "I don't care what people think. Those who truly care about either of us will be happy that we've found each other. I hope you will be one of those people. If not, it changes nothing for me. You can say the marriage would be unacceptable as often as you like, but it will have no effect. I plan to marry her with or without your blessing."

"You would choose her over your inheritance?"

"Money is your first love, Mother, not mine. You've let it rule your life, and look at what it has done. Do you so quickly forget how you badgered Father until he agreed to pilfer money that belonged to the Amoskeag Company? And then you arranged that lottery." He shuddered.

She folded her arms across her chest. "The lottery proceeds are going to do some good. I've agreed to the committee you suggested."

"As I told you before, it also caused much heartache and pain. Besides, you didn't originate the lottery for charitable purposes. You set it up to serve your own purposes."

Mrs. Stark dabbed a handkerchief to her eye. "You believe I'm a terrible woman."

He took her hand. "No, I believe you're a misguided woman who can change if you truly desire to do so. I also believe you need to seek God's forgiveness."

She paused before nodding. "You're right. I know what I did was wrong, but I dislike admitting my mistakes." She hesitated a moment longer. "After I've asked for God's forgiveness, I suppose I should ask for your father's, as well. I know how much he loves me. I've become accustomed to getting my way with him—and with most everyone else." She looked up and gave him a weak smile. "It appears you're going to change that."

Although the talk with his mother hadn't begun well, it had ended better than Morgan had expected. She now understood that he wasn't going to let her control his future.

Chapter

TWENTY-EIGHT

SINCE HER RECENT TALK WITH MORGAN, MELLIE HAD been able to think of little else. She'd been at work for only an hour when Cora left her looms and nudged Mellie to point out broken threads in her cloth. Later, when the breakfast bell rang, Clara had to call her name twice before she turned off her machines.

"What's wrong with you today, Mellie?" Cora glanced over her shoulder as she descended the winding stairs. "Your mind seems to be everywhere but on your looms. You're lucky Mr. Fuqua didn't see those broken threads before me."

"I know. Thank you for coming to my rescue." Mellie looped arms with Cora at the bottom of the steps.

Clara came alongside and linked arms with her sister. "Did you receive some bad news from home, Mellie?" She didn't wait for an answer before continuing. "Are you ill? I heard some of the girls haven't been feeling well."

Mellie shook her head and smiled. "No, I haven't had any

bad news from home, and I'm feeling fine. I didn't sleep very well last night, however."

Clara nodded. "I know how that can be, but do whatever you can to stay alert for the rest of the day. Maybe you should stay home and rest this evening instead of going to the photography shop. I can go to town and tell Mr. Harrison you're not well."

Mellie loved these two girls. They'd been kind to her since the day she'd arrived. The two of them had even begun to joke that she was their triplet. She hadn't told a falsehood. She truly hadn't slept well last night, yet that wasn't the only reason she couldn't concentrate at work. Her mind jumped from one thought to another as she attempted to make sense of everything Morgan had told her. She longed to talk with someone else and gain an objective opinion, but she didn't know if anyone could understand everything that had happened. After all, she was having difficulty sifting through much of it herself. And her questions regarding the lottery hadn't been completely answered yet.

Though the Christmas party for the children had been lovely, she wondered where the remainder of the lottery money had gone. She hoped none of those funds had been used to pay for the extravagant gala for Mrs. Stark's society friends. Surely no one who avowed to be raising funds for a charitable organization would use a portion of the money for such a thing. Judging from the number of tickets sold at the photography shop, she estimated over a thousand dollars must have been raised. And the winner had received only one hundred dollars. Perhaps Mr. Stark could shed some light on the use of the lottery funds.

The thought of meeting with Mr. Stark was enough to send a shiver of fear through her belly to the tips of her toes. Morgan had been certain his father would speak to her, but she now worried that meeting him could prove a terrible mistake. If things didn't go well with his father, would she and Morgan ever be able to mend their differences?

She sighed. *First things first.* Morgan hadn't yet arranged the meeting.

Clara pulled open the front door of the boardinghouse. "Did you hear me, Mellie? I said I could speak to Mr. Harrison if you want to rest this evening."

Mellie followed Clara and Cora into the house. "No, I need to work tonight and earn as much money as I can. With Christmas approaching, I want to have enough to purchase gifts for my sister and her children. I know she won't have the money to give them much. If I work every evening, I may have enough to purchase coal to last her through the winter, as well." She smiled at the girls. "And if I have a little extra left over, I'm going to purchase a train ticket and go to Concord for the day. It's been so long since I've seen them all. I worry the children aren't going to remember me."

"Don't be silly, Mellie. They're old enough that they won't forget you. But I think it would be wonderful if you could go and enjoy Christmas with them. I wish we could go home." Cora directed a doleful look at her sister.

Clara smiled. "Maybe next year. Besides, we will need more than one day. Concord is close enough for Mellie to travel there by train and return on the same day. Traveling to Albany is much farther—and more expensive."

"I know, Clara. I was just saying it would be nice if we could be at home with the rest of our family. Still, we have each other, and we'll have a good Christmas here in Manchester with the other girls."

Along with the rest of the girls, they rushed to the dining table and gobbled down their breakfast, braved the cold to take turns at the privy, then hurried back to the mill, repeating the same process when the noonday bell rang. By midafternoon Mellie stood at the looms and allowed her lack of sleep, the humidity, and the thrumming of the looms to lull her into a stupor.

At a tap on her shoulder, she startled, spun around, and came face-to-face with Mr. Fuqua. The kindness that usually shone in his eyes was replaced by a hard stare. He gestured for her to turn off her looms, gather her belongings, and follow him. She could feel the eyes of every operator watching them as they crossed the room. He opened the door leading into the stairwell and motioned her forward.

Even with the door closed, he was required to yell so that she could hear him. "You're to report to Mr. Walters over in the main office at Stark Number One. You would have gone there to turn in your papers before you started working here." He glanced toward the stairs. "Do you remember where it's located?"

"Yes, but why am I to go there? Have I done something wrong?" Her voice trembled with fear.

The overseer shrugged and cupped his hands to his mouth. "Not that I know of. I haven't reported you for anything, but I never know what's going on in the main office. Hurry. You best not keep Mr. Walters waiting too long."

After rushing down the winding stairs, Mellie shrugged into her cloak, yanked the hood over her head, and pushed open the heavy door. There wasn't much distance between the two buildings, but traversing it took more than enough time to give her emotions full sway. If Mr. Fuqua hadn't reported her for anything, why would Mr. Walters order her to the main office? This couldn't be good.

She came to a halt when she was struck by another thought—

one that landed like a punch to the midsection. What if Morgan had spoken to his father and Mr. Stark sent word to Mr. Walters that she should be terminated? If Morgan's parents wanted him to stop seeing her, the easiest method would be to terminate her employment and make certain she was blackballed from working at any of the other mills. She would be forced to leave Manchester, and she would be out of Morgan's life.

Step by step, Mellie forced herself to move forward while she recalled stories of employee terminations and how they'd been blackballed and unable to secure work at any of the other mills. There was an unwritten agreement between the agents and overseers at the various mills. They shared the names of employees who'd been terminated and agreed among themselves that they wouldn't hire a man or woman who'd been fired by another mill. They used their blackballing method to make certain that employees remained for the full term of their employment contract and that they followed all the rules of the mill and the boardinghouse. They did the same in Lowell—at least that was what Mellie had been told by a girl who had once worked there. No doubt many of the rules and regulations in Manchester were the same as those practiced in Lowell.

By the time she stepped inside the main building, she was trembling with fear. She crossed the vestibule and entered the outer office. The clerk gestured to the door leading into Mr. Walters's office. "Go on in. He's expecting you."

She swallowed hard. Even the clerk had anticipated her arrival. This couldn't be good. Although she'd been told to go into the agent's office, she tapped lightly on the door before entering.

Mr. Walters looked up from a sheaf of papers atop his desk and squinted over his glasses. "Miss Blanchard?"

Mellie met his gaze. "Yes, sir."

"I received a message from Mr. Stark that I was to send you to the front gate at two-thirty this afternoon. It is near that time, so I suggest you make your way there as quickly as possible." He extended a note to her. "Give this to the watchman so he knows you have permission to leave early."

"Am I to return, sir?"

His brow furrowed. "Unless I receive word to the contrary, I will expect you to report back to your overseer as usual. I've been told nothing more than what I've just told you." He returned his attention to his papers. "As I said, you should hurry if you want to be at the gate on time."

She nodded and mumbled her thanks before leaving the office. Moments later, she made her way across the mill yard, where the watchman stepped out of his small enclosure while rubbing his beefy hands together. She handed him the note.

He read it and nodded. "There's a buggy waiting for you, miss."

The heavy iron gate groaned as the older man pulled it open wide enough to permit Mellie space to exit. Once outside the gate, she caught sight of the buggy parked a short distance away.

Morgan jumped down and hurried to her side. "I hope none of this has frightened you."

Mellie stared at him a moment. "Frightened?" She shook her head. "No. I'd say *terrified* more aptly describes what I've experienced over the past fifteen minutes. Is all of this your doing?"

"Yes, I'm afraid it is, and I'm sorry to have alarmed you." He escorted her to the buggy and helped her up. Once settled inside, he turned to her. "I went to visit my father earlier today. He agreed to visit with you this afternoon, but the only way to arrange for you to meet him was to have you leave work early."

"I thought I was going to be terminated, and then I didn't

know what to think when Mr. Walters said I was expected to be at the front gate at two-thirty." She inhaled a deep breath. "So, we're going to meet with your father right now?"

"Yes. My mother has gone to visit an ailing friend, so it will be just the three of us." He picked up the reins and flicked his wrists.

Her momentary relief at knowing she wasn't going to be fired was replaced by the knowledge that she was now heading to the Stark mansion to meet Morgan's father. She doubted the owner of the Stark Mills was going to be pleased to confide in one of the company employees, especially one of her station.

"I've spoken to both of my parents, but my father more fully understands why I needed to keep my identity a secret, and he can detail the circumstances surrounding the lottery."

Her fear mounted as they neared the mansion. "I can't do this, Morgan. Not now." She touched the fabric of her worn dress. "Look at me. I'm in a work dress that is frayed and dusted in lint. My hair is coming loose from the pins, and my boots are wet from the snow."

While holding the reins in one hand, he covered her hand with the other. "You look perfect no matter what you're wearing. My father isn't going to judge you by your appearance, Mellie. He knows that you work in the mill and you're coming here from work. Please don't worry. You'll find him to be kind and gentle." He tipped his head to the side. "Sometimes too kind—at least where my mother is concerned."

A short time later, Morgan pulled back on the reins and brought the horses to a halt in front of the portico. A groom appeared out of nowhere and took the reins from Morgan while he helped Mellie down from the buggy.

He held her elbow as he led her inside through the front door.

Thoughts of the gala, cutting silhouettes, and her time with the precious children flooded her mind as they continued down the long hallway. He tapped on the door before leading her inside one of the mansion's many rooms.

A gentleman with white hair stood and smiled when they approached. Before Morgan could introduce her, his father gestured to a chair. "I'm William Stark, and you must be Miss Blanchard, the woman who has captured my son's heart. I'm pleased to meet you."

Heat rushed up Mellie's neck and across her cheeks. "Thank you, Mr. Stark. The pleasure is mine."

After they'd removed their coats and were seated, Mr. Stark leaned forward and rested his arms on the top of his desk. "I understand you have some concerns about Morgan concealing his identity from you. Going into the mills as a workman was his idea, and at first I thought it foolish. However, once I understood that his plan was to discover how to create better conditions for the workers and hopefully increase production, I was in favor of the idea." Mr. Stark continued to detail Morgan's involvement with the new bagging looms and that secrecy had been a necessity. He pointed a finger toward his son. "I can attest to the fact that Morgan's motive was always honorable, miss."

Mellie smiled. "I appreciate that you're willing to explain the reason for his hidden identity, but I continue to have some questions about the lottery. You see, Morgan had voiced his aversion to gambling and the lottery to me. So I'm sure you can understand my confusion and anger when I discovered his mother—your wife—had organized the event. I was certain he knew and had withheld that from me. It eroded my trust in him."

"Yes, I can see how that occurred. Let me enlighten you on what happened, then—and I would request that you keep what I'm about to tell you in confidence."

Mellie nodded her agreement and then listened carefully as Mr. Stark described the financial difficulties that prohibited moving forward with the bagging looms and his wife's insistence that he transfer funds from the Amoskeag Company to the Stark accounts and later repay the funds with money from her father. "When the money didn't arrive from her father as quickly as expected, she concocted the lottery idea so I could replace the funds."

"And did her father ever give her the money?"

Mr. Stark nodded. "Yes."

"And the lottery proceeds? Where is that money? Surely it wasn't all used for the party."

"No, it wasn't." Mr. Stark folded his hands atop the desk. "My wife originally planned to use a portion of the proceeds for the children's party, but we decided against that idea. I myself paid for the party. There's an accounting of the proceeds and ticket sales from each merchant, and the money has been deposited into a separate bank account at First Bank here in Manchester. Mr. Frederick, the bank president, has agreed to take charge of a committee that will be appointed to distribute the money in an appropriate manner."

Morgan nodded. "The committee will consist of members of the working class who volunteer to be involved." He glanced at his father. "Neither my parents nor I will serve on the committee."

"That's right." His father turned back to Mellie. "This has been an ugly business. All of it. I blame myself for not having had the courage to tell my wife no when she wanted me to transfer funds from one company to another. When the money didn't arrive from her father, she decided upon the lottery as a way to repay the Amoskeag Company. Believe me, Morgan didn't know anything about the lottery, Miss Blanchard. Truth be told, my wife had already moved forward with her plan before I knew about it. I'm not attempting to absolve myself in the matter, but I do want you to know that the lottery was conducted without Morgan's knowledge." He exhaled a long breath. "Again, I'd appreciate it if you wouldn't discuss this matter with anyone else. I do plan to take steps to resign my position and set this whole affair aright within the week."

"You need not worry, Mr. Stark," Mellie said. "I will maintain your confidence." She met the older man's gaze. "Do you think your wife plans to continue holding lotteries in the future?"

"I do not. Once the lottery proceeds—"

"Did I hear someone mention the lottery funds? I thought we'd resolved that matter."

Mellie and Morgan jerked around. Mrs. Stark stood in the doorway. She was wearing a sable-trimmed velvet cloak, one hand still enclosed in a matching sable muff.

Morgan pushed to his feet. "You're correct, Mother. Why don't you join us? You know Miss Blanchard, of course."

Mellie nodded. "Good afternoon, Mrs. Stark."

The older woman nodded. She didn't appear particularly surprised to see Mellie. Perhaps because Morgan had already spoken with her about their relationship. Or perhaps the maid had warned her upon her return.

Mr. Stark stood and pulled another chair close to his desk. "I thought you went to visit Eugenia Higgins." He lifted the cape from his wife's shoulders and draped it across a settee on the other side of the room.

"I did, but apparently her illness was overstated and she'd gone on an outing. I left the chicken soup, however."

Mr. Stark tugged on his earlobe. "I'm glad you've returned, my dear. We were just talking about the lottery. Miss Blanchard was curious if you were planning to conduct future lotteries, and I assured her you wouldn't be doing so. Isn't that correct?"

She nodded. "That's right, my dear. I've already given you my word." She leaned toward Mellie. "I hadn't considered the ill effects a lottery could have upon some people, but Morgan didn't hesitate to show me the error of my ways." She looked over at her son. "Did you, Morgan?"

"I believe you needed to know, Mother."

"You're right, I did. After considering all the facts, I realized I'd pursued something that resulted in hurting the people I love, as well as hurting people I don't even know." She paused and gave her husband a sweet smile. "And for that I am exceedingly sorry." Then she turned back to Mellie and added, "So Mr. Frederick is forming a committee to distribute the lottery proceeds where they are most needed. Perhaps you'd like to serve on the committee, Miss Blanchard. Any ideas how you would distribute the money if you were in charge?"

Mellie was taken aback by the question—shocked that Mrs. Stark would ask her opinion. "I think I would start a school for the children who work in the mills. One within the mill yard so they could come and go with ease." She looked the older woman in the eyes. "Of course, I tend to lean toward giving children a good education. I was a tutor before I came to Manchester, and I have always cherished the fact that I received a good education."

Mrs. Stark nodded her approval. "That sounds like an excellent idea. I hope you'll serve on the committee. I'm sure you could offer other excellent ideas as well on how best to spend the lottery funds."

Until Mrs. Stark said the words *lottery funds*, Mellie hadn't given thought to the fact that she was making suggestions for money that had been raised through a lottery. Could she even consider such an idea? She shook her head. "I don't think I'm one to serve on the committee, Mrs. Stark, but I'm certain there are many in the city who would be willing to get involved."

Mrs. Stark nodded. "As you wish. I won't insist. Would you mind if I passed your idea along to Mr. Frederick?"

"Not at all, although I'm sure Mr. Frederick will receive numerous ideas and a good number of volunteers, as well."

His mother glanced at the mantel clock. "Why don't you join us for supper, Miss Blanchard? We still have much to discuss."

Chapter

TWENTY-NINE

MORGAN MAINTAINED A CLOSE EYE ON HIS MOTHER throughout supper and was careful to lend an ear each time she spoke. Much had been accomplished this afternoon, and he didn't want her to say or do anything that might cause a setback.

Mellie had attempted to refuse the supper invitation due to improper attire, but his mother had been quick to ease Mellie's misgivings. She'd immediately stated that their evening meals were quite informal. After a bit more encouragement and assurance, Mellie finally agreed to join them.

They'd just finished their beef and barley soup when his mother looked across the table at Mellie. "I didn't have an opportunity to speak with you before you departed after the party, but my guests were all delighted with your renderings. They said their silhouettes were the best Christmas gift I've ever presented at any of my parties. That's quite a compliment, as I've hosted a party for more than fifteen years now." Her shoulders squared to a new height.

Mellie broke off a piece of her roll and picked up her butter knife. "Thank you. I'm pleased to hear you didn't have any complaints."

"Complaints? Dear me, no. In fact, several of the ladies asked how they could contact you. I wasn't certain what hours you worked at Mr. Harrison's shop; however, I did tell them you were sometimes there during the evening. That's correct, isn't it?"

Mellie nodded. "Yes. I'm there most evenings after seven-thirty and after five-thirty on Saturdays, since the mills close earlier on Saturday."

"Tell me, Miss Blanchard, how did you and my son first meet? Was he strolling through the mill one day and you struck up a conversation with him?"

Mellie suppressed a chuckle. "No. The first time I saw Morgan was at the train station. I dropped my book, and he kindly returned it to me, although we didn't introduce ourselves then. The next time I saw him was in the photography shop, yet I didn't recognize him. I don't believe Morgan has been on the weaving floors at the mill. If so, I have never seen him there. Besides, having a conversation while the machinery is in operation is impossible, Mrs. Stark." She hesitated a moment. "Have you ever visited the mills?"

She clasped a hand to her bodice and shook her head. "No. Never."

"Well, the noise created by the machinery makes it impossible to be heard unless you shout. Even then, you must be nearby or you won't be heard. It's so loud that I sometimes stuff small pieces of cloth in my ears."

"That could permanently injure their hearing, William. You and Morgan should do something to help in that regard. You don't want to be responsible for ruining the hearing of the Manchester citizens, do you?"

Morgan tilted his head, surprised to hear his mother had any concern for the company employees. In truth, he'd never heard her make mention of the mills until recently. "When did you become such an advocate for the working man and woman, Mother?"

A blush colored her cheeks. "Don't make fun of me, Morgan. When I didn't discover Eugenia at home, I made a brief stop at church before returning home. As it turned out, the pastor was there. We had a long talk, and he prayed with me." She leaned toward him. "It was your talk with me earlier in the day that prompted my stop at the church. The pastor pointed out that because of my position, there is much I could do to help the community. And it sounds as though there's much that can be done to help the workers in your mills, William."

His father chuckled. "I understand there's much to be done. If you'll recall, that's why I gave Morgan permission to hide his identity and accept a position as a mechanic—so that we could make changes where needed."

Mrs. Stark lifted her chin and nodded. "Perhaps you should speak to Mellie and ask what changes will help the female employees, as well. It sounds as if their working conditions need immediate attention."

His father sighed. "Yes, dear. We're going to be working on it."

"I'm pleased to hear that, and I'm offering my assistance, if it should be needed."

"Thank you, my dear." He gave her a warm smile. "I will keep you apprised of any assistance you might provide." He accepted the platter of roasted chicken from the maid and set about carving the bird. "I do believe that's enough talk of the mills for one evening." He looked up from his carving. "How do you plan to spend your Christmas holiday, Miss Blanchard?"

Before she could answer, his mother shifted in her chair. "Why, you could spend the holiday with us. We would all be delighted to have you join us—unless, that is, you have already made other plans." She beamed at Morgan, obviously hoping the invitation would please him.

"Thank you, Mrs. Stark, but I do have other plans. My sister and her children live in Concord. I'll be taking the early-morning train and spending the holiday with them. I've not had an opportunity to visit them since I moved to Manchester, and I miss them very much."

Mrs. Stark appeared momentarily thoughtful before giving a slight nod. "I do understand. Family is important. What about Christmas Eve? You could attend church with us. We open our gifts when we return home from church. You could spend the night here and leave in the morning, or you could return home for the night, if you prefer." She took the platter of chicken from her husband and passed it to Mellie. "Do you live in one of those boardinghouses near the mills?"

"I do. The accommodations aren't perfect, but I've become friends with some very nice young ladies since I arrived." Mellie forked a piece of chicken and passed the platter to Morgan. "I do thank you for your invitation. Perhaps Morgan and I can discuss it a bit further and come to a decision."

"Yes, of course, but I hope you'll accept. We're a small family, and we would enjoy your company for the evening. Christmas Eve is such a special time, don't you think?"

Mellie nodded. "I do, and I promise—Morgan and I will discuss possible Christmas plans."

His mother's demeanor since her return surprised Morgan. He'd hoped his talk with her would have an impact, but he hadn't expected her to welcome and accept Mellie so soon. Perhaps the change had more to do with the conversation she'd had with the pastor than anything he'd said. Then again, it was likely the combination of the two.

After they'd completed their meal and retreated to the parlor to visit for a brief time, Morgan leaned close to her. "Do you need to work this evening, or can you stay a while longer?"

"I need to go to the photography shop. Mr. Harrison is expecting me, and I'm sure Mrs. Richards has already made a notation in her ledger that I missed supper."

He stood and extended his hand toward Mellie. "We must return to town so that Mellie can attend to her work at the photography shop." When his mother and Mellie walked toward the foyer to retrieve her coat, Morgan moved to his father's side, whispered in his ear, then followed him to his office.

"William! Where have you and Morgan gone off to?"

Morgan stepped to the office door. "We're in here, Mother."

Moments later, the two ladies joined them. His mother clasped Mellie's hand in her own. "I'm sorry you must rush off, but I'm glad we had this time to visit." His mother turned to Morgan. "Promise you'll bring her back soon."

"I will, Mother." He was certain she'd wanted to add something about Christmas Eve but restrained herself. He smiled at the thought.

On the buggy ride to town, Morgan reached for Mellie's gloved hand. "What are you thinking now?"

"I enjoyed meeting your parents. Your mother was far more attentive than I expected, and your father seemed genuine."

He chuckled. "I think my mother has examined her priorities, and I believe with God's help she can truly become the woman He wants her to be." He squeezed her hand. "Mellie, please tell me you understand all of the subterfuge now. Please tell me you believe me. I don't know what else I can do to restore your trust in me."

She searched his face. "I do wish you would've confided in me, but like your mother, I've had the chance to examine my heart. I was hurt and angry. A part of me even wanted you to suffer as I had. But as I look in your eyes, I know you are still the good, kind—and honest—man I fell in love with."

"So you trust me?"

Her eyes glistened with tears. "With all my heart."

He leaned forward and pressed a kiss to her forehead. "I will do everything in my power to prove I am worthy of both your trust and your love."

Their spirits were high when they arrived at the shop, and they were surprised to discover a number of customers awaiting Mellie's arrival. Mr. Harrison scurried to the front of the shop when he caught sight of her. "I was concerned when you didn't arrive on time. And then Cora stopped in to see if you were here. She said you'd left work early, and nobody knew where you were."

Morgan inched through the crowd. "It's my fault, Mr. Harrison. She was with me, and I failed to get her to work on time."

He accepted Morgan's apology, but clearly he remained unsettled. "All these customers are here because they met Mellie at your mother's party and want additional silhouettes or want her to cut silhouettes at their own parties." He shook his head. "She's not going to have time to attend all their parties and work here, as well."

Before Morgan could respond, Mr. Harrison hastened to the rear of the shop to help a customer choose a frame. For the remainder of the evening, Morgan waited quietly and watched Mellie as she assisted each customer. Though he could see she was exhausted, she offered them care and kindness. He marveled at her ability to create the perfect silhouette for each person who sat down in front of her. He offered a silent prayer of thanks that God had sent this woman into his life. And now that he'd found her, he planned to love her for the rest of his life.

When she'd finally bid the final customer good-bye, Morgan retrieved her cape and placed it around her shoulders. "Ready?"

She nodded. "It's been a long evening. I'm thankful we can ride in the buggy rather than walk home tonight."

He smiled and reached into his coat pocket. "You can give this to Mrs. Richards. It's a note from my father. After reading it, I don't think she'll mark you absent for supper."

"Thank you, Morgan." She grinned. "She may not mark me absent, but I'm going to guess she'll keep the note just to show her friends that she received a personal message from the company owner. It will be quite a feather in her cap."

Morgan laughed and helped her into the buggy. Once settled close to him on the leather seat, she rested her head on his shoulder. "There is something I'd like to ask you." He nodded, and she inhaled a deep breath. "If I join you and your family on Christmas Eve, would you consider going to Concord with me on Christmas Day? I'd like for you to meet my sister and her children. Having you at my side would make the day a true celebration." She lifted her head from his shoulder and smiled at him. "I think you'll find my niece and nephew quite entertaining."

He squeezed her hand. "In that case, how could I refuse?"

Chapter
THIRTY

WITH THE HELP OF CORA AND CLARA, MELLIE STEPPED into the emerald green shot-silk gown that had been packed at the bottom of one of her trunks. When leaving Concord, she'd packed it with little expectation of ever wearing it again. Yet she'd been unable to leave it behind. Worn only once for a gathering at Governor Dinsmoor's mansion in Concord, she was pleased she'd elected to bring it with her. After fashioning Mellie's hair, Cora inserted a wreath of miniature silk roses and white feathers. The overall effect was stunning.

Cora stepped away and gave a firm nod. "You look absolutely beautiful. Morgan won't be able to look at anyone else."

Mellie chuckled. "The guest list is very short, so I don't think I'll need to worry overmuch. Other than the two of us, his parents are the only ones who will be present."

"How disappointing when you look so lovely, but I suppose Morgan is the only one that truly matters." Cora adjusted the thin green ribbons that circled the puffed tulle sleeves of the dress. "Are you giving his parents a Christmas gift? I'm not certain what you would give wealthy people who can afford to purchase whatever they want for themselves."

"I'm not sure if they'll be particularly pleased, but I made and framed silhouette cuttings for each of them. For Mrs. Stark I made a silhouette of the mansion, and for Mr. Stark a cutting of the Stark Mills. I hope they'll be well received."

"Oh, that was a wonderful idea. I'm sure they'll be delighted." Clara moved closer and sat on a trunk. "We received a letter from our ma yesterday. They didn't wait to open their gift from us, and she said they already hung the silhouette you made of Cora and me on the wall. She sure thought it was a good likeness."

"They went ahead and opened it because you put a note in the parcel, telling them they didn't have to wait until Christmas." Cora shook her head. "Clara didn't tell me she'd done that until after we mailed the package. If I had known beforehand, I would have taken it out. Now they don't have a gift to open on Christmas."

Clara shrugged. "This way they have more time to admire it. Besides, they'll have gifts from the young'uns. They always make things for ma and pa."

"Well, I'm pleased to know they liked their gift." Mellie stood, walked to her small trunk, and opened the lid. "I have a gift for each of you that you can open tomorrow." She extended a small package to each of them.

Cora grasped the gift, then stared at the gaily tied bow. "I know it's selfish of me, but I wish you were going to be here with us. It's going to be lonely without you and Phebe. Still, I'm glad you're happy and that Phebe decided to go and see her folks." Cora offered a fleeting smile. "I must say, though, I'm a little jealous that you get to spend the night at the Stark mansion."

"Don't make her feel sad or apologetic, Cora. Mellie should enjoy her time with Morgan. Even if she wasn't going to spend the night at the mansion, she'd be leaving Christmas Day to visit her family. And I think it's grand that he's going with you." She laid her right hand over her heart. "It's all so romantic. I hope I find a man like Morgan one day."

Mellie smiled. "I hope you do, too. You both deserve fine men who can see how special each of you are, and who will understand your need to live in houses beside each other."

Mellie had told Phebe and the twins the truth regarding Morgan's identity. They thought him a hero for seeking to better conditions for the employees. While they were quick to question Mellie's acceptance of Mrs. Stark despite the woman's involvement in the lottery, Mellie had been as truthful as possible without betraying anything she'd promised to keep in confidence. They understood she still didn't agree with the lottery and that there was little chance Mrs. Stark would be initiating future lotteries. As expected, Phebe had been more interested in the lottery than the others, but even she had expressed her support of Morgan.

"I'd be willing to face some adversity if, in the end, I had a man like Morgan at my side." Clara toyed with the ribbon on her package. "Are you sure we must wait until Christmas to open our gift?"

"Very sure." Mellie retrieved one more packet from her trunk. "Would you give this to Mrs. Richards tomorrow morning? I wasn't certain if she'd like a silhouette of herself or one of the boardinghouse."

Cora arched a brow. "Which did you finally choose?"

Mellie grinned. "I couldn't decide, so I cut her profile standing in front of the boardinghouse."

"A perfect solution." Clara picked up Mellie's traveling case. "I'll carry this downstairs for you." She turned as she neared the door. "And did you cut a silhouette of Morgan as a Christmas gift?"

"No, I . . ."

"Don't tell her, Mellie." Cora placed her index finger against her pursed lips. "She's liable to tell Morgan when he arrives to call on you."

"You may be right, Cora." Mellie turned to Clara. "Upon my return from Concord, I promise to tell you."

"You're a spoilsport, Cora. You know I wouldn't tell."

All three of them laughed as they descended the attic stairs and continued along the upper hallway. They were midway down the stairs leading to the foyer when a knock sounded at the front door.

Cora glanced over her shoulder at Mellie. "That must be Morgan."

Mellie's pulse quickened. She prayed all would go well with his family this evening and with her family tomorrow. There hadn't been time to write Margaret that Morgan would be arriving with her, so she hoped his appearance wouldn't distress her sister or the children.

⤙⤙⤙⤙⤚

Morgan stomped the snow from his boots on the front stoop of the boardinghouse. Before arriving, he'd stopped and set a fire in the fireplace and shoveled the path leading to the house his grandfather had given him. He'd not yet told Mellie about the house and thought this would be the perfect evening to give her a tour. Last week he'd hired two cleaning ladies, who had scrubbed and polished the house from top to bottom. And while the house was free of dust and dirt, it lacked furniture and the amenities that would one day make it feel like a home. Still, he wanted her to see it and know that if she agreed to marry him, they would have a place to call their own.

Cora opened the door, but it was Mellie he saw when he stepped inside. His breath caught at the sight of her. "You look beautiful." He didn't care that the twins were hovering nearby and giggled at the remark.

"Thank you," she whispered as she handed him her cloak.

He lifted her wrap and carefully placed it around her shoulders before leaning down to grasp her bag. After bidding the twins good-bye, the two of them departed. "I hope you don't mind, but I thought we'd make a stop before going to my parents' home. There's something I'd like to show you."

"A surprise?"

He didn't miss the apprehension in her voice. The recent surprises she'd experienced hadn't always been pleasant. "I think this is one you'll like. At least I hope so."

Her shoulders relaxed. "Then I'm eager to see what it is. How far away is this place where we're going to stop?"

"You're not fooling me one bit. You think you're going to figure it out before we get there. But since I don't think that's possible, I'll tell you that it will take us only fifteen minutes by carriage." He placed her bag in the carriage and assisted her up.

"I'll take you at your word, and I won't ask any more questions about the surprise." She settled in her seat. "I do hope your mother didn't have a change of heart and invite additional guests to dinner."

He grasped her gloved hand in his. "Not unless she invited someone after I left the house a short time ago. I think our evening should be quiet but enjoyable."

The snow that had fallen earlier in the day clung to the trees and bushes and created a wintry scene that rivaled the beauty of any snowy landscape she'd ever seen. A gust of wind rustled the trees nearby, and she leaned closer to Morgan.

A short time later, they stopped in front of a two-story stone house, where Morgan assisted her down from the carriage. He offered her his arm. "Right this way."

Candlelight shone through the bare windows, and as they neared the front door, they could see the fire glowing in the front room fireplace. She looked up at him. "Are we visiting friends of yours?"

"No." He withdrew a key from his pocket and inserted it into the lock. After opening the door, he bent from the waist and gave a sweeping gesture. "Please enter my home."

She gasped as she stepped into the foyer. "This is your house?"

"It is. A gift from my grandfather, a very wise man, who thought I should have a home of my own." He led her into the parlor. "I came over earlier and started the fire. I had hoped it would ward off the cold, but I don't think it did much good."

She stepped closer to the fireplace and held out her hands. "One fire for so large a house is probably not near enough, but it is lovely. You and your grandfather made a good choice."

He took her hand. "Come see the rest." He led her from room to room. After they'd inspected the entire house, they returned to the parlor.

She stepped back to the fireplace and hugged her chilled body. "It's a beautiful home, though rather big for one person. I hope you won't be lonely."

"I hope so, too." His pulse thundered, and his voice, swelling with emotion, nearly betrayed him. "Mellie, I was hoping you would agree to marry me. Until we can fill this house with children of our own, I thought you might want to use one or two of the bedrooms to hold classes for some of the children who work in the mills. Or you could use part of the house as a studio for your Scherenschnitte." He paused and drew a long breath. "I know you may need more time still—and I don't mind waiting for you—but when you're ready, I want you to be my wife."

"Yes."

"What?"

"Yes, I'll marry you." She beamed at him, her tears reflecting the light of the fire. "I don't need any more time, and I didn't need to see this house to know you are the man I love. I believe you, Morgan, and I believe *in* you. You have my heart."

⁓

After making her declaration, Mellie held her breath. Perhaps Morgan hadn't expected an immediate answer.

As a wide grin spread across his face, he withdrew a wrapped package from inside his coat. "Then perhaps you'd do me the honor of opening this Christmas gift in private."

She met his gaze before tugging on the gold satin ribbon and lifting the lid from the box. She gasped as she removed a crudely cut paper silhouette of a man and woman standing beneath an arch. "Did you cut this?"

"I know it's far from a work of art, but—"

"No, Morgan, it's the perfect silhouette." She smiled at him. "It's us."

His Adam's apple bobbed as he slipped a ring from his pocket. The facets of the garnet gemstone in the center gleamed. "It was my grandmother's." He lifted her hand and slid the ring onto her finger. "Merry Christmas, Mellie Blanchard, soon to be Mellie Stark."

She giggled. "Mellie Stark. I hadn't thought about the change of name."

He drew her into his arms. "Too late now."

Then, before she could say another word, he lowered his lips to hers and kissed her with tenderness, passion, and love all at once. Mellie knew this man would never give her reason to doubt him again.

Special thanks to . . .

My editor and the entire staff at Bethany House, for their devotion to publishing the best product possible. It is a privilege to work with all of you.

Wendy Lawton of Books & Such Literary Agency, for her guidance, dedication, and spirit of encouragement.

Malia Ebel, reference librarian and archivist at the New Hampshire Historical Society, who cheerfully gave of her time to dig through archives and find valuable material for me to examine.

The staff at the Manchester City Library.

The staff at the Manchester Millyard Museum.

Mary Greb-Hall, for her ongoing encouragement, expertise, and sharp eye.

Lorna Seilstad, dear friend, remarkable traveling companion, and critique partner.

Mary Kay Woodford, my sister, prayer warrior, and friend.

Tom McCoy, my brother, supporter, and friend.

And always to Justin, Jenna, and Jessa, for their support and the joy they bring me during the writing process and the rest of my life.

Above all, thanks and praise to our Lord Jesus Christ, for the opportunity to live my dream and share the wonder of His love through story.

Judith Miller is an award-winning author whose avid research and love for history are reflected in her bestselling novels. Judy makes her home in Overland Park, Kansas. To learn more, visit www.judithmccoymiller.com.

Sign Up for Judith's Newsletter!

Keep up to date with Judith's news on book releases and events by signing up for her email list at judithmccoymiller.com.

More from Judith Miller

Zanna Krykos eagerly takes on her friend's sponging business as a way to use her legal skills and avoid her family's matchmaking. But the newly arrived Greek divers, led by Nico Kalos, mistrust a boss who knows nothing about the trade. Yet they must work together to rise above adversity after the mysterious death of a diver and the rumor of sunken treasure.

The Lady of Tarpon Springs

More Captivating Historical Fiction from Bethany House

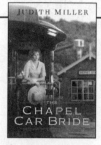

Hope Irvine always sees the best in people. While traveling on the rails with her missionary father, she attracts the attention of a miner named Luke and a young mine manager. When Luke begins to suspect the manager is using Hope's missions of mercy as a cover for illegal activities, can he discover the truth without putting her in danger?

The Chapel Car Bride by Judith Miller
judithmccoymiller.com

Mary is one of the best sharpshooters in the country, but unless the man who killed her brother is brought to justice, her accomplishments seem hollow. Journalist Christopher is covering her show, and he is immediately captivated by Mary—but getting close to someone would threaten to bring his past to light. Can they find healing from the past together?

Wherever You Go by Tracie Peterson
Brookstone Brides #2
traciepeterson.com

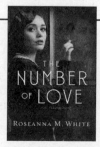

In the midst of the Great War, Margot spends her days deciphering intercepted messages. But after a sudden loss, her world is turned upside down. Drake returns wounded from the field, followed by a destructive enemy. Immediately smitten with Margot, how can Drake convince a girl who lives entirely in her mind that sometimes life's answers lie in the heart?

The Number of Love by Roseanna M. White
The Codebreakers #1
roseannamwhite.com

◊BethanyHouse

You May Also Like . . .

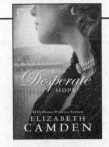

A female accountant in 1908, Eloise Drake thought she'd put her past behind her. Then her new job lands her in the path of the man who broke her heart. Alex Duval, mayor of a doomed town, can't believe his eyes when he sees Eloise as part of the entourage that's come to wipe his town off the map. Can he convince her to help him—and give him another chance?

A Desperate Hope by Elizabeth Camden
elizabethcamden.com

With a Mohawk mother and a French father in 1759 Montreal, Catherine Duval finds it easiest to remain neutral among warring sides. But when her British ex-fiancé, Samuel, is taken prisoner by her father, he claims to have information that could end the war. At last, she must choose whom to fight for. Is she willing to commit treason for the greater good?

Between Two Shores by Jocelyn Green
jocelyngreen.com

In spring 1918, British Lieutenant Colin Mabry receives an urgent message from a woman he once loved but thought dead. Feeling the need to redeem himself, he travels to France—only to find the woman's half sister, Johanna, who believes her sister is alive and the prisoner of a German spy. As they seek answers across Europe, danger lies at every turn.

Far Side of the Sea by Kate Breslin
katebreslin.com